Jo Carnegie lives in London and Cardiff. She spent her early career as a fledgling reporter on Bedfordshire's *Biggleswade Chronicle* before working at *More!* and *Glamour*. Most recently she worked as Deputy Editor of *Heat* and has interviewed stars from George Clooney, Justin Timberlake and Will Smith to Posh and Becks and Kylie Minogue.

Country Pursuits is Jo's first novel. She is now ⁣⁣⁣⁣⁣ting her second, *Naked Truths*.

⁣⁣⁣ more information ⁣⁣⁣⁣⁣⁣⁣⁣⁣⁣
⁣⁣bsite at www.churc⁣⁣

Country Pursuits

JO CARNEGIE

CORGI BOOKS

TRANSWORLD PUBLISHERS
61–63 Uxbridge Road, London W5 5SA
A Random House Group Company
www.rbooks.co.uk

COUNTRY PURSUITS
A CORGI BOOK: 9780552157063

First published in Great Britain
in 2008 by Bantam Press
a division of Transworld Publishers
Corgi edition published 2009

Addresses for Random House Group Ltd companies outside the UK
can be found at: www.randomhouse.co.uk
The Random House Group Ltd Reg. No. 954009

The Random House Group Limited supports The Forest
Stewardship Council (FSC), the leading international forest
certification organisation. All our titles that are printed on Greenpeace
approved FSC certified paper carry the FSC logo. Our paper
procurement policy can be found at www.rbooks.co.uk/environment

Typeset in 11/13 pt Palatino by Falcon Oast Graphic Art Ltd.
Printed in the UK by CPI Cox & Wyman, Reading, RG1 8EX.

2 4 6 8 10 9 7 5 3

To Mum, Dad, Ali and Joe

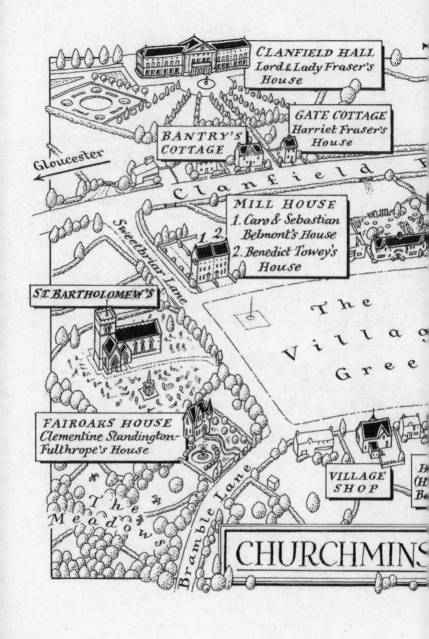

CLANFIELD HALL
Lord & Lady Fraser's House

GATE COTTAGE
Harriet Fraser's House

BANTRY'S COTTAGE

Gloucester

Clanfield

Sweetbriar Lane

MILL HOUSE
1. Caro & Sebastian Belmont's House
2. Benedict Towey's House

1. 2.

ST. BARTHOLOMEW'S

The Villag Gree

FAIROAKS HOUSE
Clementine Standington-Fulthrope's House

VILLAGE SHOP

H (H Be

The Meadows

Bramble Lane

CHURCHMINS

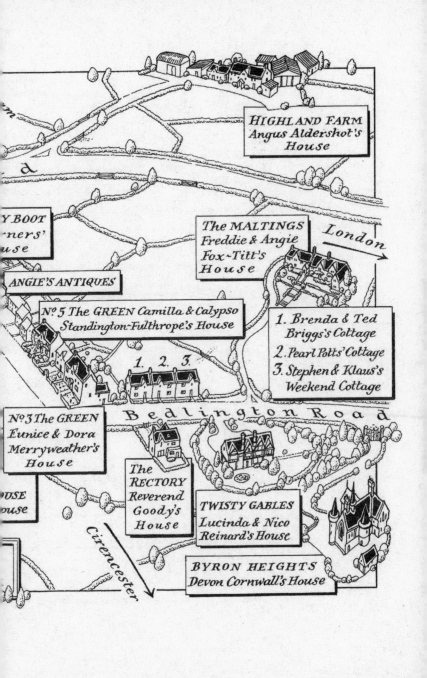

HIGHLAND FARM
Angus Aldershot's
House

Y BOOT
ners'
se

The MALTINGS
Freddie & Angie
Fox-Titt's
House

London

ANGIE'S ANTIQUES

Nº 5 The GREEN Camilla & Calypso
Standington-Fulthrope's House

1. Brenda & Ted
Briggs's Cottage
2. Pearl Potts' Cottage
3. Stephen & Klaus's
Weekend Cottage

1. 2. 3.

Bedlington Road

Nº 3 The GREEN
Eunice & Dora
Merryweather's
House

The
RECTORY
Reverend
Goody's
House

TWISTY GABLES
Lucinda & Nico
Reinard's House

Cirencester

BYRON HEIGHTS
Devon Cornwall's House

USE
ouse

Acknowledgements

Thanks to my literary agent Amanda Preston for believing in me and inspiring me to write a juicy bonkbuster in the first place. I would also like to say a huge thank you to my wonderful editor Sarah Turner and the team at Transworld for their support and enthusiasm, which has turned *Country Pursuits* from a happy dream into an even better reality. Not forgetting the real life, very female (and very glamorous) DC Helen Rance for all her words of wisdom on police matters. Finally, thanks to Sotheby's Leonora Gummer and Mark Griffiths Jones, and Caroline Offord and Andre Farrar from the RSPB.

Chapter 1

Sebastian Belmont admired his naked body in the full-length mirror. Not bad for a chap of thirty-six, he thought smugly, his eyes taking in the broad shoulders, tapered waist and muscular thighs. He turned sideways to study his washboard stomach. Maybe to compensate for a lack of height (much to his chagrin he only reached five foot nine in his Ralph Lauren loafers), Sebastian worked out furiously four times a week. Squash on a Monday, weights on a Tuesday, a hellish ten-mile run with his personal trainer on a Thursday, and, on a Friday lunchtime, a ninety-minute Pilates session with an adorable little Spanish girl called Lola. His rugger-playing work colleagues might take the piss out of him for doing what they considered a girly activity, but they hadn't got a set of abs you could bounce coins off. Yes, it was fair to say Sebastian was bloody proud of his physique.

He was also very taken with his teeth, freshly whitened by a Harley Street dentist a week ago. Sebastian flashed a wolfish grin at his reflection. God, he was irresistible! Bright blue eyes dazzled back, made even more distinctive by the perfect caramel tan he sported all year round, thanks to regular skiing and sailing jaunts. The teeth and eyes managed to deflect from a slightly weak chin, the only flaw in his handsome yet bland face. Sebastian ran a hand through his blond, slightly bouffant hair in a self-satisfied gesture and turned back to look at the bedroom.

She'd done a good job on it, even if it was slightly too boudoir for his tastes. The walls were decorated in toffee and mocha striped wallpaper, giving the room an extravagant yet intimate feel, and thick, rich cream curtains hung ceiling to floor from the sash windows, now filtering in the milky early morning light.

A black and white picture of the two of them laughing into each other's eyes stood in a solid silver frame on the dressing table. It had been taken several months earlier, on the terrace of the romantic five-star Ferreti hotel in Capri. Sebastian had whisked her off as a surprise on their first anniversary, and the couple had spent four magical days there, only occasionally surfacing from the penthouse suite to wander round the vibrant cobbled streets. The concierge, well accustomed to love-struck newly weds on their honeymoons, had exclaimed he'd never seen a more beautiful and blissfully happy couple. Sebastian stretched out on the bed like a cat basking in the sun, and smiled expansively at the memory.

Despite his luxurious surroundings, the room was in a complete state of disarray. Expensive designer clothes lay strewn across the floor, where they had been ripped off or stepped out of, and the dressing table's surface was covered with pots of

2

Crème de la Mer, Dior make-up and various Asprey jewellery sets he had bought her. She was a messy bitch, thought Sebastian. God knows how many thousands of sparklers there were just lying there for any old Tom, Dick or Harry to pick up.

Speaking of dick . . .

'Sabrina!' he called out lustily through the en suite bathroom door. The sound of running water stopped.

'I'll be out in a sec, darling!'

He lay back and waited. Shortly after, the door opened, followed by a gust of steam, and Sabrina sashayed out. Fresh from the shower, her head was encased in a fluffy white towel and her damp, magnificent body was bare. Sabrina wasn't the kind of girl to cover up her assets. Almost as tall as Sebastian – even when he was wearing his Gucci shoe lifts – Sabrina was the kind of woman who made Range Rovers and BMWs crash into each other when she walked down the nearby King's Road. Endless tanned legs reached a pert, peach-shaped bottom and a tiny waist. Further up were a pair of even more pert boobs you could rest your champagne flute on. In fact, Sebastian often did. Sabrina's face didn't disappoint either: heart-shaped with full red lips, it had a delicate, haughty nose that turned up ever just so, and bewitching, green eyes. When she wore it down, her expensively streaked, wavy blonde hair cascaded over sun-kissed shoulders.

Yes, Sabrina was a bloody good catch, thought Sebastian, his eyes travelling lazily down her perfect form. All his mates and business colleagues told him so. Even if she was a God-awful housewife.

'Come here, sexy, I've got something for you,' he said, watching his erection grow upwards like the Eiffel Tower.

Sabrina giggled. 'We can't, you'll be late for work.'

'Bugger work. Nothing starts without me, anyway,' said Sebastian.

Sabrina adopted that sexy come-to-bed look that made him just want to shag her brains out (not that she had many) there and then. She knelt on the bed above him and slowly lowered a tantalizing nipple into his mouth.

'Mmmmm. God, you taste good,' said Sebastian, sucking and biting hungrily.

'Not as good as you.' Sabrina pulled herself away and travelled down his body, kissing it hungrily. Her turban fell off and wet hair spilled out.

'Oh, Christ,' moaned Sebastian, as her mouth found his penis. She ran her tongue up and down the shaft, slow at first, and then faster and faster, like a snake flicking its tongue. Sebastian felt himself about to explode. 'Come up here, you dirty bitch.' He pulled her up by her arms until she was on top of him, her neat Brazilian nestling against his throbbing cock. 'Ride me,' he instructed. Sabrina needed no further encouragement as she manoeuvred his penis to slip inside her. She began to rock rhythmically back and forward, throwing her head back and arching her spine in ecstasy.

'Oh God, oh God,' they both moaned in unison.

'Faster!' said Sebastian urgently, gripping her hips and pulling her deeper and further towards him.

Small rivulets of sweat formed and fell between

Sabrina's perfect breasts. 'Yes, yes . . .' she gasped.

'Oh God,' Sebastian groaned again. 'Keep going, that's it . . . OH GOD!' They both let out a cry as they climaxed together and then Sabrina flopped down on top of him, her heart hammering against his.

'Who needs Ready Brek to start the day when they've got you?' Sebastian said huskily several minutes later, as he eased himself out of her and stood up.

'Well, I do like to wash and blow in the mornings,' she giggled. She pushed herself up on one elbow. 'Darling, remember we're meeting the Coutts-Nobles at Ciprani for dinner tonight. Oh, and the garage called. The Porsche is back from being serviced. Shall I get them to drop it round?'

'Yah, that'd be great,' he said. 'Maybe you can compare notes . . .' He headed into the bathroom, and was just about to turn on the power shower when Sabrina called out. 'Darling, your phone's going!'

'Who the hell is it?' asked Sebastian irritably, even though he knew the answer.

Sabrina reached across to the bedside table, looked at the phone and threw it across the bed, sticking her tongue out suggestively.

'It's your wife.'

'Hi, darling, how are you? Is Milo OK?' Sebastian rolled his eyes at Sabrina. 'Yah, yah, mmm.' He was only half listening as he started to insolently swing his now flaccid willy back and forth between his legs, making Sabrina burst into a fit of giggles.

'Who's that? Oh, it's just my secretary, Bethany. I

5

came, er, in early this morning.' Sebastian shot a wicked look at Sabrina. 'Mmm. Oh, I don't care, chicken or fish or whatever . . .' He listened again for a few moments. 'OK, fish then, it's only a bloody meal!' Sebastian checked himself. 'Sorry, sweet pea, it's just been a tough week at work. I'm exhausted.' He shot another saucy look at Sabrina, lounging on the bed like a wanton cheerleader. 'I'm fine, I'm getting the 5.03 train from Paddington tomorrow, I'll see you about seven. Love you, too. Bye, darling.'

Sebastian flung the phone on to the bed. 'Who gives a flying fuck what we eat? Honestly, the old girl needs to get out more. Still, at least I'll get a good nosh-up this weekend.' He advanced on Sabrina. 'You, my dear, are stunningly gorgeous, but it has to be said that any man who ended up with you would starve to death.'

'I've always been quite good with meat and two veg,' breathed Sabrina provocatively.

Sebastian flashed his best wolfish grin.

'Well, Nanny always told me to eat my greens, so I'd better take you up on your offer.'

'What about work?' asked Sabrina.

'Bugger work.'

Chapter 2

Nearly a hundred miles away in the picturesque Cotswold village of Churchminster, 34-year-old Caro Belmont put down the phone and sighed. She knew she annoyed Sebastian with her mundane little details, but she couldn't help it. Mundane was her life now.

She looked round the designer kitchen, spotless after Mrs Potts's morning clean. It looked like a spread from *Wallpaper* magazine. A huge, polished Aga that Caro hardly ever used dominated the room. The concrete floor was set off by sparkling stainless steel worktops, and exposed brickwork and chrome finishes gave the room a modern, trendy feel. That was the brief Sebastian had given the interior designer he had hired to decorate the whole house. Caro would have preferred to do it herself, with a more homely approach, but Sebastian wouldn't hear of it. 'You're exhausted from looking after Milo. Just concentrate on him and leave the rest to me. Besides, you know you're not very good at things like that, darling.'

Actually, having spent every minute of the last six months with their first child, Caro was screaming for a break. Her brain had turned to mush, and she could hardly remember life before she was two stone overweight and regularly covered in baby sick. But Sebastian was probably right: she was pretty useless at decorating. So she had let the interior designer, a flamboyant red-headed stick insect from Hampstead, come in and decorate their six-bedroom, three-storey half of the converted Mill House on the village green.

Aside from the kitchen, the place was white throughout, with exposed floors, overstuffed chaise longues, and dramatic pieces of graffiti art Sebastian had bought for a huge sum from a dread-locked Hoxton artist who had been touted as the next Banksy. In their bedroom was a huge four-poster bed with a frame carved from burnt timber, lights that came on as you walked into the room, and two floor-to-ceiling ladder radiators that the designer had assured them would 'make a statement'. Sebastian loved the masculine, stark feel of the house. Caro, on the other hand, hated it. The place felt like a museum, and she was terrified that once Milo started crawling he would hurt himself on the sharp edges of the granite stairs or Perspex furniture. She envied her sister Camilla's pretty little cottage on the other side of the green, with its soft furniture, low ceilings, little nooks, and pink roses curling round the front door.

It had been eighteen months since Sebastian had suggested moving from their Georgian townhouse in posh Holland Park to Churchminster, the village where Caro had grown up, and she hadn't been sure about it back then. After all, her parents had emigrated to Barbados, and she could pop back and see her sisters and grandmother whenever she wanted. She loved her life in London, her work friends and yoga buddies, their lively social life of dinner parties and long weekends skiing in Verbier. The idea of returning to her childhood home, with its one pub and endless memories of an awkward, chubby girlhood, had held absolutely no appeal.

But then Caro had fallen pregnant and, almost overnight, Sebastian had decided they should leave the rat race and retire to the country. She had protested weakly at first, but Sebastian had known how to manipulate his wife's soft nature, and before Caro knew it the Holland Park house had been sold and Sebastian had bought one half of the mill conversion in Churchminster. He had also bought a loft apartment in Clerkenwell, close to his trading job in the City, to live in during the week – although he had neglected to tell her about it until later. 'To avoid that hellish commute, darling. You understand, don't you?'

Of course Caro had murmured her assent, as Sebastian had expected her to, but inside she hadn't really understood. She was being shipped out to the country, going from living a sociable, full life with her husband to seeing him only at weekends. She'd feared the whole dynamic of their marriage would change, but Sebastian had carried on as though nothing was happening. And he had been so persuasive: 'Think of all that fresh air, it will do you tons of good. Your complexion has been looking quite pasty lately. And I know your grandmother will be *thrilled* to have her first grandchild living so close. You wouldn't let her down, would you, darling?'

Of course Caro wouldn't. So she had dutifully left her London life behind, with friends' hollow promises of coming to visit ringing in her ears. That had been nine months ago, and she had been suffocating ever since.

Caro wandered into the hall and stared at herself in the full-length mirror on the wall. A pretty, natural blonde with soft brown eyes and an attractively curvaceous figure looked back. What Caro saw was a tired, spotty old wreck facing an uphill battle with her baby fat. Sebastian hadn't said outright she needed to lose weight, but they hadn't made love in months, and she had caught him looking at her critically several times as she had got changed for bed. Already not someone with the highest self-esteem, Caro's confidence had plummeted.

Milo started crying upstairs, snapping her out of her moment of self-loathing. He was going through a grizzly stage at the moment. In a rare bout of forcefulness, Caro had declined Sebastian's suggestion to get a nanny, and declared she would bring their son up by herself, but Milo was a difficult baby and Caro hadn't had a good night's sleep since he was born. She was exhausted, but she didn't want to admit to anyone that she couldn't even bring up her child.

Milo's cries intensified. 'All right, darling, I'm coming!' Caro called. Running up the stairs, she stubbed her bare toe on one of the sharp steps, and tears of pain sprang into her eyes.

'How did my life get like this?' she sobbed, as she flopped down on the stair, rubbing her injured foot.

Chapter 3

Across the green, Caro's sister Camilla was going through her own drama. Camilla was the middle daughter of Johnnie and 'Tink' Standington-Fulthrope. Until four years ago, Camilla and her younger sister Calypso had lived with their parents in the family home – a beautiful, Jacobean country house called Twisty Gables, close by on the Bedlington Road.

Everyone had loved having Johnnie and Tink as neighbours. He was such a darling, so tall and dashing, and often taking time to help the old ladies of Churchminster across the road. His wife (whose real name was Tessa, but who had been called Tink since girlhood on account of her girlish, tinkling laugh) was the life and soul of the village, with her warm character and sunny disposition. But gradually, over the years, Tink's ubiquitous laugh had started to dwindle, until one day she couldn't get out of bed. The doctor had diagnosed clinical depression and seasonal affective disorder, and put Tink on anti-depressants.

The pills had helped, but not as much as the family's biannual trip to their holiday home in

Barbados, where the sun, bright colours and warm climate had lifted Tink out of her black cloud. Shortly after returning home to England, she had become severely depressed again, and, after a family summit and much soul-searching, Johnnie and Tink had decided the only thing to do was to move to Barbados permanently. After all, Caro had left home years ago and at twenty-seven and nineteen respectively, Camilla and Calypso had been more than old enough to live by themselves.

Their parents had bought them No. 5 The Green, a gorgeous, three-bedroomed chocolate-box cottage on Churchminster's beautiful village green. It had been ideal for Camilla, who was working two mornings a week as a secretary for an upmarket surveyor's in Cheltenham, and a perfect base for Calypso, who had been about to study History of Art at Bristol University. The girls had been devastated to see their parents go, but they had hated seeing their bright, breezy mother reduced to such a sad, listless shadow. Besides, they were still only a short walk from their granny, Clementine Standington-Fulthrope, who was Johnnie's mother.

All three daughters were very different in character, even though they looked alike with their blonde hair, soulful hazel or brown eyes and – until Caro had fallen pregnant – identical slim, full-bosomed figures. Caro was kind and sweet, Camilla was the more practical, sensible of the three, and Calypso . . . well, she was the wild one, with a spiky attitude, impetuous nature and anti-establishment views. Being the youngest, she was often indulged by her family, and had grown up to be a very controversial young woman.

As Camilla was finding out right now. Again.

'You can't give up your job!' she wailed down the phone to Calypso. 'You've only been there three months!' After graduating with a Third, Calypso had taken a year off and spent most of it sunbathing with her friends on various beaches around the world. On her return a few months ago, her parents had delicately suggested she might find a job, and Calypso had ended up working at an art gallery in Brighton. But, apparently, she'd had a huge row with the owner of the gallery over her bad time-keeping and had told him where to go. Camilla suspected she'd actually been sacked, but Calypso was much too proud to admit to that. And now, she informed Camilla, she was coming to live with her again.

'But have you thought it through?' asked Camilla, looking longingly round her little cottage. She had done it up so perfectly since Calypso had moved out, and now the thought of her sister coming home and unleashing her messy ways all over the Laura Ashley furniture was making her faintly queasy.

'Have you told Mummy and Daddy?' An angry babble erupted from the phone. 'OK, I was only asking. I'd better get your room ready, then.'

She replaced the receiver with a sense of foreboding. Her sister was temperamental at the best of times, but now she sounded positively unhinged. Camilla had a feeling that, in two days' time, hell would be unleashed on quiet Churchminster.

On the other side of the green, at Fairoaks House, Clementine Standington-Fulthrope was deadheading the narcissi in one of her many flowerbeds. Clementine, seventy-six, known as Granny Clem to her three granddaughters, was a formidable, energetic woman, often spotted taking her black Labrador Errol Flynn (on account of his whiskers) on his daily five-mile walk.

The Standington-Fulthrope clan had lived in the village for generations, and the family was seen as the unofficial royalty of Churchminster. Clementine was the head of the Standington-Fulthrope Committee (SFC), which had been founded by her husband's great-grandmother Augusta over a hundred years ago. Money raised by the SFC was spent, amongst other things, on keeping the village church maintained, and providing funds for the nearby children's home. In her time, Clementine had organized many a sponsored walk and charity function, calling on all and sundry to get involved. Often brusque and imperious, she did not suffer fools gladly. But under the prickly facade there was a good heart, and she adored her granddaughters, keeping a watchful eye on them in her son's absence.

Clementine was a tall, handsome woman with steely grey hair neatly pulled back in a bun – a hairstyle she hadn't changed since 1957. Today she was clad in her usual uniform of navy-blue waxed jacket, green Hunter wellies and Jaeger cashmere jumper, set off by an impressive pearl necklace her parents had given her as a coming-out present for her debutante ball.

Behind her loomed Fairoaks, a tall, imposing Victorian building, softened by beautiful, sweeping gardens. Clementine had lived alone there since her darling husband Bertie had died from an unexpected heart attack two decades ago. The gardens had become her pride and joy. Apart from a local boy who came in to cut the grass, she looked after the entire plot herself, which included six apple trees, climbing plants, and a deep, glossy pond with ornate stone fountain. A well-known presence at the Chelsea Flower Show, Clementine opened her gardens to the public for a small charge every summer, with all donations going to the SFC Fund.

'Anyone home?' A familiar voice cut across the still morning air. Clementine looked up to see Caro carefully manoeuvring Milo's pushchair through the wrought-iron gate. It was a rather chilly February day, and the little boy was wrapped up in swathes of blankets.

'Darling, how nice to see you!' Clementine stood up from the gardening mat, pulling off her gloves.

'Hello, Granny Clem.'

Caro walked over and gave her a kiss. She looks terrible, Clementine thought, taking in the wan complexion and dark circles under Caro's eyes. Although she had been delighted to have her back in the village again, Clementine privately worried that her granddaughter was too isolated. And Caro had become very defensive recently whenever Clementine offered to help with Milo. It would be a lot easier if Sebastian actually spent some proper *time* with his wife and son instead of staying in London and gallivanting off on all those blasted work trips, thought Clementine archly. But she often had to remind herself that Caro was a grown woman; she didn't want her silly old grandmother poking her nose in her business.

Milo let out a happy gurgle, and Clementine's face softened.

'Where's my favourite great-grandchild?' she said, walking happily towards the pushchair.

'He's your *only* great-grandchild,' Caro pointed out with a smile, as they made their way inside the house for a much-needed cup of tea.

Chapter 4

Friday dawned, and Sebastian yawned as he walked in through the doors of Harwells Bank at 7.04 a.m. It was one of the biggest, most prestigious corporations in the financial world, but Sebastian was feeling anything like work at that precise moment. Sabrina had kept him up till four in the morning, wanting to be shagged every which way senseless. Sebastian enjoyed sex as much as the next red-blooded adulterer, but he had to admit he was worn out. He was almost looking forward to going home for a change, and falling asleep on Caro's soft bosom.

To Sebastian, there was absolutely nothing wrong with having a wife and mistress. Most of his friends were doing the same, and as he had never been faithful to a woman in his life, he had no intention of starting now. Spurned by his father, Sebastian had spent his formative years shuttling round various countries as his glamorous mother Evie had fallen in and out of love with different suitors. He had grown up in an environment completely free of morals, respect and mutual affection. Eventually he'd been sent away to boarding school, staying with his flighty mother in the school holidays, wherever she happened to be in the world. He had never respected her, and it was fair to say he hadn't respected a woman since. A psychologist treating him on the couch might have put his caddish behaviour down to his peripatetic, insecure childhood. But it was simpler than that. Sebastian was just a complete shit.

Sebastian had married sweet, trusting Caro because she could give him an heir and provide a comfortable home, but that was where their union had stopped. And so, when, two years earlier, he had met Sabrina at a drinks function, he had instantly known they'd end up having an affair. A model by occupation, Sabrina often graced the pages of *Hello!* magazine in sumptuous 'at home' shoots. She was a well-known face on the Belgravia circuit, and was used to Arab businessmen spending thousands of pounds on taking her out for the evening. Like Sebastian, she loved money, power, glamour and sex. They really were a perfect match.

Back in Churchminster, someone else was feeling the effects of sleep-deprivation. The central heating in Harriet Fraser's cottage had broken down sometime around two in the morning, and she had spent the remainder of the night wrapped in pyjamas and four jumpers, shivering madly. Forgoing her normal morning shower, Harriet threw on her old cords and fleece jumper and tramped up to the main house to ask for some help.

At the age of thirty, Harriet had left home. Sort of. What she had actually done was move from Clanfield Hall, the grand estate home of her parents, Sir Ambrose and Lady Frances Fraser, and down the drive to Gate Cottage, a small stone two-up two-down at the estate's entrance. For someone who had grown up in a house with corridors so wide it took five minutes to jog across them, Gate Cottage couldn't have been more different. Harriet adored it. For the first time she was her own boss and she also loved the peace and quiet.

Clanfield Hall was very quiet as well, today, she reflected as she arrived at the top of the main drive. It was nine o'clock, but the morning mist hadn't lifted yet, and the vast lawns were shrouded in an ethereal white cloak. The gardens were historic and breathtakingly landscaped, the *pièce de résistance* a huge, ornate fountain in front of the house. Rumour had it that Queen Victoria had once bathed her feet in there during a summer party.

A hot bath was foremost on Harriet's mind as she skirted round the east wing of the house to the back, and in through the kitchen entrance. There she found Cook, busy decapitating a dead pheasant.

A cheery, red-faced woman, Cook had been in the family's employment since Harriet was a little girl.

'Miss Harriet, what are you doing here so early?'

'Blasted heating's broken down again,' said Harriet gloomily, shaking her muddy wellingtons off by the door. 'It's got to be the fourth time in the last year. Do you know if Jed's about? I need him to take a look at it.'

'I think he's out by the lake, fixing some fencing,' replied Cook. 'Now then, do you want breakfast? I could do your favourite pancakes . . .'

Harriet looked down at her bulging waistband. 'I'm meant to be on a diet.'

19

'Just a few,' said Cook conspiratorially, whose motto in life was 'If it moves, feed it.'

'Oh, go on, then!' said Harriet, with a cheeky grin. 'Just don't tell Mummy. Speaking of which, where are they?'

'Her Ladyship is in the drawing room, Sir Ambrose is in his study,' informed Cook.

'I'd better go and say hello, then,' said Harriet. 'Can you hold off on the nosh for a bit, Cooky?'

She left the warmth of the kitchen and padded down the long, wood-panelled corridor to the drawing room. The house had been in her father's family for three hundred years, and family crests adorned the walls, alongside creepy looking portraits of her ancestors. A meek and mild only child, Harriet had found growing up at Clanfield Hall a daunting experience. She had much preferred hanging out with Cook and the other staff in the cosy servants' quarters, than with her parents in the huge chilly rooms 'front of house'.

Harriet arrived at the drawing room door and tentatively pushed it open. Her mother was sitting in a Regency chair by one of the room's huge windows, reading. Lady Frances Fraser was a well-preserved woman of fifty-one, her slender figure encased in a silk shirt and long tweed pencil skirt. As always she was immaculately made-up, with her blonde hair pulled up in a chignon. She looked up as her daughter walked in.

'Have you put on weight, Harriet?' Lady Fraser never failed to comment on her daughter's weight, even if she'd only seen her the day before.

Harriet edged into the room. 'No, Mummy, I've been on my diet. Honestly, I've been really good . . .' She thought of the pancakes and blushed guiltily.

'Hmm,' her mother offered up her cheek, which Harriet kissed dutifully. 'Maybe we should get you a personal trainer as well.' Lady Fraser loved her daughter, but despaired at having produced such an ungainly, overweight lump. In contrast to her own sleek blonde hair, Harriet's was a brown, frizzy mess she usually scraped back in a ponytail that looked like it was exploding out of her head. The famous Fraser cheekbones were hidden beneath red, chubby cheeks. In fact, the only thing Harriet had going for her, as Lady Fraser often pointed out, were her calves and ankles, which stayed enviably slim no matter how much weight Harriet piled on.

Frances was twenty years her husband's junior and had given birth to Harriet when she was only twenty-one. Afterwards, due to a medical complication, the couple were told she would be unable to have any more children, and with this news Sir Ambrose's hopes of carrying on the family line had been dashed. Once he'd got over the shock, some years later, he had gone about trying to marry Harriet off to any blueblood available. Harriet's debutante ball had been the most horrific evening of her life: her frame crushed into an unflattering taffeta dress, and every eligible young bachelor firmly giving her a wide berth. Harriet had retreated behind a wall of books ever since, and much preferred a dashing hero in a Mills and Boon novel to real life. As a result, and to her complete mortification, she was starting her third decade still a virgin.

'Well, I just came to say hello,' she said, hovering on one foot.

'Do stand up straight, darling,' instructed her mother.

'Sorry, Mummy,' apologized Harriet. 'I need to find Jed, my heating's broken down.'

'Again?' her mother raised a perfectly plucked eyebrow at her daughter. 'Honestly, I don't know why you persist in living in that hovel when there's a perfectly good wing here for you.'

'I'm fine, really!' replied Harriet hastily. 'I'll get it fixed.' She turned to go out of the room. 'I might go and say morning to Daddy as well.'

'I wouldn't, if I were you,' said her mother, returning to her book. 'The post boy delivered the *Daily Star* instead of the *Telegraph*, and he's in a frightful mood.'

Her father's short fuse was legendary: he'd once smashed a priceless oriental vase when his horse lost in the 11.28 at Cheltenham.

'I think I'll leave it for a while,' said Harriet.

An hour later Jed Bantry was standing in the kitchen of Gate Cottage, iron wrench in hand. Harriet, who had ended up having seconds of Cook's delicious pancakes with maple syrup, was now feeling vaguely sick, and vowed not to eat another thing for the rest of the weekend. She watched Jed as he rummaged around in the kitchen cupboard that housed the building's heating system.

'The fuse has gone,' he announced, pulling himself out to face Harriet. The morning sun caught his face, lighting up his chiselled features. Harriet blinked as she was reminded again what a gorgeous man Jed had grown up to be. Jed was the son of her parents' housekeeper Mrs Bantry. They lived in one of the workers' cottages at the edge of the estate. Mr Bantry had run off years before 'with some old tart from the dairy' as Cook had put it. Similar in age, Jed and Harriet had practically grown up together, worlds apart but side-by-side. Jed was now the estate's handyman and sometime gardener. He had always been a boy of few words, and even now, in adulthood, Harriet still couldn't work him out. But they existed in companionable silence, a familiarity that had grown over the years.

Jed had grown over time, too. Once a skinny, rangy kid, he was now a strapping six-footer with wide shoulders and a lean, muscled physique from doing hard manual work all year round. With a tousled mop of black hair, eyes the colour of faded khaki and a flawless complexion, Jed Bantry could have walked straight off the set of a Hugo Boss advert. Not that he seemed aware of this. All the local girls fancied him madly, but Jed showed little obvious interest in the opposite sex, preferring to spend his time working on the estate or tinkering with his motorbike. Harriet had wondered in recent months if she should start fancying him, too, but her parents would have had a heart attack if she had. Besides, Harriet's libido was so dead and buried, she doubted any man other than a dashing Victorian hero called Heathcliff Montgomery would ever make her heart flutter.

'I've got a spare fuse – I'll go and get it, then, yeah?' said Jed, bringing Harriet out of her daydream. She watched him pack away his toolbox, his rock-hard buttocks straining against the material of his overalls.

'Oh, yes, that would be lovely, Jed,' said Harriet gratefully, giving herself a shake. 'Thanks awfully.' She watched him tread off down the path and shivered again. The temperature was reaching arctic proportions, while the waistband of her trousers pinched miserably. In a decisive moment, Harriet decided to kill two birds with one stone, and went to dig out her Davina McCall workout DVD to do in front of the telly.

Chapter 5

On the other side of Churchminster, Freddie Fox-Titt was inspecting his wife's overgrown bush. His beloved Angie was a keen amateur gardener and had planted something gooseberry-related by the entrance to the Fox-Titts' estate. God only knows why, Freddie cursed to himself. It had mutated so much it was in danger of blocking off the driveway. Not good when you made your living hiring out your land for various shooting and fishing parties. This was why he was armed with a large pair of rusty, antiquarian hedge clippers he'd found in Meakins's shed.

Unfortunately the gooseberry bush, with its sturdy stems and prickles, was proving quite an adversary. Freddie had been going at it for forty-five minutes and had hardly made a dent. When a branch pinged back in his face and scratched his cheek, Freddie decided enough was enough. 'Bugger this,' he said to himself, and turned back to the house, making a mental note to get Meakins in for an extra day that week instead.

Halfway up the drive, Freddie was nearly mown aside by a black GTI, bass pumping as it sped towards him at tremendous speed. 'ARCHIE!' Freddie yelled, squeezing up on to the verge to avoid being mown down. The car screeched to a halt in a cloud of dust and then reversed back to where Freddie was standing.

The tinted window slid down, and drum and bass music blasted out, making Freddie's eyes water. In the driver's seat sat a youth with a shaved head, tramlines round the sides. His eyebrows had been shaved into strips and he was wearing a baggy tracksuit and a big gold pendant. This was Freddie's 17-year-old son, Archie.

'Wassup?' he asked insolently, smoothing his hand across his shaven head and admiring it in the rear-view mirror.

'Do you have to drive like a bloody maniac?' yelled Freddie again, straining to be heard above the music. Archie sucked his teeth at his dad in response. 'Where are you going?' asked Freddie, this time more reasonably. He hadn't had such a long conversation with his son in months.

'College, innit?' replied Archie, casting his eyes around and looking bored.

'Are you back for supper with us this evening?' asked Freddie hopefully.

Archie sucked his teeth again. 'I'm not hanging out with you *olds*, man! Me and Tyrone is going to this house party. Laters.' And with that, the window rolled up and Archie revved his car, disappearing down the drive.

Freddie watched him go and sighed. Christ, who would have teenagers? Until he turned sixteen, Archie had been a model son. At Eton he had excelled at sports and science and planned to become a vet, much to the delight of his parents. But almost overnight, Archie had changed beyond recognition. He had announced he was sick of private education, dropped out of school, and enrolled in the local college to do his A levels. Instead of spending weekends with his old friends Tarquin and Rupert, Archie started hanging around with some local lads from the nearby town of Bedlington. Shortly afterwards, he had shaved off his mop of Hugh Grant hair, swapped his chinos for ridiculously baggy-crotched jeans, and started to talk like someone who had just absconded from a Harlem ghetto. Freddie didn't know what to do with this walking, talking, Vanilla Ice lookalike who was suddenly living under his roof.

His wife Angie was more understanding. 'It's just a stage he's going through,' she soothed Freddie. 'Don't worry, Freds, he'll soon grow out of it.'

'Bloody well hope so,' said Freddie gloomily. 'Still, at least we haven't got to fork out for school fees any more. It's been a tough few years.'

So it had. The Maltings, the handsome Cotswold stone house the Fox-Titts lived in, was in the middle of the Maltings estate. It had once been a stud farm, but when Freddie and Angie had moved in twenty years ago, Freddie had seen the potential of the two hundred acres of land it came with. As well as the shooting parties, Freddie rented his pastures to local farmers and organic produce businesses. However, the foot and mouth disaster a few years ago had hit him hard, and he was still recovering from it.

Angie Fox-Titt ran Angie's Antiques on the village green. She was a short, petite woman with lively brown eyes and a mane of bouncing chestnut hair. Freddie thought she was the most beautiful thing he'd ever seen, even after over two decades of marriage. Freddie, in his fifties, balding and slightly portly, often wondered how he'd managed to snare such a gorgeous creature, but Angie, her heart broken by too many handsome bastards before she'd met him, had finally decided to go for personality over perfection. Freddie and Angie worked very well together, their marital harmony only slightly marred by the metamorphosis of their only child.

Screeching up the Bedlington Road, Archie patted his pockets to make sure the cash was in there. Tyrone had called half an hour ago to tell him he had scored some weed: 'This is like, shit hot bruv, get your ass over here.' Archie had needed no encouragement. Who needed an afternoon of double chemistry when he could smoke himself into oblivion with Tyrone? As he rounded the bend far too fast, Archie nearly careered into two little old ladies, tottering up the road holding on to each other.

'Christ!' Archie yelled, his Eton accent resurfacing in the surprise of the moment. He slammed on his brakes and came to a smoking halt twenty metres down the road.

Heart still hammering in his mouth, he rested his head on the steering wheel until a knock on the driver's window made him look up. Eunice and Dora Merryweather, eighty-two if they were a day, smiled at him through the window. Archie reluctantly wound it down.

'Ooh, young Archie, you were going a bit fast then!' said Eunice, the slightly older-looking one. The two sisters had lived for years in a cottage on the green two doors down from Camilla's and were something of a village institution. Most residents had a scratchy lurid woollen jumper hidden at the back of a wardrobe that had been knitted for them by Dora or Eunice.

'Never mind, I know how you young people like to have fun,' said Dora. 'Where are you off to, dear? Eunice and I are just taking a walk before *Countdown* and . . .'

Shock over, and attitude back, Archie scowled at them both. 'Yeah, well I'd love to stay and chat to yous Miss Marples,' he said, adding '*not*' under his breath, 'but I gotta see a man about a smoke, er, dog.' He smirked and rolled up his window, started the car up and drove off. When he looked in his rear-view mirror, Eunice and Dora were still standing in the middle of the road, waving gaily at him. Archie wrinkled his brow in dismissal and thought about the big fat joint he'd presently be inhaling.

That evening, Caro sat in the kitchen, pouring out her fourth glass of Bollinger. The bubbles fizzed against the flute, a cruel antidote to Caro's flat mood. Sebastian had arrived home a few hours ago, looking every inch the city slicker in his Savile Row suit and Jermyn Street shirt. But no amount of expensive tailoring or deep tan could have hidden the purple shadows under his eyes.

'Darling, you look knackered,' Caro had said in concern as she met him on the doorstep. 'You know, you work too jolly hard.'

'Oh, stop fussing, sweetheart,' Sebastian had replied, dropping a cursory kiss on her forehead. 'Where's my son, then?'

Caro had bitten her lip. 'His bedtime was an hour ago. I did tell you you'd have to get an earlier train if you wanted to see him . . .'

'Yah, well I got held up,' Sebastian had said evasively, thinking of Sabrina's hold-ups in the back of the cab on the way to Paddington. They'd just had time to book into some grotty little Travelodge for a quickie, but then Sabrina had insisted on putting on an impromptu floorshow with her new vibrator. Sebastian had ended up missing the 5.03 and, as a result, he'd lost his seat in first class and had had to stand most of the two-hour journey back. Cursing Sabrina and her insatiable libido, he hadn't arrived home in the best of moods.

'Darling, pour me a stiff G and T, will you?' Sebastian had strode down the corridor, straight past the dining room where Caro had spent ages laying an intimate table for two complete with soft lighting and candles. 'Can we eat in front of the telly?' he had continued. 'I've eaten out at Daphne's three times this week already. Don't think I can hack another stuffy dinner.'

Without waiting for an answer, he had disappeared into the comfy room. Caro had stood for a moment in the hallway, then gone into the dining room and slowly blown out the candles.

After two courses, which Caro had spent all afternoon preparing and which Sebastian wolfed down in a matter of minutes, he had fallen asleep on the sofa. Sighing, she had carefully taken his shoes off and fetched a blanket to put over him, before going into the kitchen to comfort-eat her way through the lemon tart she had made for pudding.

At No. 5 The Green, Camilla and Harriet were tucking into large glasses of wine. They were ensconced on opposite ends of Camilla's comfy, flowered sofa, James Morrison on the stereo and the remains of a Waitrose fish pie for two on the floor beside them.

Camilla and Harriet had been friends since they were little. They'd both been born in the village, gone to the same prep school, and then boarded at Benenden, the exclusive girls' school in Kent. Over the years, they'd shared midnight feasts, exam pressures and unrequited crushes. Both homely types at heart, the pair had spurned the bright lights of London unlike many of their contemporaries, and, after a prerequisite ski season as chalet maids (Camilla in Courchevel and Harriet in Meribel) had hurried home to Churchminster as quickly as possible. Now Harriet worked as a sometime PA to her father, actually spending most of the time watching daytime TV and reading romance novels, while Camilla had her part-time job. Her boyfriend of three years was local farmer Angus Aldershot. Everyone expected Camilla and Angus to marry in the next few years, and for her to move up to his sprawling farm on the outskirts of the village. There she would readily churn out sturdy heirs to inherit the family business Angus had received from his own father.

At the moment, though, thoughts of that were far from Camilla's mind as she discussed her younger sister with Harriet. 'I just don't know what to *do* about her, Hats,' she said, as she refilled their glasses again from the rapidly disappearing bottle of Chablis.

'You know Calypso, she's always been a first-rate rebel,' Harriet replied. 'I'm sure she'll grow out of it, don't worry, Bills,' she said, using the nickname Camilla's closest friends and family gave her.

'Somehow, I can't see that happening any time soon.' Camilla sighed. 'You know, this job had given her the first bit of proper stability she'd had for ages and Mummy and Daddy were *so* thrilled she'd found something to apply herself to.'

'Has she told them yet?'

'No, that's been left to me, obviously,' said Camilla. 'Apparently Calypso's pay-as-you-go has run out and she can't afford to call them.' She raised a wry eyebrow. 'And she's coming home to live with me for a while until she sorts herself out.'

'Oh gosh, good luck!' said Harriet.

At that moment there was a violent banging on the door, followed by a loud, drunken voice.

'BUTTERCUP! It's the Shagmeister. Let me in, you horny little rabbit. I'm going to scamper up your warren and pork your brains out!'

Camilla blushed and looked apologetically at Harriet. 'Oh God, that's Angus. I *told* him not to come back blotto from the pub. Sorry, Hats.'

'Don't mind me,' said Harriet good-naturedly. 'I'd better scoot off, anyway.' She fetched her coat as Camilla went to open the front door.

A large, red-faced young man with dishevelled floppy brown hair fell in. Angus was wearing a quilted green jacket which was flapping open to reveal the checked blue and white Thomas Pink shirt Camilla had bought him last Christmas. He looked like he'd fallen in a ditch on his way over: his brown cords and Timberland loafers were covered in mud. His blue, slightly bulbous eyes were crossed as he breathed a tsunami of beer fumes through the cottage. Angus went to stick his tongue in Camilla's mouth but missed, and licked her cheek instead. She winced. He'd clearly been at the cheese and onion crisps in the pub.

'An-gus!' she reprimanded. 'I told you not to come over if you got in this state.'

'Yah, but "Little Angus" wants to come out to play,' he boomed. Camilla winced again, and he slapped her on the bottom. 'I thought I'd come and give you a good seeing-to, you naughty filly.'

Behind them, Harriet cleared her throat. 'Er, I'll be off then,' she said politely. 'Hah!' Angus rounded on her. 'Fancy a threesome, Hatty?'

This time Camilla kicked him on the ankle. 'Angus! Don't be so vile!'

'Only joking, she's not my type anyway!' Camilla kicked his ankle even harder, but he had such thick red socks on he didn't notice.

'It's all right,' said Harriet, sliding out the door gratefully. 'I'll see you soon, Bills.' With that, she got in her Golf and drove off, eager to get back to her book and a dashing young hero who didn't stink of beer and paw her like a randy bear.

Behind the closed front door the randy bear was advancing, somewhat unsteadily, on Camilla. 'Come here, my fair lady!' he slurred. Angus fumbled with his zip, and a rather mediocre-sized cock popped out, weaving like a snake being charmed out of its basket. Camilla couldn't think of

33

anything less charming at that moment than being bonked by her drunk, sweaty boyfriend. Equally, she couldn't bear to think of him fumbling around her nether regions all night when she wanted to sleep, so she guided him upstairs to her bedroom. There he fell on top of her, one leg still in his cords, and with his socks still on. As he thrust in and out of her, with all the tenderness of a bucking bronco, Camilla tried to make a mental list of what she had to do for Calypso's imminent arrival. God, Angus hadn't been this plastered since Tilly Motson-Bagshot's thirtieth last summer. He and his best friend Ed 'Sniffer' Clevedon had set fire to the moose's head in the Great Hall before putting on an impromptu *Puppetry of the Penis* show at the head of the table. Lady Motson-Bagshot had not been amused.

Roaring like a wounded bull, Angus finally came, and collapsed on top of her.

'Angus, you weigh a ton, get off me!' she protested a few seconds later. He snored loudly in her ear.

'So much for romance.' Camilla heaved his sweating bulk off her before retreating to the other side of the bed.

Chapter 6

The Reverend Arthur Goody was a bright, cheery and enthusiastic man, very popular with the parishioners of Churchminster. He lived alone at the rather gloomy village rectory, but was often seen propping up the bar at the Jolly Boot, passing the time of day with the landlord, Jack 'the Lad' Turner. The Reverend's sermons were peppered with gentle humour, which had attracted more young people from the village, and, as a result, congregation levels were at their highest in years. Mid-forties, portly with glasses and a Friar Tuck hairstyle, you wouldn't say he'd exactly sexed-up religion, but Arthur Goody had definitely put a more human face on it.

It was the first week in March, and Sunday dawned bright and sunny. The morning service at St Bartholomew's was being held at eleven in the morning, and the villagers were beginning to file up the path outside the ancient, pretty church. The Reverend stood by the door and greeted them.

'Freddie, Angie; beautiful day to enter the House of God.'

'Better that than the House of Fraser,' replied

Freddie Fox-Titt good-naturedly. 'Angie was in there yesterday afternoon, burning up my credit card.'

Angie rolled her eyes affectionately as the Revd Goody chortled. 'Come on, Freddie, or we'll miss out on our pew. See you in there, Arthur.'

Next to arrive were Clementine and Camilla. The former was resplendent in a maroon fitted velvet jacket and skirt, brandishing a large brown handbag that could have given Mrs Thatcher a run for her money. Her grey bun was immaculate as ever, as was the slash of coral pink lipstick across her mouth.

'Good morning, Reverend,' said Clementine briskly. 'I did think the committee meeting went *extremely* well last week.' She eyed him beadily. 'I am still waiting to hear from you on the subject of the new pews, though.'

'I'll get on to it,' he replied hastily. 'Sorry, Mrs Standington-Fulthrope.' Clementine reminded him of his old headmistress at prep school, a terrifying old dragon called Mrs Belcher. He always felt like a quivering schoolboy in her company.

'Excellent,' replied Clementine, sweeping past him. 'I shall be in touch. *Do* come on, Camilla.' The Revd Goody and Camilla exchanged weak smiles as she trailed after her grandmother.

Camilla had the most beastly hangover. The night before, she and Angus had gone out for dinner in Bedlington, and afterwards he'd insisted on off-roading back across the muddy fields on his quad bike, with Camilla hanging on for dear life behind him, rich food and wine churning uneasily inside her. She'd been on the verge of vomiting ever since.

The rest of the villagers filed in. This was the Revd Goody's favourite part of his services: seeing the kaleidoscope of people that came from a village like Churchminster. Babs Sax, a forty-something artist who lived in a cottage next to the village shop, skinny as a rake, and swathed in brightly patterned chiffon. Next was harassed-looking mum Lucinda Reinard, trailed by her three sulky children. Dora and Eunice Merryweather, throwing out cheery hellos and passing the children butterscotch sweets when their parents weren't looking. The Turners from the pub, and Caro with baby Milo. Oh, thought the Reverend, and the husband too; nice to see families turning out together.

In fact, Sebastian was looking round impatiently, constantly checking his watch. After forty-eight hours in the country he was going stir crazy, itching to get back to London. Caro hadn't had the nerve to tell him yet that they were expected at her grand-mother's for lunch.

An hour later, Camilla stretched her toes gratefully as the Revd Goody concluded his service. The fresh air had helped her nausea, and she was starting to feel human again. As the family pew was at the front of the church, Camilla and Clementine were the last people to leave. Outside, most of the villagers were still milling around, chatting or waiting for the pub to open. Consequently, virtually the entire population of Churchminster was on hand to witness what happened next.

Shattering the tranquil calm of the surroundings, a black cab zoomed round the corner and screeched to a halt in front of the church. The passenger door was flung open, and a pair of impossibly long, slender legs encased in fishnet stockings and tipped with spiky black stilettos swung themselves out. The villagers looked on agog.

Camilla, with a growing feeling of dread, thought she recognized the legs. They were followed by the hem of a bedraggled fur coat, a green sequin cocktail dress that couldn't have been more inappropriate for the surroundings, and, finally, the head of an extremely pretty girl with wild, tousled long blonde hair, and black mascara streaked across her cheeks.

'Yah, you can go to hell, too!' she screamed at the red-faced cab driver. She hauled out a huge, battered old suitcase, which promptly fell open, spilling lacy G-strings, cigarette lighters, and bundles of creased clothes all over the ground.

'Stick your tip right up your derrière!' she screeched. 'How dare you call me a rude bitch!' She kicked the door shut and the driver roared off, yelling obscenities as he went.

Calypso Standington-Fulthrope watched him speed off, and then, sensing the stunned audience behind her, turned to face the sea of gaping faces. As soon as she spotted Clementine her face crumpled and she suddenly looked only twelve years old.

'Oh, Granny Clem,' she sobbed, and rushed through the crowd into her grandmother's arms.

'You silly child, what *are* we going to do with you?' asked Clementine that afternoon, stroking Calypso's long hair as her granddaughter cuddled up to her. The family, including Caro and Sebastian, were sitting in the huge living room at Fairoaks.

They had just finished the Sunday lunch that had been sloppily prepared by Clementine's house-keeper, Brenda Briggs. As Camilla nearly broke her tooth on a rock-hard roast potato, she had wondered for the umpteenth time why her grand-mother didn't get rid of Brenda and get in someone who could actually cook and clean properly. But Clementine wouldn't hear of it. 'Brenda's a treasure, I get all the gossip from her, which is *invaluable* when one runs the village committee.'

Despite claiming she was too distraught to eat, Calypso had wolfed down a large helping of lunch, cramming in seconds of the shop-bought sticky toffee pudding. In-between mouthfuls, she had told her family about her screaming row with her old boss: 'Honestly, he was such a lech, and expected me to work all the hours God sent. And I'm convinced he was involved in some fraud stuff.'

Camilla raised her eyebrows. She knew her sister's overactive imagination, plus the fact she was extremely difficult to get on with sometimes. Suspecting Calypso wasn't entirely the innocent party in all this, she bit her lip.

Clementine, on the other hand, was being far more sympathetic. Putting aside her initial shell-shock at having her granddaughter, dressed like a Parisian hooker, fling herself on her in front of the entire village, she was now taking everything in her stride – fussing over Calypso, instructing Camilla to call their parents in Barbados to tell them the news, and calling for Brenda to unpack Calypso's suitcase.

'I'm staying with Bills, actually,' said Calypso,

sitting up to face her grandmother. 'You don't mind, do you, Granny Clem? It's just that I'd really like to be in my old room, and I left lots of stuff there from last time . . .'

Which is now packed away, nice and neatly, in the attic, thought Camilla irritably.

Clementine cast her eye over Camilla, and then back to Calypso. 'I suppose not. I do worry about you moping about, though. Maybe you should try and find some work with your sister to keep yourself busy.'

Calypso threw a horrified look at Camilla, who looked equally shocked. 'No, it's fine, I'll find lots of stuff to do. Besides, I do feel so exhausted. I think I should rest for a while . . .' She shot a sheepish look at Camilla, and snuggled back up to her grandmother.

Sebastian, sitting next to Caro with one hand proprietorially on her knee, was rather enjoying all the drama. He did love a scandal, especially when it involved one's own family (just as long as *his* little secret didn't get out). He also couldn't believe what a complete *fox* Calypso had grown into. Last time he'd seen her she'd been a bratty teenager with braces on her teeth. Now she looked like a funkier version of the Caro he'd first met: all long legs, a slender waist you could fit your hands round, and flashing eyes. He wondered momentarily how difficult it would be to get another S-F sister into bed. He could get hard just thinking about it . . .

Sebastian hastily crossed his legs and covered up the growing bulge in his chinos with one of Clementine's embroidered cushions.

Chapter 7

One week later, chaos had descended on the previous tranquillity of No. 5 The Green. It seemed wherever Calypso went, she left a trail of sluttiness behind her: half-drunk cups of coffee with fag butts floating in them (despite Camilla's pleas for her to smoke outside the back door); tossed-aside magazines; food; and items of clothing – mostly impossibly skimpy underwear. When Camilla tentatively poked her head around the door to Calypso's bedroom, it looked like a cross between Courtney Love's boudoir and an Ann Summers shop: there were leopard-print clothes, lacy G-strings and pots of make-up spilled everywhere. Incongruously, there was also a half-deflated blow-up dildo lying forlornly in a pile of scuffed stilettos. Camilla had recoiled in horror, and not returned since.

Now Camilla made her way downstairs, picking up two discarded coffee cups, an empty wine glass, and a half-eaten crème brûlée as she went. She found her sister in the living room, sprawled across the sofa, remote control on her chest, watching *The Jeremy Kyle Show*. She was wearing Camilla's favourite Boden pyjamas with what looked suspiciously like make-up stains down the front.

'Calypso, it's great you feel so at home, but do you think you could try and be a little bit tidier?' sighed Camilla from the doorway. 'I've got to go to work in half an hour, and so far I've spent all morning tidying up your mess.'

'I thought Mrs Briggs cleaned for you,' said Calypso dismissively, not taking her eyes off the screen.

'Yah, well, that's only two days a week, and even then, I can't really tell if she does anything.' Camilla hovered in the doorway, looking at her sister. 'Calypso, what *are* you going to do with yourself? You've barely moved off the sofa since you came here, and you still haven't phoned Mummy and Daddy. They're frantic to hear from you.'

'I KNOW!' snapped Calypso fiercely. 'I just can't handle all the stress at the moment. Oh God, my life is shit. I'm bored out of my brains here.'

Nothing a new job wouldn't fix, thought Camilla in frustration. One of their father's friends had already offered Calypso a position in his art gallery on the King's Road in London. She had flatly refused: 'I am sick of bloody artists and their stuffy bloody owners. I need something *new* in my life.'

Exactly what that was Camilla had no idea, unless it involved lying on a sofa and turning lovely flowered wallpaper yellow with nicotine. The only person Calypso did want to talk to was her new boyfriend, Sam, who she spent hours on the phone to every day. Camilla had picked up the phone to him a few times. He sounded rather a gruff chap, but when she had tried to ask her sister about him,

42

Calypso had grunted non-committally and cut her off.

'My life is just *shit*!' repeated Calypso, rolling over into the back of the sofa. Camilla's heart softened, and she put the cups, the glass and the crème brûlée on the floor, and sat down next to her sister's back.

'Come on, Muffin,' she said, using Calypso's childhood nickname. 'It can't be all *that* bad.'

'It is!' wailed Calypso from the depths of the sofa. 'I've got no life, no job, and I'm missing all my friends.'

An idea popped into Camilla's head. 'Hey, why don't I put on a dinner party, and you can be the guest of honour? It can be your official welcome home party.'

Calypso turned around, slightly placated. She loved being the centre of attention. 'Can I bring Sam?'

'Of course!' replied Camilla. 'How about next Friday?'

'Not like I'm doing anything else,' said Calypso moodily.

'I'll make lemon meringue pie,' cajoled Camilla.

For the first time since she'd been back in Churchminster Calypso smiled, making her beautiful features light up.

'OK, you've won me over.'

Camilla smiled back, relieved beyond measure. 'Thank golly for that! Now come and give me a hug.'

As well as cleaning for Clementine, Brenda Briggs worked part-time at Churchminster's village shop.

43

She hadn't taken a day off sick in twenty-six years, and was chatty and hawk-eyed, with an exceptional nose for gossip. Brenda lived with her husband Ted in one of the cottages opposite the rectory, and knew about every affair, bankruptcy and scandal going on in the village.

This morning Brenda was positively beside herself. Ted had just phoned to tell her the most exciting bit of news she had ever heard, and Brenda was itching to share it with someone. Luckily, she didn't have to wait long.

The door tinkled and one of her bingo friends walked in.

'Ooh, Sandra, am I pleased to see you!' said Brenda. She stopped marking up the Jammy Dodgers and leaned conspiratorially over the counter.

'You'll *never* guess what I heard.'

Sandra was over there like a shot. 'Go on then, duckie, fill me in!'

'Well,' said Brenda dramatically, savouring the moment. 'I think we might have a new owner for Byron Heights.'

Byron Heights was a turn-of-the-century Gothic mansion that stood on the outskirts of Churchminster. With its turrets and forbidding iron gates, it looked like something out of *The Addams Family*, and stuck out like a sore thumb among the golden stone houses of the Cotswold countryside. Byron Heights had been empty for eighteen months, since the previous owners, a couple who had made their fortune selling dried dog biscuits, had moved to Monaco. There had been several viewings since, but it had seemed no one

44

wanted to pay the £4.5 million price tag or take on such an imposing house. Until now.

'Well, y'know my Ted's in the building trade. He's been given some work on the house! Apparently it has just been bought – for the *full* asking price. And you'll never guess who the new owner is!'

'Des Lynam?' asked Sandra hopefully. She'd always had a thing for him.

'Nope. But it is someone famous.'

'Ooh! Joan Collins!'

'It's a man. And he's in the music industry.'

'Oh Lord! Michael Jackson!'

Brenda tutted, as if she was disappointed by Sandra's apparent lack of telepathic powers. 'No, dear. He's British, from round these parts originally, had a No. 1 hit with 'Hot Dang!' Ring any bells?'

Sandra clutched her hand to her mouth, eyes like saucers. 'Not *Devon Cornwall*!!'

'The one and only!' announced Brenda. 'Coming to live here. In *Churchminster*. Any day now!'

'Oh, swoon!' said Sandra, and giggled like a schoolgirl.

Anyone under the age of forty-five would probably never have heard of the preposterously named Devon Cornwall. Born plain old Neville Boyle in the quiet, unassuming village of Chipping Sodden twenty miles south of Churchminster, he had itched to get out of there from the time he could pick up a toy instrument. With dreams of becoming a professional musician, he'd moved to London as soon as he'd left school. Unlike so many before and after him, Neville had struck lucky within a few months with his own particular brand of pop rock. He had got a deal with Parlophone records, and Devon

Cornwall, music legend, had been born. In the seventies and early eighties, Devon had been more famous than Elvis and Victoria Beckham put together. Every record he released had gone straight to No. 1, including 'This Heart's for the Takin' Not the Breakin'' and 'Lusty Leggy Lady'. Four times married, Devon had developed a fond taste for cocaine in the mid-eighties, and his music career all but dried up. Last thing anyone heard, he had been living off his fortune in New Mexico post-rehab, doing the occasional 'at home' shoot for glossy magazines extolling the virtues of spirituality and clean living. Now, at the age of fifty-five, Devon Cornwall had decided to come home. His arrival would barely make a splash in the fickle tabloids which had once chased him so obsessively, but to middle-aged ladies like Brenda and Sandra, who had pinned posters of him to their teenage bedroom walls, and saved up their paper-round money to go and see him in concert, he was still a god.

'*Hot dang! Give me your sweet tang!*' trilled Brenda, shaking her hips.

'*Give me your stuff, your sexy steamy stuff. Ooh, hot dang!*' responded Sandra. They both collapsed in fits of giggles, thirty years momentarily slipping from them.

Exactly four days later, Devon Cornwall did move in. His entrance was remarkably low-key; just one blacked-out Mercedes driven by his long-time PA, Nigel. Nigel was to live at Byron Heights as well, and run Devon's day-to-day life. Not that it needed much running these days, but Nigel had been with Devon for so long, he was part of the furniture.

Speaking of which, Devon's belongings had been shipped over from Mexico, and the removal men had already installed them in Byron Heights. The huge, hand-carved wooden furniture fitted the sweeping contours of the house perfectly.

'Here we go, Devon,' said Nigel, pulling up outside the colossal arched front door. It was a beautiful, sunny spring day and the red-brick building was silhouetted invitingly against the pale blue sky. 'Home sweet home.'

Devon Cornwall looked up at the house. He had had a tough couple of years. His last wife Lina had run off with the pool boy a year earlier, not before cleaning out Devon's current bank account. He was glad to be shot of her – she had had a temper like Mount Vesuvius erupting – but he was missing the three million that she had taken as well. According to the Mexican police, her whereabouts were still unknown. He'd also been involved in a bitter legal wrangle with some no-mark hippies from Denmark who claimed that he'd stolen the third line of 'Lusty Leggy Lady' from them in the 1970s. Devon had won the case, but it had exhausted him, and when he had narrowly avoided a kidnapping attempt by guerrillas to ransom him off to the Mexican government, he had decided enough was enough.

'That's right, Nige, home sweet home,' he said, stretching contentedly in the back seat. 'Peace and quiet, fresh air and not much else. It's a country bumpkin's life for me.'

Little did he know the dangers of crime-ridden Mexico would pale in comparison to daily life in Churchminster.

Chapter 8

Another property was waiting for its new owners
in the village. The Mill House had been converted
into two luxury homes; while Sebastian and Caro
had bought one side, the other had stayed empty.
Then, the previous week, a 'Sold' sign had
appeared in the front garden. Caro noticed the sale
had been managed by Harbottle & Brunswick, a
very exclusive estate agent in Cirencester. She
wondered who the new owners would be. 'Oh,
please let it be a young mum who's lots of fun,' she
prayed. Caro envisioned a nice couple with two
adorable children; they would all get on fabulously
well and have riotous dinner parties. She and the
woman – whose name would be Sara – would have
giggly glasses of wine together and babysit each
other's kids while the other one went for a facial.
The husband – his name would be Hugh – would
get on equally well with Sebastian and they'd
spend weekends shooting together, before returning home to their families, flushed, triumphant and
happy. Caro bit her lip; perhaps Sebastian would
spend more time with her if there were interesting
people next door.

She looked at her watch. It was time for Milo's morning walk. It was a crisp, beautiful day, so she wrapped him up warm, put him in the stroller and set off. As she crossed over the road, the birds were chirping and the sun was shining, making the green look plump and fresh. Caro's heart lifted a little. It *was* lovely here. She decided to push Milo around the green and then go and buy herself a Galaxy bar from the shop. 'I'll burn it off on the walk,' she thought to herself guiltily.

As she drew level with her sister's cottage, Caro thought she really should go in and see how Calypso was doing. But she decided, with another stab of guilt, that she really couldn't face her youngest sister's traumas. She had enough on her plate with Milo. It was ironic really: when she had lived in London she had loved catching up with Calypso on the phone – when she'd been able to get hold of her. And once their parents had moved abroad, all three sisters had become closer than ever. But over the months since she'd moved back home, Caro had gradually withdrawn. Camilla had tried to broach the subject with her a few times, sensing her older sister was not herself, but Caro had brushed her off. She felt like she was on autopilot, acting the role of perfect wife and mother that everyone expected of her. She didn't know how to break that cycle.

Caro hurried past No. 5 The Green, and she was thinking longingly of her chocolate bar when the door of No. 3 creaked open and Dora and Eunice Merryweather came wobbling out. Their living room looked out directly on to the green and they had two armchairs positioned right in the window, which they seemed to sit in all day, just watching the world go by. Or stopping the world go by. They lay in wait for Caro on her morning walks, and the second she walked past, they'd be out in the front waving garish hand-knitted booties for Milo, and pinching his chubby cheeks. Caro didn't mind really, they were harmless old dears.

'Caroline, dear, how are you?' exclaimed Dora. She and Eunice did indeed look like they had just stepped off the set of Miss Marple. They were wearing almost identical floral-patterned dresses, strings of pearls round their necks, and cardigans draped round their shoulders.

'Dora, Eunice, how nice to see you!' The two ladies clustered round the pram, cooing, and Milo stared up at them, nonplussed.

'We've got a present for you, Master Milo! Haven't we, Dora?' said Eunice.

Dora's eyes twinkled. 'Oh yes, indeed!' From behind her back she produced something knitted in sludge green and orange. Caro's heart sank; she'd already got a drawer at home bulging with bits and pieces they'd made for Milo, most of a similar ilk. She had once tried to put Milo in a maroon and cream romper suit complete with knitted bow tie, but Sebastian had thrown a fit and said no son of his was going to be pushed around looking like a Romanian gipsy.

'Oh, you really shouldn't have!' said Caro truthfully. It was a knitted striped jacket with alternate green and orange buttons, and a bright blue 'M' embroidered on the front. Caro had never seen anything so horrific. She resolved to find the number of the nearest charity shop when she got home.

'It's lovely! Thank you so much,' she exclaimed brightly.

'It's our pleasure, we do so love a little one to knit for,' said Dora.

'Oh yes,' said Eunice, her eyes misting over.

Caro made what she hoped was a sympathetic noise. The rumour that had been around since she was little was that Eunice had once been married to a dashing air force pilot who had been killed in a ferocious dogfight over the Channel in the Second World War. Eunice, pregnant at the time with their first child, had miscarried at the shock and vowed never to marry again.

'Anyway, we won't keep you, dear,' said Dora. 'Besides, *The Archers* is on in a minute.'

'Thanks again for the jacket,' said Caro, quickly putting it under the pram.

'Bye, dear,' said Eunice. 'Say hello to that nice husband of yours.' She and Dora turned and walked slowly up the path. Caro made a mental note to steer clear of the sisters for a while, before poor Milo was swamped in a sea of itchy woollens.

As Caro got up to the shop, she found an extra fiver tucked in amongst Milo's bottom wipes. Oh good-oh, she could buy that month's *Tatler* as well. The perfect treat to go with her Galaxy. It was always quite tricky getting the stroller through the narrow door to the shop, and even more of a chore to steer it round the cramped aisles. Luckily Babs Sax was coming out, a copy of *Watercolour Monthly* under one bony arm. She lived next door to the shop in a pretty little cottage rather ambitiously named Hardwick House. (Also known by the locals as Hard-On House, because of the number of arty young men who went through the front door.) Today she was dressed in an aquamarine turban and matching kaftan, her lips and long nails painted firebox red.

'Darling!' she exclaimed huskily. 'You look radiant. And how, er, is the little one?' She peered into the pram the way a person might look at the sole of their shoe after treading in dog poo. Caro seized her chance. 'Fine, thanks. Babs, would you mind looking after Milo while I pop in the shop? I won't be a sec.'

'Well, er, I . . .' Babs flapped her skinny hands anxiously.

'Thank you!' Caro rushed into the shop before Babs had time to change her mind. Inside, she grabbed her mag and chocolate and an impromptu purchase of a pot of organic honey, and headed to the counter.

'Miss Caro!' said Brenda, appearing from under the counter like a genie from a bottle. 'How are we? Milo? Sebastian? Your parents? Heard from them recently?'

'Er, yes, I spoke to Mummy and Daddy a few days ago,' replied Caro, slightly bamboozled.

'Keeping well, hmm? When are they over next?'

'I think it will be Christmas,' replied Caro, thinking wistfully of London, where she could step outside her front door without facing the Spanish Inquisition at every corner. 'Must be off, I've left Milo outside in his pram.'

Brenda raised one over-plucked eyebrow. 'You want to be careful of those baby snatchers, I've been reading all about it in *Take a Break*.'

'Babs Sax is minding him, Brenda,' sighed Caro.

Brenda gave a snort of laughter. 'As if she'd be any good! Too busy trying to have it off with the getaway driver, I bet.'

Caro gave a forced smile and headed for the door. Brenda stopped her again.

'Ooh, have you heard who's moved in? Devon Cornwall! He's bought Byron Heights!'

Caro wrinkled her brow. 'Wasn't he in *Coronation Street*?' she asked, leaving Brenda open-mouthed. Outside, Babs Sax was standing by the pram, trying to look as if it was nothing to do with her. Caro relieved her of Milo, who was starting to squawk hungrily, and trundled home.

Chapter 9

Over in Farm Cottage, Stacey Turner was enjoying her third orgasm in thirty minutes. 'God, you are *so* good at that,' she breathed as Jed Bantry looked up from between her legs. They were in Jed's bedroom at the poky two-bedroom home he shared with his mother. Speaking of whom—

'You better push off,' said Jed, not unkindly. 'Ma will be back from the big house soon.' He stood up and kissed her quickly on the mouth, then turned to put his boxer shorts back on. Stacey propped herself up on one shoulder looking at him as his firm, muscular buttocks worked in front of her. What an arse! In her eyes, Jed would give Colin Farrell a run for his money. Colin Farrell was Stacey's favourite actor, and she had seen every film he'd been in.

At the age of eighteen years and two months, Stacey Turner was pert, buxom and curvy. She looked like a poor man's Kelly Brook. Stacey was a barmaid at the Jolly Boot, where her dad was landlord, and she loved it. She'd inherited her mum Beryl's flirtatious manner and her dad Jack's charm and gift of the gab, and she was always the centre of attention at the bar, with men for ever wanting to buy her drinks. If only there were more about like Jed Bantry, she thought to herself, watching him step into his overalls. Stacey had her pick of the local boys, and she'd had a fair few of them, but Jed was definitely the best shag she'd ever had – and the fittest. He never suffered from brewer's droop or shooting his load too early; Jed could keep rock hard for hours. In fact, he wore *her* out sometimes, and that was a first. There was something unrestrained and wild about him that none of the others came close to.

Still, Jed was a strange one. Theirs was a strictly sexual relationship, and she never expected anything more, but he'd still barely utter a few sentences when they were together. He just used his mouth to communicate in different ways ... Stacey shivered at the recent memory of Jed pleasuring her. Getting physical was just fine by her. And besides, she would be the envy of all her mates if they ever found out.

Stacey stretched luxuriantly, her magnificent boobs standing up to attention. Jed glanced at them momentarily and Stacey smiled. That would keep him ticking over until next time. 'Pass me my bra, lover. I'm working at noon, Dad'll wonder where I am.'

Jack Turner was notoriously protective of his only child, and had once chased one of the locals down the road with a poker from the fire when they'd made a suggestive remark about Stacey's chest. 'You'd better get your skates on then, lass,' said Jed. No one in the village knew about their fling, and that was just the way Jed intended keeping it.

*

The market town of Bedlington was five miles east of Churchminster. It lacked the prettiness and charm of the village, but had a functional, rustic charm that hadn't been completely diminished by the arrival of such places as Iceland and All Bar One. It helped that Bedlington held a very popular organic farmers market each month in the town square.

There was a small council estate on the eastern outskirts of the town, where farm workers had been housed in the seventies when their employers had sold off farm buildings to private owners. Nowadays, the Orchards Estate, as it was known, was home to young, non-farming families as well as some of the original tenants.

It was on the rec, a small, muddy piece of grass at the back of the estate, that Archie Fox-Titt and Tyrone lay on their backs, staring up at the sky in stoned oblivion. Archie had missed college yet again. Tyrone, who was meant to be studying to be a civil engineer, hadn't been to a lecture since before Christmas.

A fresh wind gusted across the field, making Tyrone shiver. 'Man, it's freezing out here. Me nuts are about to drop off.' He cackled at the thought.

'Can't we go back to yours?' slurred Archie.

Tyrone sucked his teeth derisively. 'As if!' He lived round the corner in a cramped house with his mum, her second husband and two stepbrothers and sisters. There wasn't enough room to swing a cat.

In a moment of clarity, Tyrone slapped his thigh. 'Why can't we start hanging at yours, man? It's, like, perfect to get well stoned.'

'I don't think my parents would approve,' slurred Archie again, getting his words out with some difficulty.

'Use your *brain*!' retorted Tyrone. 'Your place is massive, man! We could chill for days in there and your olds wouldn't even know. What you say, bro?' But Archie had passed out, smouldering joint still in his hand.

Tyrone reached across and rescued it, then lay back again and took a decisive drag. As far as he was concerned it was sorted; no more hanging around the poxy rec freezing to death. Archie's place was perfect for a wicked house party as well; he'd just have to find out when Archie's parents were going to be away.

'Bring it on!' said Tyrone to himself.

Chapter 10

It was the Tuesday before her dinner party and
Camilla was in full organizational mode. The small
dining room at the back of the cottage was dwarfed
by her mother's Regency dining table and chairs,
which her parents had donated to her when they
left Churchminster. Camilla hadn't really entertained there properly since she'd moved in, and for
a long time the room had been a dumping ground
for more of Calypso's possessions. She didn't think
Brenda had ever stepped foot in there, preferring to
stay next door and run her cloth up and down the
mantelpiece as she watched *This Morning*. But now
new life had been breathed into the room. Camilla
had cleared all the junk and polished the furniture
until it shone like amber. Fresh flowers stood in the
middle of the table and pieces of the Standington-
Fulthrope family silver sparkled like diamonds in
the mahogany cabinet. It was a room worthy of
cultured conversation, fine food and exquisite
wine, Camilla decided, as she stepped back to
admire her handiwork. Then she thought about the
dinner guests and winced slightly.

There would be Angus, of course, and Calypso

and her new boyfriend Sam, who everyone was very excited about meeting. Maybe she'd found a decent man at last. At least his name sounded normal; Calypso's previous boyfriends had all had names like Snake, Rabid and Rev.

Caro was coming by herself, as Sebastian was off on a boys' weekend in Monaco (which was actually the truth, for once). Harriet would be on her own as well. Camilla had been fretting about the male to female ratio, until Angus offered to bring two of his friends, Ed 'Sniffer' Clevedon (called that on account of the way he was always after the opposite sex), and someone mysteriously known only as 'Horse'.

'Are you sure they'll behave themselves?' Camilla had asked Angus anxiously. 'Caro hasn't been out properly since she had Milo, I don't want to scare her off before the first course.'

Angus had winked and slapped her bottom affectionately. 'No party is a party without the Horse and Sniffer there, they'll be a riot!'

'That's what I'm afraid of.'

The prospect of out-of-control dinner guests aside, Camilla had the menu to think about. She and Caro could put on a jolly good spread, having both done a course at the Prue Leith cookery school. Although Camilla was ashamed to admit she relied mostly these days on M&S and the gourmet range at Waitrose. She was determined, however, not to have a cellophane wrapper or foil lid in sight for this meal. After much deliberation she'd decided to go for smoked salmon mousse for starters, rack of lamb with dauphinoise potatoes for the main course, and the promised lemon meringue pie for pudding.

This would be followed by petit fours she was going to attempt to make herself, and cheese and biscuits. Calypso had made a half-hearted offer of help, but after Camilla had come down one morning and found her absent-mindedly dropping cigarette ash into her bowl of Alpen while chatting on her mobile, she had firmly put her on drinks duty in the living room.

Caro had just flopped down exhausted on the sofa after putting Milo down for his nap, when there was a knock at the door. Her heart sank. She really wasn't in the mood for visitors, but she hauled herself up and went to answer it.

'Caro! Have you got a minute?' Caro's heart sank even more. Standing on her doorstep was Lucinda Reinard, the current owner of Twisty Gables. In her early forties, she had moved to the village three years earlier with her second husband, a rangy laconic Frenchman called Nico, who Caro always caught staring at her bosom. Lucinda once confessed, after one too many G and Ts at the Jolly Boot, that the reason they had moved away from London was to make a fresh start after her husband's affair with a glamorous blonde boutique owner. Even though the two women were entirely different, Lucinda had taken a shine to Caro, calling them 'kindred London spirits'. Caro knew they were anything but, but that didn't stop Lucinda.

'Er, yes. Is everything all right?' Caro asked. 'You look a bit stressed.' Lucinda was a well-fleshed horsy blonde woman who reminded her of Princess Anne in the throes of a minor breakdown.

'I am! Bloody Julien's been at my Cacharel

pashmina with the scissors. I just caught the little horror flying around the garden in it pretending to be Superman!' Julien was Lucinda and Nico's five-year-old son. She also had a precocious pair of eleven-year-old twins, Hero and Horatio, by her first husband. 'Anyway, I was just passing and wanted to know if you fancied coming along to the pony club quiz night with me next week. I'm organizing it, thought it would be a good chance for you to meet some of the other girls, see what you think of it all. You'd better not leave it too much longer to put Milo's name down, they are *dreadfully* over-subscribed at the moment.'

Caro sighed. Lucinda had made it her mission to try and get Caro to sign up to practically every club and society in the district. 'Can't have you at home all day while your husband's away!' she had told her. Since decamping to the country, Lucinda had forgone her townie roots with a vengeance. 'Integrating with the village is *so* important for one's family,' she had insisted. Caro tried to hide her irritation. 'Milo's not one until next year, Lucinda, I'm sure it won't matter just yet. Besides, he might not like horses.'

Lucinda looked at her as though she was speaking some foreign, incomprehensible language.

'Of *course* he'll like horses!' she cried. 'The twins are quite besotted with their ponies; I don't know what I did to keep them from under my feet before.'

At that point, Milo started crying upstairs. Caro had never been so pleased to hear the sound.

'Look, I'm going to have to go—' she started. Lucinda looked past her down the hall and smiled sympathetically, revealing large white teeth with a gap between the front ones.

'Of course, bloody nightmare at that age. Bloody nightmare at any age! Ha ha ha.' She looked at her watch and panic flittered across her face. 'Christ, look at the time! I've got to take Hero to cello practice and I've a mountain of paperwork to get through. Let me know what you want to do about next week.'

I won't be coming, thought Caro as she watched Lucinda's ample rear disappear down the path towards a muddy Range Rover. She knew Lucinda was just being kind, really, but the thought of spending the evening in a room full of loud, domineering women and their rowdy offspring held about as much appeal as watching John Prescott do a naked pole-dance. Upstairs, Milo's cries had developed into blood-curdling yells. Once again, Caro ran up the stairs to placate him.

Chapter 11

The day of the dinner party arrived, and from mid-day Camilla had been in the kitchen roasting, basting, tasting and whisking. The smoked salmon mousse now resting in the fridge was a triumph. The lamb had been studded with rosemary and garlic and was ready to go in the oven later. Potatoes and vegetables were under control. Camilla had ended up cheating on the petit fours and buying them from the Swiss confectioner's when she was dashing through Cirencester on her way home from work, but they were exquisite. The only thing that was a slight let-down was the lemon meringue pie. She had followed Nigella's recipe to the letter, but it hadn't looked, well, quite so messy in the picture in the book. Camilla's version looked more like a pile of vomit than a gastronomic triumph, but she figured she could smother it in cream and dim the lights when she brought it in.

It was 6.45 p.m. The guests were arriving in forty-five minutes. Calypso had just told her Sam was stuck in bad traffic on the M4 and would be there by 8 p.m. at the latest. The Bollinger was chilling in the fridge, and several bottles of red were opened and resting comfortably on the table in the dining room.

Camilla was upstairs in her bedroom getting ready. She had on her favourite black dress from Alice Temperley, her mother's pearl necklace, and black pumps from French Sole, deciding heels were not a good idea if she was going to be rushing to and from the kitchen all night.

Calypso materialized in the doorway. She was wearing the shortest of T-shirt dresses, with a thick, low slung belt around her slender waist. Her legs were bare, apart from a silver ankle chain and patent stilettos that were easily six inches high. Her streaky blonde hair was pulled back in a high, unforgiving ponytail which only served to highlight her cheekbones and kohl-rimmed eyes. Huge silver earrings in the shape of anchors hung from each ear.

Calypso gave her sister a cursory once-over.

'You wearing that?'

'Yes, why?' said Camilla defensively. 'What's wrong with it?'

'Oh, nothing, it's just like, a bit . . . blah,' replied Calypso, turning to walk down the hall. 'I'm fixing a Screwdriver, d'ya want one?'

Camilla declined. Knowing the strength of her sister's cocktails, she didn't want to be on her back before the main course. She turned to the mirror. OK, she might not look as cool as Calypso, but convenience outweighed style tonight. 'Blah it's going to have to be,' thought Camilla, and tugged her dress down a bit before heading downstairs.

The first guest to arrive, at 7.21 p.m., was Caro, clutching a bottle of Pinot Grigio. Camilla helped her out of her coat. Caro was wearing a black skirt that looked slightly too tight, and a purple see-through blouse with a built-in camisole underneath it. She also had a bright red lipstick on that didn't suit her, so that, unfortunately, she resembled a tacky barmaid, rather than the glamorous model from the pages of *Tatler* that she had been hoping to imitate. She also had a smear of something white across her right boob, which looked specifically baby-orientated.

'You look lovely, Caro,' said Camilla dutifully. 'There's some kind of a stain on your top, though.'

Caro looked down. 'Bugger! I thought I'd wiped all Milo's sick off me. Bills, can I borrow a cloth?'

Calypso, coming out of the kitchen with her second super-sized Screwdriver, heard the tail-end of the conversation and looked horrified. 'Urgh, gross!' she said, and whisked past them into the living room. By the time Camilla had got Caro settled in there with a drink, the doorbell rang again.

This time it was Harriet, brandishing a bottle of wine and a beautiful bunch of flowers. 'Oh Hats, they're beautiful,' said Camilla, taking them. 'Thank you!'

'They're off the estate, actually,' said Harriet grinning. 'I went and picked them this arvo; at least that flower-arranging course I went on taught me something!' She shrugged off her coat to reveal a plunging red dress which showed off an enormous, milky white cleavage. Harriet had obviously tried to tame her frizzy hair and failed, as it was now scraped back in an unflattering bun with bits sticking out everywhere. The whole effect was a rather unnerving blend of Dolly Parton meets Worzel Gummidge.

'Golly, Hats!' giggled Camilla, staring down at her friend's décolletage. 'Where did they come from?'

Harriet looked anxious. 'It's too much, isn't it? I've been standing in front of the mirror for hours. Mummy bought it for me; she said I have to stop dressing like an old maid. I don't think it looked as revealing as this on the hanger, though.'

'It's fine! You look great,' said Camilla, stretching the truth for the second time that night. 'Come on, let's get you a drink.'

A few minutes later, the doorbell rang again, and this time the door was nearly knocked down as someone hammered on it. Camilla ran to open it and was confronted by Angus, dressed in black tie, a Santa Claus hat incongruously perched on his huge head. Flanking him were two equally enormous men. One was dressed in full drag, complete with blonde wig and fishnet stockings, and the other was dressed as a giant fairy with wings, a wand and a pink tutu. They looked like clones of Angus, with their big meaty bodies and ruddy red cheeks, except the one on the left had a huge, Desperate-Dan-style chin, and the fairy on the right was sporting an inane, gap-toothed smile. Camilla's heart sank.

'Hello, you foxy filly!' boomed Angus, clapping a hand around the men either side of him. 'You've met Sniffer,' he said, cocking his head to the one dressed in drag. 'And this is Horse.' The hulk of a man next to him flashed his gap-toothed smile and curtsied in his tutu.

'Angus, it's not fancy dress,' said Camilla faintly, as they all thundered in, filling the narrow corridor completely.

'Yah, I know,' said Angus. 'But me and the chaps

thought it would be jolly good fun; keep you ladies entertained all night!'

'If you know what we mean,' leered Sniffer, looming over her. Camilla pretended she didn't, and wondered just what Angus had been saying to his friends about her.

It was too late to do anything. Camilla stood aside helplessly and watched them barrel into the living room. Cool as a cucumber, Calypso lit her cigarette and looked at them.

'Didn't know there was a dress code, lads.'

'Yah, we decided things needed livening up a bit,' boomed Sniffer, his eyes travelling up and down her endless legs. He took in the make-up and earrings. 'Are you a pop star or something?'

Calypso ignored him and took a drag.

'So!' said Camilla brightly. 'Let me introduce everyone. Caro, this is er, Sniffer and Horse. Guys, this is my sister Caro, and that,' she indicated Calypso, 'is our younger sister, Calypso.'

Horse bared his substantial teeth in what Camilla took to be an inviting smile. 'Yah, well I can see good looks run in the family. I do have a liking for sisters.' Sniffer elbowed him conspicuously, and they fell about laughing.

Camilla ploughed on. 'This is my best friend, Harriet Fraser.' All three of them rounded on Harriet, who until that point had been trying to shrink unobtrusively into the armchair in the corner of the room.

'*Mamma mia!*' said Sniffer, looking down into the acres of cleavage.

'You don't get many of *those* to the pound,' chortled Horse. Harriet went bright red and put a cushion over her chest. Angus, sharply prodded by a furious Camilla, realized his friends might have gone slightly too far. 'Come on, you two, leave the poor girl alone. What's a chap got to do for a drink around here, anyway?'

'So why are you called Horse?' asked Calypso sarcastically.

A smug smile spread across Horse's face and he gestured down to his crotch. 'Can't you guess, gorgeous?'

'Urgh!'

Sniffer stepped in. 'Stop lying, Horseman! Your name has got nothing to do with how big your dick is,' he said. Horse's red cheeks paled slightly.

'No?' asked Calypso, leaning forward and showing her first spark of interest so far. 'Why's he really called Horse, then?'

Angus guffawed. 'Because he used to have huge front teeth at prep school!' He turned to Horse. 'Isn't that right, you goofy twat?'

Angus and Sniffer roared with laughter, while Horse looked thoroughly put out. 'Leave it out, you bastards,' he said petulantly. 'I had to wear a brace, so what?'

His friends roared with laughter again. Just then the doorbell rang. Camilla looked at the clock on the wall; it read 8.08 p.m.

Calypso's eyes lit up. 'Sam!' she exclaimed, and ran out of the room.

'Who's Sam?' boomed Angus.

'Sam is Calypso's new boyfriend, and Angus, you *must* behave around him!' implored Camilla. 'Don't challenge him to arm-wrestle you or anything! Calypso is frightfully keen on him.'

Angus gave Sniffer and Horse a knowing look. 'As if we would.' They turned to face the door of the living room like everyone else, awaiting the new arrival.

Camilla could hear Calypso giggling coquettishly in the hall. Suddenly she appeared in the doorway, looking flushed and excited. 'Everybody, I'd like you to meet my lover, Sam!' she announced and pulled Sam in next to her. There was utter silence in the room, and then Camilla, as if in slow motion, dropped the glass she was holding.

'Bugger me!' exclaimed Angus, open-mouthed. Even with the short spiky hair and oversized man's shirt and jeans, there was no disguising the swell of breasts or the vaguely feminine face.

Sam was a she, not a he.

After an excruciating twenty seconds, Camilla realized how rude she must look, and managed to stop staring. Beside her Angus was making no such pretence; he was looking rather like a goggle-eyed fish as he gaped at the muscular, squat build, the multiple body-piercing and the leather dog-collar. For her part, Sam seemed remarkably unfazed by the reception, surveying the room with amused contempt.

'Sam, hi!' Camilla trilled in what sounded to her like an unnaturally high voice. 'I'm Camilla, Calypso's sister and this is Caro, our other sister . . .' She turned beseechingly to Caro, who looked like a rabbit caught in headlights.

'Hi!'

'I know who you are,' replied Sam in a gruff, cockney accent. 'Cal's told me all about you.'

Cal? thought Camilla. Dear God, had her sister been leading a double life? She managed to carry on with the introductions: 'This is my dear friend Harriet, and my boyfriend Angus, and his friends Sniffer and Horse . . .'

'Are you a lezzer now, then?' Angus asked Calypso.

She gave him a scathing look. 'Sam and I don't define sexuality; we're lovers and partners.'

'Look like a pair of rug-munchers to me!' said Angus cheerfully, helping himself to another drink.

'Angus!' hissed Camilla. Sam scowled at him.

'Oh, it doesn't bother me,' said Angus. 'As long as you promise to put on a girlie show later. Haw haw haw!'

'He's only joking,' Camilla said quickly, as Sam looked ready to throw the iron door stop at his head. 'Don't mind Angus, he's just got, er, a very peculiar sense of humour.'

Sam looked slightly pacified until Horse said in a stage-whisper to Angus, 'Are you sure it's a woman? It's got a bigger neck than I have!'

'Champers time!' announced Camilla brightly.

A few hours later everyone had relaxed visibly. In fact, they were all so drunk they wouldn't have noticed if the lemon meringue had come to life and started breathing. After several bottles of Bollinger, the eight of them had worked their way through copious amounts of an obscenely expensive red Angus had found in his wine cellar at home. They were now on extremely alcoholic Irish coffees, remnants of Brie and Camembert melting and oozing on a cheese board in the middle of the table.

Caro was having her glass refilled by Sniffer for the umpteenth time and telling him she hadn't had a shag in ages. 'With my huzzband of course,' she said unsteadily. 'I'm not slutting it around. Babies, you know, once you have them you get all fat and your sex life goes up the sprout.' She slapped a hand to her forehead. 'I mean spout.'

Sniffer, sensing a damsel-in-distress situation, leaned in. 'You look pretty sexy to me, Mrs Belmont.' He tried to blow cigar smoke out of his mouth seductively, no easy feat when you're six foot four and dressed like an extra from *The Rocky Horror Show*.

'But you *are* pleased you've got Milo, aren't you?' interrupted Camilla. She had been eavesdropping on the exchange, and even through her haze of alcohol could sense something was definitely not right with her sister. But Caro was already talking wistfully about the days when she could fit easily into her size-ten jeans. Sniffer had leaned in even further, and Camilla resolved to switch to water and keep an eye on them. She didn't want that awful lech taking advantage. Sebastian did that enough already. Although Camilla had never been openly rude to her brother-in-law, she didn't hold a very high opinion of him in private. She'd seen the change in Caro. But every time she'd tried to talk to her about it, Caro had suddenly changed the subject. However her sister was feeling at the moment, she clearly didn't want to talk about it when she was sober.

On the other side of the table, Calypso was happily telling Harriet how she and Sam had got together. Sam was leaning back listening, one arm laid possessively around Calypso's shoulders. 'Yah, we met at this club in Brighton. I was like, going out with Henry at the time, but he was rah-ly doing my head in. Anyway, when my friend Lizzie decided we should go to this gay club because, like, it would be a total laugh, I totally said yes! As soon as I walked in, I saw Sam, and that was it, really.'

'Yeah, I always hang round the entrance to corrupt new innocents,' said Sam in her gruff voice. She smiled, but it didn't reach her eyes, and Harriet wondered if she was joking. She suddenly felt very depressed. Here she was at thirty, and still with her bloody hymen intact, while Camilla's bloody younger sister had moved on to women! Where was she going wrong?

Harriet stood up to go to the loo, lurched and fell straight in Horse's lap. She realized she was absolutely plastered. 'Scuse me,' she slurred as she stumbled past him. His hands were suddenly on her bottom, 'helping' her past.

When she got to the loo, Harriet stared at herself in the mirror. A wild-haired, mascara-smudged woman, with a chest barely contained within her flimsy dress, stared back. She pulled down her tights and sat heavily on the toilet. 'My love life's a messh,' she murmured drunkenly.

When Harriet returned to the dining room about fifteen minutes later, after dropping her lipstick down the toilet, a fuggy, pungent haze hung over the table. Calypso was inhaling an enormous spliff, which she passed to Sam. Caro had passed out, her head on the table. Harriet sat down again.

'I say, anyone fancy an E?' said Horse suddenly. He produced a small packet of Ecstasy from inside his tutu and waved it around in front of them. 'I got them off Dodgy Dave in town earlier.'

'I'll just stick to this, tonight,' said Calypso, drawing on the joint. 'I'm trying to cut back on my narcotic intake.' Sam nodded assent. Camilla tried not to look shocked – she thought her sister only smoked joints. Angus went to say yes, but Camilla shot him one of her rare steely looks. He was wrecked enough already.

'No, old boy, thanks anyway.'

At the other end of the table, Sniffer had passed out next to Caro, face down in his third helping of lemon meringue.

That left Harriet. Horse turned to her. 'What do you say, foxy?' He pressed his considerable thigh against hers under the table.

Maybe it was because she was drunk. Maybe it was because of talking to Calypso and Sam earlier. Maybe it was because she was already stoned from passively inhaling smoke from the joint, but something inside Harriet snapped. She was tired of being boring, safe Harriet. She wanted to live a little. 'Go on, then,' she said.

'Hats, I don't think that's a good idea—' Camilla started, but Horse leaned over and put one arm round Harriet.

'Don't worry, I'll only let her have a little bit, she's in safe hands, I promise.' He guffawed and Harriet felt one of those safe hands creep round and squeeze her boob. Something inside her stirred slightly as she watched Horse fish a small pill out of the packet and cut it up clumsily with one of Camilla's cheese knives.

Horse gave a little bit of the pill to her and kept a

bit for himself. He picked up his glass of wine and Harriet did the same. 'Here's to getting totally trashed. One, two, three!'

Thirty minutes passed. Harriet still felt drunk, but not really any different. Conversation had resumed around the table. Calypso was now telling a story about the time a millionaire businessman had offered two thousand camels for her when she was working as a promotions girl in Annabel's night-club. 'Like, I'm worth so many more than that!' she joked indignantly. By now it was two in the morning and everything was slowly winding down. Camilla was snuggled into Angus's broad shoulders, Calypso into Sam's even broader ones. Sniffer and Caro were still conked out, heads down side by side on the table.

The smoke from the joint had been making Harriet feel drowsy to the point where she thought she might drop off. Then suddenly – or was it gradually? – every part of her body started to wake up. She stopped eyeing up a remaining chocolate as a feeling of energy rushed through her body, eradicating her appetite. Her head and neck started tingling, as though she had been given a very pleasant electric shock.

Harriet looked round the table; everyone looked the same but somehow so *different*. Shinier, happier, more alive. Her senses were sharpened, colours more vivid, conversations louder. Harriet smiled to herself as a feeling of warmth and elation tucked itself around her. God, she loved these people, this room, this life!

'Hats, are you OK?' Camilla's voice seemed a

million miles away, but it brought her face back into focus. 'Your eyes look like saucers!'

'I'm cool,' sighed Harriet happily. 'Everything's cool. Live life!'

'Er, OK,' replied Camilla. 'Look, I'm awfully tired and Angus is about to pass out. You will be all right if we go to bed? Horse, you had better look after her!' She turned to him, but he was gazing in happy fascination at a watercolour of a hunting scene on the wall.

'The colours . . .' he said in wonder. 'It's, it's . . . like something out of *Joseph and his Techno Dreamcoat.*'

'I think you mean *Technicolor*, you bloody pill-head,' said Calypso, who had managed to hold herself together remarkably well throughout the evening. 'Don't worry, sis, I'll keep an eye on them.'

It was only when Calypso interrupted Harriet's monologue – about why Howard was the sexiest member of Take That – to say she and Sam were going to bed, that Harriet realized she had been talking non-stop for two hours.

'Are you going to be OK, Hats?' asked Calypso kindly.

'Drink loads of orange juice when you start to come down,' was Sam's gruff instruction. Then Calypso and Sam left them there, Horse still staring in wonder at the watercolour, Harriet just sitting, pulsing with new-found confidence and energy.

Finally Horse dragged his eyes away and focused them on Harriet. They glittered sexily, and Harriet was suddenly struck by how good-looking he was: like a younger Colin Firth. Horse, in turn, seemed mesmerized by her chest. It was practically hanging out now; Harriet had stopped tugging her dress up long ago.

'You're . . . stunning!' Horse said in wonder, coming over and running his hand through her hair. 'Your hair, it's like a beautiful Brillo Pad.'

'And I love your teeth, they're so big and white . . .' breathed Harriet, looking up at him.

'All the better to eat you with,' said Horse lasciviously. He leaned down and stuck his tongue down her throat.

Any sober, innocent bystander would have seen this for what it was: a slobbering, wet and disgusting tongue sandwich. But to Harriet, her senses crying out in a chemical haze, having Horse's tongue thrust around her mouth was the most erotic experience ever. The last person she'd French-kissed was a nine-teen-year-old viscount at a black tie two years ago. That had been a disaster, but somehow this was so different; she felt so uninhibited.

After a few minutes, they were groping each other like randy octopuses. Horse raised his tutu to reveal white M&S underpants. He dragged them off, pulled Harriet's dress down so her breasts were completely exposed, and started rubbing his erect manhood up and down between them. Harriet looked down at the purple, knobbly member that bent like a banana to the left, and thought it was the most exquisite thing she had ever seen in her life.

'Fancy riding my knob, little lady?' whispered Horse in her ear. Through her drug-enhanced mood, Harriet was still aware that normally she wouldn't have put herself in this position in a million years. But this wasn't normal. And she was tired of waiting for Prince Charming to come and whisk her off to be deflowered in a grassy meadow somewhere. She just needed to grab the bull by his horniness and get on with it. She *wanted* it.

Harriet led Horse into the living room and lay back on the sofa. 'Have you got something?' she whispered, feeling like she was reading the script of a teen drama. Horse smiled and retrieved his wallet from under the tutu, pulling out a square silver package. Before he put it on, he rubbed Harriet's clitoris the way one might rub a horse's nose affectionately ('Was that why he was really called Horse?' wondered Harriet fleetingly).

Horse crudely stuck his fingers up her, and Harriet winced. 'Christ, you're tight! Are you a virgin?' he asked.

'Of course not!' said Harriet, her euphoria momentarily dissolving. Then, before she knew it, her dress was up, her Janet Reger control knickers were completely down and Horse was on top of her. After a few attempts, he finally thrust his cock into her. Harriet felt a momentary stab of pain, and then it seemed like she and Horse were one, rocking and moaning in unison. She ceased to feel him in her; it was like he was part *of* her. Harriet looked past Horse; the room was spinning in a maelstrom of light. Feeling passion she'd never experienced before, she raked her nails down his back, and Horse whinnied as his orgasm exploded inside her. He fell back gasping and sweating, while Harriet lay still, every nerve in her body tingling. It wasn't just the ecstasy coursing through her veins making her feel euphoric.

She'd finally popped her cherry – hallelujah!

Chapter 12

'How's the wife, Sebbo?' asked Barnaby Smith-Rourke, one of Sebastian's oldest friends from Harrow. They and two other friends of similar ilk were lounging in the hot tub of Barnaby's presidential suite at the five-star Regency hotel in Monaco. They'd had a thoroughly top weekend, including a night spent gambling at the hotel's world-famous casino, where Sebastian won thirty thou, which he promptly spent on a table at Alfie's, one of the most exclusive – and expensive – clubs in Europe. With Moët and bottles of vodka starting at eight hundred pounds a pop, and lap-dances by delectable, obscenely young Russian girls, the four of them had got through the money in no time. And Sebastian had been in a particularly generous mood. He'd just received a large bonus at work, he had a son and heir and a ravishing mistress who he was bonking the life out of, and earlier that week his personal trainer had told him he'd almost got his body fat down to the level of an Olympic athlete.

'Yah, she's OK,' he said dismissively, taking another glug out of the champagne flute by the edge of the hot tub. 'Still a bit chubs after Milo, but I'm thinking of getting her a trainer. That or lipo; a client recommended a great guy in Harley Street who tidied his wife up.'

'Not like Sabrina, eh?' said Barnaby, a leering grin crossing his face. 'Any more where she came from, Seb? Has she got a sister or something?'

'Keep your fucking grubby little paws off her, Barno,' said Sebastian lazily. 'Sabrina is mine, and I have no intention of sharing her.'

Actually, back in London at that exact moment, Sabrina was licking Fortnum & Mason hazelnut spread off a very handsome pair of buttocks in her bedroom. The owner of the bottom was a twenty-something aristocratic model called Piers. He had been coming round to have sex with Sabrina most afternoons for the past six weeks. Sabrina had a predilection for toyboys, and this was the seventh in the last two years. Sebastian might have expected her to stay faithful, but Sabrina had no intention of living like an old maid while he played happy families with his dreary wife in the country.

Not that she'd ever tell him that. She'd had richer lovers, but Sebastian looked after her pretty well. And she had every intention of keeping it that way.

It was Monday morning, and Caro was lugging the recycled rubbish bag out for the cleaners when she noticed a sleek, silver grey Porsche parked next door. The new neighbours! she thought excitedly. Maybe they've decided to leave the 4×4 at home for this visit.

At that moment, the front door opened and

someone came out. Caro's heart stopped momentarily. Striding down the path towards her was the most handsome man she had ever set eyes on. In his late thirties, with dirty blond hair, sculpted face, and blue eyes the colour of stormy seas, he looked like an even more gorgeous Brad Pitt, something Caro had never thought possible. His six-foot-plus frame was dressed in jeans and a pale blue shirt which couldn't hide the broad shoulders and muscular contours of the body underneath. Caro felt her heart flutter.

Unfortunately, the man also had a face like thunder, his gorgeous, manly features overshadowed by a fierce scowl. It looked like he was going to completely ignore Caro even though she was standing mere feet away. She finally found her voice.

'Morning!' she squeaked. 'I'm Caro Belmont. You must be our new neighbour.' She stuck out her hand nervously.

The stranger stopped in his tracks and looked at Caro as though she had just climbed down from a space ship. He glanced down at her hand and then stepped forward and shook it in a cursory fashion. His hand was large, firm and warm. Caro didn't want to let go.

Still the stranger didn't say anything, just stared at her. Caro was starting to feel a bit intimidated. 'Er, I'm Caro,' she repeated. 'I live next door . . .'

'Towey,' the man barked, cutting her off. 'Benedict Towey.' His voice was deep and well cultivated, although it showed no signs of warming up.

'Have you bought the house, then?' asked Caro. Benedict Towey looked at her as though she had just announced she'd killed his mother.

'Yes.'

'Oh, and your wife and children . . .' Caro trailed off.

'No, it's just me,' he answered shortly, and started to walk towards the car, terminating the conversation.

Caro couldn't help her curiosity. 'It's an awfully big place for one person, isn't it?' she called after him.

Benedict Towey turned and fixed her with a cold stare. 'It's none of your damn business,' he said, and with that he got into the Porsche and screeched away, leaving Caro standing there, speechless.

'What a *horrible* man!' she finally exploded.

Chapter 13

The following evening, Devon Cornwall was walking around the grounds of Byron Heights. The property was set in six acres of gardens complete with gazebos and ornamental ponds, bridges and statuettes galore. The main choice of shrub seemed to be rhododendrons and yew trees, giving the grounds a slightly 'churchyard' feel.

Somewhere an owl hooted. Devon shivered slightly. He was standing at the bottom of the vast lawn, looking back up at the house. The turrets were silhouetted against the twilit sky, and the house loomed ominously over the grounds. This place hadn't looked so creepy when he'd viewed it in daylight.

A fox suddenly ran out in front of him. 'Jesus!' he yelled in surprise, then checked himself. 'You silly old sod,' he muttered out loud. 'Let's go and see what Nige has knocked up for dinner.'

As well as being Devon's PA, Nigel was a fabulous cook. Devon had had many chefs over the years, and each had come with the highest recommendation, but in his opinion none of them had been as good as Nigel. So he'd upped Nigel's wages and now let him do all the cooking. It was Nigel's passion and hobby anyway, so it was an arrangement that suited them both very well. The only other member of staff was a daytime house-keeper Nigel had hired from some agency. Devon had yet to bump into her along the twisty, cavernous corridors of Byron Heights.

In the kitchen, which boasted a huge wooden table and ornate cupboards, Nigel was busily chopping vegetables, Radio 3 in the background. One of Devon's stipulations when he moved in was built-in stereos and speakers in every room, so he could wander through the house listening to his favourite music.

'All right old fella, what's for dinner?' Over the years, Devon had managed to eradicate his Gloucester accent, and now spoke a muso style of cockney, much like his contemporary, Mick Jagger.

'Feta cheese and asparagus pie, your favourite,' replied Nigel. 'It'll be ready in about an hour.'

'Nice one!' said Devon, taking a smoothie out of the enormous American-style fridge. There was time for him to practise some yoga in the specially converted gym before dinner.

'You don't think this place is haunted?' Devon asked. They were sitting in the grand hall, at one end of a dining table that could accommodate up to a hundred people.

Nigel paused, a piece of asparagus speared on the end of his fork. 'No, why? Oh, you're not having flashback hallucinations, are you?' Despite his now ultra-clean lifestyle, Devon still suffered very occasional flashbacks from all the LSD he'd taken in the early days of his career.

'No, of course not,' said Devon. 'It's just this place. Well, it's a bit spooky innit? I'm half-expecting Scooby Doo and Shaggy to come running around the corner pursued by something in a white sheet. All those dark nooks and crannies, it's getting me a bit on edge.'

Nigel rolled his eyes. 'It's an old house, Devon. It's bound to be a bit creaky. It doesn't mean it's infested with spirits, though.'

Devon thought for a moment. 'Nah, you're right. I just got the heebie jeebies. Christ!' he laughed at himself. 'Anyway, what's for pud?'

After dinner, Devon retired to bed. The master bedroom was enormous, a four-poster bed in the centre, expensive rugs on the stone floors and pieces of art deco that Devon had collected on his travels arranged tastefully by Nigel on the walls.

Devon was deep in the autobiography of an Indian yogi when he suddenly heard a strange shuffling noise from somewhere downstairs. He stiffened and put his book down, his ears straining to hear in the silence. Was that Nigel? But he was in a room at the other end of the house. Devon picked up his book. Must have been imagining . . .

There it was again! It sounded like someone walking about downstairs. But there was no one down there, Nigel had gone to bed before him! Burglars wouldn't be that noisy, would they? Summoning all his courage, Devon flung back his covers and tip-toed to the door. It creaked as he opened it, and he hesitantly stuck his head into the blackness outside.

'Nige? Nigel?' he called. 'Is that you?'

Silence. Then, just out of the corner of his eye, a movement made Devon look through the banisters of the staircase down into the grand entrance hall. Something white, something non-human, was slowly walking – no, *gliding*! – across the floor.

It was too much for Devon. He screamed loudly, slammed the door shut and dived back under the bedclothes.

'It was probably just mice or something,' said Nigel fifteen minutes later. He was sitting on Devon's bed in a dressing gown, putting some herbal calming remedy drops into a glass of water for his boss. The house was ablaze like a lighthouse because after Nigel had rushed to Devon's aid he'd been told to go around putting every light on.

'Yeah but mice aren't s-s-s-six feet tall, an' they don't dress in white and glide across the f-f-f-floor!' said Devon, gibbering with terror.

'But they *do* shuffle around,' pointed out Nigel. 'As for the white shape, I am sure you were just seeing things. You'd taken your contact lenses out, hadn't you?' Devon nodded.

'Well that solves that!' said Nigel. 'Now you try and get back to sleep. I'll get the exterminators out in the morning to catch the nasty little buggers.'

Devon lay back on his pillows, pacified but not entirely convinced. He might be an ex-druggie but he was *sure* he'd seen something.

*

The next day, a local pest-control firm from Bedlington were called out. Despite a thorough examination, no traces of mice, rats or anything else vermin-like were found. What they did find, however, were strange claw marks running along one of the skirting boards. 'No mouse is big enough to make those, they'd 'ave to 'ave paws the size of bleedin' shovels,' said Len from Rodent-Kill.

'For God's sake, keep your voice down,' hissed Nigel. Devon was only in the music room down the hallway and Nigel didn't want any more silly ideas put in his head.

Len wasn't to be deterred. 'Looks like you've got a bleeding werewolf or summin!' He laughed heartily at his own joke, and Nigel paid up and got rid of him before Devon appeared.

'So what was it, Nige?' asked Devon nervously a few minutes later, appearing in the study, where Nigel was going through some bills.

'Just mice, as we suspected!' Nigel lied. 'It's all cleared up now, nothing to worry about.'

Devon's face brightened. 'Thank Christ for that, I thought we'd moved into the house of living dead or something!' He turned and walked out.

Nigel smiled thinly. He'd encountered enough of his boss's drug-fuelled visions over the years. Once, in a hotel room in Rio, Devon had thought he was being mounted by a sex-crazed Margaret Thatcher when it was actually just a navy-blue cushion. No, Nigel didn't believe his boss had seen anything spooky; he just had an over-active imagination. Without giving it another thought, Nigel went back to his paperwork.

Chapter 14

It was a mid-week evening at No. 5 The Green, and Camilla was just going up to bed with a hot chocolate and a copy of *Cotswold Life* when she got the shock of her life. Walking down the corridor from the bathroom to Calypso's room was Sam, as naked as the day she was born. Camilla stopped dead at the top of the stairs, mouth open in shock. Try as she might to look *anywhere* but at Sam, she couldn't stop herself. It was quite a sight. Sam had both nipples pierced with what looked like large silver studs. A tattoo of a dragon ran down one shoulder, and her pubic bush had been bleached blonde and cut in the shape of a lightning flash. Sam's man-sized thighs, rock-hard stomach, and rippling biceps were still glistening wet from the shower.

'Oh!' squawked Camilla.

'Sorry, I forgot my towel,' said Sam casually. 'I didn't know you were in.'

'That's fine, honestly,' replied Camilla, trying not to appear flustered. She didn't want to, but she couldn't help giving Sam's bush another glance, she'd never seen anything like it before. Sam caught her doing it and smirked slightly. Oh God, thought

Camilla. She's going to think I'm one as well! Before Sam could say anything, Camilla flashed a nervous smile. 'Anyway!' She edged past Sam and fled into her room, shutting the door. Almost immediately, the phone beside her bed rang. Camilla put her mug down and snatched it up. 'Hello?'

'Darling! Is that you, Bills? You and Calypso sound identical on the phone!'

Camilla sat down on the bed, relieved to hear the warm, familiar tones of her mother. 'Mummy!' she said weakly. 'How are you?'

'I haven't caught you at a bad time, have I?'

Fifty seconds earlier and you would have, thought Camilla. 'No, no,' she replied, composing herself. 'How are things? Are you and Daddy OK?'

They were on a slight time delay. 'Everyone's wonderful,' replied her mother a moment later. 'I was actually phoning to speak to Calypso.' The day after the dinner party, her sister had finally phoned her parents and re-established contact and relative harmony between them.

'Er . . .' said Camilla. 'She is in, but I think she's a bit tied up at the moment, Mummy.' Camilla tried not to think how true her words might be.

There was a questioning silence down the phone.

'She's in her room,' blurted out Camilla. 'With her, er, with Sam. They've been seeing each other for a while.'

Her mother laughed. 'Oh, that's wonderful!' She shouted to Camilla's father. 'Johnnie, Calypso's finally got herself a proper boyfriend.' A muffled voice could be heard in the background.

'Your father says he'd better be a dab hand at

squash, so they can escape us girls gossiping when we come over!'

Camilla privately thought Sam would be more than a match for her father at any sport, including shot-putting and rugby. 'Mmm, great!' she said evasively. 'Shall I get Calypso to call you?'

'Super, yah,' said her mother. 'I just wanted a catch-up with her.' She changed the subject. 'Anyway, do tell me what you've been up to. I spoke to Granny Clem and she says Devon Cornwall has moved into the village! Ooh, I used to fancy the pants off him when I was younger . . .'

A few days later, at the Maltings, Freddie Fox-Titt was standing in the kitchen, gazing out at the paddocks. Angie was at the shop and Archie was in his bedroom with his new friend Tyrone, listening to some awful rap music. Minutes earlier, Freddie had noticed a pungent smell of smoke in the upstairs corridor.

Bloody Archie's taken up smoking, the silly little sod, he thought furiously. He ran upstairs and hammered on his son's door.

Instantly, the music stopped.

'What?' called a hostile Archie from behind the door. Freddie pushed it open and was hit by a wall of smoke. Archie and Tyrone, who had a shaved head like his son, and a goatee beard etched into his pale, spotty skin, looked up at him from the bean bags they were lounging on.

'Christ!' spluttered Freddie, and strode over to open the window. The two boys watched as Freddie turned back to face them. 'Now look here, Arch, we don't mind you drinking here, but you *know* we don't have smoking in the house. Especially after your mother's cancer scare.'

'Yeah, but it's not smoke.' Archie looked at his father as if he were stupid. 'It's incense, innit?' Freddie looked around the room; there were indeed several strong-smelling sticks alight, their heady fumes wafting around the room.

'Hmm,' said Freddie dubiously. 'Just make sure you air the room once in a while. I don't want the place smelling like some bloody hippy's caravan.'

'You got it, Mr FT,' said Tyrone. As soon as Freddie had closed the door behind himself, Tyrone retrieved the joint he'd been hiding behind his back and re-lit it. He and Archie cracked up laughing.

Downstairs in the kitchen Freddie was starting to get a real craving for chocolate. Funny that, he thought. I never normally have a sweet tooth. In fact the nearest Freddie got to sugar was crème brûlée for pudding about twice a year. He pulled open the cupboards and started searching for Angie's Twix fingers.

Chapter 15

The morning after Horse had climbed aboard and galloped off with her cherry, Harriet had woken on the sofa in Camilla's living room feeling like she had been dragged through hell and back. Her red dress, ripped at the front in the moment of passion, had been bunched up around her waist. A chocolate stain and another mark of dubious origin had been streaked across the front of it. Harriet's bra had been hanging from a lampshade, her huge flesh-coloured knickers lying crotch-up on the floor in the middle of the living room.

'Oh no!' she had groaned, attempting to sit up. Her head had been banging, and everything had been a little blurry round the edges. She had stood up and fallen over something large lying beside the sofa. Horse. He had been naked except for his tutu, lying on his back snoring gently, a bubble of spit blowing out between his huge teeth. Harriet had looked at him in horrified fascination. God, how could she ever have thought he looked like Colin Firth? Then she had remembered taking the Ecstasy, albeit somewhat fuzzily. She had lived to tell the tale, but there was no way she'd be doing that again. Especially not with the awful Horse; if that's what E did to her, she might end up in an orgy with him and Sniffer next time. The thought had made her head spin even more.

The rest of the house had been quiet, the clock on the DVD player reading 8.07 a.m. Harriet had scurried around, quietly retrieving her belongings and trying not to wake up Horse. She had poked her head round the dining room door, seeing that Caro had obviously made it home at some point, but Sniffer was still there, snoring loudly, his head encrusted in a half-eaten bowl of meringue. Harriet had dressed, borrowed a large Barbour jacket that was hanging in the hallway and let herself out of the cottage.

As she had walked unsteadily across the green, Dora and Eunice's curtains had twitched violently, but Harriet hadn't cared. She had felt a burden had been lifted from her shoulders; even if the man of her dreams hadn't been the one lifting it, and even though she had been in the throes of a monumental hangover and narcotic comedown. What had Sam said about orange juice? Harriet had kept her head down and hurried home to Gate Cottage, thinking of bath and bed.

Unfortunately for her, someone had been there to witness her arrival home. As she had walked up the path to the front door, Jed had come round the corner with a piece of drainpipe in his hand.

'Jed, what are you doing here?' she had squealed. 'You scared me to death!'

He had eyed her curiously, taking in her dishevelled appearance. Harriet had wrapped the coat tightly around herself; hoping she didn't stink of raw sex. Whatever that smelt like.

'Fixing that guttering for you,' he had said, putting down the bit of pipe and leaning on it. 'You been out all night?'

'Of course not!' Harriet had said hotly. 'I was just er, taking a walk.' Jed had looked at her more closely, a smile starting to twitch at the corner of his mouth.

'Is that spunk on your chin?'

Harriet had turned puce with shameful mortification. 'NO!' she had yelled. 'Let me past. And DON'T tell anyone you saw me.' She had fumbled with the lock while Jed watched in amusement, finally falling in through the front door. She had slammed it behind her and rushed straight to the downstairs loo to look at her reflection. She had seen she had mascara down her cheeks, but her chin was free of any bodily fluids. Jed must have been winding her up.

'Little shit!' she had said to herself furiously, and plonked herself down on the toilet for a much-needed wee.

'There's something different about you,' remarked her mother a few days later, observing her daughter over the huge, polished dining table. Harriet blushed and buried herself in her beef bourguignon. She had been summoned up to the Hall for her weekly dinner with her parents. The family normally ate together on a Sunday evening, but Sir Ambrose and Lady Fraser had gone to a charity function in Cheltenham the previous Sunday. 'I mean, on a Sunday!' Ambrose had stormed. 'How bloody *provincial*!'

He was looking at his daughter as well now, his hair as white as snow against florid cheeks. 'Still looks hefty to me!' he said, returning to his plate.

'Ambrose!' Lady Fraser chided her husband.

Sir Ambrose Fraser was not a cruel man, but he came from a generation and class that had taught him to bloody well say what he thought and to hell with anyone else's opinions. He had the tact of a five-year-old and was thoroughly thoughtless into the bargain. His relationship with his daughter mainly consisted of Harriet trying desperately to please him or stay out of his way, with Ambrose overriding her on everything she said, did or wore, always convinced he knew better. It had been his idea that Harriet become his PA, 'So I can keep a firm eye on you.' But her role mainly involved being shouted at when her father couldn't find his reading glasses.

Harriet shrank down further into her chair. 'Though I do agree with your father, your diet *clearly* isn't working still,' said her mother. As if to make a point about her own self-control and slim figure, Frances purposely put her knife and fork together on her plate, even though she had only eaten half her meal.

Harriet hated these dinners. Every week, she would arrive at the house hoping that maybe, just maybe, this time would be different and she could laugh and joke with her parents like Camilla did with hers. That they'd actually be interested in her day, tell her she looked nice or that she was a good daughter. It never happened. Each week, they would pick apart her appearance and love life and talk about her as if she wasn't there. The tragedy was that they genuinely believed this criticism was the only way to reach out to their daughter. Harriet left each Sunday feeling fat, worthless, and personally responsible for ruining the centuries-old Fraser bloodline.

'How was Camilla's dinner?' asked her mother, dabbing delicately at the corners of her mouth with a pristine cloth napkin.

'Any chaps there that would consider taking you on?' asked her father hopefully.

'It was good, and no, Daddy,' said Harriet, hoping she wasn't going red again.

'Hmm,' said her mother cryptically. 'Well, there is definitely *something* different about you. You look a bit "off" for some reason.'

Yah, maybe that's because I took loads of drugs last weekend and had a Horse's cock up me! Harriet wanted to yell. Instead she replied dutifully, 'I'll get an early night and put on one of those face packs you bought me, Mummy.'

'Good girl,' said Frances.

Harriet managed to extricate herself some time later, and wearily made her way down the drive to her cottage. She'd left the upstairs landing light on, and a warm glow seeped out of her bedroom window. Suddenly Harriet felt like crying. She let herself into the cottage, shivered, put the heating on, and was just heading to the cupboard to get out the half-finished pot of Green & Black's organic chocolate spread she'd had for lunch, when her mobile went. Camilla's home number flashed up.

'What ho, Bills,' said Harriet, trying to make her voice sound cheerful.

'You OK? You sound like you've got a cold or something,' replied Camilla.

'I'm fine, honestly,' said Harriet, not in the mood to talk. 'What can I do for you, sweet pea?'

'Angus and I are going to a Young Farmers' do next week, and we wondered if you and Horse would like to come and make it a double date?' Camilla had heard most of the grisly tale from her best friend the day after the dinner party. Now she sounded overly hopeful.

'God no. I mean, that's awfully nice of you, but I don't know, Bills,' said Harriet falteringly. 'I mean, I'm sure Horse is a jolly nice chap when he's sober and everything, but he's really not my type. Why, has he asked if I'm going?'

'Er yes,' lied Camilla. What Horse had actually said to Angus, faithfully translated back to her word for word was: 'She's got pubes like tumbleweed but I'd give her another go.' Camilla, a hopeless romantic, had hoped Horse was just showing off, and secretly liked her friend, but she was becoming less convinced. 'OK, if we really can't persuade you . . . I'll look out for other eligible young bachelors for you, though!'

'You *are* a treasure, thinking of me,' said Harriet, before wishing Camilla goodnight. At this moment in time, she felt so low she'd take chocolate and bed over meeting her Prince Charming any day.

Chapter 16

Angie Fox-Titt was in a slight predicament. With a good eye for art and an even better one for a bargain, she'd been running Angie's Antiques at a very tidy profit for years. It had given the Fox-Titts a comfort blanket to fall back on during the lean times at the Maltings, meaning Angie didn't have to give up her beloved half-bottle of Taittinger every evening, nor Freddie his caviar sandwiches for lunch.

Now, on a sunny spring morning in Churchminster, her predicament was leaning against the wall in the back room of the shop. Its owner and creator Babs Sax had just dropped it off. 'Let me know what price you'll give for it,' she'd said grandly, before sweeping out of the shop.

Angie had bought a few pieces from Babs in the past out of simple good-heartedness, but had come to regret it. Babs's avant-garde style had not gone down well with Angie's customers, who had more conservative tastes. One piece that had been languishing in her store for months was a picture of an African woman's breasts, made from the excrement of Ghanaian dung beetles especially imported for an extravagant fee. To Angie, the painting could have been produced by a toddler with sticky, chocolate covered fingers, but Babs had insisted the painting represented 'a fusion and vision of when woman meets earth'. Needless to say it hadn't sold. Nor had a picture which resembled a vomit-splattered canvas and was simply titled 'PMT'. The lack of interest in these works had been embarrassing and Angie had had to hide them whenever Babs came into the shop, telling her that a client had put them on hold.

The last thing she wanted was the latest offering, a four foot by six foot monstrosity of swirling reds, nuts and bolts and what looked like bits of string. Babs had explained that it captured Princess Diana's mood just seconds after she had married Prince Charles. Angie was interested in anything to do with royalty, indeed she'd hunted with Princess Anne on many occasions, but even she doubted that anyone could avoid looking at this picture with distaste and horror. Christ, how was she going to get out of buying the bloody thing?

The shop bell tinkled.

'Anyone home?' Caro's voice called out. Angie left the painting and went out to the front of the shop. She and Caro kissed each other warmly on both cheeks, and Angie stooped down to land a kiss on Milo's forehead.

Despite the age gap, Angie and Caro got on extremely well. Angie recognized a lot of herself in the younger woman. She could also see Sebastian for what he really was. Not that she would ever tell her friend that.

'Darling!' exclaimed Angie. 'How are you?

Looking radiant as always, God I wish I had your skin.'

'Yah, but not my thighs, I bet,' said Caro, sinking down into a Regency armchair. Milo threw his dummy on to the floor and Caro absent-mindedly scooped it up, wiped it on her coat and stuck it back in his mouth. 'I just popped in to say hello and see how you were, darling.'

'*I'm* fine, but come and have a look at this,' said Angie conspiratorially, leading her friend out to the back. Babs's painting glowered at them like some angry abomination.

'Oh, heavens!' giggled Caro. 'I take it that's our resident artist's latest offering?'

Angie nodded. 'Isn't it vile? Heaven knows what I am going to do with it.'

'Maybe you could sell it to Sebastian. It's the sort of thing he'd go nuts for. Just as long as he kept it in his London flat,' said Caro.

Angie looked sideways at her. 'How are things going with his nibs?'

Caro sighed. 'Oh, you know.'

Angie linked arms with her. 'Do you fancy lunch at the pub? I'm gasping for a vino, anyway.'

'Why not?' replied Caro. 'But it's on me, I've got Seb's Coutts credit card.'

'Better make it a bottle of bubbly, then,' said Angie wickedly, turning the 'Open' sign to 'Closed' on the shop door.

The Jolly Boot dated back to 1839 and there had been a Turner running the pub ever since. It was a pretty, quaint building with low ceilings, a roaring fire in the winter, and a delightful, flower-scented garden that opened in the summer. The pub claimed a star-studded past – Joan Collins used to pop in when she had a house in the area – and, in their heyday, film legends like Oliver Reed and Richard Harris had enjoyed raucous, all-day sessions there. It maintained a strong sense of history and occasion, and as soon as you walked in it was impossible not to be charmed by the delicious smell of cooking wafting through from the kitchen, or the gleaming brasses hanging on the stone walls. Owing to the area and the clientele, the Jolly Boot also boasted the most extensive selection of champagne of any licensed establishment in the South West of England.

Angie and Caro found themselves a nice table by the window and tucked Milo in the corner. 'What can I get you two charming ladies?' Jack Turner was over like a flash, hovering above them with his huge frame, red hair, and twinkly green eyes.

'Hello, Jack,' replied Angie, taking off her pashmina and draping it across the back of her seat. 'We'd like to see the lunch menu, please. What's Pierre rustled up today?' Pierre was the hugely expensive Michelin-starred chef Jack had managed to steal away from the renowned five-star Cartouche restaurant in Knightsbridge. Pierre had transformed the pub's menu, and now the restaurant at the back was booked up months in advance. But lunchtimes were quieter, and Jack always had a place for locals, particularly when they were as buxom and attractive as Angie and Caro.

'He's got some huge prawns on the go. I had some earlier and they were facking lovely!' said

Jack. 'I'll get you both menus. What about refreshments? Got some vintage Laurent-Perrier delivered last night, it's on ice in the cellar . . .'

Jack knew how to tempt his customers. Caro nodded vigorously. 'Mmm, we'll have a bottle, thanks.' The landlord drew himself up like a genie in front of them. 'Your wish is my command, ladies,' he said, and disappeared off behind the bar.

Thirty minutes later and three glasses in, Caro was confiding in Angie about her marriage. 'Things have just changed so much between us, Angie, with me and Milo stuck down here, and Seb up in London, carrying on his life as normal. I try not to feel bitter, I mean, Seb is really very generous, and I don't want for anything . . .' she trailed off.

'How's the sex?' asked Angie, draining her glass and nodding to Jack to bring another bottle over.

'That's the problem, we aren't having any,' said Caro miserably. 'I feel like a bloody heifer . . .'

'You are not. *At all*,' interjected Angie firmly.

'Then why won't Sebastian come near me?' said Caro. Her eyes clouded over suddenly. 'You don't think he's having an affair?'

That was precisely what Angie was thinking. After all, she knew the warning signs from her own experiences before she met Freddie. 'Darling, I really don't know,' she lied, refilling their glasses. 'But you must remember you have a wonderful son, a family who love you, and good friends.' She put her hand on Caro's and squeezed it.

'Thanks, but I wouldn't blame Sebastian for having an affair, I look so revolting at the moment,' said Caro gloomily.

'Nonsense!' said Angie briskly. 'You're gorgeous,

and Sebastian is bloody lucky to have you.' She paused. 'At least you don't wear shoe lifts.' Much to her delight, Angie had noticed them one day when Sebastian had crossed his legs in front of her at a lunch.

Caro stared at her, and for an awful second Angie thought she'd gone too far. But to her relief, Caro's face suddenly creased into a smile. 'I haven't even told you what he does to his chest hair!'

Their peals of laughter could be heard all round the bar.

Chapter 17

Speaking of the devil, at that moment Sebastian was standing butt-naked in a tanning booth in Soho. Watching himself in the mirrors at the gym that morning, he'd decided he was looking a bit off-colour, and promptly ordered his secretary to book him in for a session at the Club Deluxe salon on Berwick Street. Now he could barely breathe through the blasted fumes as the brown mist spray filled the tiny cubicle.

He emerged, spluttering, and after waiting a minute or two to dry off, got dressed again. This had better bloody not rub off on his Turnbull & Asser shirt, or Club Deluxe would be landed with a whopping great dry-cleaning bill. Sebastian slicked his hair back in the mirror, flashed a smile at his reflection, and stalked upstairs, ignoring the camp receptionist behind the counter as he left.

Just then his phone rang. 'Yah?' he said, looking up the street for a cab to hail.

'I'm in the bath soaping myself,' breathed back a familiar voice. 'I'm all wet, and rubbing the soap into my nipples . . .'

'Are you a dirty little girl, then?' asked Sebastian,

flagging down a cab and climbing in, indicating that the driver should turn left.

'Ooh yes, I am *so* dirty. Filthy in fact,' answered Sabrina huskily. 'When are you going to come back and make me clean again?'

'Keep soaping those luscious titties for the time being,' said Sebastian. The cab driver glanced in his rear-view mirror and Sebastian shot him a conspiratorial wink. 'I'll be home about seven,' he said and rang off. 'Yah, pull over here, driver.'

He threw down a note, jumped out, and was immediately accosted by an equally tanned, pinstriped man, who slapped him heartily on the back.

'Belmo!' he brayed. 'You look like shit!'

Sebastian pretended to pummel his arm. 'Cleevy, you utter arse! How the fuck are you?'

'Wankers,' muttered the cabbie as he drove off.

Later that evening, after he'd shagged Sabrina against every wall in her flat, and finished off with a quickie over the bath, Sebastian took her out for a well-deserved meal. They went to a sweet little French bistro around the corner, a favourite of Hugh Grant's, that did the most exquisite lobster ravioli. As Sebastian sat down in his chair, he winced. 'Christ, you really raked my back with your nails, you evil bitch. I better not get blood on this shirt.'

'Well, my love, no pain no gain,' said Sabrina, sexily narrowing her eyes at him over the table.

'Yah, but that doesn't mean ripping my back to shreds,' said Sebastian. At that moment, two effeminate-looking men with quiffed hair and fur coats bounded over to their table. Sabrina stood up and squealed. 'Edgar! Columbo!'

'Sabrin-a!' they chorused in unison. Air-kisses all round.

'Darling, I'd like you to meet Edgar Fortune. He is, like, this amazing photographer who can always get rid of all my wrinkles.'

'Oh, like you've got any!' simpered the slightly taller of the two men, playing perfectly to her cue.

Sabrina fluttered her eyes coquettishly. 'You are too much! And darling, this is Edgar's assistant, Columbo. Isn't he adorable?'

'Delighted,' said Sebastian, clearly anything but. He hated Sabrina's fashion friends; so OTT and vulgar. He looked pointedly at the menu. 'Anyway, shall we?'

'We'll leave you to it, darling!' cried Edgar. 'I'm shooting you next week aren't I? Ciao for now!' He and Columbo scampered off to greet another flurry of friends across the room.

Sabrina looked like she wanted to shoot Sebastian instead. 'You could try being a bit nicer to my friends.'

'They're not your friends,' said Sebastian dismissively, without looking up from the menu. 'They're a pair of ghastly nancy boys who throw themselves all over you because they know what a shit-hot model you are, and they know you're their next pay packet. And *you* entertain *them* because, my darling, you're a vain little madam who likes the way Edgar shoots you.'

Sabrina stuck her tongue out at him in a not entirely unfriendly manner. 'Sebastian, sometimes you are such a shit.'

'And you can't get enough of it,' he answered, reaching for the wine list. 'Now, what year are we drinking from tonight?'

Back in Churchminster, Caro had turned off the upstairs landing light and was peeking out through the window. Benedict Towey's Porsche was parked outside. Caro glanced at the Cartier watch Sebastian had bought her for her thirtieth: 10.32 p.m. Towey had only just got there, so was he moving in?

Suddenly his front door slammed shut and she watched as his broad, lean back strode down the path. Then Benedict stopped and turned, looking back at her house as if he suddenly sensed she was there. Caro shrank behind the curtains until she heard the Porsche rev up and disappear down the road. Looks weren't everything. She'd had such hopes of a nice family moving in, and instead she'd ended up living next to the most unpleasant man in south west England.

At one in the morning, over in the rectory, the Revd Goody in his warm bed happily dreamt of becoming the next Archbishop of Canterbury, while down the road an exhausted Caro was roused from sleep again by a crying Milo. At Gate Cottage, Harriet put down her romance novel, decided to start a new diet the very next day, and turned the light off. In Camilla's bedroom at No. 5, Angus sighed contentedly as she gave him a hand-job in the darkness, her wrist aching, and body full of pent-up sexual frustration; while in the room next door Calypso and Sam, their bare legs entwined on the bed, shared a final joint. Archie was also glassily dragging on a joint at the Maltings, probably *not* his last of the day, while a rerun of *The Simpsons* played on the TV in the corner of his bedroom. Over at Fairoaks, Errol Flynn cocked his head momentarily before settling back to sleep in the basket at the end of his mistress's bed.

Outside, the leaves in the trees ruffled slightly as a breeze blew across the green. The night was dark, the moon obscured by dense cloud, so that even if anyone had looked out of their window, they wouldn't have seen the tall, hooded figure in black, gliding silently across the dewy grass.

An unwelcome presence had unleashed itself on the village.

Chapter 18

The Revd Goody was on one of his walkabouts in the village. He'd dropped in on Eunice and Dora to see how they were, and had only managed to extricate himself two hours later. Full of fruit cake and over-sugared tea, he made his way across the green towards Bramble Lane. A vehicle screeched to a halt behind him.

'Morning, Reverend!'

He turned to see Lucinda Reinard smiling out of the open driver's window of her Range Rover, which was parked up on the grassy verge. As he got closer, the Reverend could see Lucinda was wearing a lime-green headband and what looked like a rather shiny pink, tight vest which showed off a large, wobbly bosom. The Reverend didn't know where to look.

'Just been for my first session with my personal trainer,' she trilled. 'You know, at that new Fit 4 U place off the market square in Bedlington.'

The Revd Goody had no idea what she was talking about, but smiled weakly: 'Oh?' Lucinda seemed in rather a good mood, and he wondered if she'd been in the Jolly Boot.

She was obviously in the mood to talk.

'Yah,' she said. 'My stress levels have been through the *roof* recently and Nico threatened to divorce me if I didn't do something about it!' She laughed raucously. 'To be quite honest I was simply dreading it, but I have to say that Henry, my personal trainer, is really something.' A dreamy expression clouded her eyes. 'He owns the place and I was expecting some ghastly bull-necked type, but my goodness! He's ex-Horse Guards, you know, and an absolute *dead* ringer for that gorgeous black showjumper, Oliver Skeete. I've signed up for three sessions a week, and Henry says he's going to make a new woman of me.' She glanced up the street before tilting her head conspiratorially. 'He wears these *extremely* tight cycling shorts, and between us, Reverend, his packet makes Linford Christie's lunch box look like a carrot stick and a couple of mini scotch eggs.'

The Revd Goody visibly blanched at this revelation, stepping back from the car. Lucinda stared at him aghast, as if she'd only just realized who she was talking to. She clapped a hand over her mouth.

'Oh, Reverend! Do excuse me. I don't know what came over me.' She leaned towards him again, anxiously. 'You're not going to ban me from attending Sunday services are you? I'd never live it down!'

The Revd Goody opened and shut his mouth a few times like a goldfish. 'It's fine, really,' he managed.

Lucinda sighed with relief, and flashed a gappy smile. 'Thank heavens! Mind you, I suppose you must have people confiding in you all the time. Must be off!' She cranked the car into first gear, turned up the stereo and screeched off, 'Girls Just Want To Have Fun' blasting from the windows.

The Revd Goody sighed and continued on his travels. Next stop was Fairoaks House and Clementine. He'd been dreading this visit, but after that last encounter the Spanish Inquisition on the church's affairs would be a walk in the park.

'So you've put the new advertisement for the church cleaner in the shop? I *do* hope we don't get someone as flighty as the last one,' said Clementine. They were sitting in her drawing room, facing each other in overstuffed straight-backed chairs. Clementine was expertly pouring Earl Grey from a Wedgwood teapot. The Reverend had just tried one of Brenda Briggs's homemade fruit scones and nearly broken a tooth.

'Yes, that's all done,' he said hastily. 'And the new pews are being delivered next week.'

'Excellent,' responded Clementine crisply. 'Now, there is something else I wanted to discuss with you. I suppose you've heard about this Devon Cornwall character moving into Byron Heights?'

The Revd Goody murmured his assent. Clementine continued, 'I can't say I've ever listened to any of his songs, but apparently he was rather big in his day, and still has quite a following round here. Well, quite a few of the villagers have approached me about putting on some kind of welcome bash. He was born in the area, as I am sure you are aware.'

'Er, it sounds like a marvellous idea,' replied the Revd Goody, wondering what part he was going to play in this.

'I think it should be a drinks party and we should hold it at the rectory,' said Clementine.

The Reverend spluttered into his tea cup. 'But, but . . .' He thought of the year-old cobwebs he still hadn't got round to dusting.

'I think it will send the right message,' continued Clementine. 'I haven't seen Mr Cornwall at any services yet, and I think it would be a wonderful way to get him involved in the village community. Think of the donation to the church fund!' Clementine appeared to go dreamy for a moment.

That convinced the Revd Goody. Fundraising had been quiet of late and St Bartholomew's was looking a bit tatty around the edges. 'Do you want me to pay him a visit? I was planning to go round, anyway.'

'Leave it with me,' she replied. 'I can be extremely persuasive when I want to.'

The Revd Goody felt a fleeting flash of sympathy for Devon Cornwall.

Chapter 19

Devon was at home practising his yoga. He had been doing a thirty-minute routine every morning for the last fifteen years of his life. These days Devon was also strictly vegetarian, practically tee-total and, oddly enough for someone who had once got through sixty Marlboro Reds a day, hated smoking so much that no one was allowed to spark up within fifteen feet of him.

Just as Devon was a disciple of detox living now, he had spent most of his rock star years doing exactly the opposite. Countless doctors had told him he should be dead. Breakfast back then had often been a giant spliff and a bottle of Jack Daniels, lunch a couple of acid tabs, and dinner enough cocaine to make an elephant high. Large parts of the seventies and eighties were a complete blank to Devon, as were the women he'd slept with and married along the way. None of them had been capable of saving him – only rehab had done that – and Devon had emerged a new, if slightly neurotic, man.

He was just getting into his 'downward dog' when there was a knock on the gym door. He exhaled irritably; Nigel knew never to disturb him during his yoga. He ignored the knock, but it was simply followed by a louder one and Nigel sticking his head round the door.

'What?' barked Devon crossly.

'You've got a visitor,' said Nigel apologetically. 'Someone from the village.'

'Can't they come back?' asked Devon, his red face looking up from in-between his legs.

'I don't think this is the kind of person who is used to being kept waiting. I'll see you in the front reception room.'

Five minutes later, Devon wandered moodily down the corridor, a towel around his shoulders, and his hair slicked back with water from the water-cooler fountain. In a large reception room at the front of the house, with huge windows and twenty foot velvet burgundy curtains to match, Nigel was sitting on a velvet chaise longue pouring tea. An older, smartly dressed woman was sitting upright on a wing-backed chair facing him. Must have been quite a looker in her day, thought Devon, as she looked pointedly at her watch.

'Devon, this is . . .' began Nigel, but the woman interrupted.

'Clementine Standington-Fulthrope,' she said crisply, in a cut-glass accent, holding her hand out imperiously for Devon to shake. He took it, feeling slightly uncomfortable in his own home, in the presence of this well-mannered stranger.

'Er, pleased to meet ya,' said Devon, flinging himself down on the chaise longue so that Nigel almost spilled the tea. He ignored the disapproving looks Nigel and the visitor flung him.

'Mr Cornwall,' said Clementine.

'Devon, please,' responded Devon.

Clementine nodded her head slightly. 'Devon, on behalf of the residents of Churchminster, I would like to welcome you to our splendid village. You have settled in?'

It was a question that required only one answer. 'Er yeah,' said Devon weakly.

'Excellent, excellent,' said Clementine. 'Church-minster is a wonderful place to live: it has a warm community spirit, beautiful countryside, one of the finest parish churches in the district . . .' At this she let her eye linger on Devon for a second longer. He wondered what the old bat was here for; he wasn't going to open some bloody church fete or something.

'Are you available next Friday?' asked Clementine, interrupting his thoughts. 'Because I have been speaking with the Reverend Arthur Goody, the vicar of St Bartholomew's, and I, we, think it would be an excellent idea to put on a little drinks soirée at the rectory. It will be a wonderful chance for you to meet your new neighbours, get acquainted with the village.'

'That sounds super, thank you,' said Nigel, before Devon had the chance to turn Clementine down.

She rose out of her seat. 'Excellent! Well, I shall see you both then. You know where the rectory is? Good, good. Seven o'clock sharp, please.'

'What the hell did you say that for?' Devon rounded on Nigel as soon as Mrs Nutkins, the housekeeper, had shown Clementine out.

'It will do you good,' said Nigel firmly. His boss

114

had become increasingly reclusive over the years and Nigel didn't approve; Devon's social skills were appalling. If he'd had any in the first place.

'That woman did my bleedin' head in after five minutes. How am I going to hack a whole evening with her?' complained Devon.

'I am sure there will be lots of nice people to talk to, don't be silly,' said Nigel. Besides, he was dying for a night out. Devon was normally in bed by nine o'clock these days.

Over at the rectory, a frantic spring clean got under way. Although she hadn't said anything when she had last visited the Reverend, Clementine had been horrified by the state of the place. It clearly hadn't been cleaned for years. When the sun shone in the window, dust particles had hung in the air. Piles of newspapers, cuttings and books had been heaped up in every room, even the downstairs loo. The whole place had stunk of neglect. When Clementine had left, she had felt she needed a bath. No wonder the Reverend always smelt so musty.

Clementine had known Brenda wasn't up to the task, so with a little diplomacy – 'Brenda, I simply *can't* spare you from Fairoaks' – Clementine had enlisted the help of Pearl Potts, Brenda's next-door neighbour. At the age of seventy-four, Pearl was tiny, wiry and sprightly. A demon with a duster, she always stood in for the church cleaners when they were away. Pearl had jumped at the chance to clean the rectory. 'Those windows give me the shivers every time I pass them Mrs S-F!' she had said, spending the two days before the party cleaning every inch of the house. Or rather, every inch downstairs; the Reverend had banned her from going upstairs. 'Pearl, a man must keep his privacy and dignity.' She'd been disappointed. She'd been looking forward to rummaging through his drawers; and especially to getting her hands on those greying underpants she often saw hanging on his clothes line, so she could bleach them. Pearl's husband, Wilf, had died several years earlier, and she missed having a man to look after.

It was like a different house after she'd finished: the windows sparkled, the wooden floors had been polished, and the curtains and rugs beaten to within an inch of their lives. Even the Reverend had to admit the place looked better. 'Pearl, you've done a marvellous job. I'll have to start entertaining more,' he chortled.

The Jolly Boot was donating several cases of wine. ('Not *too* many, thank you, Jack,' Clementine had said. 'We don't want Mr Cornwall to think we are *all* drunken degenerates.') And the Revd Goody had found several dusty bottles of sherry left over from a Christmas do several years ago. Jack had also kindly volunteered his daughter to serve drinks; he was still punishing Stacey after finding her bra hanging off the pub sign one evening three weeks ago. The more time she spent working the better, as far as he was concerned.

Chapter 20

At half past six on Friday evening Clementine walked briskly over to the rectory. It was just getting dark; the dusky sky casting a bewitching light over the luscious curves and swells of the Cotswolds countryside. She breathed in the fresh, pure air, and sighed contentedly. She had always loved this time of day: it reminded her of the first glass of bubbly at all the parties she used to go to, when a night of fun and debauched company had stretched ahead. Those days were long gone, but Clementine still liked to keep up with a nightly glass of champagne.

She turned into the rectory gate. The house was lit up welcomingly and snatches of classical music filtered gently through one of the open windows. Clementine had to knock a few times before the Revd Goody answered, looking slightly flustered and red-faced. 'I do apologize! I've been having a bit of a last minute tidy-up. Please, come in.'

Clementine stepped in, pulled off her leather gloves and cast an appraising eye around. 'It looks *wonderful*. Pearl really has done a splendid job.' She sighed. 'I only wish Brenda shared her enthusiasm for household cleaning.'

Stacey Turner bustled over with a tray of sherry. She was clad in an extremely short black skirt and tight white shirt, which was opened one button too many to reveal a lacy push-up bra. Clementine had been about to say something, when she remembered the spandex cat suit Calypso had been wearing when she had come round that morning.

Fifteen minutes later, Clementine and the Reverend were standing in the drawing room. Clementine was sipping a glass of the Reverend's ancient sherry, which tasted horrific. She'd already made a discreet emergency phone call to Brenda to ask if her husband would be so kind as to pop round to Fairoaks and collect a case of Laurent-Perrier from the wine cellar.

At 6.55 p.m., the doorbell chimed. It was the Reverend Brian Bellows, the vicar of All Saints Church in Bedlington. Clementine knew him from various religious functions and clasped his hand. 'Vicar, how nice to see you!'

'P-p-pleased to see you too, Mrs Standington-F-f-fulthrope,' said the vicar. He was a tall, gangly man in his late thirties. Sermons at All Saints had been known to take all morning, thanks to his unfortunate stutter.

Shortly afterwards, Brenda and her friend Sandra arrived, giggling and red-faced. They were both clutching autograph books, and Sandra was wearing a bedraggled scarf with the slogan 'Devon is Heaven' printed on it.

'Is he here, yet?' asked Sandra breathlessly.

Clementine frowned. 'I hope you two aren't

going to pester Mr Cornwall all night,' she said severely. 'I've invited the poor man to a civilized drinks party, so *please* don't follow him around all night like a pair of love-sick puppies.'

Brenda pulled a mock curtsey, 'OK, Mrs S-F.' They gravitated over to where Stacey was, Sandra pulling a face behind Clementine's back.

Gradually more people filed in: the Fox-Titts, a few of Clementine's bridge-playing friends, Lucinda and Nico, Eunice and Dora Merryweather. Camilla was there with Angus, who goggled at Stacey's cleavage each time she passed by. Babs Sax swayed into the room with her eyes slightly crossed and red lipstick all over her front teeth.

'She's obviously been at the sherry already,' Stacey whispered to Camilla.

Lady Fraser had even made a rare village outing with Harriet. Normally she and Ambrose wouldn't have been seen dead at any social gathering with a head count of less than five hundred, but, although she would never have admitted it to anyone, Lady Frances Fraser had had rather a crush on Devon Cornwall in her youth. Tonight, curiosity had got the better of her: would he still be a bit of a dish after all these years?

'Camilla, where *is* your sister?' Clementine beckoned Camilla over to the other side of the room, where she had just been discussing the quality of afternoon tea at Claridges with Mitzy Gibbs-Bourke. The room had filled up nicely; there was a buzz of conversation above the tink of glasses. But the guest of honour hadn't turned up yet, and there was only an hour to go.

'Calypso?' replied Camilla. As far as she knew

Caro had been let off coming because Milo wasn't very well.

'Yes, she was meant to be here an hour ago!' Clementine looked at her watch. 'She promised she'd be here on time. Honestly, that girl won't be on time for her own funeral.'

Which is what it will be if Calypso leaves it any longer, thought Camilla. As if on cue, her younger sister sashayed in. With Sam, who was dressed in camouflage army trousers and a tight pink T-shirt with 'Helmet Hater' emblazoned across it. Camilla's innards curdled.

'Good lord!' said Clementine. 'Who on *earth* is that? I thought I'd seen it all with Calypso's wardrobe.' She sighed. 'I don't know, when one was young one dressed how God intended; like a *lady*.' She suddenly spotted an old friend and bustled off, much to Camilla's relief. Watching her grandmother cross the room, Camilla noticed that Freddie Fox-Titt had been cornered by Eunice and Dora, who were both talking at once, while Babs Sax was deep in conversation with Nico Reinard, spilling her glass of wine as she gesticulated madly.

Camilla was about to walk over to her sister and Sam, when there was a loud scream from the corner of the room. Brenda and Sandra were looking out of the window on to the drive, clutching each other. Everyone turned to look.

'It's him!' they shrieked in unison. 'Devon Cornwall!' Sandra pretended to swoon and Brenda caught her, giggling.

'Kevin Who?' said the husband of Mitzy Gibbs-Bourke, who was rather hard of hearing.

'Oh, for goodness' sake,' said Clementine,

bustling out to the front hall to open the door. A grim-faced Devon stood on the step with Nigel, who was smiling broadly. Another shriek came from behind Clementine. She winced in embarrassment and smiled back. 'Mr Cornwall, Nigel, we're *delighted* you could make it. Come in, please.'

Devon was certainly not delighted to be there. He'd been engrossed in a really good book about spiritual practices in the Himalayas, and Nigel had practically had to drag him out. And now here he was, in this fusty old house full of people gawking at him. Especially the two old trouts in the corner. They looked like they wanted to take him upstairs for a threesome. Devon shuddered at the thought.

'Do come this way,' Clementine artfully steered Devon past Sandra and Brenda into the drawing room. Instantly, Babs Sax was on them, fluttering two-inch-long false eyelashes and breathing sherry fumes in Devon's face.

'I'm Babs,' she said, holding out a gnarly hand decked with rings. It was as cold as ice. 'Darling, as a fellow artist I know the pain of living amongst cultural heathens,' she slurred. 'You *must* come and see me if you feel like you are *dying* a death and need to spread your *wings* of creativity!'

Who is this hideous, insect-like creature? thought Devon as Babs staggered off in search of Stacey and the drinks tray. Clementine propelled him onwards. 'Come and meet our host for the evening, the Reverend Arthur Goody. He does quite marvellous work here in the parish, you know, and . . .'

From across the room, Lady Frances Fraser eyed Devon surreptitiously. He *was* rather handsome still. One could have let oneself go like that scruffy

Keith Richards, but Devon looked more like Sting, instead, with a healthy complexion and a lean, strong body. He was slightly crinkly around the eyes, but at least he had all his own hair. Which was cut respectably short and not in some awful eighties throwback ponytail.

Devon was scanning the room, and immediately caught her eye. There was a strange, electrically charged moment between them before Frances blushed and lost her usual composure. She quickly looked away and feigned interest in a watercolour on the wall. Devon had only a second to contemplate the elegant, attractive blonde woman, before being steered firmly towards a man in a dog collar who reminded him of Penfold from *Dangermouse*.

An hour later, Devon was getting bored. The party was thinning out and he hadn't seen the elegant blonde again. For the past twenty minutes, he'd been stuck talking to a stuttering vicar about the damp in his pulpit. Before that, he'd enjoyed a quick chat with Angie Fox-Titt, who'd proved sexy and fun with her enticing eyes and lively wit. Some of the women round here were lookers, Devon reflected to himself, even though he'd sworn off them for life after his last marriage. But that ice queen . . . Devon shook himself and looked round for Nigel, who was chatting to a slightly worse-for-wear Freddie. Nigel noticed his boss was becoming restless, and a moment later excused himself and appeared at Devon's elbow.

'Nige, I'm dying. I've talked to the Reverend Toody or whatever his name is, I've been harassed by two women who wanted me to sign their norks, and I got stuck with some old dear banging on about how good-looking Richard Whitely used to be. Me 'ead's about to explode. Can we do one?'

'I'm having rather a good time, actually,' Nigel chortled, an empty glass of wine in his hand. 'I've met some real characters.' Devon's brow darkened. 'All right, all right, let's say our goodbyes. Better get you back home before you turn into a pumpkin.'

It was ten thirty and the Reverend had just poured the last guests out of the front door. Jack Turner hadn't listened to Clementine's plea and ended up providing a huge amount of wine: 'It was bargain bucket stuff I couldn't sell in the pub anyway.' And most of the guests had stumbled home completely blotto. Including Eunice Merryweather, who had to be retrieved by Lucinda Reinard from the Reverend's privet bush.

Clementine, Camilla and Angus were in the drawing room. Calypso and Sam were nowhere to be seen. 'They must have gone already, I barely had a chance to talk to them all night,' remarked Clementine. 'Samantha seems like a rather odd girl, though.'

'That's one way of putting it!' chortled Angus, who was several sheets to the wind.

Clementine shot him a quizzical look and Camilla squeezed his knee a little too hard just as the Revd Goody came back into the room, rubbing his hands. 'That all went rather well, didn't it?'

'Yes, there was a good turnout,' said Clementine. 'I hope Mr Cornwall enjoyed himself. I did hear you extolling the virtues of St Bartholomew's, excellent work, Reverend. Now, we must be off.'

The Revd Goody showed them out to the hall-way and helped Clementine with her coat.

'Hold on, ladies,' boomed Angus. 'I must pop to the little boys' room, first.' He pulled open the door of the downstairs loo, which was situated right off the hallway. Camilla's hands flew to her mouth as they were all confronted with a full view of Calypso and Sam, frantically snogging the faces off each other. Her sister was sitting on the sink, with her legs wrapped around Sam's trunk-like middle. They were so engrossed in each other that they didn't realize they had an audience.

'Good lord!' exclaimed Clementine. 'Calypso, what *are* you doing?' Calypso screamed in horror and leapt apart from Sam like a scalded cat. She then burst into tears and rushed down the hall and out of the front door.

Sam looked at them belligerently. 'Well, excuse me!' she huffed and pulled the door shut.

Outside in the hallway, there was a deathly silence. Then Clementine continued fastening the buttons on her coat, her face like granite. 'Reverend, I do apologize for my granddaughter's *disgraceful* behaviour.'

'Oh no, really . . .' he spluttered.

'I will be having words with her, I can assure you,' Clementine announced. 'Goodnight.' She swept out, a stunned Camilla and Angus following in her wake.

'Of all the things!' Clementine said, as they walked down the front path.

Camilla hurried to catch up as she strode along. 'Granny, I am so sorry you had to find out about Calypso like that . . .'

'I have never seen such a disgusting thing in all my life!' continued Clementine.

'Granny, please!' Camilla pleaded. 'I know it's a shock, but just because Calypso's dating a – er – girl, well, it doesn't make her a bad person.'

Clementine stopped dead in her tracks. 'Oh, I'm not worried about *that*!'

'You aren't?' Camilla was confused.

'Of course not. Heavens, my first crush was on a wonderful creature called Angelica Featherbrook. She was in the year above me at school, gave me my first orgasm in the fourth-floor dormitory you know. Girls will be girls; I'm sure it's a phase, anyway. No, what I am *extremely* cross about is the way Calypso has conducted herself. She is a Standington-Fulthrope and cannot be seen carousing like a gutter tramp in downstairs lavatories! She must learn to conduct herself correctly in public, and I for one will be telling her so.' With that, Clementine swept off ahead of them.

Camilla's jaw was still sitting on the road where it had just dropped after her grandmother's revelation. A strange gargling noise sounded in her throat, and she couldn't seem to speak. Angus was more vocal.

'What, your grandmother used to be a lezzer?' he asked in a horrified tone.

Camilla finally found her voice again. 'Oh Angus, *shut up!*'

Chapter 21

The annual parish meeting was on 1 May. After an unseasonably grey and wet April, the weather had changed for the better. Fluffy white clouds scudded across bright blue skies, like a frieze in a child's nursery. The sun had finally decided to make an appearance, and shone down on the village. The countryside, wet and sodden for most of the last month, now looked green and lush. The hedgerows were full of life: wild flowers peeked out from the shiny dense foliage, while rabbits and birds nestled beneath them.

Held in the back room of the Jolly Boot, the parish meeting usually turned into a rather raucous, lively occasion in the bar next door. But, first and foremost, it was a chance for the local residents to raise and address any pressing issues, fundraising ideas and forthcoming social events, and indeed anything village-related.

The day before, Clementine had received a very worrying phone call from one of her old friends, Humphrey Greenwood, who was high up in the county council. Clementine was surprised to hear from him – he was a busy man these days and normally sent one of his representatives to parish meetings on his behalf. Humphrey's usual jovial voice sounded strained.

'Humph? What's up?' Clementine wasted no time with preamble.

He hesitated. 'Clementine, I just wanted to let you know I shall be attending the meeting tomorrow. I am afraid I have some rather serious news that I want to tell you all personally.'

'Good God, man, out with it. What's wrong?' she asked.

'I'm afraid I can't tell you at the moment. Damn procedures,' Humphrey said. 'So sorry to keep you hanging like this, old girl, but I just wanted to warn you there is going to be a rather big announcement tomorrow. I'll see you then.'

As Clementine replaced the receiver, she knew it was bad news. Her hand clutched her throat. What on earth could it be?

Desperate for someone to talk to, Clementine mentioned the phone call to Brenda later that day, and, predictably, by that evening the news was all round the village.

Still, it wasn't a bad thing, reflected Clementine, looking round the warm, cosy room at the back of the pub as she waited for the meeting to begin. They had never had such a large turnout. All the chairs were taken and people were even standing up, squashed against the walls. Tension hung in the air. Freddie and Angie Fox-Titt were there, the Revd Goody, Lucinda and Nico, the Turners from the pub, Mrs Bantry, Camilla and Harriet ... Even Sir Ambrose and Lady Fraser were present, looking slightly uncomfortable as they squeezed round a small table.

Stephen and Klaus had also made an appearance, looking wonderfully flamboyant in matching white jeans, cowboy boots and flowing flowery smocks. Aged sixty-two and forty-three respectively, the two men ran a hugely successful furniture-making business just off Sloane Square. Despite the age difference, the couple had been together for years and were utterly devoted to each other. They lived in London, but had a weekend cottage next door to Pearl Potts and loved coming down to recharge their batteries. Last year *Harpers Bazaar* had hailed them the new Lord Linleys of the bespoke cabinet world.

Jed was also there, sitting beside his mother. As Stacey squeezed past to go to the loo she rubbed herself against him provocatively, but Jed just stared stonily ahead. The villagers would never have guessed that, just two hours earlier, Stacey had been bouncing around on top of him screeching like a banshee.

At 7.32 p.m., Humphrey bustled in with his secretary, and two other colleagues from the council who Clementine recognized vaguely. The room went quiet.

At the front of the room, Humphrey got straight down to it. 'Good evening, ladies and gentlemen. I'd like to say it was a pleasure to be here, but I do have a rather serious announcement.' He cleared his throat. 'Four days ago, I received correspondence from Whitehall. I don't know if any of you have been following the news recently, but the Prime Minister Gordon Brown has been under huge pressure to address the issue of overcrowding in our cities. Last week's riots in Stockwell, over families being forced to share houses by Lambeth Council, have provoked what some might say is a knee-jerk reaction. Consequently, a new law is about to be passed that will allow areas of Green Belt land to be put up for sale around Gloucestershire.'

A pin could have been heard to drop in the room as Humphrey continued. 'One piece of land within this area that could be affected is the Meadows.'

Clementine started to feel faintly sick. The Meadows was a fifty-acre woodland site on the south-western outskirts of Churchminster. It was not far from her front door. Until a hundred years ago, it had been used for farming, and then it had been left to grow and flourish as an unofficial area of natural beauty. Clementine had spent her childhood summers playing in the Meadows, and now spent many an hour walking Errol Flynn there.

As if sensing her thoughts, Humphrey looked over at Clementine briefly before continuing. 'Due to the new law, that piece of land has been earmarked for development, and it is now going to be sold off.'

'Sold off for what?' asked a confused Freddie Fox-Titt.

Humphrey looked very apologetic. 'For housing.'

'We're going to get a bloody big housing estate in Churchminster?' boomed Sir Ambrose Fraser, looking appalled. Frances put a placatory hand on her husband's arm.

'It looks that way,' said Humphrey. 'Er, in fact an offer has already been put in by a developer called Sid Sykes. Sykes Estates are big in the building industry. There are quite a few of them around the country.'

Howls of protest went up round the room. Only a few months ago, Sykes Estates had been the subject of a *Watchdog* programme, and accused of exploiting cheap labour and using building materials unfit for purpose. The estates were notorious for squeezing as many cheap, ugly, box-like houses in as possible, but somehow Sid Sykes had escaped investigation. A brash, vulgar, self-made millionaire, there were dark mutterings that he had paid the right people off.

'This is awful! We can't have a Sykes Estate here! It will dwarf the village!' exclaimed Lucinda. Even the normally laid-back Nico was nodding vigorously in agreement.

'We'll have bloody young kids trying to get served in the pub and causing no end of bother,' shouted Jack Turner.

'And they'll all have ASBOs, I've seen *Crimewatch*,' squawked Brenda Briggs. 'Oh lawks, this is awful!'

The room erupted into a babble of worried and angry voices. Humphrey tried to restore calm. 'Ladies! Gentlemen! PLEASE. I understand this is unsettling news to take in, but do try to keep some perspective.'

'Easy for you to say. You don't live here!' someone shouted angrily. Humphrey flushed various unbecoming shades of red.

Clementine couldn't bear it any longer. She stood up. 'Humphrey, is this definitely going to happen? Have we *no* say over the future of our village?'

'It's ninety-nine per cent likely to happen,' he

admitted. 'All I know at the moment is that the Meadows is coming up for auction. The council will accept an offer from the highest bidder.' He looked round the room, pleading for some support. 'Even if it does get sold to Sykes Estates, think what the money can do for the county. Improve public transport, local schools . . .'

Angry jeers and boos echoed around the room. Humphrey began to fear for his personal safety; the crowd was becoming distinctly mob-like. But Clementine suddenly felt the faintest glimmer of hope. She interrupted the hubbub, her loud, strident voice claiming attention.

'Hold on, hold on everyone! Right.' She turned to Humphrey. 'What you are saying is that the land is going to be sold off to the best offer? It doesn't automatically have to be sold to that horrible little man for a grotty housing estate?'

'That's right,' answered Humphrey weakly. 'The land won't even be up for sale for six months or so. Sid Sykes just got to hear about it . . .'

'I bet he did, he's probably giving all you lot bloody back-handers!' someone heckled.

'Shush!' said Clementine crossly. 'So if I am correct, *we* could put an offer in for the Meadows? To save the village and keep it how it is?' This was met with loud cheers.

Humphrey looked round the room dubiously. 'I suppose so . . .' he said. 'But you will be up against some seriously stiff competition. Prices for land in this area have quadrupled over the last eighteen months.'

'How much?' asked Clementine bluntly.

Humphrey looked distinctly uncomfortable.

'Developable land has reached a premium,' he told them. 'With the price of the land round here shooting up by the week, it's been valued at . . .' He ummed and aahed for a few moments.

'Oh, for God's sake, Humphrey!' said Clementine faintly. 'How much?'

Humphrey looked at her. 'Fifteen?' he said hopefully.

'Fifteen thousand?' said Freddie. He looked rather relieved. 'God I was expecting much more, that's a bargain! I'm sure we can all dip in our pockets and get this sorted out right now.'

'No, Freddie, you don't understand,' Humphrey was sweating now, beads forming on his forehead. 'I meant fifteen million.'

'*Fifteen million pounds?*' asked Clementine, each word perfectly, painfully enunciated.

Humphrey nodded. 'That is at the high end of the estimate, though,' he added hopefully, as if it would soften the blow.

It didn't. Silence enveloped the room once again as stunned, white faces struggled to take it in.

'Christ on a bike,' said the Revd Goody.

Chapter 22

The next day, the village was buzzing with the shock announcement. The *Cotswold Journal* sent a reporter, who was quickly accosted by Brenda when he popped into the shop to buy some cigarettes. It was all they could talk about in the Jolly Boot, with various scurrilous tales about the evil villain Sid Sykes flying around, while Beryl Turner quickly raised a petition amongst the regulars to send to the county council headquarters in protest.

Clementine had had a very trying morning. She'd woken up with a splitting headache and momentarily wondered why, until the events of last night had come flooding back. She had spent the night tossing and turning. How on earth were they going to raise fifteen million pounds to buy the Meadows? Clementine, like a few other village residents, could put her hand in her pocket and stump up a decent sum towards it, but it would still fall way short of the amount they needed.

Before he'd died of gout in 1978, Clementine's darling husband Bertie had tirelessly run the Standington-Fulthrope Committee and this was just the sort of challenge he'd have relished. She could almost hear him shout: 'Let's get the buggers!' Now Clementine felt the future of the village rested on *her* shoulders, and twenty years ago she would have approached the challenge with gusto. Now she just felt daunted and helpless, and too old for the fight.

The phone rang, briefly snapping her out of her gloom. She picked the receiver up wearily. 'Hello?'

'Clementine? It's Fred.'

'Oh, Freddie, hello.' Clementine stared out of the kitchen window in the direction of the Meadows. Memories of her son Johnnie swinging from the trees pretending to be a superhero all those summers ago suddenly flashed into her mind. She blinked back a tear.

'I've been thinking . . .' There was a note of excitement in his voice that snapped Clementine out of her black mood. 'Look, we can't let this happen! I've lived in Churchminster all my life and the Maltings is my livelihood. It's Angie's and Archie's too. We can't let that Sykes character buy the Meadows and destroy our village!'

Clementine let out a sigh of despair. 'But Freddie, the only option is to buy it ourselves, and where are we going to find that kind of money? I mean, I could put some in myself or even sell Fairoaks . . .' The thought made her feel sick to her stomach.

'You'll do no such thing,' said Freddie, his voice strong and resolute. 'There are other ways to raise the cash without making you homeless. Look, between you and me finances aren't that great for us at the moment, otherwise I'd stump up for the lot myself. But Angie and I have been talking, and there are other ways to raise money. I'm sure I can put on a few deluxe shooting weekends and Angie says she can try and pull some strings in the antiques world, see if we can get some donations. Maybe auction them off? It may seem like little things, but if we all pull together and do what we can, then who knows, we might just raise enough. Better than us all just sitting on our arses! Er, sorry, I mean bottoms.'

'I wonder . . .' Clementine murmured thoughtfully.

'Tam Spinker-Butworth for example,' said Freddie. 'He made a few cool mill with that sponsored yacht race last year, do you remember?'

The fighting blood suddenly coursed back through Clementine's veins. She sat up straight in her chair and banged her hand firmly on the table. 'Fred dear, you are absolutely right! An auction is just what we need! We are not going down without a jolly good fight. I survived the war and I'll get through this as well. I'll go to my grave before this village is swallowed up by some ghastly tin-pot housing estate!'

'Hear hear!' cheered Freddie down the phone and rang off, promising to start making plans for the shooting and fishing parties that very morning.

Clementine got out her address book and picked up the phone, her mouth set in a resolute line as she made the first of many phone calls that day.

By mid-afternoon, the offers were flying in. Babs Sax had donated several of her paintings ('Are you sure that's a good idea?' asked Caro when she found out), and Sir Ambrose and Lady Fraser had generously offered to donate a wantonly expensive

Louis XV table and chairs from one of the many rooms at the Hall. 'Bloody uncomfortable to sit on, makes one's backside go numb,' boomed Ambrose down the phone. 'Be glad to see the back of the blasted things.'

Caro had phoned Sebastian to see if his bank could make a substantial donation (he'd refused to give up his Christmas bonus), while Lucinda was going to organize a sponsored ride with the pony club. Spurred on by her increasing fitness levels at Henry's attentive hands, she also put herself down for the Churchminster Fun Run in July. Jack Turner was to put on a French evening at the pub with all proceeds going into the fund. Stephen and Klaus popped round on their way back to London to offer their services. 'Anything, anything at all Clementine, dah-ling,' Stephen drawled through a haze of menthol cigarette smoke.

'Ve are sure ve can persuade some of our clients to contribute to *such* a good cause,' Klaus added in his distinctive German accent. By five o'clock, her ear burning from being pressed to the phone all day, Clementine was quite overwhelmed by the villagers' goodwill and generosity.

That evening, Clementine invited her three grand-daughters over for supper. So while the smell of Brenda's burnt asparagus tart wafted out of the kitchen, they made themselves comfortable in Clementine's cosy reading room, and discussed the day's events.

Clementine recounted the response from the village. 'That's marvellous news, Granny Clem,' said Caro, taking a huge glug of Chablis. Milo was asleep upstairs in one of the spare rooms and she was taking advantage of the break. He had been crying on and off all day, and her head felt like it was about to explode. Sebastian hadn't helped by calling just as Milo was screaming blue murder in the background, and saying, 'Christ, what are you doing to him?'

'Nothing, he's doing it to himself,' she had replied furiously.

'Yah, well, maybe you should get a nanny. Face it, darling; you're really not coping, are you?' Then he'd rung off, leaving Caro making a V-sign at the phone. Childish, but it had made her feel better. As did this huge glass of wine.

'So you're going to put on an auction?' asked Camilla.

Clementine nodded. 'That is the idea, yes. And there will be all the other money people are going to raise.'

'And this is going to get fifteen *million* pounds?' asked Calypso, one eyebrow arched.

'It's a start, Calypso!' responded Clementine hotly. 'What else are we going to do: stand by and watch our village ruined?'

'I didn't mean it like that,' said Calypso thoughtfully. 'I think the auction and the other stuff is like, a really, really good idea. But will it be enough? Suppose we put on a ball as well? I have always, like, *totally* wanted to do that.' She smiled. 'Especially as I've been thinking about a career as a party organizer.' Calypso had only just started looking her grandmother in the eye again after the downstairs loo incident. She'd packed a grumbling Sam back off to Brighton the next day.

'You've got a new job? Oh, how marvellous!' exclaimed Clementine.

Calypso flushed. 'Well, not exactly. But I've been thinking about getting involved with organizing parties and stuff for ages. You know what great contacts I've got, especially with the girls from school.' Unlike her sisters, Calypso had spurned the country comforts of Benenden and had boarded at Vespers, an achingly cool girls' school in Notting Hill. Currently it counted two pop stars, seventeen It girls, four supermodels, and an Oscar-nominated actress among its alumni. 'What better place to start than with Churchminster's very own ball?'

Clementine looked doubtful. 'There will be an awful lot to do, darling. I know from experience.'

But Calypso was on a roll. 'We could have the auction at the ball! Make it like Elton John's White Tie and Tiara Ball. We could invite loads of celebrities and stuff. Honestly, Granny Clem, I've got great contacts.'

'Like Kate Moss!' interjected Caro. 'She's got a country house round here. So has Liz Hurley.'

'And I nearly ran over Paul McCartney in Stow-on-the-Wold last week,' said Camilla excitedly. 'He didn't look very pleased at the time, but this is just the sort of thing he'd support. Ooh, tickets will go like hot cakes!'

'*Totally*,' said Calypso confidently. 'We could get, like, loads of press with people like that coming. You need to think about media coverage,' she told Clementine knowledgeably. 'This is just the kind of thing people go *nuts* for.'

Clementine looked round at her granddaughters. They were right. 'Do you think we can really do it?

Put on an auction *and* a ball?' she asked. 'I will need all of you to help me.'

'*Deffo!*' they all chorused.

'We'll make *double* fifteen mill!' shouted Calypso, jumping up and down on the sofa. Errol Flynn, who had been asleep at the end, woke up grumpily and climbed off, leaving a rather noxious smell in his wake.

'Let's not get too carried away,' said Clementine, but her eyes were shining with excitement. She raised her wine glass. 'To Churchminster!'

'Churchminster!' they chorused, toasting each other.

Clementine called an impromptu meeting at Fairoaks the next evening, and phoned round the village again. 'No excuses, you *must* be here,' she crisply informed Babs Sax after hearing her say she needed to attend a talk about the art of life-modelling genitalia. Babs meekly acquiesced: you didn't say no to a woman like Clementine Standington-Fulthrope, especially when she was on such a mission as this.

As a result, everyone in the village turned up. Even Archie Fox-Titt, red-eyed and tousle-haired, was dragged along to stand between his parents. 'Little bugger's been lying in bed all afternoon!' Freddie Fox-Titt informed Lucinda Reinard. 'These students are a lazy lot, I tell you.'

Archie was, in fact, feeling terrible. He and Tyrone had been on a mammoth smoking session all day – Tyrone had managed to score some really strong weed called skunk – and he was still feeling completely out of it. He pulled his baseball cap further over his eyes and hoped no one would talk to him.

Once everyone was there, Clementine brought them up to speed with the events of the past twenty-four hours. Many people present, including Lucinda and the Fox-Titts, were already on the Standington-Fulthrope Committee, but Clementine needed more volunteers. With help and interjections from her granddaughters she put forward the proposal for the Save Churchminster Ball and Auction, or SCBA as it was to be known from then on. They were to start a fund now, for any other monies raised in the interim.

The suggestion went down a storm.

'Bloody marvellous idea!' yelled Freddie Fox-Titt.

'Rather!' echoed Angie, who was sitting beside him, looking ravishing in a gold and chocolate pashmina.

'We are going to form a new committee, and I would be extremely grateful if people would put their names forward,' said Clementine. 'Those who can spare the time and are *one hundred per cent* committed please come and see me afterwards.' Around the room heads were nodding vigorously.

'So I suppose you need somewhere to hold the ball,' boomed Sir Ambrose Fraser, looking like Toad of Toad Hall in tweed plus fours, walking stick, and cap pulled down over his florid face.

Clementine nodded. 'Yes, Ambrose, we are looking for somewhere, so if anyone has any suggestions—'

'Lady Fraser and I have just had a quick discussion,' Ambrose continued, as though

Clementine hadn't spoken at all. 'We would be delighted if it was held at Clanfield Hall. What ho! Got a bloody great ballroom that hasn't been used for years, anyway.'

Clementine beamed at him. 'Ambrose, what a fabulously generous offer. Thank you!' More cheers echoed around the room.

'Just as long as no one tramples on my rose garden,' interjected Lady Fraser.

'I'm sure Jed can build a fence around it,' whispered Harriet, who was sitting behind her. 'Oh, how exciting! A ball!'

'That does mean you will have to wear a dress, darling,' her mother replied, speaking through clenched teeth as she smiled graciously round the room. 'Maybe that nice red one I got you.'

A vision of Horse, red-faced and sweating above her, came back to Harriet in a flash. 'I might buy a new one for the occasion, if that's OK, Mummy.'

Humphrey rang Clementine three days later. It had been confirmed – the Meadows was being put up for auction. Offers from interested parties were to start at five million pounds, but, as Humphrey explained, it was expected to go for a lot more than that. The accompanying red tape and paperwork was a hell of a job, so the auction wasn't scheduled until the end of the year, on 10 December. The Standington-Fulthrope Committee had decided the Save Churchminster Ball and Auction would take place nine days earlier, on 1 December.

Sid Sykes had already put out a statement in the trade press to say he would be making an offer, and Clementine had read the article grim-faced. This was war. Six months later all their lives could change for ever. For the better or for the infinitely worse.

Chapter 23

It was a beautiful sunny afternoon in the village, and Caro was taking full advantage of the weather. She and Milo were in their back garden on a huge Boden picnic rug. Caro had put up one of the garden umbrellas and Milo was under it, gurgling happily. Caro lay on her side next to him. Milo's soft brown eyes looked innocently into hers and crinkled round the corners as she tickled his tummy. When he was like this, it was all worth it and nothing else mattered to Caro. She got her phone out and switched it on to camera. 'Smile, darling!' Milo obliged happily. Caro switched the picture to 'Send' and keyed in Sebastian's mobile. 'We'll send this to Daddy at his office, just so he can see what a *gorgeous* boy you are.' Caro was determined to show her husband she was capable of achieving domestic bliss at home, as well as screaming chaos.

Caro looked round the garden. It was a long, walled piece of paradise, the brainchild of an exotically named landscape gardener from Cirencester. Caro was hopeless with anything botanical, and she had to admit they had done a marvellous job. The French windows at the back of the house opened out on to a huge, decked patio. Exotic green plants and an oak table big enough to seat fifteen stood on it, and a decked path led down the sixty-foot garden. In the centre of the lawn a polished brass sundial stood glittering in the sunlight. At the far end was a beautiful wooden summer house painted a rustic white, and brightly coloured flowerbeds provided a stunning background. They had a gardener in once a week, even though Caro felt guilty about it, with so much time on her hands. Sebastian had insisted. 'I remember all those dead pot plants in your flat when we first met, darling,' he had drawled. 'There is no way I am letting you anywhere near the garden, especially when I've spent a small bloody fortune on it.'

There wasn't a cloud in the brilliant blue sky. The sun beat down as the scent of the blue wisteria clambering up the back of the house wafted across the garden. Caro lay back, luxuriating in the moment. Right here, right now, the black cloud which seemed to have followed her around for so long had finally lifted. If only momentarily. Goodness, it was hot! Secure in the privacy of her garden, Caro peeled off her long-sleeved Whistles T-shirt and lay back in her bra and shorts. She didn't need sun cream in this weather, did she? She only had Milo's factor 50 and she wouldn't get *any* colour wearing that.

As she relaxed even more, Caro's thoughts once again drifted to her next-door neighbour. On the phone the next day, she had recounted to Sebastian, word by word, her heated encounter with Benedict Towey, but Sebastian had been predictably uninterested. 'Probably working like a dog to keep his family in the manner they've become accustomed to. Like me,' he had added unnecessarily. And untruthfully. Sebastian had spent about three hours at his desk that week, the rest of his time having been spent dining in offensively expensive restaurants, working out, having his weekly manicure and rutting with Sabrina on a thrice-nightly basis.

'That's not fair!' Caro had responded hotly. She had paused. 'Besides, I don't think he's got a wife and family.'

'Man's got the right idea if you ask me.' So much for defending her honour.

Caro had only seen Benedict Towey a handful of times in the past couple of weeks. From what she could gather, he had moved in on a part-time basis, spending a few nights there in the week and then disappearing God knows where at weekends. 'Probably ravishing some long-legged blonde mistress just as vile as he is,' Caro had ranted to Angie over a spritzer in the Jolly Boot. 'I don't know why he doesn't just push off and let a nice family move in, some people who are actually going to live in that lovely house. It's such a waste.'

Now Caro started to wonder what *his* garden looked like. Was it as nice as theirs, or would it be wild and overgrown? The front of the house looked like a show home, with the curtains up but nobody home.

Milo was now fast asleep on the rug. All of a sudden, Caro had an overwhelming urge to look over the high stone wall that separated the gardens. Benedict hadn't been home for days, and if anyone else caught her, she could always say she had heard a funny noise and gone to investigate. But first, she needed to stand on something. She jogged back to the house and dragged out one of the extremely heavy Philippe Starck bar stools from the kitchen. Huffing and puffing, Caro pulled the stool across the grass, praying it wouldn't leave skid marks.

She glanced at Milo. He was still out like a light, so she positioned the stool carefully against the wall. Then Caro carefully climbed up and, wobbling slightly, looked over into Benedict Towey's garden.

It was the same size and shape as hers, the lovely Cotswold stone wall circling the length and breadth of it. There was a set of French windows as well, but instead of looking out on to an impressive deck, they faced a smaller paved patio which was woefully bare. A few chairs were scattered randomly about the slightly overgrown lawn, and the flowerbeds stood empty, as if waiting for someone to fill them.

Disappointed, Caro turned her attention back to the house. If she just hoisted herself up a bit higher, she could see in through the kitchen window. It was huge and square, the units made from some kind of light wood. There was a breakfast bar there, too, bare apart from an empty fruit bowl. Ooh, if she leaned in a bit more she could see through the French windows . . .

'What the hell do you think you're doing!' Caro squeaked in surprise and almost lost her balance as a man's voice boomed across the garden. She looked up, and to her absolute horror, a fuming Benedict Towey was leaning out of one of the upstairs windows.

'I er, well actually . . .' she stuttered, her ready made excuse going straight out of her mind. Christ, did he have to be so bloody gorgeous? Benedict was wearing a crisp white shirt which showed off his tanned skin and blue eyes perfectly, a dark blue tie casually pulled away from the collar.

'I said: What. The. Hell. Are. You. Doing?' This time he lowered his voice to a menacing growl. Caro quivered even more.

'Er, I just wanted to know, er, what kind of garden furniture you've got. We're thinking about getting a new set you see . . .' The excuse sounded hollow, even to her ears.

Her neighbour narrowed his eyes and leaned further out of the window. 'Don't give me that crap! If I see you spying into my property one more time, I'll call the bloody police on you!'

Caro felt her temper rise. 'There's no need to be so rude,' she yelled back. 'And don't you dare threaten me!' The window slammed shut.

Behind her, Milo had been woken by the angry exchange and started to cry. The tranquillity of the afternoon was shattered. Caro, still shaking from her encounter, climbed down off the stool, and as she went to comfort her son caught sight of her reflection in her own windows. Her hands flew to her mouth in horror – she was still in her bra. 'Shit!' she wailed, gazing at her sunburnt, wobbly chest, unflatteringly encased in the shell-pink maternity contraption she still hadn't stopped wearing.

Caro's mortification made her hatred for Benedict Towey burn ever more strongly. She swore never to speak to the detestable man again.

Somehow, by the time Caro popped round to see her grandmother the next day, Clementine had heard all about Caro's shouting match.

'How did you find out?' asked Caro, appalled.

'It doesn't matter,' Clementine replied crisply. 'But darling, in future do try and refrain from screaming like a fishwife with one's new neighbour in public.'

'I was in my own back garden!' protested Caro indignantly.

'Noise travels,' was all her grandmother would say, enigmatically. But, in fact, Caro's row was the least of Clementine's troubles at the moment. She had also had a very unsettling experience in the village that morning.

Clementine had taken Errol Flynn to stretch his legs, and had decided to pop into St Bartholomew's to see if the new pews had been delivered. And indeed they had. The Revd Goody had been in the church sitting on one, stroking the shiny wood happily.

'Aren't they marvellous?' he had said when he saw her. Clementine had agreed, and after a quick discussion about the order of service for Sunday, she had left the Reverend and started for home. She had just reached the start of Bramble Lane, which led off the green towards her house, when a gleaming blue Bentley had pulled up beside her. The window on the driver's side had glided down silently.

'Which way to the Meadows, luv?' the oily looking man inside had asked. He had had a rough, estuary accent, jet-black hair slicked back, and hooded, dark eyes. Clementine had thought he looked like some kind of mafia gangster, especially with the flash pinstripe suit he was wearing and chunky gold rings littering his hands, which rested on the cream leather steering wheel. She had taken an instant dislike to him, and besides, Clementine Standington-Fulthrope was not the kind of woman you called 'luv'.

'Carry along the road, half a mile on your right,' she had said frostily, tugging Errol away from peeing on the Bentley's spotless wheels, and turning to walk briskly home. The car crawled along beside her.

'You live round here, then?' the driver had asked.

'Yes, I do,' Clementine had stared straight ahead. God, he was one of those awful nouveau riche types that came nosing about here sometimes. But when he had made no move to drive on she had begun to feel distinctly unsettled. 'Well, good day, then,' she had said, nodding to him curtly. He had stared at her for a second and then smiled wolfishly, revealing a set of teeth more gold than they were white.

'See ya,' he had said casually, before the tinted window slid up again. The Bentley had revved, and poor Errol Flynn had nearly fallen into the ditch in fright. As it had passed her, Clementine had caught sight of the car's registration and nearly choked: SYKES 1. It had to be Sid Sykes! What a revolting man! He was even worse than she had imagined. And to have the audacity to show his face round here! Thoroughly ruffled, Clementine had hurried the rest of the way home.

Over at No. 5 The Green, Calypso was trying not to giggle at a pair of nipple tassels Sam had bought for her. 'Don't you like them?' asked an affronted Sam, as if she'd just handed over a pair of knickers from M&S.

'Yah, they're fun, babes, but I don't really think they're me.' Calypso was lounging on her bed, long legs crossed, while Sam stood in front of her holding a nipple tassel in each hand, like a pair of dangly earrings. Sensing a mood coming on, Calypso tried to placate Sam. 'Honestly, they're totally cool. I do like them.'

'Maybe you could wear them to Pink Rush?' asked Sam hopefully. Pink Rush was a girls-only nightclub in Brighton. 'I've even got a pair of dungarees I can coordinate them with.'

Calypso sighed. She didn't know why Sam insisted on dressing like a stereotypical dyke whenever they went out; it was as if she was trying to ram the point home. Luckily Calypso's mobile rang at that moment, and she pounced on it gratefully and peered at the screen. 'Granny Clem!' she exclaimed warmly, and listened for a few moments. 'Mmm, yah. OK, I'll be over in two ticks.'

'You're going out?' grumbled Sam.

'You can come if you want,' offered Calypso half-heartedly.

'No way!' she replied. 'Your grandmother thinks I'm the devil's spawn.'

'Better than the devil's sperm,' said Calypso cheekily, and swung her legs off the bed. She planted a quick kiss on Sam's mouth. 'See you later.'

She had no doubt Sam would be perfectly happy

rolling a joint and settling back to watch a DVD. Sam was a mature student at Brighton University, and for someone who claimed they were on a very demanding art course, she seemed to be spending an awful lot of time in Churchminster.

Clementine had decided she wanted to do a bit of research on Sid Sykes to see exactly who they were up against. On the advice of her family, she had acquired a computer and had Broadband installed in her house last summer, but she hadn't used it once. 'Blasted newfangled things, what's wrong with using one's library?' she had said. But Clementine knew there would be nothing about the likes of Sid Sykes in any of the hundreds of books which adorned the walls of the library at Fairoaks.

'Calypso, I need you to get me on that Goggle thing,' announced Clementine as Calypso walked into the study.

'Google,' corrected Calypso, pulling off her electric-blue raincoat.

'Precisely,' said Clementine impatiently. 'The search motor.'

Calypso rolled her eyes. 'Search *engine*. Look, let's switch the computer on and I'll show you . . .'

A few minutes later, they were sitting at Clementine's huge mahogany writing desk, staring wide-eyed at the screen. Sid Sykes had done a lot in his fifty-three years, and not much of it was good. Born in East London as the eighth child of a poor family, Sid Sykes had run away from home at thirteen and joined a travelling fair. He had then worked in a series of betting shops, taking only a decade to rise from shop boy to owner. He sold his business for a huge profit and moved into property. Fifteen years on, Sykes Estates was one of the most formidable building firms in the country. Sid Sykes lived with his wife Gloria and two children in a five-million-pound Tudor mansion in Essex.

That was the official history. The unofficial one was a record of money laundering, extortion and trading in stolen goods. And of course, his infamous appearance on *Watchdog*. The police had tried several times to press charges, but each time Sykes had hired the best defence lawyer money could buy and the case had been picked apart and blown out of the water. The notoriety had stuck though: Sid Sykes was not a man you messed with.

'Granny, he sounds horrible!' Calypso shuddered and wrapped her arms round herself.

'Not the most savoury of characters, I have to agree.' Clementine closed her eyes tightly for a second. Oh Bertie, I wish you were here! she said silently to herself.

'Lumme, did you hear that Sid Sykes was here yesterday?' Brenda asked Pearl Potts. The two neighbours were standing in their gardens, having their usual gas over the fence. Benedict Towey would have had a fit if one of them had moved in next door to him.

'Here?' Pearl raised a scandalized eyebrow. 'In Churchminster?'

Brenda nodded knowingly. 'Mrs S-F ran into him yesterday. Driving around in a bleedin' great motor like he was lord of the manor!'

'Which he might well be soon,' Pearl pointed out darkly.

'Oh, Pearl, don't speak like that!' Brenda scolded her. She shivered dramatically. 'Quite a nasty character by all accounts. Dressed completely in black he was, and he hasn't got teeth, he's got fangs! All yellow and dripping from what I heard . . .'

'Is that what her nibs told you?' asked Pearl archly. Brenda's overactive imagination was well known in the village. Brenda flushed. 'Not exactly, but that was the feeling I got from her, anyway.'

Pearl glanced at her watch. 'Ooh, lordy! It's Friday and the bummers are arriving in two hours. I promised I'd go water their plants and turn the heating on.'

'Pearl, you can't call Stephen and Klaus that!' said Brenda, overcome by an unfamiliar attack of political correctness.

'That's what they do, isn't it?' Pearl gathered up her washing basket. 'Each to their own and, besides, they don't mind. Nice boys, they are.'

'You say it to their faces?' asked a horrified Brenda, but the tiny pensioner was already bustling across the lawn to her back door, arms full of clean washing.

Chapter 24

Spurred on by her run-in with Sid Sykes, Clementine called an SCBA committee meeting at her house. Sykes's visit had somehow contaminated the village, his residue still lingering, and Clementine was determined to eradicate it as soon as possible.

It was a warm evening, and the committee sat out on the huge veranda at the back of the house. Clementine glanced around; yet again, it was a jolly good turnout and she had been touched by the number of new members who had flocked to put their names down. Alongside stalwarts such as Freddie and Angie were some younger residents like Jed Bantry. Stephen and Klaus had commitments in London, but Clementine had decided they could be absent members and represent the committee in the influential London circles they moved in.

Clementine had already been elected chairperson. 'As many of you are aware, I have many years of organizing charity events,' she addressed the room. 'I don't have to tell you that it is *extremely* hard work, but of course, most rewarding at the end. In the meanwhile, you have to be motivated, well-connected and resourceful. We don't have much money in the pot, but this ball needs to be the best bash the Cotswolds has ever seen. This means calling in as many favours as one can from friends, business associates and any sponsors we can get on board. Understood?'

Heads nodded vigorously. Clementine looked down at the list in front of her. 'Right, I have a list of what needs to be done, and the people I think would be suitable for each task.' She put on her reading glasses and started scanning a bony finger down the page.

'As chairperson I shall be overseeing everyone. I shall also be in touch with the council about the Meadows to make sure they keep us abreast of all arrangements.' She glanced round the room. 'As you know, it is extremely important we get VIP guests to attend.' She looked at her youngest grand-daughter. 'Calypso, I am leaving you in charge of this. Also you will be responsible for getting us media coverage for the event. I don't know much about that, so I am entrusting you with it.' Clementine tried to fix Calypso with her infamous beady eye, but she was already furiously scribbling into a pink leather Filofax.

'Caro, you are going to be in charge of the guest list overall. You will take my address book for starters, and phone your mother and father to make sure we haven't left anyone off. We need an Hon sitting on every table. Any suggestions from others would be gratefully received. I am also leaving you in charge of the most important part of the evening, the seating plan.'

Caro gulped. She had seen grown women

reduced to tears over seating arrangements for a simple dinner. It was such a political process; she might have to take a crash course at the House of Commons.

'We will also be having a sit-down dinner,' Clementine continued. She looked beseechingly at Jack Turner and his wife Beryl. 'I was rather hoping you would be able to help . . .'

'We've already spoken to Pierre,' said Beryl. 'He's going to think up a top-notch menu using produce donated from local sources.' Jack nodded in agreement.

Freddie spoke up. 'As far as alcohol, I've got a friend who runs a rather good vineyard in the south of France. He says he's happy to provide the wine *and* the fizz. Says it's great PR for him.'

Clementine clapped her hands. 'Wonderful! This is turning out better than I could have hoped for. Now Camilla, I want you to be in charge of entertainment . . .'

As the meeting went on, more roles were dished out. Harriet was going to be the site manager at Clanfield Hall, to ensure everything was put in place and ran smoothly on the night. She was to oversee the ballroom, cloakrooms and toilets and the car park. Camilla's friend's brother ran his own fireworks company in London, so Camilla was going to ask him if he'd do some kind of show for them. 'He was involved with the Sydney Harbour display at the Millennium, so, yah, he does know what he's talking about,' she explained.

Calypso had also insisted on being in charge of music on the night: 'We'll get like, a totally amazing band and DJ!'

'I don't want any of that dreadful car-alarm music,' warned her grandmother.

'Hey, maybe we could get Devon Cornwall on board,' suggested Freddie. 'He might be able to get Mick Jagger or something, I bet they're mates.'

'Good idea, Freddie!' said Clementine. 'Can you go round and talk to him about it? Now, Angie, I was wondering if you could be in charge of securing donations for the auction? The more expensive and inventive the better my dear . . .' And so it went on.

After two hours the committee had covered all aspects of the ball, and everyone was exhausted. But they had a gleam of something else in their eyes.

Hope.

Chapter 25

To kick-start the fundraising the Jolly Boot was putting on a French evening the following Friday. Tickets were fifty pounds a head and, for that, guests would receive a champagne (French, naturally) cocktail on arrival, followed by a set five-course dinner. The tickets sold out in a day.

Camilla managed to bag herself and Angus two, as well as tickets for Calypso and Harriet and, much against her better judgement, a pair for Sniffer and Horse. She gave them strict instructions via Angus to behave themselves. When Harriet found out they would be there she tried to pull out, but Camilla talked her round. 'Come on, Hats, it will be such fun! Pierre is putting on quite a spread, from what I hear.' Harriet eventually agreed, on condition that she didn't have to sit next to Horse.

Caro was also going along, with Sebastian and a couple they were friendly with from skiing called Tilly and Tobey. Clementine had graciously forgone a ticket to babysit Milo: 'That place is *ghastly* when it's busy, no matter how good Pierre's escargots are.' Milo was going to sleep in the old nursery Caro used to stay in as a little girl.

*

On the evening, Caro was waiting for Sebastian to come home, hovering in the kitchen, hands curled round a chilled glass of Pinot Grigio. She was wearing a new black dress from Amanda Wakeley in Cirencester. She had been thrilled to find she could fit in a size twelve. Caro hadn't been consciously dieting, but she had found herself picking at her meals recently. Her ebbing lust for life had affected her appetite, too. She might be bored, lonely and miserable, but at least she was losing weight, she thought ruefully. Caro twirled around and looked at her reflection on the cooker window. And she was looking forward to tonight. Tilly and Tobes were a giggle, and it would be nice to have a few glasses of bubbly and let her hair down.

Her phone beeped. A text from Sebastian popped up. *'Train is crawling, will be late. Have U ironed my dark blue Turnbull & Asser shirt?'* Caro took another glug of wine, hoping they wouldn't lose their table.

Meanwhile, Harriet and her party were arriving at the pub. Beryl and Stacey had done a marvellous job of decorating: blue, white and red flags hung everywhere alongside strategically placed garlands of garlic. A covered marquee had been set up in the back garden with even more tables, so they could seat a larger number of diners. The staff were all dressed in cute berets and striped blue and white T-shirts. Sniffer and Horse nearly fell over when they saw Stacey, her chest straining like a pair of wriggling puppies trying to get off the leash.

The place was packed. The front bar had been commandeered for diners as well, and every table was full of people chattering, pulling their bread baskets apart and drinking red wine. Chirpy young waiting staff rushed around to accommodate them, while delicious smells floated out of the kitchen.

Harriet took a seat next to the wall, and then pulled Camilla in next to her. To her relief, Calypso sat down opposite as well. Angus was most put out. 'I say, what happened to boy girl, boy girl?' he complained.

'Not tonight, darling, us girls have got lots to catch up on,' said Camilla quickly.

'Yah, at least we get a good view of that bird's massive hooters!' announced Sniffer, taking his seat at the end of the table. Camilla cringed and hoped Jack Turner wasn't in earshot.

Across the green, Sebastian had finally arrived home.

'Do you like my new dress?' asked Caro hopefully, as she watched him get ready.

He looked up from tying his shoelaces. 'It's all right. A bit frumpy. At least it covers all your lumps up.'

Caro had an insane urge to boot her husband in the shin with her LK Bennett kitten heel. Finally they left the house, Caro trying to hold on to her husband's arm as he strode across the grass with no thought for her suede shoes. At the door of the pub, Sebastian stopped and smiled at her. He reminded Caro of a wolf baring its teeth. 'After you, dear,' he said, and swung the door open.

They were hit by a wall of warmth, noise and heady smells. 'At bloody last!' a male voice shouted out, followed by a woman's cut-glass tones. 'We'd just about given up on you!'

Caro and Sebastian swung round. 'Guys! Sorry we're late,' said Caro, going over and kissing the woman on both cheeks.

'Seb taking too long in the bathroom again?'

'Fuck off, Tobey,' said Sebastian, grinning. He turned to the woman, who at five foot four and barely eight stone, looked adorable in a tight black waistcoat and trousers. 'Tils, you look as radiant as always. Can't you take Caro shopping with you? She's dressing like her bloody grandmother these days.'

'Ignore him, darling,' said Tilly, smiling at her friend over Sebastian's shoulder.

For once Caro did. She was here to have a jolly good time with her friends, and to hell with what Sebastian said to her.

'Glass of bubbly?' Tobey asked her, holding a bottle of Moët aloft.

Caro picked up one of the flutes from the table. 'Rather!'

Over on Camilla's table, the three girls were having an earnest discussion about the ball. Calypso had even brought her hit list of people and press she wanted to get. 'So obviously I *must* try to get the Goldsmiths. Zac should be a deffo for sure because he's like, a totally massive environmentalist, and this should be just the kind of thing he'd support. If I can get him there maybe I can get his sister Jemima Khan as well, and you know Kate Moss has a weekend cottage, like, round here ... then there's Stella and, ooh, they might bring Madonna!' She flicked efficiently through the pages on her clipboard. 'As far as press goes, you know my friend Octavia? Well, her sister is a freelance journalist and *totally* well connected and she said she'll, like, try and write something. *And* Octavia has a dad who is on the board at Condé Nast, which publishes *Tatler*, so I am sure we can pull a few strings there.'

The two others looked at her in admiration. 'Muffin, you have done a marvellous job,' said Camilla. She had been secretly delighted at the way her younger sister was throwing herself into the ball. It seemed to be giving her a much-needed purpose in life.

Calypso scowled. 'Don't call me that! It's events organizer *extraordinaire*.' A smile spread across her face, and she laughed, Harriet and Camilla joining in.

'What are you fillies tittering at?' boomed Angus, turning away from a conversation with his two friends about how much a healthy pair of bull's testicles should weigh.

'Who's got their tits out?' asked Sniffer, and he and Horse burst into guffaws. Calypso rolled her eyes. 'Oh please! We're not in the playground now, boys.'

Horse shot Harriet a lascivious glance. 'Sorry ladies! I must apologize for old Sniff Dog's revolting manners, we normally leave him tied up outside, you know.' Angus chortled and summoned Stacey over to get them another bottle of champagne.

'A bottle of your best bubbly, please!' he hollered. As Stacey turned to go to the bar, Sniffer made silent 'honk honk' movements with his hands. The three men collapsed, eyes watering with tears as they slapped each other on the back.

Calypso looked at her sister in pity. 'Honestly

Bills, what *do* you see in him?' she whispered. Camilla had to admit that, at that precise moment in time, she had absolutely no idea.

Pierre had really pulled the stops out with the menu. There was foie gras to start, followed by organic orgasmic French soup, the top oozing with delicious cheese and crusty toasted croutons. Then huge bowls of moules à la provençale were carried out, the smell of garlic and fresh tomatoes filling the pub, and after that, an utterly delicious boeuf bourguignon with a creamy potato gratin and crisp green beans.

'God, this is delicious!' exclaimed Tilly, forking up another slice of succulent beef. Caro enviously eyed the waiflike woman, who had finished both her soup and moules and was now attacking her main course with gusto.

'Honestly Tills, where do you put it?' she smiled through a mouthful.

'It's the shagging!' said Tobey. 'Like a dog on heat, I tell you.' Tilly nudged her husband in mock-annoyance.

'I am not! Take that back Tobey Sedgewick-Lough-Ainswick-Fotherington!'

'Help, I surrender,' said Tobey, shooting a smirk over the table at Caro.

Caro was, in fact, trying to dodge Tobey's knee, which had been pressed firmly against hers for the last hour. At first, she had put it down to the fact they were all squeezed in round a rather small table, but when a hand had suddenly reached across and squeezed her knee, she had known she wasn't imagining things.

For dessert, Pierre had conjured up a crisp tarte Tatin accompanied by an exquisite crème anglaise, but by that time most of the guests were too drunk to appreciate it. One of the Fox-Titts' party was stretched out comatose on top of the table. The rest of his dining companions were resting their drinks on him, and carrying on as though it was completely normal to have a six foot two, sixteen stone unconscious man sprawled in their midst. Lucinda Reinard had come back from the toilet with her skirt tucked into her knickers, and everyone had been laughing too much to point it out, until Beryl Turner had taken pity and come out from behind the bar to tell her.

Caro had just had her umpteenth glass of Chablis when the room suddenly started spinning. She thought she might be sick, so leaving Seb regaling Tobey and Tilly with a scandalous sex story about some big shot in the city, she quietly excused herself from the table. The queue for the ladies was a mile long, leaving Caro no choice but to make her way unsteadily outside.

The fresh night air hit her, and she gratefully sucked it up. Spying the bench on the village green, she wove across the lane and plonked herself down on it. Her head was still turning like a merry-go-round, and in the clear sky the stars were moving about like a giant kaleidoscope.

'Are you feeling OK, darling?' Tobey was standing in front of her, holding his blazer out. 'Look, I brought this in case you get cold.' He sat down beside her.

'Tobes, thank you,' said Caro, as he put the blazer round her shoulders, leaving one arm draped around her. 'I'm fine, just a bit too much to drink. Since I had Milo, my tolerance levels seem to have shot down.' She tried to ignore Tobey's hand, which was creeping over her shoulder like some randy, sex-starved bit of ivy.

'Mmm, yah, I completely understand,' said Tobey abstractedly. Suddenly, his hand found her nipple and squeezed it firmly.

'Tobey! What do you think you're doing!' exclaimed Caro, and tried to push him off. But by this time he'd slipped his hand inside her dress, his fingers groping the soft flesh of her right bosom.

'Oh come on, darling! You and me, we've always had a thing, haven't we?' He was slurring and Caro realized he was more drunk than she was.

'No, we haven't!' she cried. 'Now get off me!'

Before she knew it, Tobey was being dragged off her and thrown a good few feet over the ground. 'Argh!' he yelled, landing in a heap. Caro looked up to see Benedict Towey standing over him, breathing slightly heavily. Tobey remained on the floor, groaning.

'What did you do that for?' she yelled at Benedict, forgetting she had vowed never to speak to him again. 'He's a bloody friend of ours!'

'Looked like more than that,' replied Benedict archly.

Caro watched him warily from the bench, trying to collect herself. 'What are you doing here?' she demanded.

'Taking a walk. Look, sorry if I intruded, but it looked like he was getting a bit tricky. I would have thought any *sane* woman would have appreciated someone stepping in.'

165

'What, were you *spying* on us?' said Caro, trying to stand up.

Benedict Towey looked at her in utter disgust. 'For Christ's sake,' he said, and stalked off.

Desperately trying to sober up, Caro went over to Tobey, who was still lying prostrate on the ground. 'Are you OK?' she asked.

'Bloody shoulder is killing me,' he mumbled. 'Sorry if I got a bit heavy with you, old girl, plonk does give one the horn, you know.'

Caro sighed. 'It's fine, really, Tobey. Come on, let's get you back inside.' She pulled him up and they staggered back towards the pub.

Inside, someone had put Queen on the juke box and 'We Will Rock You' boomed throughout the pub. Two gorgeous young blondes were dancing on one of the tables, while Horse, Sniffer and Angus downed shots of flaming sambucas at the bar, guffawing hysterically as they rammed lemon slices into each other's eyes. Pierre had given up on the cheese course and gone home.

Camilla was busting for a pee. The queue for the ladies hadn't got any shorter, so she went in search of another loo. There was a door marked 'Private', which obviously led to the Turners' private accommodation. Camilla knew that she shouldn't, but she was so desperate she pushed through the door and up the stairs. Bladder full to bursting, she came to another, wider corridor with rooms leading off it. At the end of the corridor, a door was ajar and Camilla could see it was the bathroom. She was hurrying along to it when a sound from one of the rooms made her glance in. She stopped short.

166

Jed Bantry was standing there, pants and jeans around his ankles while Stacey Turner, naked as the day she was born, had her legs wrapped round his waist. Her back was against the wall and her eyes were closed in ecstasy as he drove into her. Suddenly, as if aware of another presence, she opened one eye, and seeing Camilla there, screamed. 'What are you doing up here!'

Camilla covered her mouth with shock. 'Oh my God! I only came to find a loo to use, I really am terribly sorry . . .' Jed, far from being ruffled, just stared at Camilla with a look she couldn't quite place.

'It's along the corridor, yeah?' said Stacey crossly. 'Just don't tell Mum and Dad you saw us, OK?' Camilla felt rooted to the spot with embarrassment. Stacey gave her an incredulous look: 'Can you *go* now?'

Camilla jolted out of it. 'Of course. Look guys, I am so sorry . . .' The door swung shut as Stacey kicked it with her foot, leaving Camilla dying of mortification.

When her cheeks had calmed down and she eventually arrived back downstairs, the place was in uproar. 'CAMILLA!' yelled Calypso as soon as she saw her. 'Sniffer and Horse are having a punch-up in the car park!' They both rushed out, along with the rest of the pub. By that time, Sniffer, with a streaming bloody nose, was on top of Horse, beating him round the head with his own Timberland loafer.

'I do not shag my bloody mother, so take that back, you bloody arse!' he roared.

'Fuck off!' shouted Horse in-between the blows

that rained down on him. 'That's what she told me when I had her this morning! Ow!'

Camilla turned to Angus. '*Do* something!'

Jack Turner was there first. 'All right you two, break it up!' he shouted, pulling them apart. Sniffer staggered back and, loafer still in hand, ran off into the night. The wail of sirens could be heard in the background. Someone had called the police. '*Merde!*' groaned Jack, and stalked back into the pub.

Detective Inspector Kevin Rance was not amused. He had been looking forward to a quiet evening in front of the box at Bedlington police station when the call had come out on the radio. 'Two IC1 males engaged in a fight, one armed with an unknown weapon. Outside the Jolly Boot in Churchminster. Crowds gathering. Can we have a unit to deal?'

'Bloody Hooray Henrys,' grumbled DI Rance to the panda car's driver PC Penny. 'They've probably got in a dust-up over who finished the last of the Bolly.'

'Or it could be something really serious, Guv!' squeaked PC Penny. Paul Penny, pink-cheeked and sandy-haired, had been fresh out of police training college six months earlier. He had all the youthful enthusiasm and blissful ignorance DI Rance vaguely recalled from when he had joined the force twenty years ago. Rance gave him two years before it was knocked out of him.

'I doubt it, Penny,' he said as the car pulled into the car park, sirens still wailing. Rance turned to look at his young cohort. 'I think you can turn those off now,' he said drily. He'd only let Penny turn them on on the condition he went to buy biscuits once they'd got back to the police station.

Rance entered the Jolly Boot, pausing on the doorstep to take the room in. It was past 2 a.m. by now, and most of the diners had gone home. Camilla and Angus were sitting at a table with Horse, whose right eye was bloody and swollen. DI Rance drew himself up to his full height and addressed the room. 'Can anyone tell me what has been going on here?'

Angus stood up. 'Look here, officer, it's just a fight that got out of hand. Nothing to worry about.'

'I'll be the judge of that, son,' said Rance. He looked at Horse, who was holding a sodden bar towel against his head. 'Looks like we should start with you.'

After the full sorry story – 'I only said he porked his old mater for a laugh!' – Rance sent PC Penny out to look for the weapon. He came back fifteen minutes later, triumphantly holding the loafer in a clear evidence bag. He'd found it in someone's front garden, and the owner was nowhere to be seen.

'I really don't want to press charges,' Horse insisted. 'The Sniffster would never forgive me. Besides, he didn't complain when I set fire to his pubes at Henley last year. I need to return the favour.'

'We don't want any trouble here, bad for business,' added Jack Turner, who was busy wiping down tables.

Rance let out a disgruntled sigh. What a bloody waste of time. 'Penny, we'll leave these people to the rest of their evening.' He waited until the young PC had opened the door for him. 'Let's stop at the twenty-four-hour garage on the way back, eh? I quite fancy some of those choc-chip Boasters.'

Chapter 26

The French evening raised a staggering twenty thousand pounds. 'Jack, that's wonderful!' Clementine exclaimed when he dropped the takings round for her to put in the fund. The committee had opened an account with the private bank in Bedlington.

'Only another fourteen million, nine hundred and eighty thousand or so to go,' said Jack gloomily.

'Oh nonsense, it's a good start!' said Clementine. 'I'll bank this later. Now, what's this about a dust-up? Camilla's terribly upset Angus's friends were involved . . .'

That afternoon, Clementine was driving up the Bedlington Road in her ancient Volvo estate, Errol Flynn sitting with his head hanging out of the passenger window, when the Revd Goody suddenly appeared outside the rectory and flagged her down.

'Everything all right, Reverend?' asked Clementine, when he'd trotted up to her window. She looked at him. 'My dear man, what's wrong?' The Reverend looked pale and clammy, as though he'd just had a nasty shock.

'I was down at the church this morning,' he started, 'when some people came in. I told them there wasn't a service today but they just stood there.' He gulped. 'That's when I recognized *him*.'

'Who?' asked Clementine.

'Sid Sykes!' replied the Reverend. His mouth trembled. 'Not a nice man, is he? He had two awfully menacing chaps with him, as well.'

'Reverend, did he threaten you?' asked Clementine quietly.

'No! I mean, not as such.' The Revd Goody smiled weakly. 'He wanted to know if I could slip a couple of lines into my sermon about what a good idea the housing estate would be for the village. Something about growth and prosperity as I recall ... Anyway, he said he would make it worth my while financially.'

'He tried to bribe you?' gasped Clementine, appalled.

'I guess that's what you would call it,' the Reverend replied. 'Of course, I told him no such transaction would take place in the house of God and sent them on their way.' He shivered. 'I don't have a good feeling about him; he seems like a nasty character.'

'Indeed he is,' she said grimly. 'And if he comes down here intimidating anyone else, I will inform the police. Good day, Reverend.'

'Good day, Clementine,' he responded, and stood for a long time in the road after she had driven away.

'Darling, you in there? Your bedroom light's on. Wake up!'

'Jesus fucking Christ!' Sabrina yelped when she heard Sebastian's voice crackling through the intercom. She leapt up from bed, hurriedly pulling on her silk pyjamas. Piers's ruffled head looked up sleepily from the pillows. Panicking, she threw his clothes at him and told him to get out. Even though they were on the second floor. Once he'd actually realized she was serious, Piers muttered something about how lucky it was he'd done an abseiling course at school, sat on the window and tentatively lowered himself out. As far as he was concerned, it was actually a lucky escape. Bloody older women were nothing but trouble!

'What took you so long?' asked Sebastian irritably. They were standing in the hall, Sabrina locking the door carefully behind him. 'One of Caro's friends lives in the next street. I can't be seen hammering on my mistress's door.'

'Sorry, darling,' purred Sabrina. 'I just wasn't expecting you yet.' She caught sight of her bed-head hair in the hallway mirror and hastily smoothed it down.

Sebastian looked at her. 'You seem on edge. What's wrong?'

'Nothing, nothing!' she trilled. 'I was just er, having a bit of a spring clean before you came. It's left me a bit worn out.'

'Now I know you're lying,' said Sebastian, a half-smile playing at the corner of his mouth. His eyes bored into hers. 'Have you got someone up there?'

'Don't be ridiculous.'

But Sebastian was already leaping up the stairs two at a time. 'Seb, wait!' cried Sabrina. 'I can explain!' She took off after him and got there just as

Sebastian wrenched the door to her bedroom open.

The bed lay unmade, but it was empty. Sabrina did a lightning sweep of the room but, thankfully, there was no incriminating evidence, just an open window, the curtain flapping in the slight breeze. She breathed a silent sigh of relief.

Sebastian turned to look at her. 'You see!' said Sabrina haughtily, regaining some of her composure. 'I can't believe you would accuse me of that.'

Sebastian lifted his hand and gently stroked her cheek, before his fingers found their way around her throat. 'I'll give you the benefit of the doubt this time, my precious, but if I ever find out you've been making me look stupid . . .' For a second his fingers pushed into her skin: 'I'll bloody kill you.'

Later that night, Freddie was on his way home from a dinner with some old rugger friends in Cheltenham. As he turned left at the green on to the Bedlington Road, something caught his eye. A shadowy figure was standing back from the road, against the wall outside the rectory, as if it didn't want to be seen. Freddie frowned. What on earth were they up to? He stopped the car and let down the window slightly.

'I say, are you lost? Can I help you?' Freddie's words trailed off. The figure had vanished. The moon went behind a cloud, making shadows dance on the dense leaves as they rustled in the breeze. Freddie rubbed his eyes. Had he imagined it? He started up the car again and drove off, checking the rear-view mirror for as long as he could, but seeing nothing.

Chapter 27

The next morning, the sinister figure was firmly out of Freddie's mind. He had more important things to think about. Today was the day he would tackle Devon Cornwall about getting involved with the charity ball. And each time Freddie had been round to see him so far, the housekeeper had politely informed him that her employer wasn't in.

Devon was still going through one of his more anti-social periods, spending all of his time reading or practising yoga. A suggestion from Nigel that he should go to the French evening had been met by a look of horror. 'Nige, I haven't been in a pub since 1989 and I don't intend to start now,' he had informed him. 'Besides, you know I don't like eating refined carbs after eight o'clock.'

At the same time, Devon longed for some time away from this strange house, which seemed to creak and groan constantly. At night he'd been hearing the strange shuffling noises downstairs again. Nigel put it down to the fact that Byron Heights was an old house and that, structurally, of course it would make the odd creak; but Devon wasn't convinced. Since the night he'd stuck his head out of the door and seen that horrifying white apparition, he'd been too scared to go and investigate, instead lying fearfully in bed waiting for the door handle to slowly start turning. 'You've been watching too many horror films,' Nigel had said firmly, and promptly banned Devon from watching anything with a certificate 18.

It was a dull morning, warm but sluggish. Freddie decided he could do with some exercise and would walk across to Byron Heights. For some reason he'd been feeling a bit foggy-headed lately and, as he was still diving into the biscuit tin every five minutes, his waistbands were a little tighter. Freddie just couldn't understand it. Maybe he was going through the male menopause or something.

As he walked up the vast drive to Byron Heights, Freddie took in the turrets and gargoyles looming over him. He could never live here. It was like something out of a horror film.

He rang the large bell on the doorstep and heard it reverberate through the bowels of the house. After about thirty seconds, Nigel appeared.

'Frankie!' he said.

'Freddie, actually,' Freddie said apologetically.

'Oh, gracious!' squawked Nigel, going red. He was furious with himself; he hadn't forgotten a name in thirty years.

'Don't worry,' Freddie smiled kindly. 'I was wondering if Devon was at home?' He looked expectantly past Nigel.

Like the housekeeper, Nigel had been instructed by Devon to say he was unavailable to callers. But Freddie had such a nice demeanour and open, friendly face that Nigel couldn't resist. Besides, he was fed up with Devon shutting himself away.

'Of course, do come in,' said Nigel. 'Can I offer you anything to drink? Tea, coffee, something a little stronger?' He led Freddie into the drawing room and went off to find Devon.

As he expected, Devon was furious at being called down to see Freddie. 'I bloody moved to the country to get away from people, and it's like Piccadilly bleedin' Circus here!' he grumbled.

'Oh, shush,' said Nigel firmly. 'Mr Fox-Titt is a perfectly nice man, and it won't be too much of a hardship to spend a few minutes in his company, will it?'

'No, Nanny,' replied Devon sulkily as he followed Nigel down the corridor.

Nigel had to hand it to his boss; he knew how to turn on the charm. As soon as he entered the drawing room Devon was all smiles, and shook Freddie's hand heartily, inviting him to sit down again, and making sure he had the beverage of his choice. After a few minutes of pleasantries, Devon found himself warming to this easy-going visitor. Then Freddie steered the conversation round to the Meadows.

'Yes, we saw that on the local news the other week. Dreadful business,' said Nigel, taking a sip of his Earl Grey.

'The guy's a first-class crook from what I hear,' Devon commented.

'Well, we have decided to put in our own bid for the land,' explained Freddie. Devon whistled. 'You must be talking millions, the prime estate around here.' Byron Heights had cost him a small fortune. Well, actually quite a lot of his dwindling fortune.

'Rather,' Freddie agreed, and he outlined the plans for the ball and auction. 'I'm on the committee, you see. It's our job to get as many people involved as possible.'

'You want some Devon Cornwall signed merchandise?' asked Nigel perceptively. 'That should be no problem at all.'

Freddie shifted forward in his seat. 'Well, actually, we would like a bit more than that.'

Devon groaned. 'You're not wanting me to do a bleedin' meet and greet as well?'

'It's nothing like that,' said Freddie hurriedly. 'It's actually something a lot bigger.' He paused, making sure he had their undivided attention. 'We'd really love it, Mr Cornwall, if you would perform at the ball.'

Nigel's cup had paused half-way to his mouth. Devon sat upright, stiff in his chair. 'Are you 'aving a laugh?'

'We're hoping to get Mick Jagger or someone as well,' Freddie added hurriedly. 'You'll be in similar esteemed company.'

Nigel cut in. 'Sorry, Devon doesn't mean to be rude, Freddie. It's just that, well, he hasn't performed for nearly *twenty* years.'

'Left it all behind when I went to rehab and cleaned up me life,' said Devon. 'To put it bluntly, Mr Fix-Tott, wild horses wouldn't drag me back on stage.'

'Er, it's Fox-Titt.'

'Besides,' Devon carried on. 'No offence meant, me old mucker, but if I was going to make a comeback, it would be at Wembley, not some posh ball in the friggin' Cotswolds.'

The colour drained from Freddie's face and he stood up. 'Well, then, I'm sorry to have wasted your time, gentlemen,' he said stiffly, turning for the door.

'Freddie, wait!' cried Nigel, leaping up. He shot a murderous look at Devon. 'I think it sounds like a marvellous suggestion. I think Devon just needs a bit of time to come round to the idea—'

'I do not!' interrupted Devon indignantly.

'Leave it with me, I'll talk to him,' Nigel continued.

Freddie looked at him, slightly mollified. 'Thanks, Nigel.'

'I'll show you out,' offered Nigel.

Two minutes later he bustled back into the drawing room. Devon was standing by one of the huge windows, gazing out on to the gardens.

'Did you have to be quite so rude?'

Devon waved his hand dismissively. 'Don't start!'

'Well, I'm afraid I'm going to! This is a really good thing they're putting on, and it's for a wonderful cause. One which affects you, too, may I point out. I don't know if it has escaped your attention, but it's not exactly down and out country round here. It's the society event of the year and you're dismissing it as some little village knees-up!'

'Whatever,' said Devon, sulkily. This enraged Nigel even more.

'Performing at this ball might be the best thing you've ever done, Devon!' he shouted. 'You know, I look at you cooped up in here for weeks on end and it makes me want to weep. You've turned into a grumpy, lonely old man, and do you know why?'

'No, but I'm sure you're going to tell me.'

'Because you're bored! You're bored with your life and you don't like yourself very much any more either. And you say you're over music! Devon – you were *born* for music. I can't stand seeing you in here, day after day, just existing, refusing to face up to things.'

By now Devon had turned quite pale. 'Enough.'

But Nigel hadn't quite finished. 'I think a comeback at this ball would be just the thing to turn your life around. The trouble is, you're just too bloody stubborn to admit it.' He turned and stalked from the room, trembling.

Devon stood motionless, still staring out of the window.

Chapter 28

It was July and Churchminster was looking almost indescribably lovely. The heavy rains of spring had left the countryside even more fertile and blooming. There had been clear blue skies and soaring temperatures for a week now, and people were slowing down their normal hectic routines and making the most of it. The Jolly Boot's beer garden was filled every afternoon with relaxed punters enjoying jugs of Pimms and al fresco lunches. Delicious smells of barbecues wafted from people's back gardens, while Stacey Turner and her equally nubile young friends almost caused a riot when they sunbathed in thong bikinis on the green one day, until an outraged Jack Turner rushed out of the pub and told them to cover up.

On this particular morning, the sun was already beating down at eleven o'clock. Calypso had joined her grandmother for a walk around the Meadows. They headed down Bramble Lane, Errol Flynn trotting in front of them with his pink tongue hanging out. Calypso filled the older woman in on how far she'd got with the VIP list for the ball; the next committee meeting was scheduled for the following week. Clementine was impressed by the number of names Calypso was chasing, even if she had never heard of most of them. 'This DJ Dawg, who is he?' she asked, her clipped vowels struggling with the unfamiliar slang.

'He is totally, like, the hottest rapper ever!' Calypso exclaimed. 'P Diddy, like, discovered him when he came over here, and has made him, like, this massive star! Here and in America. I read in the *Sun* last week that Dawg was going out with this totally famous supermodel called Fifi B but they had a huge row and split up. According to Octavia's sister's friend's cousin who is, like, a *really* cool stylist, Fifi is really upset about it.'

They turned off the lane on to a grassy path which led down to the Meadows. The long grass tickled Clementine's ankles as Calypso ran in front chasing Errol Flynn. Clementine watched her granddaughter. With her bare legs and long hair flying, she looked like a child again. Which Clementine still thought she was, no matter how hard Calypso tried to pretend she was grown-up.

'Do you remember when we used to come down here and look for fairies when you were little?' she asked when Calypso skipped back, slightly breathless.

'Yah, what a dolt I was!' Calypso scrunched up her face disparagingly, then smiled. 'It was fun though, wasn't it?'

They clambered over a rickety wooden stile into the first of the many grassy, rolling fields that constituted the Meadows. Wild flowers grew in abundance, while birds chirped from the shady knolls of huge oak trees. It was idyllic.

Clementine couldn't bear to think about how it would change if Sid Sykes got his hands on the place. 'How are things going with Samantha?' she asked briskly, forcing her thoughts elsewhere.

Calypso gulped. Her grandmother always went straight to the point. 'Er, OK.'

'Is it a long-term thing?' Clementine pressed. 'Or just a bit of fun? She does seem to be spending an awful lot of time at No. 5.'

'Has Camilla been moaning about it?' flashed Calypso defensively.

'No, of course not,' replied Clementine. 'You know she adores you. No, I was just wondering myself, darling. Sorry if I'm being a dreadful busybody.' Clementine admittedly also had an ulterior motive in finding out the state of play in Calypso and Sam's relationship. She wanted to know whether it was worth telling her son his daughter was going out with someone so butch she made Frank Bruno look effeminate. Johnnie kept asking her about this 'Sam chap' whenever he phoned up, and Clementine was fast running out of excuses to change the subject.

'It's going fine,' said Calypso. She felt a bit weird talking about this with her grandmother. 'We're just having fun, you know . . .'

She trailed off and Clementine shot her a kindly glance. 'I *do* know, darling. Even though you probably find the idea of an old dinosaur like me having fun somewhat ridiculous.'

'Really? Were you a bit of a wild child, then?' Calypso loved the idea of her grandmother hiding a colourful past, but before she had a chance to interrogate her Clementine stopped suddenly in her tracks.

'Look, smoke!'

From a large tree in front of them, they could see white wispy puffs trailing around the trunk. Errol Flynn bounded ahead towards it. 'Do you think it's a dry grass fire?' asked Clementine anxiously. 'Errol, come back here!' But he was too busy barking at something around the other side of the tree.

Suddenly there was a shout. 'Get 'im off me, bro! I 'ate dogs!'

They both dashed for the tree. Behind it sat a very stoned Archie Fox-Titt and Tyrone, who was being licked to death by Errol Flynn. Archie stared up at them blearily, a huge spliff smouldering in his hand. He took a few seconds to focus. 'Shit! Mrs Standington-Fulthrope! I, er . . .' In vain, he looked around for somewhere to hide the spliff.

'Archie, I can see perfectly well what you are doing,' Clementine informed him sternly. Calypso tried not to giggle.

'You're not going to tell my dad, are you?' he moaned, trying to stand up. Tyrone was still being slobbered on by Errol, and Clementine decided not to call him off just yet.

'Well, that depends,' she said crisply.

'On what?' Archie looked hopeful.

'On whether you are able to take time out of your *busy* schedule to hand out flyers in Bedlington town centre. Lucinda Reinard is putting on a fun run and we need to advertise it.'

Tyrone finally pushed off Errol and started laughing at his friend. 'Bruv, that is so uncool. All da homies are gonna *rip* it out of you!'

Clementine eyed him with her frostiest stare and Tyrone shut up. '*Both* of you.'

'What? I ain't handing out no leaflets!'

'Oh yes, you are,' she said firmly. 'Unless, Archie, you want your father to find out about this?'

'OK, OK, we'll do it,' groaned Archie. Tyrone started to protest but received a kick in the shin. 'I'll get my allowance stopped!' Archie's money from his dad bought most of their weed.

Tyrone eyed Clementine balefully. 'Whatever.'

'Excellent! I knew we could come to an agreement. Now get out of my sight, the pair of you!' The boys scrambled to their feet, trying to gather the various cigarettes, Rizlas and matches lying around.

'Oi!' shouted Tyrone. 'Bring that back!' Errol Flynn had got his Burberry cap between slobbering jaws and was making off across the field. Tyrone took after him, followed by a queasy looking Archie, who promptly tripped over the undone laces in his trainers and fell head-first into a dry ditch. Clementine collapsed into gales of laughter.

'Granny Clem, you are so naughty. You blackmailed them!' scolded Calypso, before she too fell about laughing. Clementine composed herself and wiped her eyes.

'All's fair in love and war when it comes to charity, darling,' she said.

Chapter 29

It was Camilla's thirty-first birthday. As she'd had a black tie do in a marquee at Fairoaks for her thirtieth, she wasn't that bothered about doing anything special this time. But to her surprise, Angus had offered to cook a birthday supper at his place. Highlands Farm was one of the biggest in the county, and to Angus's credit, the outbuildings and land were well looked after. It was inside the actual farmhouse, a rambling low-roofed building that had been magnificent in its day, that the problems started.

Since his widowed father had gone into a home five years ago, Angus had been living there alone. Algernon Aldershot had subsequently died, leaving the farm to his only son and rightful heir. Having spent most of his childhood at boarding school, it was fair to say Angus didn't know the meaning of 'domesticity'. The house had become the ultimate bachelor pad – and not in a good way. On the rare occasions Camilla had been persuaded to stay there she had found old pizza boxes and empty bottles of beer strewn across every room. Even the downstairs loo. She had once found a dead rat in the cupboard under the sink, which Angus had left there because he thought it was some kind of scrubbing pad. Not that he did any cleaning; the whole place was covered with a thick layer of grime. Camilla always brought her own towels and bedsheets when she stayed, and always felt she had to have a shower the minute she got home. Thankfully Angus was fairly hygienic himself; it was just unfortunate that he lived in the domestic equivalent of a compost heap.

So far, Camilla had had a lovely birthday. Calypso had woken her up with breakfast in bed and a pretty pair of handmade silver-drop earrings. 'You have got good taste, thank you!' Camilla had said as her sister had carefully put them in for her. Next had come a call from Barbados, with her parents singing 'Happy Birthday' down the phone. They had already generously offered to buy her a new Golf to replace her rather battered old one, it was just up to Camilla to go to the Volkswagen garage in Cheltenham and choose what she wanted. After that Harriet had popped round with a beautifully wrapped, deliciously scented candle set from Jo Malone. 'They're gorgeous!' Camilla had said, hugging her friend. 'You will join us for lunch at Fairoaks, won't you?'

Even though Camilla had told her she didn't want any fuss, her grandmother had insisted on holding a lunch in her honour. 'Just family, darling.' Harriet was practically part of the clan, anyway, so just before one o'clock, two Standington-Fulthropes and one Fraser made their way round to Clementine's, where Caro and Milo would also be joining them.

After champagne in the drawing room and another round of presents, Brenda announced lunch was being served and they moved into the dining room. For once, she hadn't burnt anything and they ate a perfectly respectable chicken dish, followed by raspberry fool. One of Brenda's friends had even made a wonderful birthday cake in the shape of the gold signet ring Camilla always wore on her little finger.

'So Angus is cooking for you tonight, then?' Caro raised an eyebrow in jest as she tucked into a slice of cake.

'Oh, don't!' said Camilla. 'God knows what it will be. I don't think he's ever cooked a proper meal in his life.'

'Do you know what he's getting you?' asked Harriet.

'No idea,' Camilla replied, leaning over and feeding Milo a bit of icing as he sat gurgling in his high chair.

'Probably a lifelong membership to *Tractor Weekly* or something,' suggested Calypso wickedly.

As she clattered up the muddy mile-long track to the farm that evening, Camilla wondered what present she *would* receive from Angus. She didn't hold out much hope. Last year he'd proudly presented her with a hideous cashmere tartan dressing gown with her initials monogrammed on the breast pocket. It had been swiftly recycled by Clementine into a lining for Errol Flynn's basket.

The lights of the farmhouse twinkled in front of her, and as Camilla drew into the stone courtyard she was surprised to see Angus already waiting for her by the front door. What's more, he was dressed in black tie, his huge shoulders straining to get out of his dinner jacket.

He rushed over to the car and opened the door for Camilla. 'Angus, what's all this?' she said. 'You've made such a special effort. I'm afraid I didn't dress up. I feel like a right scruff, now.'

'You look beautiful to me,' said Angus. He looked extremely nervous, his left eye twitching slightly and sweat gathering at the back of his neck.

Camilla had never seen her big, oafish boyfriend like this. She stared at him. 'Are you OK?'

'Of course, of course!' he replied in an over-hearty fashion, before leading her through the front door and into the kitchen.

Camilla's jaw dropped. It was like a different house. The pots and pans hanging from the over-head range were polished and shining brightly. The stone floor had been washed so you could almost see your face in it. A jug of fresh flowers stood on the wooden table where a pile of old newspapers used to be. Instead of the usual musty, damp smell the scent of fresh lemons permeated the place.

'I hired a cleaner to come in and tidy the place up,' Angus said shyly. He grabbed her by the hand. 'Let me show you the rest of the house.'

He led her from room to room, and they had each been given an injection of new life. There wasn't a cobweb or muddy footprint to be seen. All the antique wooden furniture had been polished until it glowed. Clean curtains hung from the crystal clear windows. Now all the dirt and dust had gone, Camilla could see just what a beautiful place it really was.

'Angus, it looks wonderful!' she gasped.

'I'm not finished yet,' said Angus, and dragged her back to the drawing room, where, as if from nowhere, a butler appeared with two flutes of champagne.

'Madam,' he said solicitously, and presented her with one.

'I hired him from "A Night to Remember" in Cirencester,' Angus explained, after the butler had graciously backed out of the room. The clatter of pots could be heard from the kitchen. 'Er, he cooks as well,' said Angus apologetically.

Camilla finally found her tongue again. 'I can't believe this! I'm gobsmacked.'

'So you like it?' he asked.

'I love it!' she cried. 'But, why . . . ?' This was such a turnaround from the Angus she knew, and Camilla was struggling to take it in. Angus was sweating even more now, his fingers pulling at the collar of his shirt. Camilla half-laughed. 'What *is* wrong with you?' she asked, kindly.

Before she knew it, Angus was down on one knee in front of her, with a small blue box in his bear-like hands. He opened it and a stunning diamond ring glittered up at them. 'Camilla Beatrice Candida Leonora Standington-Fulthrope,' he said, his voice wobbling slightly. 'Since I met you, I've been the happiest chap alive. Would you do me the honour of becoming my wife?'

Camilla felt like she was dreaming. 'Goodness! I wasn't expecting this. Er, er . . .' Why was she stuttering like such a bumbling idiot? Angus looked at her beseechingly, his brown eyes like a puppy dog's, and Camilla felt her heart melt. 'Oh Angus, of course I will!' He slid the ring on her finger and they collapsed to the floor clasping each other tightly.

After that, it was like a whirlwind. Angus had already phoned Johnnie to ask for his daughter's hand in marriage, but it didn't stop Tink crying tears of joy when Camilla phoned her parents to tell them the news. Camilla had barely had time to admire the sparkling ring before Clementine was on the phone, with Caro and Calypso in the background. 'Darling, that's wonderful news! We're all so pleased for you both.'

Later, after they'd phoned Angus's relatives, the couple sat down to an exquisite supper of oysters and lobster, followed by strawberries dipped in rich dark chocolate sauce. Neil, the butler, discreetly washed up and left, and Angus carried Camilla upstairs to the bedroom. He'd even sprinkled red rose petals on the bed. There, he made tender love to his future bride. (As tender as a big oaf like Angus could manage.) Afterwards, holding Camilla in his arms, he took her hand in his and looked at the ring, turning it this way and that so it caught the candlelight and sparkled.

'Camilla Aldershot! That has a good ring to it, don't you agree?'

'Yah, deffo,' said Camilla, laying her head against his chest.

'I can't wait to make babies with you,' Angus declared, before he drifted into a happy sleep.

Camilla, on the other hand, spent half the night lying there awake. It was meant to be one of the happiest moments of her life. So why did she feel so empty inside?

'You're engaged! Oh my God!' squealed Harriet, throwing her arms around her best friend. It was the next morning and Camilla had popped into Gate Cottage on her way home to tell Harriet the news. They were standing in her small, charmingly rustic kitchen, which looked out on to the garden. 'How does it feel? Is it any different?' asked Harriet excitedly.

'To be honest, it all feels a bit weird,' Camilla admitted.

'Oh, it's bound to take some getting used to,' Harriet reassured her. 'So you'll be moving to Highlands Farm?'

Camilla nodded. 'I guess so, but not for a while yet. There's so much to do! We're going to set the date for next summer.'

'Let me know if there's anything I can do to help,' offered Harriet. Camilla eyed her for a second. 'Well, there is, actually.' She took her friend's hand. 'Darling Hats, how do you feel about being my matron of honour?'

'Oh my God!' squealed Harriet for the second time in ten minutes. 'I would love to!' They hugged each other again, Harriet jumping up and down in excitement.

'What's going on here, then?' A deep voice came through the open window. Jed was standing outside, toolkit in hand.

'Oh Jed, Camilla's just got engaged!' cried Harriet. 'Isn't it wonderful?'

His mysterious green eyes clouded over.

'Marriage is a load of crap if you ask me.'

'Jed!' reproached Harriet, shocked.

He was still staring at Camilla. 'Whatever makes you happy.' He shrugged and walked off.

'What on earth has got into him?' said Harriet.

Chapter 30

It was the SCBA Committee's first official meeting since everyone had been given their roles. After the glorious sunny start to July, it had now been raining solidly for two days, so everyone retreated to the biggest living room at Fairoaks. It was west-facing and looked over the garden. Rivulets ran down the window panes, while Clementine's normally glorious flowerbeds had been turned into a muddy, sodden mess.

Everyone had much more pressing things on their mind than the weather, however. Clementine was still reeling from a phone call she had received that morning from Coutts bank. A mystery benefactor who wished to remain anonymous was donating a million pounds to the fund. When Clementine told everyone there was a stunned silence.

'That is fucking a-mazing!' cried Calypso eventually. 'Sorry, Granny Clem, but it is! Who the hell is it?'

Clementine tried to look as if she disapproved of her granddaughter's language but failed miserably. 'I agree with your sentiments entirely, darling!' she said, eyes twinkling. After a brief discussion about who the benefactor could be, with suggestions ranging from Paul McCartney to Prince Charles ('after all, Highgrove is only down the road, really'), to JK Rowling and even the Sultan of Brunei, Clementine insisted they moved on.

Calypso was bursting to bring them up to date on her progress. As well as inviting every young Honourable and titled amongst her friends and acquaintances, it looked like the entire Goldsmith clan would be attending. Calypso was also 'like, totally new best friends' with Kate Moss's PA. 'Hopefully she can talk to Kate about it. Just think if she comes . . .' After much begging and pleading, Calypso had also persuaded Annabel Trowbridge, features editor for renowned glossy magazine *Soirée*, to put a piece about the ball in their November issue, pinpointing it as *the* social event of the Christmas calendar. 'So, like, we have got to make this the best thing ever,' said Calypso dramatically. 'Or I can never show my face in SW3 again.'

Lucinda had taken on the role of chief organizer for the fun run. She had done a marvellous job, handing out leaflets from the back of her Range Rover in Bedlington's market square one lunchtime, and personally marching into the *Bedlington Bugle* editor's office one day to bully him into running a front-page story on the fun run. As a result, over three hundred people had entered, most of them raising money towards the SCBA fund; and it had been sponsored handsomely by the rich patrons of the district. The plight of Churchminster had reached beyond the hedgerows and fields of the village.

Lucinda herself was walking on air, anyway. After weeks of heavy flirting her sweaty private workout sessions with Henry had moved up a gear. Yesterday afternoon had unexpectedly culminated in him taking her on the stretching mats for the most energetic, passionate shag of her life. Years of self-conscious sex with the lights off had flown out the window and she'd ridden him like Frankie Dettori riding the winner at Cheltenham. Afterwards, they'd had to go round picking up all the exercise balls that had been kicked round the gym in the throes of passion. Lucinda was expecting to feel racked with guilt afterwards, but to her surprise, she didn't. For the first time in so many years, she felt alive. Caro had even remarked on how well she was looking when she walked in.

'Oh, it's just this new wrinkle cream I've got, it's been working wonders,' she lied.

'You must tell me what brand it is, you look marvellous!' Caro had said admiringly, and Lucinda had smiled and hastily changed the subject. She felt she practically had the word SEX tattooed across her forehead.

On a more mundane note, tickets were now going on sale for the ball, with ten people to a table for dinner. Using money from the Standington-Fulthrope Committee fund, Harriet had managed to secure all the tables and chairs from an events firm in Bristol. The firm, sensing some lucrative future business with the calibre of guests attending, was delighted to be involved, and had offered a hefty discount, even promising to supply people for free to set the ballroom up.

Angie Fox-Titt was still putting the feelers out in the antiques world. Through an old friend, she had secured a much coveted two-week work-placement with an uber-cool designer who had been the darling of London Fashion Week. Some adoring parent was bound to snap it up for their darling Tabitha, fresh out of a textiles course at St Martins, she explained to the rest of them. Even more exciting was her Tiger Tomlinson connection. Tiger was a billionaire entrepreneur, and many years ago his wife Candy and Angie had given birth in the same private hospital, right next door to each other. They had struck up a firm friendship and stayed in touch ever since. Angie had been on the phone to Candy at the Tomlinsons' palatial mansion in Mustique and told her about the SCBA. Candy, an ardent fundraiser herself, thought it was a 'simply super' idea. Provided Tiger gave it the go-ahead, Candy offered their own private island in the Bahamas for a week's holiday for a party of ten. The island, a two-by-five-mile stretch of paradise, had been named by *Traveller* magazine as one of the most luxurious holiday spots in the world. You couldn't just buy your way on; you had to be personally invited by the Tomlinsons. As far as an auction prize went, it was social dynamite. 'Angie, that is *wonderful!*' exclaimed Clementine. Even Calypso looked impressed.

*

Poor old Freddie wasn't having as much success. He had heard nothing from Nigel since he'd been round to Byron Heights.

'Do you think he'll do it?' asked Clementine anxiously.

'I honestly don't know,' replied Freddie. 'He was going to be my lead to Mick Jagger as well . . .' He trailed off.

'Look, I'm still going to try and get a big-name DJ,' offered Calypso. 'I'm sure it will come together.'

'Just hate to let the lot of you down, blasted unreliable rock stars,' said Freddie gloomily. 'You've all done such a bloody good job so far—'

'So have you!' interrupted his wife. 'We'd all be drinking tap water if it wasn't for you sorting out all the booze and bubbly.'

'Hear hear!' piped up Caro. But Freddie didn't cheer up until Clementine asked Brenda to go down into the cellar to bring up a magnum of his favourite champagne. After the group had stopped for a glass, Freddie's spirits lifted. 'I'll get that Cornwall man if it kills me!'

'There's no need to go that far, Freds,' said Clementine.

Over at Byron Heights later that morning, the atmosphere between Devon and Nigel was slowly returning to normal. After their argument, Nigel had retreated to his wing of the house, and the pair hadn't crossed paths for two days. Bloody-minded as he was, Devon wasn't going to apologize, and it was only when Nigel offered to cook him conciliatory buckwheat pancakes for breakfast that things had started to thaw. They hadn't spoken about the fight, but secretly Devon was still reeling from Nigel's words. He'd been shocked at the outburst from his usually mild-mannered PA, especially as a lot of it had hit home.

To prove that he *wasn't* turning into a complete hermit, Devon decided to go for a walk. Since he'd moved in, the nearest he'd got to exploring the local countryside was a few laps of the garden. Shouting to a surprised Nigel that he was off out, Devon dug out his old panama hat – the one that made him look rather raffish and handsome – and set off.

At last the rain had stopped and it was now a beautiful day. Outside his house Devon turned left on to the road, the verges framed by sturdy stone walls the colour of honey. On the lawn by Hollyhocks Cottage, home to Brenda Briggs, a big ginger cat lay stretched out, dozing. As Devon passed, the curtains twitched and an excited shriek came from inside. The noise made the cat jump up like it had been scalded and it shot off over the wall. Despite himself, Devon laughed, feeling slightly flattered. 'Still got the magic, you old dog,' he said to himself wryly. Meanwhile, inside, a palpitating Brenda Briggs was being fanned back into consciousness by her bemused husband and a copy of the *Bedlington Bugle*.

Devon carried on walking. The smell of cut grass lingered in the air and he breathed in deeply. An old biplane hummed gently in the cloudless sky above him; otherwise the countryside was restored back to a quiet, lazy serenity.

God, it's good to be alive, thought Devon. He felt a sudden surge of creativity flash through him, something that hadn't happened for a long, long time. Devon smiled wistfully. Those days were far behind him. Weren't they?

Suddenly, his thoughts were interrupted by a black horse rounding the corner at a fast trot and nearly trampling on him. Devon jumped up on the verge with a yelp. He was scared stiff of animals, and this huge beast looked like some horse from hell, all flashing eyes and flaring nostrils.

'Watch where you're bleedin' going!' he shouted at the rider. He put his hands up to shield his eyes from the sun and get a good look. There, looming above him, looking impeccable in snow-white jodhpurs and a blue velvet riding hat, was the elegant blonde from the drinks party.

'Firecrest, calm down!' Lady Fraser ordered the horse, as it started pawing the ground.

Devon stared at her. She was just as lovely as he remembered, her light blue eyes looking down at him imperiously.

'It's you,' he finally managed to say, immediately feeling a complete fool. He took a step towards her, and quickly jumped back when Firecrest's nostrils flared menacingly at him. 'Er, you were at that party at the rectory?' he asked, from the safety of the verge.

'Yes, I was,' said Frances crisply. Devon thought she sounded like Joanna Lumley.

'I'm Devon. Devon Cornwall,' he offered. 'I've moved into Byron Heights.'

'I know,' she replied, and her face relaxed slightly. 'One can't help but hear everyone's business round here. I'm Lady Frances Fraser. I live at Clanfield Hall.' She motioned her head slightly towards the fields at her left. 'I'm sure you've heard of it.'

'Er, yeah,' lied Devon. He couldn't stop staring at this aloof, regal woman.

Frances, despite her cool exterior, was trying desperately to think of something to say. That hat made Devon look irresistibly dashing. 'So, I hear you've been asked to sing at our ball?' she asked.

'Your ball?' said Devon.

'Yah. It's being held at Clanfield. We haven't hosted a function since the African orphan night, so I'm rather looking forward to it. *Are* you going to perform?' she asked rather bluntly, inwardly cringing at how gauche she must sound.

Devon's mind was all of a flutter. She looked so sexy in those jodhpurs, the tight fabric emphasizing her long, slender thighs. 'Er, I haven't decided yet.'

Frances gazed down at him. 'It would be wonderful if you could. I mean it.' She blushed momentarily and corrected herself. 'I meant *we* mean it.'

Devon plucked up the courage to give her a rakish grin. 'I'll think about it. Not promising anything, mind.'

Firecrest started whinnying impatiently, pawing the ground again with his giant hooves. 'Please do consider it, you would be a wonderful addition to the evening.' Frances smiled at him, and the smile softened her demeanour and made her look younger and prettier. She gathered up the reins. 'Goodbye, Mr Cornwall.'

'I'll be in touch, then,' said Devon, watching as she trotted expertly off down the road. What an arse!

Chapter 31

Sunday, 1 August dawned. The day of the Save Churchminster Fun Run. The sky was crystal clear already, the sun rising steadily in the east. At Mill House, Sebastian was already up, strutting round the bedroom in an obscenely small pair of under-pants. To Caro's surprise, he had signed up for the fun run. She had thought it would be far too small and rustic an affair for him to be bothered with, but Sebastian was trying to push his physical fitness as far as he could. Besides, he had told her loftily, a five-mile run was nothing when one was in such supreme shape as he was.

Watching her sprightly husband getting ready, Caro just felt even more exhausted. Sebastian had banished her to the spare room the night before, to ensure he got his optimum eight hours. Milo had been grizzling, and Caro, terrified he would wake Sebastian and all hell would break loose, had spent most of the night walking around the nursery with him in her arms.

The run was scheduled to start at ten in the morn-ing. At 9.35 a.m. Sebastian, clad in an extremely expensive skintight black and pink running vest and shorts, strutted out of the house. Caro followed, struggling to get Milo down the step in the pushchair. Sebastian stopped at the end of the path and looked back impatiently. 'Oh hurry up, darling, we're going to be late.'

'Morning,' a gruff voice said from next door. Caro looked up from trying to double-lock the door. 'Oh, hello,' she replied, attempting to sound nonchalant.

Benedict Towey was standing outside his own front door. He was wearing a pair of faded blue shorts and a simple white T-shirt, his bronzed forearms and calves rippling impressively. Caro noticed they were sprinkled with blond hair, and wondered fleetingly what they would feel like to stroke. Then she saw he was also wearing running shoes and carrying a water bottle.

Sebastian looked him up and down. 'Are you entering the race?' he asked rudely. Benedict looked at him steadily. Next to Sebastian's over-the-top get-up he looked cool and casual.

'Sure am,' he answered. The two men stared each other out for a few seconds. Caro could see what was coming and inwardly groaned. Why were men so bloody competitive?

'Well,' said Sebastian lightly. 'May the best man win.'

Benedict nodded, and without a backward glance strode off down the road.

The fun run was starting on the green. Flags and bunting festooned the grass around it, and a long piece of rope was stretched between two posts. Someone had even found an umpire's chair – which looked suspiciously like it had been stolen from

Wimbledon – for the race starter to sit in. This person was Clementine, who could be seen bustling about in top-to-toe white, and a straw boater with a blue and white striped ribbon round it.

The five-mile route would begin with two laps round the green, then continue down the Bedlington Road before turning left on to a track which ran round the back of the Maltings. The runners would then go along Sweetbriar Lane and back towards the village, ending with a final sprint down the back of the green and through the finishing posts. Crowds of spectators milled around, watching the runners limbering up, while a St John ambulance was on standby in case anyone wilted in the fierce morning heat.

There were still a few minutes to go, and Caro was at the refreshment stall, buying herself a diet coke. She paid, turned round and bumped straight into Benedict Towey. 'Oh!' said Caro. Benedict glared at her, his eyes looking incredibly blue against his tanned face. She took a deep breath: 'I haven't had the chance to apologize for my appalling behaviour at the French evening. I know you were only trying to help and—'

'Forget it,' Benedict interrupted. 'I have.' He looked away, as if bored with the conversation.

Caro gritted her teeth. 'Are you running for the SCBA Fund?' she asked.

He glanced at her momentarily. 'No, Meningitis Trust,' he said shortly, and strode off, leaving Caro standing there clutching her ice-cold can. The least he could do, if he was going to live here, was support the village in its hour of need, she thought crossly. But before she could get any more annoyed, her grandmother was upon her, brandishing the starting pistol.

'Careful with that thing, Granny Clem!' cried Caro.

'Oh darling, it's not loaded,' Clementine assured her. 'Haven't we had a wonderful turnout?'

Indeed they had. The Bedlington Running Club were there in their entirety, looking very snazzy in their bottle-green and gold running strips. Angus was enthusiastically discussing tactics with Sniffer and Horse, who had obviously managed to repair their friendship. All three were dressed in rugby shirts, shorts and socks, and looked more like they were off to stick their heads between some burly man's thighs than take part in a run. Camilla, playing the dutiful fiancée, was standing nearby with Harriet, laden down with energy drinks and towels. Jed Bantry, lean and agile, was stretching out his hamstrings by the side of the road. Even the Revd Goody was taking part; pulling off a pair of tracksuit bottoms to reveal milky white legs, while Eunice and Dora Merryweather clutched each other and looked on admiringly.

Then Caro caught sight of Lucinda, wearing a black all-in-one and looking very trim indeed.

'God!' said Caro admiringly to Clementine. 'Lucinda is looking fabulous! I really must stop being so lazy and get the name of her trainer. Harry or something, I think it was.'

Looking at the scene unfolding in front of them, Clementine guessed correctly that Lucinda's new shape was to do with a quite different kind of workout. A tall, handsome black man had just strolled up to her, Nico and the three children, and Lucinda had promptly gone puce, a tight smile etched across her face. The newcomer, who had No. 147 tacked to his back, looked like a professional athlete, his carefully honed physique shown off in a tight unitard which left nothing to the imagination. Despite Lucinda's rictus grin, Clementine could see the sexual chemistry sizzling between them. Nico, who wasn't taking part in the run, seemed not to notice. He was too engrossed in watching a pert blonde in tiny shorts stretch out her quad muscles.

After a few moments, No. 147 said something to Lucinda, smiled and walked off. Lucinda looked round furtively and made eye-contact with Clementine, blushing again as she waved awkwardly. 'Just my trainer,' she mouthed. Clementine nodded and suppressed a smile.

'Mummy, why did that man have a banana stuck down the front of his shorts?' Lucinda's daughter asked loudly, just before Henry was out of earshot.

The loudspeakers crackled into life. 'Right, can everyone make their way to the starting line please!' Clementine's voice boomed over the green. The competitors finished their last-minute stretches and started to walk over, wishing each other good luck. All except Sebastian, who had already positioned himself at the start, a grim look of determination on his face.

'Quiet, everyone!' ordered Clementine, sitting aloft in the umpire's chair. She held the pistol up: 'On your marks, get set. GO!' A shot fired, and the spectators cheered as the competitors surged forward, Sebastian at the front. Homemade banners saying 'Go on Super Dad!' and 'Bedlington Racers Do It Better' fluttered in the air above the crowd as they watched the runners disappear around the green.

After two miles, the pack had separated into three groups along the Bedlington Road. The fastest and fittest at the front, the majority of runners in the middle and the stragglers bringing up the back. Angie Fox-Titt had already retired after slipping on a cow pat and twisting her ankle. Calypso, who had excelled at sports at school and entered despite not doing a minute's training, was soon mortified to discover her twenty-a-day habit had affected her fitness considerably. In hot pants and cropped vest, she was still attracting a lot of attention from the crowd, and they shouted lewd suggestions to her as she passed. In turn, she smiled sweetly and stuck up her middle finger.

'Lovely day, Reverend,' puffed Freddie as he drew alongside.

'Freddie,' the vicar wheezed back. His normally pale complexion was bright red and blotchy, and Freddie wondered in alarm if the Revd Goody was about to have a heart attack. He was struggling himself. He had been feeling tired and lethargic for weeks now, and just couldn't understand why. As he tried to push his tired legs onwards, he made a mental note to book an appointment with his private doctor.

The front group, which consisted of Sebastian, Henry, Jed Bantry, Benedict Towey and several members of the Bedlington Running Club, had already turned off the main road. By now, they really were running at a fast pace, silently concentrating on their rhythm and breathing.

After a few minutes, Sebastian glanced over his

shoulder. Some of the runners had fallen back. Now he only had to worry about a scarily fit-looking woman who resembled Martina Navratilova and, just behind him, Benedict Towey. Benedict was looking resolutely ahead, running mechanically and effortlessly.

Sebastian led them left on to Sweetbriar Lane, where a group of spectators cheered them on. They were on the homeward straight now, heading down towards the village. Sebastian's calves were starting to burn, the searing agony of exhaustion setting in. Christ, this was pushing it! He checked his watch; he'd never run a mile so quickly. He glanced behind him again to see Martina had fallen behind. Great! Now it was just that infernal Towey. Sebastian was pleased to see the grimace of pain on his sweating face; at least he was suffering too.

Finally, the two men reached the village green. The cheers and shouts of encouragement whipped up into a cacophony. Sebastian, hotly pursued by Benedict, started to pelt down the road to the finishing line. His heart was hammering so hard he thought it might jump out of his chest. In the distance, the bunting and flags fluttered like the Holy Grail, and the cheering spectators lining the road disappeared into a blur of colour and noise. Gasping and wincing through his screaming muscles, Sebastian put his head down. He was going to win . . .

Suddenly, just a few hundred yards from the finishing line, Benedict appeared like an apparition at his shoulder. 'You bastard,' croaked Sebastian, trying desperately to muster up another ounce of energy. But he was running on empty and could only watch helplessly as his rival powerfully surged past. Chest pushed forward and arms outstretched, Benedict crossed the finishing line, the tape trailing behind him.

Moments later Sebastian stumbled across and pulled up short, hands on knees as he gulped in large breaths. Even though the sweat was rolling off him, he could *feel* the bitterness of defeat coursing through his veins. Caro rushed over with Milo in her arms. 'Darling, you were wonderful! It was like something out of *Chariots of Fire!*'

'I didn't win though, did I?' he spat at her. By now other runners were starting to come in, the race officials crowding around them with Mars bars and Lucozade. A shadow fell across him and he looked up.

There stood Benedict Towey, a towel round his shoulders and a gold medal hanging round his neck. Still breathing heavily, Benedict stuck out his hand. 'The best man won, then.'

'Fuck off,' snarled Sebastian, and stalked off towards home.

Chapter 32

Sebastian's vile mood did not improve. Despite a few cajoling attempts from Caro once they arrived back at the house, he refused to talk to her and stomped upstairs. He disappeared into the en suite bathroom and Caro heard the power shower start.

Twenty minutes later, he appeared in the doorway of the kitchen. Caro withdrew guiltily from the fridge, where she'd had her hand in a jar of stuffed olives. Sebastian was fully dressed, his hair slicked back. He was carrying his Armani holdall in one hand, car keys in the other.

'Where are you going?' Caro was bemused; they were meant to be meeting the Fox-Titts down at the pub for a few post-run bottles of bubbly.

'Back to London,' Sebastian informed her.

'But you're meant to be staying until tomorrow!' Caro cried. 'We've got drinks and lunch today, and then I said we'd pop over to Fairoaks later for a drink with Angus and Camilla. Seb, you can't!'

'I can, and I bloody well will,' he said firmly. 'The last thing I feel like is being round people at the moment. Especially in this festering armpit of a village.'

'For Christ's sake, it was just a race!' Caro shouted at him. Instantly, she knew she'd said the wrong thing. Sebastian's face darkened even more.

'I'll see you on Friday,' he said icily, and stormed down the hall. The front door banged shut and Caro rushed to the downstairs loo, angry hot tears springing out of her eyes. She pressed her head against the cool tiles, trying to calm herself down.

'I hate you,' she whispered.

A few days later, everyone who had taken part in the fun run had collected their sponsorship money.

Eunice and Dora Merryweather gave Calypso a whole load of ancient, unusable halfpennies, and she didn't have the heart to point out their mistake. Johnnie and Tink had very generously sponsored their youngest daughter two thousand pounds – but only on condition she gave up smoking for a week. Calypso had begrudgingly accepted, but by 10.31 a.m. on the first day she was already climbing walls. At 11.04 a.m. she'd had a huge screaming match with Sam about something inconsequential, and had locked herself in her bedroom ever since.

Thanks to his uber-rich farming contacts, Freddie had also managed to drum up a fair amount, and with everyone else's contributions flooding in, by Thursday morning Clementine counted up a grand total of £16,792 to add to the fund. Plus the halfpennies, four buttons, a chocolate coin and something that looked like it had just been wrenched off a car's engine.

She phoned an uncharacteristically subdued Caro to tell her the good news. 'I know in the big scheme of things it doesn't seem much,' Clementine said, 'but it is just so wonderful to see the village pulling together. Things like this do so much for one's morale.' Actually Caro couldn't think of a time when hers had been lower. She hated being on bad terms with Sebastian, and even though it was the last thing she felt like doing, she'd actually tried to phone him to make amends. Of course, he hadn't returned any of her calls, and now she was angry with herself for caving in, and fed up with being fended off by his smug secretary.

Later that evening, the mood was slightly soured for Clementine. She was just settling down with her nightly tipple of Möet, and had switched on the television to get the local news when, to her distaste, Sid Sykes's rat-like face loomed up in front of her. He was being interviewed by a reporter about his bid to buy the Meadows.

'Churchminster needs dragging into the twenty-first century, and I'm just the man to do it,' he said nasally.

Clementine pushed the red button on her remote control, and his image disappeared into blackness. She could think of somewhere she'd like to drag Sid Sykes. The ghastly man seemed to be everywhere these days. Clementine took another glug of champagne and let out a heavy sigh. Tonight she might require two glasses to get her back on an even keel again.

Sebastian's sulk lasted until Wednesday. He cancelled two business lunches and turned off the mobile that was used solely for Sabrina to call him on. By the time she eventually got hold of him on Wednesday afternoon, she was positively seething.

212

He was supposed to have accompanied her to an exclusive fashion party in Chelsea on the Tuesday night, and she ended up having to cancel because she couldn't find a last-minute replacement. She had missed out on some serious networking opportunities and a goodie bag worth three thousand pounds. *No one* treated Sabrina Cox like that.

'Where the fuck have you been?' she screeched at him down the phone.

'Oh, darling!' he said dismissively. He was sitting in a new oyster and champagne bar that had opened in the City, surrounded by work colleagues. One of them had just closed a mega-bucks deal and they were celebrating. Sebastian's dark mood had finally lifted and he was back to his normal arrogant self. He took a swig of Cristal, rolling his eyes at the sniggering table around him.

'I couldn't get hold of you, what was I supposed to think?' complained Sabrina.

Sebastian's accommodating mood swiftly evaporated. 'Who the hell are you to give me a hard time?' he asked her coldly. 'If I wanted that, I'd go to my fucking wife!' His response was met by a dialling tone. Oh well, he'd sort that out with a bracelet from De Beers and dinner at Nobu later.

'Old Seb Boy's been given the heave-ho!' chortled one pink-faced man in a loud pinstripe suit.

'Fuck off, Gilly,' said Sebastian, smiling at him evilly over his glass. 'Talking from experience, are we? I mean your *wife*; you'd never have the balls to get yourself a mistress as well.'

Monty Gillsworth, fresh from the divorce courts

and paying maintenance through the nose, looked momentarily flattened as the rest of the table slapped their thighs and guffawed.

Chapter 33

Harriet was being yelled at by her father. They were standing at opposite ends of the five-hundred-foot ballroom at Clanfield. Ambrose's booming tones easily carried the length of it.

'I don't want the bloody stage down here!' he shouted, holding a crumpled room plan in his hand.

'But Daddy—' Harriet started, holding her clipboard like a layer of protective armour in front of her chest.

'What's that? I can't bloody hear you all the way over there,' he shouted again, forgetting he was the one who had started this exchange. 'For God's sake come here, girl!'

Harriet gulped and obediently trotted down the ballroom towards him. Her father was being a nightmare. Even though she had actually been doing a jolly good job, he'd already made her change the location of the car park because he didn't want people taking a short cut through the gardens. Now he obviously had issues about where she was planning on putting the stage.

'Why are you putting it here?' he complained

when she reached him almost a full minute later. 'Damn awful place.'

'Daddy, it's not,' she said patiently. 'We want the stage at that end of the room, so people can come in and see their tables first. The company constructing it want it at that end too, so it's easier for them to bring everything in.'

'Humph!' said her father. 'Well, I think it's a bloody silly idea.'

And no doubt just because it's *my* idea, Harriet thought to herself despairingly. She had actually been expecting some praise from her parents, for a change. The car parks were all set up with marshals. She was getting a specialist company in to clean the ballroom and chandeliers one week before the event. The seating arrangements had been organized. Harriet was going to turn one of the downstairs rooms that wasn't really used for anything into a cloakroom, and she'd even managed to persuade Cook to give up her beloved kitchen to Pierre and his team of chefs for the night. The committee was thrilled with her efforts, so it was discouraging, to say the least, to come home to such a negative reaction from her parents.

Unlike her husband, Frances seemed preoccupied and was showing little interest at all. Harriet couldn't understand it: her mother *lived* for things like this. Normally, she'd be on her daughter's back every inch of the way to make sure everything was up to her exacting standards.

Unbeknown to her daughter, or indeed another living soul, Lady Frances Fraser was spending every waking moment thinking about Devon

Cornwall. It was like the man had cast a spell over her, and she found herself in turn enthralled and appalled at the effect he was having. Since that chance meeting in the lane, Frances had thought of little else. Several times she had almost got in her Saab to go round to Byron Heights, under the pretence of talking to him about performing at the ball. But she had checked herself every time; she was a married woman, for God's sake! And not just to any old person either. Her husband's family had lived at Clanfield for generations, and Sir Ambrose Fraser was thirty-second in line to the throne. In truth, the physical side of their marriage had dried up years ago, and the couple now slept in separate bedrooms. But still, Frances had been brought up with a strong sense of family, and knew her duty towards her husband and the Fraser name.

A few days later, however, events were taken out of her hands. It was mid-morning and Frances was sitting in the pink drawing room reading. There was a discreet knock on the door. 'Come in,' she called, and Hawkins the butler appeared.

'A Mr Devon Cornwall is here to see you, your Ladyship,' he informed her.

Frances nearly dropped her book. Devon, here? She composed herself. 'Do send him in, Hawkins,' she told him.

As soon as the butler had left the room, Frances jumped up and looked in the mirror. She looked like a flushed, giddy schoolgirl. Get a grip, she told herself, and had just smoothed her chignon when the door opened.

'Mr Cornwall,' Hawkins announced.

Devon stood there, in white linen trousers and

some kind of smock top. He was wearing Birkenstocks and a pair of Ray-Ban sunglasses that still gave him that rock-star edge. Frances's heart skipped a beat, but she managed to maintain her composure. They were on her territory now.

The butler withdrew, and Frances waved Devon over to one of the many overstuffed chairs. 'Do take a seat, Mr Cornwall.'

'It's Devon, please,' he said, as they sat opposite each other. Again, her immaculate beauty entranced him. Frances's hair was sleek and golden, and she was in a pale-blue cashmere jumper and silk skirt that set off her almost Nordic looks perfectly.

There was a second's silence between them before Devon remembered why he was there. 'Er, I've come to talk to you about that ball.'

'Oh?' said Frances politely, even though her heart was hammering around in her chest like a ping-pong ball.

'Yeah,' said Devon. He paused. 'The thing is, I gave up performing and all that music industry shit, I mean stuff, years ago.'

And without knowing why, he told her all about his career, the drugs and the drink it brought with it, and his subsequent end in rehab.

'Gracious, you've led quite a life,' Frances said thirty minutes later. She didn't quite know what to say. Here was her one-time pop idol opening his heart to *her*. She had read articles in the paper about his battles with substances and alcohol, but had never realized quite how low Devon had sunk.

'The thing is,' Devon repeated. 'I cleaned up me

life and made a conscious decision to leave music behind. Too much temptation and all that.' He smiled wryly. 'But there's something about this place, Churchminster,' he waved his arm around expansively. 'It's making me feel all sorts of things I haven't felt for years. Creative stuff.' He looked at Frances. 'So after a long hard think, I've decided I would like to play at the ball. I've got some new stuff I've been working on recently, I mean it's only really in the early stages, but I'd love the chance to showcase it . . .' He trailed off, suddenly looking quite shy.

'I think it's a marvellous idea!' exclaimed Frances. Her eyes were shining. Several times during Devon's candid confessions, she'd found herself almost moved to tears. He was no longer just Devon Cornwall the pop star, he was Devon Cornwall the man. And what a man!

'You do?' asked Devon, uncertainly.

'Of course! The committee will be beside themselves when I tell them,' replied Frances. 'Oh Devon, it's simply wonderful!' She had become quite animated, and Devon couldn't help but smile – the ice queen had melted! He had an irresistible urge to take her into his arms, but checked himself.

'That's great.' He looked at his watch. He had a business meeting with Nigel and his accountant in twenty minutes. 'I'd better be going,' he said, and stood up. Frances followed suit. She rang a bell on the wall, formality returning for a moment.

'Hawkins will see you out.'

As they got to the drawing room door, Devon turned to face her. They were standing barely a foot apart and he could smell her light, flowery perfume. They both reached for the door handle at the same time, and for a second Devon's hand rested on hers. He looked into her eyes. 'Do you know what? I'd really like to take you out,' he said softly.

Frances couldn't speak. She could hear footsteps in the hall. 'I'd like that,' she finally managed, before there was another knock at the door and Hawkins materialized.

Devon winked at her: 'Be seeing you, then.'

'Yes, goodbye, Mr Cornwall,' she said gracefully.

Frances shut the door behind him and slid down it, letting out a huge, trembling gasp. What had she just got herself into? For the first time in her life, she feared she was about to be guilty of a severe dereliction of duty.

Chapter 34

Ever since Angus had proposed to Camilla, he'd been trying his best. He'd bought her a bedraggled bunch of flowers from the petrol station. He'd stopped his excruciating habit of rolling across from the pub completely blotto and roaring at Camilla's window that he was going to bonk her brains out. Which was just as well for Calypso, whose window was next to Camilla's. She had started complaining she felt like an unwilling extra in a pornographic remake of *Rapunzel*.

In fact, Camilla *did* feel like a princess, locked in her own self-imposed tower. Angus's proposal had been marvellous; all she had ever wished for. So why wasn't she happy? With every day that passed, and every person who congratulated her, Camilla started to feel more desperate. Of course Angus, who had the sensitivity of a forklift truck, didn't notice anything was wrong with his bride-to-be, but Calypso did. She cornered Camilla in the kitchen one sunny summer morning as she was making breakfast.

'Hey, you making tea? I'll have one.' Calypso watched her sister dig out the Earl Grey teabags, and then hopped up on the work surface next to the toaster, where two slices of multi-grain bread were toasting. 'Bills? You are cool about marrying Aberdeen Angus, aren't you?' she asked.

Camilla had her back to Calypso and stiffened. 'Of course I am. Why do you say that?' she answered in an unnaturally high-pitched voice.

Calypso stuck out a long, tanned leg and examined it. 'I don't know, you just seem a bit flat about it all. I thought you'd be more, like, totally excited about it? I know you'll probably tell me to mind my own business but . . . Oh no! What is it?' Camilla had turned round to face her, her lower lip wobbling and her eyes full of tears. Calypso jumped down from the worktop and enveloped her in a protective hug.

'I don't know what's *wrong* with me,' Camilla wailed into her shoulder. 'Mummy and Daddy are over the moon and Angus is being so adorable. It's what I've dreamt of all my life, what girl wouldn't? But I just feel so empty inside, like it's the biggest anti-climax ever. I can't bear it. Am I some sort of complete freak?'

Calypso looked into her sister's blotchy face. 'Of course you're not!' she said fiercely. She sighed. 'Look, sometimes we think we want things in life, and when we get them we don't want them any more.'

'Are you talking about you and Sam?' snuffled Camilla.

'No! Christ, Bills, will you stop worrying about everyone else and think about yourself for a change? I know Angus is a nice guy, and you've always had a dream of bringing up loads of sprogs in the country, but maybe it's happened too soon?

222

Before you know it, you'll be packed off to Highlands Farm to pop out Aldershot heirs and your life will be full of choir practices, making jam and wiping snotty noses.'

'But that's what I've always wanted!' wailed Camilla again.

Calypso tenderly smoothed the tears from her sister's cheeks. 'You still might. But what I'm saying is that it might be a bit soon, or you just need time to come round to the idea. It's, like, a *totally massive* life change.'

Camilla stopped snuffling. 'It *is* all rather a lot for me to take in,' she admitted, and looked more hopeful. 'Maybe I just need time to adjust.'

'That's the spirit,' declared Calypso, and hugged her again. 'God, this is *weird*, it's usually you having to counsel me about stuff.' She reached across and handed the kitchen roll to her sister, eyeing her as she blew her nose loudly. 'You know what you need?'

'What?' said Camilla warily. She knew that mischievous look on her younger sister's face only too well.

'A night out on the town!' Calypso said. 'I reckon that's half the problem – you don't have enough *fun*, Bills. You live in your nice little cottage with your nice little life—'

'I like it that way!' Camilla interrupted.

'Of course you do,' soothed Calypso. 'But you must admit even Granny Clem has a more exciting social life than you do. Let's go out and let our hair down. Have a proper girls' night out!'

Camilla looked thoughtful. 'I haven't been on one of those for yonks.'

Calypso clapped her hands. 'Well, guess what? There's, like, this *totally* cool club opening in Brixton tonight. It's guest list only, but Sam knows the promoter and she'll put us down as VIPs! What do you reckon?'

'Brixton in London?' Camilla asked in surprise.

'No, Brixton on the moon,' replied Calypso sarcastically.

Camilla ignored her. 'Will it be really loud fast music I can't dance to?'

'Deffo.'

'Will it be full of really trendy people who will think I'm a total frump?'

'Duh, obviously. But you can borrow something of mine and I'll do your make-up. Oh come on, it will be, like, so much fun.'

Camilla stared at her sister for a second, and a smile crept on to her mouth. 'Oh, goodness, I'm going to regret this.'

'Life is too short for regrets,' said Calypso and bounded upstairs to her room to find Camilla an outfit.

It was seven o'clock that night. 'You're going out dressed like that?' asked Angus in shock. He had popped round to see Camilla before she left.

Her hands flew to her throat self-consciously. 'It's too much, isn't it? I *told* Calypso I'd be more comfortable in my own clothes.'

Angus cleared his throat and gulped. 'It's certainly *something*.'

Camilla was standing in the middle of the living room wearing a skintight black dress that hugged every contour of her body. It was knee-length, but one side was slashed all the way up the thigh, leaving little to the imagination. The top of the dress was strapless and Calypso had persuaded Camilla to go bra-less, insisting she didn't need one. On her feet, Camilla was wearing her sister's five-inch Vivienne Westwood spike heels. Her normally loose and wavy long blonde hair had been scrunched and back-combed, her hazel eyes ringed with black kohl and lashings of mascara. A clutter of bangles adorned her right wrist and made a tinkling noise when she moved. Camilla looked like a cross between Debbie Harry and Kate Moss – sassy, sexy and edgy. Not that she was aware of it at this point in time: Angus was making her feel exactly the opposite.

'Fuck, I'd forgotten what good legs you've got!' Calypso bounded into the room, dressed in a denim all-in-one playsuit with red stiletto ankle boots. She looked her sister up and down admiringly. 'You look so hot in that dress, Bills!' She turned to Angus, who was sitting, eyes still goggling, on the sofa.

'I think it's er, er . . .' he spluttered.

'He doesn't like it,' said Camilla miserably.

'It's not that,' Angus protested. 'It's just, well, don't you think you're a bit *old* to be going out like that?'

'Oh shut up, Angus,' Calypso said sharply. 'Just because you dress like you're seventy!'

Angus looked down at his mustard yellow cords. He'd got his best brogues on and his favourite Barbour checked shirt. His sludge-green quilted jacket lay on the armchair where he'd tossed it off. 'What's wrong with my outfit?' he asked indignantly.

'Where do you want me to start?' asked Calypso. A beep sounded outside, followed by the loud, reverberating bass of house music. 'Shit, that's Tizzy. She's giving us a lift. Come on!' She pulled her sister out of the room.

'What time will you be back?' asked a perplexed Angus, sticking his head out into the corridor. Camilla shrugged her shoulders helplessly.

'Don't wait up!' cried Calypso as she slammed the door behind them.

An hour later, Camilla was seriously beginning to regret being talked into going out. The car reeked from the joint Calypso and her friend Tizzy were sharing in the front. Tizzy, who had bleached blonde dreadlocks and a ring through her nose, obviously didn't believe in keeping to the speed limits. Even before they'd reached the M4, her sporty BMW was flying at 90 mph down the country lanes, the trees and hedgerows a blur of green as they whizzed past. With the speed, the smoke and the booming stereo, Camilla was starting to feel quite sick.

Finally, the music was turned down and her eardrums breathed a sigh of relief. 'Do you want a toke?' asked Calypso, turning around and waving the joint in front of her. Camilla shook her head.

'So you're the middle Standington-Fulthrope,' drawled Tizzy from the driver's seat. 'Mummy did the same deb season as your mother. Say Iona Fitzroy-Lambeth says hi. That was her name before she married Daddy,' she explained.

'Tizzy's dad is like, the fifth Earl of Gloucester,'

said Calypso, taking a deep drag of the joint and blowing the smoke out lazily.

'Fourth, you spaz,' Tizzy corrected. She shuffled around in her seat. 'Fuck, I am so wired about playing tonight. I can't believe I got the 12 a.m. to 2 a.m. slot. That is, like, so freakin' wicked.'

'Tiz is, like, a totally wicked DJ,' Calypso explained. 'Plays under the name Blue Blood.'

'And you're, er, playing tonight, then?' Camilla asked her.

'Yah, at Zulu's in Chelsea,' replied Tizzy. She glanced over at Calypso. 'Both HRHs are going; Harry texted me earlier.'

'I thought we were going to Brixton?' said Camilla.

'*We* are,' said Calypso. 'Tiz is just giving us a lift into town; we'll get a cab the rest of the way.' She cranked up the music and sat back, putting an end to their conversation.

By now, the open country spaces of the motorway had given way to the grey sprawl of suburbia. It was nine o'clock, dusk settling over a jagged, luminous skyline. Negotiating traffic and taking short cuts down backstreets, they headed towards Chelsea. Tizzy pulled into a leafy wide street full of magnificent three-storey houses. She parked up outside one with white shutters on the windows and an imposing black front door with a gold knob in the middle of it. 'My godmother lives here,' she informed them breezily, 'but she's away in St Barts so I'm using her parking space.'

After making plans to meet up later, and flagging down a black cab, Calypso and Camilla headed for Brixton, climbing out on to the high street nearly forty-five minutes later. It was Thursday night and the place was heaving. Souped-up cars with even louder sound systems than Tizzy's thundered past. Every bar was packed with young people drinking, smoking and partying. They all looked trendy, confident and completely unapproachable. Camilla was starting to feel like a fish out of water. There was a distinct edge to the atmosphere, like something could go off any moment. She shivered. Oh, what she'd do to be back in dear old Churchminster!

Calypso was on her mobile. 'Yah, we're nearly there, babe. We'll just come straight to the club. Cool, see ya.' She ended the call. 'That was Sam, she's in there already.'

They were off the main road now, walking down a badly lit street. 'I don't even know the name of this club, what is it?' asked Camilla.

Calypso paused. 'Pussy Galore,' she said, and watched for her sister's reaction.

'Pussy Galore?' echoed Camilla, recognition dawning. 'You're taking me to a gay club?'

Calypso linked arms with her. 'Yah. *Don't* look like that. I didn't tell you because I knew you'd have a total freak and not come. No one's going to bite your head off, you know.'

'It's not like that,' protested Camilla. 'I've got nothing against lesbians. It's, er, just not really my scene.' A vision of Sam's bush flashed before her eyes.

Calypso winked at her. 'It is tonight!' They had reached a doorway with people queuing outside. A kitsch neon sign hanging above it read 'Pussy Galore' in loopy writing. A huge, menacing bouncer with a shaved head, and shoulders like a Russian shot putter was standing at the beginning of the line holding a clipboard. Calypso waltzed up. 'Yah, we're on Sam Devine's list?' She gave their names and the bouncer checked his list.

'OK, you can go in,' came the reply, in a surprisingly girlish voice. They headed down a long winding staircase, the sound of music getting louder, until eventually they reached a set of double doors, reverberating with the noise behind them.

'Ready to party?' asked Calypso, and pulled one open.

Instantly, Camilla was hit by a double whammy of lights and noise. They were in a large, square room with banquet-style seating all the way around. A long glass bar ran the entire length of the far wall, and a seventies-style flashing dance floor dominated the middle of the room. The walls, floor and ceiling were stark white, and pink strobe lights flashed intermittently against them.

The place was packed, and not a pair of testicles in sight. Gorgeous, sexily dressed women were bumping and grinding with each other on the dance floor. Two tiny, elfin-looking girls with matching pink hair were snogging right in front of Camilla. To her left, a sixteen-stone woman dressed in a latex cat suit was whipping the buttocks of the skinny, scantily clad woman she was parading around on a dog lead.

'Babe, you made it!' said a gruff voice. Sam was standing in front of them. Her short hair had been gelled into spikes, and she was holding a bottle of beer. She gave Calypso a lingering kiss on the lips and then pecked a completely taken-aback Camilla on the lips as well. Camilla thought she looked flushed and happy, like a different person. 'So we've enticed you over to the dark side?' Sam said wickedly to Camilla.

'Ignore her,' said Calypso, smiling, and grabbed her sister's hand. 'Let's get some drinks in.'

On the way to the bar, they bumped into a gorgeous creature who looked like a cross between Ru Paul and Nefertiti. She shrieked: 'Cally, babe, how are you?'

Calypso shrieked back, air-kissing her. 'Crystal, this is my sister.'

The six-foot vision, dressed in a chain-mail minidress, looked Camilla up and down. 'I can see good looks run in the family. You're a *doll*, darling!' she said with dramatic flamboyance. Camilla couldn't help but giggle.

'Thanks,' she said, smiling at her.

'Crystal's, like, a top fashion muse for all the big designers,' said Calypso as they manoeuvred their way towards the bar. 'Totally bonkers, but she's such a laugh. Let's start off with shots, shall we?'

Fifteen minutes and three potent concoctions later, the alcohol had already gone to Camilla's head. She had started to relax and take in her surroundings, rather than be terrified by them. They found Sam sitting at a table in the corner with three other girls. Calypso launched into introductions. 'Guys, this is my sister, Camilla,' she said, and they were greeted with hellos and hiyas from round the table.

'I'm Penny, love your dress,' said one, a cool-looking redhead in a silver bomber jacket. 'This is

Sadie,' she continued, and the friendly looking blonde next to her smiled and raised her glass. 'And Lola.'

'Camilla, we've heard so much about you.' Lola was a bewitchingly pretty Chinese girl with long dark hair that fell like a sheet down to her waist.

'All good, I hope,' Camilla joked, taking a sip of the cocktail she was holding. It was so strong her eyes started watering.

'Of course!' said Calypso mock-indignantly. 'Now, you lot, my sister doesn't get out much so we're on a mission tonight. Let's get hammered!' They cheered and clinked glasses.

A few hours later, everything was turning into a blur for Camilla. They'd started playing drinking games and she'd lost count of the number of times she'd lost, downing one dubious shot after another. Her bum had been pinched four times on the way to the bar and a three-foot dwarf dressed in a Wonderbra and spaceman suit had tugged on her dress and asked if she was up for a threesome.

Now they were glugging vodka from a bottle Penny had bought, giggling hysterically as Lola recounted a disastrous date she'd been on with a fire-eater who had accidentally set fire to a pub chair whilst trying to impress her. Tears were rolling down Sadie's face while Penny cackled and chain-smoked Benson & Hedges.

Camilla's stomach hurt from laughing so much. She hadn't had so much fun in ages. Everyone was well, so *normal*. What had she been expecting?

'Is that an engagement ring I spy?' asked Lola,

who had finished her story and was sitting next to her.

'Yah, I'm getting married,' sighed Camilla.

Lola eyed her curiously. 'You don't sound very happy about it.'

Before Camilla realized it, her eyes had filled up again with tears. 'Oh, how embarrassing,' she sobbed as Lola took the paper mat from under her drink and handed it to her. Camilla dabbed her eyes with it ineffectually. 'I am really looking forward to it. It's the booze talking, I'm just having a few last-minute nerves.'

Lola gave her an understanding smile. 'I know the feeling, I was going to get married once,' she told her.

Camilla was shocked. 'Really?'

Lola nodded and took another deep glug of her drink. 'Lovely guy, proposed with a three-carat ring at the Rio carnival five years ago.'

'What happened?' asked Camilla.

'Oh, I just knew it was *wrong*. Felt wrong, looked wrong,' Lola explained. 'Of course, I just assumed I was with the wrong guy, not the wrong sex.' She laughed ruefully. 'Caused an awful rumpus at the time, but I got there. We're even friends again, now.'

'I don't think I'm into women,' said Camilla hurriedly.

Lola glanced across at her. 'I know, you don't have to explain.' She clinked her glass against Camilla's. 'Just remember to follow your heart, babe.' She shot Camilla a flirty look. 'Still, it's a shame.'

Lola's face swam in and out of Camilla's line of vision. Her inhibitions had gone out of the window hours ago. I wonder what it would be like to kiss a girl? she asked herself hazily. Her sister's words came back to haunt her: 'You don't have enough fun!' Suddenly, feeling like it was happening to someone else, Camilla launched forward and locked her lips on to Lola's. Lola tasted of bubblegum and strawberry lip-gloss. After a moment her soft tongue found its way into Camilla's mouth, and they started necking like a pair of randy teenagers.

Everyone whooped and cheered around the table until a giggling Calypso eventually prised them apart. 'Bills! You don't know what you're doing. Leave my sister alone, you,' she said to Lola. 'She's getting married!'

'*She* kissed *me*!' protested Lola.

'Yes, I did!' slurred Camilla proudly. 'And very nice it was too. Hic!' She stood up unsteadily. 'Right. Who's for a boogie?'

When the club shut at three, it took two bouncers, Calypso and one of the bar staff to drag Camilla off the dance floor. She'd lost a shoe along the way and her mascara was running down her face, but she was in a buoyant mood. 'I just wanna dance with somebody,' she sang drunkenly as Calypso and Sam dragged her up the stairs. The others had left an hour earlier, but only after Camilla had typed her number into Lola's phone and ordered her to call her.

By the time they got back to Chelsea and met up with Tizzy, Camilla had passed out face-down in Sam's lap. She didn't wake up all the way back to the Cotswolds, even when Sam gave her a fireman's lift up to bed. She did have a funny dream about a beaver that night, though.

*

When the phone rang at No. 5 The Green at nine in the morning, it entered Camilla's consciousness like a sledgehammer. She peeled open one eye and winced at the sunlight filtering into her bedroom. What had happened last night? She couldn't remember much past the fifth tequila slammer.

The phone continued ringing. 'All right, I'm coming,' she groaned, forcing herself to sit up. Her head was pounding and a wave of nausea washed over her. She leaned across to pick up the receiver. 'Hello?' she croaked.

'Camilla? Darling, is that you?' Her grandmother's voice sounded distant and shaky. Camilla tried to focus. In the back of her consciousness, warning bells were chiming. 'Granny Clem, is something wrong?'

A sob sounded down the phone. Camilla was wide awake now; a cold, sick pit of fear spreading through her stomach. 'Is it Caro, or Milo?' she whispered. 'Or Mummy and Daddy?'

Another choked sob as Clementine tried to compose herself. 'Oh, Camilla, something *dreadful* has happened,' she finally said. 'The Reverend Goody has been murdered!'

Chapter 35

DI Rance looked at the body and quickly turned away. Throughout his time in the force he had learned not to be shocked when confronted with death, but that didn't mean he'd ever get used to it.

The Revd Goody was lying on his back in the middle of his large double bed. His flabby white body was completely naked, arms splayed out to the sides and legs crumpled and curled up underneath him. It looked like there had been some kind of struggle: the flowery covers and bedspread were scrunched up in disarray. His neck was disturbingly red and mottled, and tied around it – so tightly it was cutting into the soft folds of his flesh – was a white silk scarf. Above this, the Reverend's bespectacled face was purple; unseeing eyes staring at the ceiling, and a bloated tongue lolling obscenely out of his mouth. It was horrible, but the most shocking thing of all was his expression – lips curled back and teeth bared as if in a silent scream. Rance let out an involuntary shudder. Poor sod – what a way to go.

'Looks like he was strangled, Guv!' PC Penny materialized beside him in the bedroom doorway. 'I reckon the perpetrator broke in while he was sleeping, crept upstairs and POW!' Penny slammed his fist into the other open palm. 'Throttled the Reverend good and proper!'

Rance looked disdainfully at the young officer. He was positively beside himself with excitement, bulbous eyes almost popping out of his head. 'Penny,' he said grimly. 'May I remind you that a very serious offence has been committed here, so can you stop going round looking like a dog with two tails? The last thing these villagers need to see is you slavering in a frenzy over the death of their beloved vicar.'

Penny looked suitably chastened. 'Sorry, sir,' he said meekly. His eyes lit up again. 'But he *has* been bumped off, hasn't he?' he asked eagerly. 'My mates from training college are going to be pig sick when they hear about this! Most they've had so far are shoplifters and flashers!'

'Until we've done the post-mortem, I don't want to say one way or another,' replied Rance. 'Now get downstairs and set a cordon up outside the front door. There's a crowd forming outside and we don't want anyone coming in who's not with us or the crime scene lot.'

As Penny scampered off down the stairs Rance turned and looked back at the body. Even though he had just put his constable in his place, Rance had to agree with Penny. He was 99 per cent certain he was looking at a murder victim.

'Time of death was between two and three o'clock this morning,' the duty doctor informed Rance when he returned to the kitchen. 'The body is showing signs of early rigor mortis.' The doctor was a small, efficient man with an immaculate pencil moustache. Rance looked around the kitchen. The SOCO officers were painstakingly moving down the corridor now, dusting for fingerprints and any other trace evidence. Another PC from the station was blithely going through a biscuit tin next to the kettle, his mouth full of ginger snaps. Rance frowned at him, and lowered his voice. 'In your opinion, Doc, what do you make of it?'

The doctor snapped off his rubber gloves and started packing away his medicine bag. 'Not for me to say, Inspector, but it does look rather suspicious.'

The next morning Rance paid a visit to the morgue at Bedlington. The pathologist, Bernard Trump, was one year away from retirement, but looked like he had been in a nursing home for decades already. A raging alcoholic, it was a long-running joke amongst the local police that if a corpse wasn't dead before it entered his morgue, the fumes from the pathologist's breath would finish it off for good. Bernard was ponderous and portly, with a permanently red nose and watery, rheumy eyes. Eyes that were now surveying Rance over the stainless steel trolley the Reverend's body lay on. Loud retching could be heard coming from the toilet next door. Penny's orgasmic excitement at having a possible murder on his hands had been tempered slightly by having to witness his first autopsy.

'Death was caused by compression to the trachea, leading to loss of consciousness due to suffocation,' Trump intoned, leaning over to show Rance. 'The carotid arteries in the neck would also have been severely compressed, stopping the supply of blood to the brain and making it bell, I mean, er, swell,' Trump slurred. He stared off into space and burped gently. Rance surveyed him in disgust.

'So basically, you're telling me he was strangled?'

'Mmm,' replied Trump distractedly. Rance noticed his hands shaking. Probably got the DTs, the silly old sod. The pathologist peered at Rance. 'I would say the Reverend here would have been unconscious in seconds, but it could have taken up to twenty minutes for him to die. You can tell by the livid bruise marks on both sides of his neck.'

Trump pulled the sheet over the Revd Goody's ghostly white face. 'Was there anything else? Only I've got a lunch meeting.'

With a bloke called Jack Daniels, thought Rance disparagingly.

Penny came back into the room, looking decidedly corpse-like himself. 'All right, Penny?' his boss asked wickedly. 'Fancy a bit of lunch, maybe a nice rare steak? Just imagine, all that blood oozing out when you cut into it. Mmm.' He watched as Penny clapped a hand over his mouth and fled the room again. Moments later, violent retching could be heard as Penny dry-heaved the last of his bile into the toilet bowl.

Rance looked back at the pathologist to share the joke, but Trump was surreptitiously taking a swig out of a small silver hip flask. Jesus, he couldn't even wait for other people to leave the room! No wonder afternoon autopsies were unheard of in here.

*

Minutes later, Rance was getting his come-uppance for playing a joke on Penny. The PC stank of sick and sweat, and even with all the windows open the patrol car reeked all the way back to the station. Penny was too ill to drive, so Rance had to take over while he sat slumped against the passenger door, head hanging out the window. Rance hoped none of their superiors would see them as they pulled into the car park. It was hardly a good advert for the police force.

Rance had already set up an incident room at the station. Photos of the Reverend – dead and alive – were stuck on one of the walls. On another wall, a large white board covered in red marker pen indicated the victim's last movements. In the centre of the board Rance had written the word 'motive' and underlined it several times. So far they had none. In the middle of the room, surrounded by empty Ginsters pasty wrappers and cans of Red Bull, sat a mixture of grey-faced detectives in crumpled suits, moaning about being drafted in to work over the weekend, and a few young, shiny-eyed uniforms. Even with the grumbling of the more seasoned detectives, there was a certain frisson in the room. Bedlington CID had never seen such a thing before and it was causing quite a kerfuffle.

'You've had calls from the *Bedlington Bugle*, the *News of the World* and the *Sunday Mirror*, sir,' Rance was informed by the only female police officer, a small, squat, blonde woman typing away furiously on a laptop in the corner of the room.

Rance rolled his eyes. 'Not the bloody nationals as well! It'll be front-page news all over the country tomorrow. The last thing we need are hordes of reporters descending like locusts and getting their facts wrong.'

'Bound to be something to do with devil-worshippers, Guv. You know these religious types,' remarked one of the detectives, a ravaged chain-smoking forty-something called Powers. He dragged on his cigarette and blew smoke rings expertly up towards the yellowing, nicotine-stained ceiling.

Rance coughed. 'Yes, well, we don't know that yet, so I don't want any of you making assumptions from the off. We've got a hell of a job in front of us. We need someone to put out a press release, get on to the press bureau.'

'Sir,' said another detective, reaching for the phone.

'DS Powers. After the staff cuts in this area we're short on manpower. I know it's not normal procedure, but you're pairing up with PC Penny. Give him the benefit of your expertise.' Rance allowed himself a sardonic smile. Penny looked like he might pass out with excitement but Powers was outraged; detectives worked a murder case, not some pimply faced young uniform!

Rance carried on. 'I want you two to be in charge of all the house-to-house calls in the village. Talk to everyone, find out what they know, how they got along with the Reverend.' Penny jumped up like a jack-in-the-box and started fishing for his pocket book, while Powers groaned and muttered under his breath.

'Anything from CCTV?' Rance asked the room.

'Only camera in the village is in the shop, Guv,'

said Penny. 'I don't think we're going to get much.'

Rance sighed. 'What about next of kin?' he asked wearily.

'Victim's unmarried. Parents both deceased, one sister who's a missionary in Africa,' chirped Penny.

'Track her down, will you?' Rance said. 'One word to remember – sensitivity.' Penny nodded vigorously. 'Guv!' He'd got his colour and enthusiasm back.

'Right,' said Rance, sounding more decisive than he felt. 'Let's get started.'

Chapter 36

That afternoon Powers and Penny found themselves over at Fairoaks, interviewing Brenda Briggs. Brenda had been the one to discover the body, when she'd popped over to the rectory to pick up the latest copy of the parish newsletter. On finding the back door slightly ajar, her curiosity had got the better of her and she'd entered the house, calling out the Reverend's name. Five minutes later, Freddie Fox-Titt had been driving past when a hysterical Brenda had rushed into the middle of the road and flagged him down. Freddie had immediately called 999.

Brenda was still in a dreadful state. She was clasping a glass of single malt whisky in one hand, trembling as she took the occasional sip. Her husband Ted was sitting silently beside her, his huge calloused hand occasionally patting hers. Brenda hadn't been able to face going back to her cottage because she could see the rectory from her kitchen window, so Clementine had insisted they both get away from the scene – and the hordes of camera crews – to the relative serenity of her house.

'Had you seen anyone suspicious hanging

around the victim's property recently?' asked Powers, while Penny took down copious notes.

'No one!' replied Brenda tearfully. 'Oh, why would anyone want to kill him? He was such a nice man. Seeing him lying there . . .' She dissolved into floods of tears again.

'We don't know of anyone who would have wanted to hurt the Reverend,' Clementine told the officers. 'Churchminster is an extremely close-knit village and he was a very popular man.' A memory rustled distantly in her brain as she said it, like leaves blowing in a gentle autumn wind. Was there something she should remember? Oh, her mind was all over the place!

'No ex-wives with a grudge, or anything?' asked Powers hopefully. Clementine shook her head. 'The Reverend was married to the church, Detective. It was what he lived for.' Her voice wobbled but she fought to maintain her composure. 'It's simply too awful for words. Here, in Churchminster!'

Next, the two policemen spoke to a hysterical Dora and Eunice Merryweather, and were stuck in their sitting room for nearly two hours. Clutching embroidered hankies to their bony chests, both sisters were convinced the Reverend had been killed by devil-worshippers.

'It's happening all over the place!' cried Dora, her sister nodding in fervent agreement as she offered them another slice of dried-up fruitcake. Powers got quite excited until he realized the Merryweathers didn't have one shred of evidence to back up their theory, it was just that Dora had been reading a similar plot in one of her sensationalist crime novels.

'We've wasted half the evening listening to them prattle on,' complained Powers when they finally managed to escape from the suffocatingly hot cottage.

'Aah, they're harmless,' said Penny. Dora and Eunice had reminded him of his great auntie Betty, who had always spoiled him with her homemade farmhouse fruitcake. Powers looked at him like he'd lost his marbles.

Subsequent calls at Camilla's, Babs Sax's and the Jolly Boot disappointingly yielded nothing. At Benedict Towey's the lights were off and no one was home. The village shop had also been closed as a mark of respect, so there was no Brenda to stir up gossip and just maybe give Penny and Powers something to work with.

It was gone eight by the time they had reached the Maltings, and both were feeling dispirited. House-to-house calls were notoriously long and laborious, but so far they had *nothing* that gave any clue to the Reverend's death. The general consensus was that he was a kind, friendly man, committed to his job and the parish. No one could think of anyone who would want to harm him. 'The man's so squeaky clean, he makes Mary Poppins look like a bleedin' crook!' exclaimed a frustrated Powers as they parked up.

A shaken-looking Freddie welcomed them in. 'Can I get you chaps a drink?' he asked, showing them through into the living room.

'No thank you, sir, we're on duty,' said Penny,

looking around enviously at the expensive silk curtains and thick carpets you could sink ankle-deep in. What a pad!

Angie was curled up on one of the huge sofas, with one of Freddie's Arran jumpers wrapped around her shoulders. Even though it was the height of summer, ever since she'd heard the news of the Revd Goody's death she just hadn't been able to get warm. Now she was staring into the bottom of a huge G and T, still trying to take it in.

'We're trying to build up a picture of the victim's last movements,' explained Powers, trying not to stare at Angie's chest, impressive even hidden under a layer of wool. 'Can you tell us if you saw anything out of the ordinary, anyone suspicious hanging around?' he asked ponderously. They both looked at each other and shook their heads.

Then Freddie suddenly spun round to face them. 'Hang on a tick, there was something!' he exclaimed. Both policemen sat up alert in their seats and leaned forward, listening.

'Yah, it was actually a few weeks ago, which is why it didn't spring to mind immediately,' continued Freddie. 'I was driving back from an evening out in Cirencester—'

'What time was this, sir?' asked Powers, as Penny scribbled away.

'About midnight. I remember listening to the news on Radio 4. Anyway, I was just driving home on the Bedlington Road, when I swear I saw a hooded figure standing by the wall outside the rectory.'

Angie looked horrified. 'Darling, why didn't you tell me this?'

245

'Oh, I don't know, I thought I was imagining things,' replied Freddie. 'You know how badly lit it is along there. But when I stopped and pulled over, there was no one to be seen.' He looked at the police officers.

'Height, age, weight?' asked Powers.

Freddie screwed up his brow in concentration. 'He – or she – had this hooded black top on so it was hard to say. But they reached the top of the wall, so they must have been about six foot. Not fat either, they had quite a long, lean outline. But hell, I don't know if it was just the light playing tricks on me.' He turned to his wife. 'You know how you're always badgering me to get glasses, darling.'

Powers sank back in his seat, deflated. Still, it was better than nothing. Freddie couldn't give them any more than that, so the officers thanked the couple and left. They walked over to the patrol car.

'So we're looking for a tall, thin apparition, answers to the name of Lord Voldemort,' said Powers sarcastically.

Penny let out an excited squeak. 'I swear I could smell marijuana in there,' he said.

Powers snorted with laughter. 'As if you'd know what that smelt like! Besides, I can't really imagine those two sharing a joint over *To The Manor Born* of an evening, can you?'

'I have smelt it before, when we did that raid on the youth club,' protested Penny indignantly. Just then his mobile started to ring. He pulled it out of his coat pocket; it was another PC back at the station. Penny listened and rang off, his eyes shining. 'Just got a call in from a Mrs Caro Belmont, Mill House. Says she might have seen a suspicious vehicle.' He turned on the ignition and they headed back towards the village.

'I *thought* it was funny at the time,' said Caro ten minutes later. She was making both policemen coffee in the kitchen while they sat on high stools at the breakfast bar. Powers's libido was going into overdrive – another great pair of hooters! What, did they stand the women in this village in special nork fertilizer or something? He chuckled at his own joke. Pity his own wife Janet was as flat as her beloved ironing board.

'It was about ten days ago,' Caro continued, spooning freshly ground coffee into the cafetière, blissfully unaware of the lustful glances her bosom was receiving. 'Milo – he's my son – had been having a difficult night, so I was in the nursery trying to get him back to sleep. Anyway, his room looks out on to the green, and as I was standing there cuddling him, I glanced out the window and saw this black car driving around the other side, near my sister's cottage. That's No. 5 The Green. Anyway, I had to really look, because it didn't have any lights on. Like it didn't want to be seen, you know?'

Penny nodded violently. This could be their first break! 'Did you get a registration, madam?' he asked in his most efficient tone.

'Fraid not, it was too far away,' said Caro. 'It had blacked-out windows though, I think.'

'Model?' asked Powers. Caro shook her head, looking extremely flattered. 'No, I'm a housewife. I used to work in human resources but . . .' Seeing their nonplussed faces, she cottoned on and flushed bright red. 'Oh! I see what you mean. I haven't a clue. As my husband will tell you, I'm hopeless with cars. It was quite sleek and low though. Maybe a sports car? Ooh, it really was rather creepy.' As much as they could see Caro wanted to help them, 'creepy' was not going to find the vehicle. Their spirits quickly deflated again.

It was ten o'clock by the time the two policemen got back to the station. Rance was still in the incident room, going through the Reverend's phone records. His face was grey and there were violet shadows under his eyes. 'You look how I feel, Guv,' yawned Powers, and relayed both Freddie's and Caro's stories. Despite the gloomy report, Rance was pleased by the news. 'A car *and* a suspect. They'll both need following up. Great start, lads, well done.'

'Can we knock off now?' asked Powers, slightly mollified by the praise.

'Yes, but I need you back in here at eight to-morrow morning,' said Rance, going back to his paperwork.

'Bloody murders, I might as well kiss goodbye to any beers down the pub,' said Powers as they walked out of the building. Penny was still full of energy, and Powers felt even more weary as he watched him skip off across the car park to go home and watch his *Police, Camera, Action!* DVD for the fifty-third time.

Chapter 37

The next morning DI Rance was at home in Bedlington, shaving in the bathroom, when he heard the heavy thud of the Sunday newspapers landing on the doormat. He wiped his face clean, let out the water from the sink and headed downstairs.

It was worse than he had thought. There had been a little bit in the papers on Saturday, but now it was front-page news. 'Country Vicar Slain!' screamed the *Sunday Mirror*. 'Dead In His Bed!' gasped the *News of the World*. Rance exhaled heavily; public hysteria was all they bloody needed. Flicking through the coverage in the second tabloid, he noticed a small sidebar on how Churchminster was also under threat from a big property developer called Sid Sykes. Carve it all up and build the bloody houses, thought Rance uncharitably. Would stop those bloody rich gits running around like they owned the place. Which most of them probably did.

Rance wasn't a big fan of the countryside. An Ealing boy born and bred, he had joined Hendon police training college at eighteen, and six months later was patrolling the mean streets of Ladbroke Grove and the less salubrious side of Notting Hill as a fledgling member of the Metropolitan Police. He met a girl called Susan at a pub on the Portobello Road, and two years later they were married and living in a poky flat somewhere behind Paddington train station. For eight years, they existed fairly peaceably together, then all of a sudden Susan started swapping her copies of *Grazia* and *Marie Claire* for *Country Living* and *Homes and Gardens*. Against his better judgement, they found themselves living in a little cottage on the outskirts of Bedlington, Rance with a new job at Bedlington CID. Susan was blissfully happy. Rance couldn't stand it. God, he missed the action of living in a city. And all this fresh air made him feel ill, having been quite happily brought up on a cocktail of traffic fumes and pollution.

'I'm off, love,' he shouted up the stairs to his wife. 'It could be a long one.' He realized he hadn't said that in a long time, and left the house with a spring in his step. He might be going to work on a Sunday, but at least he wasn't going to be dragged around a garden centre looking at sodding petunias.

Later that evening, a predatory darkness fell over the village. Caro had just finished watching one of her old *Sex and the City* box sets, at about 10 p.m., when the doorbell rang. She sat up nervously – who could it be? Sebastian was away on a work conference in Italy (which actually translated as shagging Sabrina's brains out in a very expensive villa next to George Clooney's place on Lake Como). For the first time in the house, she was feeling very nervy. Switching on all the lights as she went, she made her way to the front door and looked through the spy hole. To her surprise, it was Benedict Towey. Caro unlocked the door and pulled it open. Benedict was standing on the doorstep in a light grey suit, blazer slung casually over his left shoulder, a crumpled white linen shirt encasing the muscular contours of his chest. His blond hair was ruffled, and there was a five o'clock shadow starting to appear on his chin. He looked like a Greek god.

'Er, hi,' she said awkwardly. Was he going to have a go at her about something again?

Benedict shifted on the step. 'I've just got back from work and I heard about the Reverend's death. I just wanted to make sure everything was all right.' As usual, his tone was flat and unfriendly. Caro had to let his words sink in for a moment.

'Oh, I'm fine,' she told him. 'Of course it's been a dreadful shock to the village and . . .' Stop wittering, she thought as she gushed on about what a lovely long service there had been that morning, conducted by the Revd Brian Bellows from Bedlington. A bored expression flickered across Benedict's handsome face and he started backing down the path again.

'Give me a shout if you need anything,' he said gruffly, making it sound like it was the last thing on earth he wanted her to do.

'Er, I will. Thank you,' Caro called after him as he disappeared into the gloom at the end of the path. She closed the door gently behind her and leaned against it for a moment. Was that his half-hearted attempt at being a friendly neighbour? She wasn't sure why he'd bothered, he clearly couldn't stand the sight of her. She checked the answering machine in the hall as she went upstairs. No red light flickering, which meant Sebastian still hadn't called her since she'd left a tearful message about the Reverend on his voicemail yesterday. 'Probably hasn't had time to charge his phone,' she thought, trying to convince herself.

Around the village, others were preparing to go to bed. Without telling her sister, Camilla double-locked the back door for the first time. Calypso noticed when she tried to go outside for her last fag of the night. She went to unlock it, thought for a second, and decided to smoke out of her bedroom window instead.

After an intense discussion at the Maltings, Freddie and Angie decided to get a guard dog. Their own dog, an adorable fox terrier called Bella, was more likely to lick an intruder to death than anything else. Up at Clanfield Hall, Harriet's parents had insisted that, after their usual Sunday night dinner, she stay in her old bedroom in the west wing of the house. For once, Harriet didn't protest.

The Revd Goody's untimely demise had got the village very jittery. Although no one had dared bring it up after the service that morning, the same question could be seen in the eyes of each of the Churchminster residents.

Was there a killer among them?

Chapter 38

It was a week of heightened emotions in the village and several people were about to do things they shouldn't.

Caro, desperate to escape the air of tension in the village, left Milo with her grandmother and drove to Fit 4 U to pick up a class schedule. If there was a murderer lurking in the village, the least she could do was be as fit as possible to defend herself and Milo if needs be. Sebastian was being his usual unsupportive self and refused to stay with her in the country for more than a few extra days. 'Place is crawling with rozzers, there's more chance of me getting mugged when I get back to London.' When she suggested getting more security for the house, he had informed her no bastard was getting past the fifty grand alarm system he had bought and, if she was really worried, she should go and stay with Clementine.

'After all, darling, I can't imagine any serial killer, no matter how psychotic, taking your grandmother on,' he had drawled. What about your son? Caro had thought, but she had to admit she was feeling better because of the regular patrols by police cars around the village.

She arrived in Bedlington and drove into the car park of Fit 4 U. Only a few cars were parked there. Pulling in near the entrance, Caro climbed out of the car and walked into the bright, airy reception. It was deserted.

'Hello?' Caro called out. Nothing. She strained her ears, but could only hear a faint gasping coming from a room at the end of the corridor. Must be a class going on, she thought, and made her way down to have a look. She passed several studios, all empty and filled with exercise equipment, and finally got to the room the noise was coming from.

A sign on the door read 'Meditation Room', and there was a small round window below the sign. Caro looked through it, but she couldn't see much, as the lights in the room were turned down low. Gradually, her eyes accustomed to the gloom and she could make out a small, square room with about a dozen exercise mats laid out on the wooden floor. On one of them, her fuchsia pink leggings round her ankles and a look of pure bliss on her face, was Lucinda. What's more, she was furiously riding the man Caro recognized from the fun run as her personal trainer.

'Oh!' For a moment, Caro stood transfixed as the two bodies ground and writhed in unison. Henry was facing away from Caro and she watched the muscles in his arms work as he kneaded and fondled Lucinda's naked breasts. Luckily, Lucinda's head was thrown back in the throes of ecstasy, so she didn't see Caro finally clap her hand over her mouth and step back quickly from the window. Blushing furiously, Caro ran back down the corridor, through the still empty reception and out to the car park.

It was only now she recognized Lucinda's Range Rover parked next to a navy-blue convertible BMW. An image of Lucinda bouncing around in pink Lycra flashed through her mind, and Caro opened her car door, climbed in weakly and sat behind the wheel.

Lucinda Reinard was having an affair! Who would have thought it? Caro didn't know whether to feel shocked or impressed.

A few days later, Lady Fraser was taking afternoon tea out on the terrace when her mobile beeped. It was a text message. Amazingly for this day and age, she'd only just got the thing. (Really, it was so vulgar to be seen in public with such a contraption clamped to one's ear.) The message was short and to the point. *'Do you fancy dinner at mine tomorrow? D.'*

Frances's heart started thudding, and a thrill of excitement she knew she shouldn't be feeling went through her. Devon! So many times she had nearly picked up the phone to call him, only to stop herself quickly. Ambrose was away for a few days on a shooting trip to Scotland – did Devon know that? But how could he?

It would be rude not to accept, she thought; he probably wants to discuss the ball. She chuckled at herself: for God's sake, Frances, who are you kidding? Hands shaking, she typed a formal reply. *'That would be wonderful. Thank you.'*

She pressed the send button and, almost instantly, her phone beeped again. *'Great! See you about 8 p.m.'*

*

The next evening, Frances stood in front of the full-length mirror in her opulent bedroom. She'd already changed twice, deciding the white beaded Chanel dress was too showy and the caramel John Rocha trouser suit a trifle dowdy. Finally, she decided on a simple sleeveless black top, and fitted linen trousers that showed off her long, elegant legs. At her neck, an exquisite diamond necklace Ambrose had bought her for their twenty-fifth wedding anniversary. At the thought of her husband, Frances felt a wave of guilt wash over her. She stared at herself in the mirror. Somehow, she looked different. Is this the face of a soon-to-be adulteress? she wondered. The diamonds glittered around her neck accusingly. Frances decided to take them off, and put on a black and white silk scarf instead.

Outside, it was a beautiful evening. The grounds of Clanfield Hall looked prosperous and perfectly kept, green lawns stretching away as far as the eye could see. Frances decided to take the MG so she could put the roof down. She tied another scarf around her hair to protect her immaculate chignon, then set off looking like Grace Kelly – but feeling like a nervous schoolgirl inside.

At Byron Heights, Devon was feeling equally jittery. He'd told Nigel to go out for the night, and Nigel had looked at him critically but said nothing. At Devon's request, the housekeeper had laid a table for two on the veranda at the back of the house. A thick white tablecloth was draped over it, silver cutlery laid out on top. On an ornate platter lay delicious slivers of smoked salmon and Serrano ham, with fat stuffed olives and other delicacies from the organic deli in Bedlington. A bottle of Dom Perignon stood chilling in a solid silver ice bucket by the side.

It was 7.59 p.m. when the huge, clanking doorbell sounded. Devon, who was in the garden doing deep breathing exercises to centre his core, hurried back into the house. He was beaten to the front door by the housekeeper, on her way home for the evening, and found Frances standing imperiously in the corridor. She was made for huge houses like these, he thought. Others might have felt dwarfed or intimidated by such grandiose surroundings, but they only served to make Frances seem even more regal.

They shook hands awkwardly. 'You have a wonderful home,' said Frances stiffly.

'Thanks, it's not everyone's cup of tea,' said Devon, looking round at the dark-red walls and massive Gothic staircase. 'It does me all right, though.' There was a silence as Frances surveyed the place, looking anywhere but at him. Do I sound really common to her? he thought. He didn't know if it was intentional, but Frances had that effect on him, and he felt like an uncultured yob beside her inherent, aloof classiness.

She followed him through the house to the veranda. 'Drink?' he asked.

'Thank you,' Frances replied. Another silence. God, this is awkward! both of them thought. Frances looked at the table pointedly and Devon jumped forward.

'Shit! I mean, do you want a seat?' asked Devon, and she nodded, allowing him to pull one of the chairs out before lowering herself elegantly into it. Devon got the champagne out of the ice bucket. He was suddenly gagging for a drink to calm his nerves. He seemed to have lost his powers of speech completely, now, grinning at her goofily while she looked back in apparent distaste.

In fact, Frances was feeling exactly the same, desperately trying to think of something to say. Her mother, had she still been alive, would have been horrified at her daughter's sudden attack of muteness. Lady Frances Fraser had been put on this earth to hold effortless, charming conversation with the rich, the royal and the privileged. So why did she feel so completely tongue-tied now?

Devon was having problems with the cork. As he subtly wrestled with it, growing gradually redder in the face, Frances pretended not to notice, and looked out across the gardens. All of a sudden, there was a loud 'pop!' and Devon watched in horror as the cork ricocheted off the wall and flew in terrible slow motion towards Frances, hitting her squarely on the right breast.

At that moment, Devon wanted to curl up and die. Frances's mouth formed an 'O' of shock, and her hand instinctively moved towards the boob in question, then stopped. There was a moment's deafening silence. Beyond shame and mortification, Devon waited for a furious, icy reaction. She probably thought he'd done it on purpose! But after a few excruciating seconds that seemed to last a lifetime, the most extraordinary thing happened. Frances laughed. Devon stared at her, utterly overwhelmed. What the hell was going on?

'Your face looks so funny!' she giggled. 'I've

never seen anyone look so horrified in all my life.'

Still unsure of her reaction, Devon looked at her worriedly. 'You're not hurt? Christ, Frances, I really am so sorry—'

She put up her hand. 'Stop. It's fine, really.' She started giggling again. 'Oh, your expression!' It was such a surprisingly light and infectious sound that Devon couldn't help but join in.

'Shit!' he spluttered. 'I thought you were going to have me bloody 'ead chopped off!' Now they both fell about laughing, Devon leaning forward with both hands on the table, while tears of mirth and relief dropped on to the tablecloth.

Three hours later, they were getting on famously. Devon just couldn't get over what a laugh Frances was! Once she'd abandoned her stuck-up exterior, he saw a very funny, interesting and warm person beneath. For the last hour, they'd been talking about Devon's career, Frances firing questions at him about his life as a pop star. 'I used to have the biggest crush on you,' she told him, delicately nibbling at a piece of sun-dried tomato. 'All the debs did, we thought you were marvellous!'

'A bit of rough?' asked Devon, grinning.

Frances blushed. 'Oh, of course not. Well, not that much.' She shot him a mischievous smile. In the half-light of evening, her pale blonde hair shone, making her look like a beautiful sea nymph.

'Do you fancy a walk around my grounds m'lady?' he asked.

'Rather!' said Frances, finishing the last of her champagne and kicking off her expensive court shoes. Devon held out his hand and she took it to climb over the low stone wall on to the lawn. Despite the dropping temperature of the evening air, the heat of electricity between them was unmistakable.

They walked down the long curving path to the small ornamental lake at the bottom of the gardens. 'This place reminds me of my grandmother's house,' Frances said, as they passed a huge pair of stone lions, jaws drawn back in impressive snarls.

'What, did she live in a bleedin' Hallowe'en theme park?' Devon chuckled.

Frances smiled. 'I didn't mean it like that,' she said. 'I think this was rather a wonderful era for landscaping, actually.'

Suddenly, her foot went from underneath her, and she tripped. Instinctively Devon went to grab her. When he pulled her up again, he didn't let go, drawing her in towards him. Frances didn't resist. They stayed like that, bodies pressed against each other, faces inches apart.

'Your heart is going like the clappers,' said Devon softly.

'So is yours,' she whispered back. 'Devon, I—'

Now it was his turn to stop her. 'You're a fine woman, Frances,' he said. 'Don't feel bad.' With that, he leaned forward and kissed her. Her lips were like the finest velvet. Frances, feeling the strange thrill of a new person's mouth on hers, responded passionately. Her hands moved over his broad, lean back: first over the shirt and then underneath, touching and caressing the firm flesh. Devon groaned and kissed her harder; she could feel his erection pushing into her pelvis. When his hands didn't find her breasts quickly enough, she guided them herself. They were small and perfect, and Devon gently felt the hardness of her nipples through the fabric of her top. A few seconds later the top was off and he was slowly lowering her on to the grass. She pulled him down with her and started unbuttoning his trousers. In the moonlight he marvelled at her slenderness and flawless, porcelain skin. She was beautiful.

'Make love to me,' she said, as Devon's fingers moved inside the front triangle of her underwear. Suddenly, he was inside her, making her gasp with pleasure. She wrapped her legs around his back, mirroring his movements with her own body. Then he was kissing her again, his tongue flickering in and out of her mouth, as his thrusting became quicker and more intense. 'Oh God, oh God,' moaned Frances as Devon eventually climaxed, just seconds before her. Her whole body felt alive, and he clasped her to him, shallow, fast breaths against her neck.

'I was a lady and now I'm a tramp,' she said softly.

Devon shook his head in disagreement. 'No you're not,' he said, stroking her hair. He added, 'I bet your grandmother never did *this* on her lawn.'

Frances smiled. 'You never know, it might run in the family.' They both laughed and Devon started to tenderly kiss her body again.

Chapter 39

Two weeks later, the village was trying to get back to some semblance of normality. The Reverend's body still lay in Bedlington morgue. Despite an extensive search, neither the mysterious black car nor the hooded figure had been found, and the story had moved from the front pages of the newspapers to a cursory mention inside.

Rance thought they might have their first suspect when Clementine strode into the station one morning, demanding to see him. She had finally remembered something that had been bothering her and relayed the Revd Goody's story of his altercation with Sid Sykes. A few swift phone calls soon stopped Rance in his tracks. On the night of the murder, Sykes had been at some fancy dinner with his wife in London. They'd gone to a casino afterwards until four o'clock and then stumbled back to their suite at the Dorchester. His wife, several hundred people, a night doorman and a good few hours of CCTV backed up his story. Sykes had a watertight alibi. And who was to say the Reverend hadn't exaggerated? thought Rance cynically.

The SCBA Committee met up and discussed, out

of respect to the deceased, whether or not the ball and auction should go ahead. They unanimously agreed to carry on. 'Arthur loved this village!' cried Angie.

The fact they now had Devon Cornwall on board was a major coup. 'How *did* you do it, Mummy?' exclaimed Harriet at one Wednesday-night meeting at Fairoaks.

'Yah, it was like getting blood out of a stone when I talked to him about it,' said Freddie admiringly.

Frances hoped she wasn't blushing; she could still feel the warmth of Devon's tongue licking her inner thigh. Since their first frolic on the lawn, they had tried to see each other as much as possible. Is it really only a fortnight? Frances wondered. She couldn't even remember life before him. Her waking hours had taken on a new energy, a colour she had never thought possible. 'Oh, I didn't do much,' she said to Freddie dismissively. 'I think Devon – Mr Cornwall – just came to his senses.'

'Is he going to try and get Mick for us?' asked Freddie.

'He might be away touring at the moment, but I am led to believe Nigel, Devon's secretary, has made a phone call about it,' Frances replied, in the most businesslike tone she could muster.

'A sort of "my people will call your people" thing?' said Caro. 'Oh, how frightfully glamorous!'

The conversation moved on then to Calypso's VIP list. The death of the Revd Goody was a terrible thing, but it had brought a certain irresistible notoriety to Churchminster. Suddenly, everyone wanted a ticket to the ball in the village all the papers had dubbed 'the real life *Midsomer Murders*'.

Celebrities' agents were ringing up by the hour, and Calypso had even managed to secure DJ Dawg, who was going to play a set. ('A what?' asked a baffled Clementine.) Calypso had even persuaded him to forgo his enormous fee, with a vague promise he might meet the Queen. *Soirée*'s features editor had been on the phone to Calypso earlier to inform her that they were planning a much bigger piece now, and were going to send a journalist and photographer down to the village. 'We're thinking an old money versus new money battle, yah?'

'Oh, it's going to be a nightmare doing the guest list,' Caro wailed, but they all rallied round her with promises of help, and cries of: 'Of course it won't!' and 'You'll do a jolly marvellous job!'

Angie Fox-Titt was still working wonders sourcing things for the auction. Somehow she had secured twenty one-hour sessions with Madonna's personal trainer (who was otherwise booked up for the next five years), and an art critic friend was going to approach Tracey Emin about doing something. Clementine hadn't got a clue who Tracey Emin was, and had to discreetly ask Calypso afterwards.

'She is, like, this totally cool artist, Granny,' Calypso told her. 'People are going to bid, like, *zillions* for that. Awesome!'

If Lady Frances Fraser was on top of the world at the moment, her daughter was about to become the opposite. She loved being on the SCBA Committee. Being the site manager gave her so much more confidence; organizing, pulling things together, making it all *happen*. People asking *her* opinion and actually listening! It had made her realize she was actually good at something. So the next Sunday, at dinner with her parents, she broke the news. She wanted to train to be an events manager.

Ambrose, who at that moment was halfway through his bowl of gazpacho soup, almost spat it out over the priceless Ming china.

'A what?' he'd spluttered.

'An events manager, Daddy,' explained Harriet patiently. 'You know, someone who is in charge of putting on social functions and corporate events, for example—'

Her father cut her off, waving his spoon around furiously. 'Yes, I do know what one is, Harriet,' he boomed. 'I've seen those women! Bloody awful big-arsed girls running around with a clipboard, looking like something out of *Challenge* bloody *Anneka*. Vulgar, pushy, common creatures. Over my dead body!'

'Ambrose,' said Frances sternly, but he ignored her.

'Your ancestors will be turning in their graves. A Fraser! Working as an events manager! For Christ's sake, girl, why do you want a job like that? Don't I give you a big enough allowance? Hmm. Is that what it is?'

Harriet went quite pale. Suddenly she pushed her chair back and ran from the room, choking back a sob.

'Ambrose!' Frances put her spoon down. 'You really have gone too far!'

Her husband's face was purple, and Frances was worried he was going to burst a blood vessel. 'An events manager!' he repeated again. 'What on earth? Can you imagine what people will think?

Bloody load of nonsense.' With that, he returned to his soup, grumbling incoherently between mouthfuls.

Across the table, Frances sighed. She had to admit, she could think of a few more glamorous careers she would like to see her daughter pursue, but she was angry with her husband's reaction. The older he became, the narrower his horizons were getting. The forthright attitude that had won her over as a young, impressionable girl was now turning him into an intolerant, grumpy old man. She reached over, putting her hand over his. 'Darling, you really shouldn't get yourself so wound up about things.' Ambrose grunted something about 'that blasted Rice woman' and carried on eating his soup.

Frances sat back and watched him. It was starting to feel as if they were leading completely separate lives. Ambrose was retreating ever more into his own world, which seemed to consist solely of shooting game and drinking claret in his study. She worried about the effect it was having on him, their marriage and family.

God, she wished she was in Devon's arms right now.

At that precise moment, Devon was sitting with Nigel in his studio at Byron Heights. For the past hour, he had been trying out some of his new songs, guitar on knee as his inimitable rich and husky voice filled the room. Finally, Devon stopped and turned to Nigel. 'So what do you think?' he asked, almost shyly.

Nigel hadn't said a word for some time, his face

blank and expressionless. From the very beginning, he had always been Devon's harshest critic, and it was his opinion above all others that Devon had always trusted most.

Nigel remained silent, and Devon leaned over to him. 'Nige? Mate? Surely it wasn't that bad,' he joked, trying to hide his disappointment.

A full ten seconds passed, but when Nigel eventually spoke, his voice was thick with emotion. 'Devon, I think this is the best stuff you've ever written.'

That night, as they were eating Nigel's delicious black bean stew, Devon made an announcement. 'You know what, I really feel like I'm on this mad, creative trip at the moment. Melodies, lyrics, they just won't stop coming. It's like I've been reborn, y'know?'

Nigel looked him straight in the eye. 'Anything to do with a certain lady?' Devon didn't answer, suddenly becoming very intent on his stew, but Nigel pressed on. 'Devon, she's married.'

'Is she? I didn't realize,' Devon joked, trying to lighten the moment. He saw the concern in his friend's eyes. 'Nige, I know you've got my best interests at heart, but it's fine, really. You're right, she *is* married. At some point, I am going to have to deal with that. But at the moment, she's bringing the kind of joy to my life I never thought I'd have again. So don't worry, OK?'

Nigel gave him a wan smile. 'I suppose at least we know she's not going to run off with the rest of your fortune. I'll put the apple pie on, shall I?'

'Nice one,' replied Devon happily.

Chapter 40

There were more tears on the Clanfield estate at the end of that week as Jed called things off with Stacey. For the first time in her young but manipulative life, Stacey had really fallen for someone. When Jed broke the news, she threw herself on his bed at Bantry's Cottage and sobbed her heart out.

Jed felt awful. He had never seen it as more than a fling, and in his mind he'd always thought that was how Stacey felt, too. She begged him to take her back, and he gently disentangled himself from her and told her again that it was over. At that point, it finally sank in that she was fighting a lost cause. Angry, surprised and humiliated, Stacey called him an arsehole. 'I've got, like, a million boys after me, what makes you so special anyway, Jed Bantry?' she spat. And with a final indignant heave of her chest, Stacey was gone, leaving a trail of sickly sweet perfume in her wake.

Despite the last fraught hour, Jed wanted to smile. She was a feisty little madam. But he still didn't care how many men wanted to take her out. It was over.

*

That lunchtime, Caro and Angie were sitting in the corner of the pub, at the window seat overlooking the green. Milo was squirming around on Angie's knee, and she was placating him with bits of her delicious chocolate torte.

Caro hadn't even been able to finish her main course, and Angie looked at her in concern. 'Darling, are you OK? Are you not eating? You know, you've lost a terrific amount of weight.'

Caro had. Her post-baby fat had melted away, and from a distance she could almost pass for her youngest sister Calypso. Newly discovered cheekbones were appearing on her face, but she still looked pale and unhappy, her eyes huge and haunted.

'I have lost my appetite recently,' she confessed. She attempted a wan smile. 'I should be happy, really, I got into a pair of my size ten jeans for the first time in yonks yesterday.'

'How are things with Seb?' Angie asked, perceptively.

Caro shrugged her shoulders. 'Oh! Fine really. I mean I haven't seen much of him recently. Poor man has been working flat out and spending most of his time up in town.'

Angie, who had just heard a rather disturbing rumour from a friend who was married to a millionaire city financier, didn't feel sorry for Sebastian at all. In fact, she felt quite the opposite. But she knew she couldn't bring herself to tell Caro her worst fear, when it was just that. A rumour.

'Surely his family is more important?' she asked Caro.

Caro shrugged again. 'He's working for some big

bonus at the moment, reckons it will change his life completely.'

Angie eyed her. '*His* life? What about you and Milo? And especially at the moment, with God knows who running around. He should be here, with you.'

Caro's eyes were filling with tears now. 'Who am I kidding?' she sobbed. Angie moved to put an arm around her, ignoring the curious stares from the next table. 'We've just grown so far apart,' Caro continued unhappily. 'He's hardly any kind of father to Milo. If I do ask him to spend more time at home, or suggest we do something as a family, he just bites my head off. We haven't made love in months, he never pays me compliments. Oh Angie, it's like I don't exist!' She broke up, shuddering.

'What are you going to do?' asked Angie softly. 'You and this adorable little chap can always move into ours if you need the space, we've got tons of rooms. It might just make bloody Sebastian realize what he could lose if he carries on like this.'

Caro squeezed her friend's hand gratefully. 'You are sweet. But I need to stay at home and give it one last shot. I can't bear the thought of Milo not having his mummy and daddy together any more.' Her eyes filled up with tears again.

'Darling, you're not exactly together at the moment,' Angie pointed out. 'Bloody Sebastian's off doing exactly what he wants while you're stuck at home. It doesn't seem at all fair.'

Caro smiled sadly. 'I know it's not right, believe me I do. But I can't just give up like that. I'll talk to him. I promise.'

'I hope you do, darling,' said Angie, smiling at

270

her. 'And give him hell from me.' She hugged Caro fiercely.

Angie spent the rest of the day worrying about her friend. When she shut up the antiques shop that evening and started for home, she wondered if she should speak to Freddie about it. Get him to have a 'man to man' talk with Sebastian perhaps? Her heart softened at the thought of dear, sweet loyal Freddie. She wouldn't swop him for a million Sebastians, no matter how big their bloody bonuses were.

When she opened the front door to the Maltings, however, her concern for Caro quite left her mind as she was assailed by a heavy waft of smoke in the hallway. She really was going to have to speak to Archie about his incense candles. They were reeking the place out. Loud music thudded from upstairs. He was obviously in, then. When her son wasn't at college, he seemed to spend all his time in his bedroom with his friend Tyrone. On the few occasions Angie had knocked on the door to ask if they wanted any food or drinks, Archie just told her to go away. Her only child was looking so pale and scruffy at the moment, it bothered her. No wonder, when he seemed to sleep half the day and stay up all night instead. Angie prayed to God he hadn't got in with the wrong crowd at college.

She made her way through to the kitchen, where she found a red-eyed Freddie toasting a Mars bar on a bit of ciabatta under the grill. 'Darling, what on earth are you eating?'

'I just really fancied it, I don't know why,' said Freddie absent-mindedly, kissing her on the mouth.

271

Angie didn't think she had ever seen her husband eat a bar of chocolate before. What was up with him? She went to the fridge to get the filtered water out and, to her surprise, found one of her husband's green Hunter wellies in there, wedged next to the leftover cold roast chicken and magnum of Möet.

Freddie came up behind her, dripping melted caramel all over the kitchen floor. 'There it is!' he exclaimed. 'Been looking for the blasted thing everywhere. Must have left it in there when I got the Green & Black's hazelnut spread out earlier.' Then, for no reason, he got the giggles and couldn't stop, shoulders shaking as he collapsed at the kitchen table.

In utter astonishment, Angie stared at her husband. God, was this how dementia began?

Chapter 41

Sebastian and Sabrina, far from having a romantic weekend, had actually had a huge falling-out in Italy, and not spoken until they were heading back home on their BA business class flight. On the Saturday night they had been having dinner at a three-star Michelin restaurant up in the mountains, when Sabrina had caught him slipping his business card to the very beautiful and very young waitress serving them.

'She's barely out of her teens, you fucking pervert!' she had hissed at him when he had returned to the table.

'Oh, for Christ's sake, Luciana is a very intelligent young woman who has just got a business degree and wants to come over and work in the City,' he had informed her smoothly. 'The least I could do is give her my business card. Give her a leg up.'

'Leg over more like,' Sabrina had spat, filing her nails out of the window furiously.

Sebastian had surveyed her coldly. 'Jealous are you, darling? You shouldn't be, it doesn't make you look half as pretty.' Vain creature that she was, that had shut Sabrina up and she had sulked the rest of the evening, not even letting Sebastian get near her in bed when they got back to their magnificent villa. She had been feeling quite twitchy anyway. She hadn't seen Piers for weeks, and had heard on the model grapevine that he'd taken up with some silly anorexic bitch from Slovenia.

She had wondered if it was about time she got in touch with the Russian businessman who'd been pestering her. To hell with Sebastian. She'd met Vladimir in Le Caprice restaurant when he'd sent an eight hundred pound bottle of Cristal over to her table, where she had been dining with a girl-friend. Short and squat with a shaved head, he had looked like a low-rent bouncer, so she'd brushed him off. But he'd still given her his business card as he left. When her girlfriend had seen his surname and squealed, saying he'd been listed in *Forbes* as one of the fifty richest and most influential men in the world that year, Sabrina had had second thoughts. Especially when she'd Googled him later that night at home and found out he was divorced, friends with the Sultan of Brunei and kept a twenty million pound yacht called Sapphire moored in St Tropez.

With this in her mind, Sabrina had calmed down enough so that when Sebastian's hand wandered up her inner thigh in business class the next evening, she hadn't pushed it off. Besides, she'd gone without sex for almost twenty-four hours, which was some kind of record for her. Sabrina needed sex like Denis Healey needed a pair of eyebrow-tweezers.

They'd ended up renewing their membership of

the Mile High Club in the toilet, only pulling apart when an air stewardess had knocked discreetly on the door and told them they were starting the descent to Heathrow. Sebastian had stopped his own descent between Sabrina's thighs and the pair had waltzed out smugly. 'What are you looking at, Four Eyes?' Sebastian had snarled at a small, bespectacled man in a suit who had quickly dived back behind his *Sunday Times* money supplement.

Elsewhere in the capital, Stephen and Klaus were on a conference call to Clementine from their six million pound art deco pad in Chelsea. As promised, they had managed to secure the services of the legendary Christie's auctioneer Belvedere Radley. As it had turned out, he'd once had a great uncle Bunty who had lived on some rolling estate a few miles south of Churchminster and had always had a great affinity with the area.

'Chaps, that's wonderful!' said Clementine when they relayed the news to her.

'Rather,' Stephen agreed. 'He's bloody merciless in action. He once got someone to pay fifteen mill for a loo seat that had apparently belonged to Van Gogh. If he can't get the likes of Jemima Khan handing over her entire inheritance for a fivesome with Take That, no one can!'

Talking of foursomes, Angus had been badgering Camilla to set up a double date with Harriet and Sniffer.

'What about Horse?' Camilla had asked.

'Oh, Horseman has been seeing some chick from Cirencester,' Angus had chortled over a late supper at the Jolly Boot one evening. 'Sniffer said he wouldn't mind a go on old Hatty now. I think you and I getting hitched has got him wondering if he shouldn't make a decent woman of some lucky filly.' With that, he'd squeezed Camilla's thigh with his huge hand in a gesture that was meant to be tender, but had made her yelp out in pain.

'OK, I'll ask her,' she had said dubiously.

Harriet's expression said it all. 'You're not interested are you? I didn't think you would be, but I had to ask, Hats,' said Camilla. It was the next evening and the two women were curled up on the sofa in the sitting room at Gate Cottage, a half-drunk bottle of Sauvignon Blanc on the floor between them.

Harriet sighed. 'He's just a bit much. Although I suppose I should be taking up every offer I get, otherwise I am going to end up an old maid, and Daddy will hate me even more.' Sir Ambrose had only just started talking to her again, but any plans of her pursuing the career she wanted had been firmly stopped.

Camilla took a sip of wine. 'So you're not going to look around?' she asked.

'Not unless I want to be cut out of the family will and made homeless and penniless,' said Harriet gloomily.

'That's such a shame,' cried Camilla. 'I think you'd make a marvellous events manager.'

Harriet smiled. 'You are a dear friend, Bills.' She changed the subject. 'How are the wedding plans going?'

Camilla shrugged. 'It's all on hold, to be honest.

Mummy and Daddy have fixed for us to get married at St Bartholomew's like them and Granny and Grandfather, but with this awful business of the Revd Goody, everything's suddenly a bit up in the air.'

Harriet shivered. 'It's horrible, isn't it? I can't believe someone murdered him.'

Caro looked round the cottage. 'Do you get scared being here by yourself?'

Harriet thought for a second. 'A little, since he was killed. But I've just had security lights installed and, besides, Jed's just down the road.'

'Ooh yes, he looks like he could knock an intruder out,' remarked Camilla. She hesitated. 'Have you ever fantasized about, you know . . . I mean, he *is* awfully handsome.'

Harriet laughed. 'No, we're more like brother and sister, I suppose. Besides, can you imagine Daddy's face? In his eyes, getting it on with the hired help is far worse than events management!'

'Oh Hats, poor you,' said Camilla. 'I'm sure your father is only like this because he wants the best for you.'

'Best for him, more like. He hasn't got a clue what I want,' Harriet retorted. She stared off wistfully into the distance, then looked back at her friend. 'Oh, to hell with getting upset about it! At least they've gone off the idea of making me move back in the Hall with them.' She stood up. 'I've got some of Cook's legendary chocolate-chip cookies in the kitchen. Do you want one?'

Camilla hesitated. 'I should be watching my weight. I've got a wedding-dress fitting next week.'

'Nonsense! If anyone should be on a diet, it's me,'

said Harriet, looking down at her straining Jack Wills tracksuit bottoms.

'Have you still got any of that delish hot chocolate from Fortnums to dunk them in?' asked Camilla hopefully.

Harriet shot her a wicked glance. 'Oh, I am sure I can dig some out.'

The Revd Goody's body was finally released to his family. He had a private funeral in London attended only by his sister, who flew over especially. As requested in his will, his ashes were to be scattered over the fields in his favourite part of Tuscany.

The village said goodbye in their own way as well, with a service at St Bartholomew's commemorating the Revd Goody's life. The Revd Brian Bellows was seconded in to take it, looking dreadfully uncomfortable standing in the pulpit where the Revd Goody should have been. Rance and Penny stood surreptitiously at the back, observing the crowd. Babs Sax, dressed in a dramatic black veil and engine-red lipstick, sobbed theatrically throughout the service.

'She's such a bloody drama queen,' hissed Brenda to Pearl Potts. The two women were sitting in a pew behind Caro and the rest of her family.

'Lawks, I know! I don't think she ever set foot in church when our dear Reverend, God bless his soul, was still alive,' said Pearl. Several people turned round and shushed them, but to no avail.

'You know she's trying it on with that handsome Mr Towey,' Brenda said. Caro's ears pricked up.

'Inviting him over to dinner and all sorts. The woman's got the morals of an alley cat.'

'Nice young man like that, can't imagine why he's divorced,' remarked Pearl. 'He's awfully rich, you know, runs some hot-shot business up in London.'

'Well, from what I heard, *he's* not much better!' said Brenda in a scandalized voice. 'Left his wife high and dry for some other woman.'

'Well, I never!' said Pearl. 'Men just can't keep it zipped in their trousers, can they?'

Clementine turned around. 'Shush!' she ordered crossly, and both women finally shut up.

Caro couldn't concentrate on the service after that. Just when she had been thinking he wasn't so bad after all, Benedict Towey's true colours had been shown up. What a complete bastard!

Chapter 42

Unfortunately, things soon went from bad to worse between Harriet and her father. The next time she visited him in his study, he informed her he wanted the car park back in its original place. 'To the left of the Hall, away from the rose gardens.' It wasn't a request, it was an order.

Harriet looked at her father in despair. He gazed out of the window at something in the distance, not even granting her the courtesy of eye-contact. Harriet had had enough.

'For goodness' sake, Daddy!' she said furiously, raking a hand through her hair. 'Why? I've had to ring the car park people and get them to draw up a new plan, because *you* didn't want it out there in the first place.' She looked at her clipboard and started rifling through the pages loudly, trying to find the contacts page.

Ambrose suddenly swivelled round in his huge, leather chair. 'Stop making that bloody racket,' he roared, staring belligerently at the clipboard. 'What, is that thing surgically attached to your chest now? I want you to move the car park because I've changed my bloody mind. And that, my girl, is a good enough explanation for you, so don't you dare question me again!' Harriet felt all of twelve years old again, and had a flashback to the time he'd shouted at her for riding her pony through the downstairs of the house. She turned and fled the room.

In the hall, she bumped into her mother. Frances was dressed in her snow-white tennis outfit, a shiny new tennis racquet in her hand. She was on her way out to the courts behind the house for her weekly lesson with her coach. 'Darling!' she exclaimed, taking in her daughter's red, agitated face. 'What on earth is wrong?' Harriet sighed in exasperation. 'Bloody Daddy wants to bloody change the location of the bloody car park again!' she said.

'Language, darling,' said Frances, guiding Harriet further down the hallway. She had never seen her placid, well-mannered daughter so uptight. 'I know he can be a trifle difficult at times, but he does know the Hall better than anyone,' she told her. 'I'm sure he must have a perfectly good reason for changing it.'

'He's just trying to ruin everything I'm doing!' cried Harriet. 'Why, Mummy? Does he really think I am incapable of achieving anything?'

'Of course not,' soothed Frances. 'It's just that he has his own particular way of doing things.' As she said it, she wondered why she was defending him. Ambrose *was* being impossible at the moment. She must be feeling guilty over Devon. Not wanting to think about Devon, she swiftly changed the subject back to one she was more comfortable with: Harriet's appearance.

'Darling, you really do need a haircut,' she said

critically, eyeing her daughter's hair. It was a hot September day and the heat had made it even more frizzy than normal. 'Do you want me to arrange for François to come over?' François was the family hairdresser who ran a very exclusive, expensive salon called Allure in Cheltenham. The Frasers had been going to him for years.

'Oh, who gives a shit about my hair?' Harriet snapped. 'I might just go to the barber's in Bedlington and get it all shaved off. At least then you wouldn't be able to have a go at me about it!' And with that, she stormed off down the corridor, leaving an open-mouthed Frances in her wake.

'She's probably just having a tough time with her hormones,' Devon said, when Frances recounted the episode to him. They were in the master bedroom at Byron Heights. Dozens of lit candles cast a bewitching light over the room. With its opulent red rugs and thick, purple velvet curtains hanging luxuriantly from the windows, it looked like a scene from *The Arabian Nights*.

'She's thirty, though, not some hot-headed teenager,' sighed Frances, lying back on the pillow. The cover fell away to reveal one milky white breast, and Devon leaned over to kiss it. They had the place to themselves whilst Nigel was out at some concert recital in Oxford. Frances had told Ambrose she was going out for dinner with a friend.

Earlier, Devon had played Frances some of his new material and, like Nigel, she had been blown away. 'Darling, that was just wonderful!' she had said when he had come to the end of 'Heart Catcher', a stirring soulful rock number that had made the hairs on the back of her neck stand up.

'Well, you're the one who inspired it babe,' he had confessed, grinning at her.

She had flung her arms around his neck. 'Oh Devon!' she had said breathlessly. In a more subtle way, Devon had definitely been having an effect on her as well. Frances had become more light-hearted, more girlish. Even her appearance had changed: the elegantly severe chignon, always her trademark, was sometimes replaced by a loose ponytail that made her look softer and even more beautiful. Cook had noticed the change in her mistress and had wondered what, or rather who, was responsible for it. It was so unlike Lady Fraser to have an affair, but Cook had to admit it suited her.

A slight wind blew in from the open sash window, making the candles flicker momentarily. All of a sudden, there was a thud from downstairs. Devon and Frances both sat up. 'What was that?' asked Frances uncertainly. The Reverend's death flashed through her mind, making her blood run cold. Was it the murderer, back for more victims? Common sense kicked in. Don't be so ridiculous, she told herself.

But then there was a second thud, much louder this time, and followed by the horrifyingly unmistakable pad of footsteps. They clutched each other tightly and listened. The noise was right underneath the bedroom now, somewhere in the hallway downstairs.

'The ghost!' croaked Devon.

Frances stared at him. 'The what?' All of a sudden, there was another thud and a terrible, low howl. It was too much for Devon. He screamed loudly and flung his arms round Frances's neck. She held him for a second, their hearts hammering as they strained their ears into the darkness. Nothing.

'What in God's name *was* that?' asked Frances. Devon was saved from answering by headlights shining in through the window. Nigel. 'Oh no!' Frances cried, leaping up, all thoughts of anything phantom evaporating from her mind. 'I can't let him see me!'

'Chill, princess, your car is parked out the front. He already knows you're here,' said Devon. He hadn't told her about his conversation with Nigel. 'Get dressed quickly and we'll go downstairs, make out you've come round to talk about the ball.'

By the time Nigel had parked, locked the car and inspected the new flowerbed by the front door, they were both downstairs in the formal sitting room. Devon was on one side of the room and Frances the other, perched ramrod straight in her chair and anxiously smoothing her hair back. 'As I was saying about the ball, Mr Cornwall,' she started loudly as they heard the front door open. A few seconds later, someone cleared their throat discreetly outside.

'Come in!' called Devon, his earlier fright forgotten. He was actually rather enjoying all this; she was even sexier when she got all flustered.

Nigel put his head round the door. 'Devon, Lady Fraser,' he said, not missing a beat.

Frances nodded her head graciously: 'Good evening.'

'How was the recital, Nige?' asked Devon.

'Very uplifting,' Nigel replied, pretending not to

notice that Frances's top was on inside out and Devon had all his shirt buttons done up the wrong way. 'Can I get you some refreshments?' Devon looked at Frances.

'A pot of tea would be wonderful. We've just been discussing the ball. That's why I'm here,' she added unnecessarily.

'Any news from Mick?' Devon asked Nigel, as he started to back out.

Nigel shook his head. 'He's still on tour in the Far East, but I am under the impression they have managed to get a message to him.'

'Maybe I'll just email him, cut out the middle man,' said Devon. 'I've got his address somewhere.'

Chapter 43

The investigation into the Reverend's murder had ground to a frustrating halt. No new leads, no more sightings of the car or Lord Voldemort, as the shadowy figure had now been nicknamed by the rest of the team. Only Rance was still doggedly trying to track down other witnesses who might have seen this stranger in the village.

It was one of the hottest autumns on record and the windowless incident room was swelteringly hot. Penny and Powers had escaped, claiming they were going to chase up some new leads. Rance suspected the real truth was that they were down the Jolly Boot, in the beer garden. He didn't blame them. He took off his suit jacket and rolled back his shirt sleeves, shifting uncomfortably as rivulets of sweat trickled down his back. What he'd do to be by a pool with a cold San Miguel right now! Which reminded him, he must get on to Susan about booking a holiday.

The phone rang and he grabbed it, holding the receiver away from his ear as the angry voice of his Chief Inspector, a po-faced man called Haddock, barked out. Haddock was on holiday in the

Dordogne and had just had the Superintendent call him up demanding to know why they still had no suspect nearly six weeks in. Haddock was not happy about having his annual break interrupted, and by the time Rance got off the phone five minutes later his ear was ringing from the severe bollocking. He exhaled furiously. What? Did the old git think he'd just had his feet up on the desk reading Mystic Meg for the last frigging month or something?

'Everything all right, Guv?' asked the lone detective in the room, cautiously.

'Marvellous,' said Rance sarcastically. 'Couldn't be better. How long have I got before I can retire, again? In fact, don't remind me.'

The following Sunday Caro attended church service with Milo and her grandmother. Sebastian had waltzed off back to London first thing, claiming he had to go into the office. They both knew it was a lie, but to be honest Caro was relieved to see him go. Sebastian made it so abundantly obvious how bored he was that Caro would rather have been by herself than having him complain and put her down every five seconds.

The Revd Brian Bellows was still standing in to take the services, until a new vicar could be appointed. Unfortunately, with his violent stutter, it was taking twice as long as normal and people were starting to grumble about having numb bums and being late to put the roast on. Sitting in the church now, wedged between Clementine and Freddie Fox-Titt, Caro was beginning to wish she hadn't come. The temperature was still in the mid-eighties, unusually hot for September, and even though the stone walls offered a cool respite, Milo was squirming around on her lap, his little face hot and bothered. About halfway through the service he started to grizzle and, what with that and the Revd Brian Bellows getting his words mixed up on some ramble about the wealth of God, Caro was getting quite a headache.

Finally, Milo had had enough. Despite whispered cajoling from Caro, he opened his mouth and let out a blood-curdling yell. Startled, everyone looked around.

'Sorry!' Caro mouthed apologetically. 'I'll take him outside and wait for you,' she whispered to Clementine, and squeezed out past Freddie.

Outside, the sky was a glorious blue. Caro sat in the shade of a gnarled and aged yew tree in the right-hand corner of the graveyard. Out in the fresh air and soothed by his mum's rocking, Milo finally fell asleep. Caro looked across the grass to where a tall, impressive white gravestone stood. 'Fortuna Standington-Fulthrope,' it read. 'Born 1885, died 1967. Beloved wife of Oscar.' Underneath was the family crest and motto: 'In work one prospers, in life one loves.' Caro sighed; she wasn't doing too well keeping the family tradition going on either account. She hoped her great-grandmother wasn't looking down at her in thin-lipped disapproval.

Fifteen minutes later the heavy wooden doors to the church opened and the congregation started filing out. Stephen and Klaus, who had been sitting two pews back from Caro, spotted her under the tree and made their way over. Caro had to smile: they stuck out like sore thumbs in Churchminster, but somehow it worked. Stephen was in his sixties, and yet today he was clad in a cream linen safari suit and velvet orange cravat, his silvery white hair under a dapper Panama hat. Klaus, the darker-haired, younger of the pair, had on a pink painter's smock top that looked very expensive, and dark-blue, knee-length shorts which showed off a pair of long, elegant calves. On his feet he wore brown, Grecian-style sandals. As they got closer, Caro enviously noticed his immaculate pedicure and clear nail-polish. She looked at her own ragged feet in dismay.

'Oh, darling, that's an awfully long face for such an exquisite girl,' Stephen exclaimed. He was so posh he made the Queen sound like she'd just stepped off the set of *EastEnders*.

Caro blushed slightly. 'Sorry, I was just thinking what a dreadful scruff I look!'

'Poppycock!' Stephen said. His blue eyes twinkled. 'We've been commanded to tell you your grandmother is speaking with the vicar about something and will be out in a few minutes.' He chuckled gently. 'That's if the poor chap can get his words out. Last thing I heard, he was attempting to ask Clementine about the merits of lavateras versus rhododendrons.'

Caro smiled up at him, shielding her eyes from the sun with her hand. Milo was still asleep in her lap. 'Just up for the weekend, then?'

'Yah,' said Klaus in his thick German accent. 'Vot vith this heat, London is unbearable at the moment. Stephen suffers vith it so badly, so ve made our escape on Friday.'

Stephen spoke again. 'Caro, my dear, do tell me.

289

What do you make of your new neighbour?'

Caro tried to sound nonchalant. 'Benedict Towey? Oh, I couldn't really say, I haven't had much to do with him.'

'He lives on the same street as us in London, you know.'

Caro was shocked. She knew the mews where the two men lived, in one of the most desirable parts of Chelsea. She had no idea what Benedict Towey did when he was off skulking away from the village, but she hadn't imagined him living on a gorgeous cobbled street with enchantingly pretty houses.

'Really?'

'Oh yes, he has a house several doors down. We must admit, we're rather taken with him, aren't we Klaus?' The German nodded impassively. 'He's been round to dinner a few times,' continued Stephen. 'Frightfully interesting fellow. Runs a fantastically successful design agency in Soho. Works bloody hard at it, too. That's how he ended up buying next door to you, you know. Benedict mentioned he was looking for a country bolthole to get away to and recharge his batteries and, of course, Klaus and I couldn't recommend Churchminster highly enough. Benedict was over the moon when he got his hands on the other half of Mill House.'

This time Caro couldn't hide her surprise. They must be talking about two different people. Benedict was horrid and unfriendly, she knew that first-hand. She couldn't imagine him being over the moon about anything in life, far less genially holding court around Stephen's dinner table.

'I can't say I've seen that side of him.' She gave

them a tight smile. 'To be honest, we haven't really hit it off. I don't think I'm his sort of person.' And he's certainly not mine, she thought forcefully.

Stephen eyed her perceptively for a second. 'Oh, I wouldn't write him off just yet, darling. I always find people are full of surprises. Sebastian down this weekend?' he asked lightly.

'He's had to go back to London for work,' Caro said, a little too brightly. 'He's simply snowed under at the moment. Some big deal or another. You know these City boys, it's all work, work, work!' She gave a forced laugh.

Stephen studied her again. 'Of course,' he said. 'Well, do pass on our regards, darling. We must be off. Oh look, there's your grandmother.'

A harassed-looking Clementine was striding out of the church, the Revd Brian Bellows, rather ruffled in his dog collar, trailed along behind her.

Chapter 44

The next month, the new edition of *Soirée* included a six-page spread about Churchminster. The extensive article, called 'A Countryside In Crisis' delved straight into the village's blueblood heritage and also the fact that it had become the scene of one of the most sensationalist murders of the past decade. It went on to describe many of the residents, including eighties rock star Devon Cornwall who, according to the rumours on the Internet, was poised to make a huge comeback. They hadn't managed to speak to the man himself, but had got a quote from a 'Nigel' confirming: 'Devon is back in the studio and will be showcasing his new music at the Save Churchminster Ball and Auction.'

Thankfully, the article's main focus was the ball and why it was taking place. To everyone's great satisfaction, they painted a rather unflattering portrait of Sid Sykes as some modern-day Fagin of dubious dealings and character. The piece concluded by questioning the sanity of allowing the new planning law to be passed, and ominously asking what it meant for the future. On the opening spread, there was a stunning overhead aerial shot of Churchminster at its sunny, most succulent best, and further drop-ins of the Reverend and the rectory, looking every inch the gloomy murder scene. There was also a fantastic picture of Devon on stage in his heyday and a rather less flattering one of Clementine in the green drawing room at Fairoaks. Unfortunately she had sneezed just as the photographer clicked the button. She was also furious to see they'd listed her as aged ninety-nine.

The piece caused incredible uproar. In the House of Commons the next day, a Conservative MP for Millford-On-Sea attacked Gordon Brown, accusing him of 'raping our country for unscrupulous financial gain'. In the papers, columnists had howling debates about the countryside, asking what place landowners had in society, and whether or not the power of the building contract industry had got out of hand.

'I have no comment to make,' said a smug, oily Sid Sykes on the six o'clock news that night, after reporters ambushed him coming out of a private golf club in Essex. 'Apart from the fact that I am a victim of persecution by those lucky enough to have been born with a silver spoon in their mouths.'

Freddie, watching the bulletin, had been so incensed he'd taken off his deck shoe and flung it at the television screen. 'Utter crap,' he howled. 'We just don't want you ruining one of the most beautiful places in the country, you bloody scoundrel!'

Within twenty-four hours, the story had spread across the national press and Churchminster had become the most famous village in Great Britain. Brenda, ever with an eye for a deal, had had some commemorative 'The charms of Churchminster' tea towels printed, and was doing a roaring trade selling them at the local shop. Coach-loads of tourists were turning up every day to visit the Meadows, making a macabre stop at the rectory to see where the Revd Goody had met his untimely end, before popping into the Jolly Boot for lunch, ever hopeful that they might discover Devon Cornwall propping up the bar.

The village felt like it was under siege but everyone tried to remain stoic. 'I'm sure when the ball is over, it will all return to normal,' Angie said consolingly when Freddie came home fuming one day after a tourist had jumped out in front of his car, only to ask if he knew Liz Hurley.

'That's all very well to say, but what if they never bugger off?' huffed Freddie. 'Place is turning into bloody Disneyland!'

It was turning everyone's lives upside down, but the added interest did wonders for ticket sales. Several more A-list stars had got their agents to ring and confirm they were coming, and the remaining few tickets were quickly sold. Some even ended up being touted on the black market for extortionate amounts of money.

Donations for the auction were also coming in thick and fast. Churchminster's plight struck a cord with many in other parts of green-belt country. Angie Fox-Titt was so overwhelmed, she seriously wondered if they might actually have to start turning things down. The *Daily Star* even tracked down nineties green activist Swampy and offered him twenty grand to sit in one of the huge horse-chestnut trees in the Meadows for a month, wearing only an 'Oo-ah *Daily Star*' jock strap and a pair of hobbit ears.

One evening in early October Devon was in his study checking through his email when a new message popped up in his inbox. Devon didn't recognize the sender, but opened it anyway. The message from Jagger's people was short and sweet. He could do it!

Excited, Devon picked up the phone and called Frances's mobile, knowing the number by heart now. After several rings she picked it up. 'Hello?'

'Frances, you sexy broad, guess what? I've got some bloody great news. I think Mick's going to do a number at the ball!'

There was a slight hesitation before Frances spoke. 'Oh, that's simply marvellous!' she said politely. 'I shall inform the committee first thing tomorrow.'

Devon clocked on. 'You with his nibs? Look, I'll call you later.'

'Yes, that is correct,' she said formally.

'What are you wearing?' asked Devon mischievously.

'Yes, I am sure they will all be thrilled,' was the gracious answer.

'Not that lace bodice with the silk ribbons?' he asked and groaned theatrically down the phone.

Frances was clearly not in the mood for indulging him. 'I hope your, er, cough gets better. Ambrose and I are just with the Duke and Duchess, we're nearly at the opera. Thank you for letting me know, goodbye.' She cut him off, leaving Devon chuckling. She was going to bend his ear for that!

Sure enough, a few minutes later a text arrived from Frances. '*You shit! Am with Charles and Camilla. Make you pay for that!*' it read. Grinning, Devon texted back. '*U better!*'

At No. 5 The Green, Camilla was on her bed, re-reading the article in *Soirée*, when there was a quiet knock on her bedroom door and Calypso peered round. 'Hey, can I come in?'

Camilla moved up the bed to make room for her. 'Of course, Muffin, come in.' Calypso threw herself down and sighed dolefully.

'Is everything all right?' Camilla asked, putting the magazine down.

Calypso propped herself up on her elbows. 'I just finished with Sam.'

'Oh!' said Camilla, not really knowing how to respond. 'But I thought you two had been getting on so well . . .'

'We had, until recently,' Calypso replied. 'I don't know. I'm just like, *soooo* busy with all the ball stuff, and she was always on at me to spend more time with her. I suppose if I'd really wanted to, I would have, but I didn't, like, want to. It made me realize how different we are. She thinks this ball is really stupid, and I should just move down to Brighton with her, but, Bills, it's really important to me!'

'It is to all of us, darling,' said Camilla.

'Exactly! You know, it's made me think about a lot of things, like how lucky I am to live in a place like Churchminster and have a family like you. But Sam didn't see it that way. It was *totally* doing my head in.'

'Have you just spoken to her now?' asked Camilla.

'Yah, she went, like, mental,' said Calypso. 'Said I'd be back sucking some toff boy's knob before I knew it. Sorry, you probably didn't want to know that. It made me realize I've deffo done the right thing, though.'

'If you're happier now, then it *is* the right thing,' Camilla told her. She gave her a hug. 'At least I won't have to go out with Lola now,' she joked. 'I can't believe I gave her my number!'

'Nah, she's cool,' said Calypso. 'She did think you were pretty fit, though!'

'Can you imagine if Angus had seen us?' gasped Camilla. 'Oh, I am naughty.'

'He'd probably have started beating Lola off with his shooting stick and thrown her out to the Labradors!' said Calypso and the sisters collapsed into uncontrollable giggles.

The next morning, Frances phoned Clementine to tell her the good news about Mick Jagger. She was understandably thrilled. They had a short conversation about all the media attention, ruefully agreeing the publicity had done them wonders.

Then Frances phoned Gate Cottage to tell Harriet. Harriet had stuck pictures of the Rolling Stones on her bedroom wall when she was younger; she'd be over the moon to hear they'd got Mick.

There was no answer at the cottage. No answer on her mobile, either. Frances guessed Harriet must have gone out and accidentally left her mobile at home. She left messages on both phones, telling her daughter she had some extremely exciting news and Harriet should call her immediately.

By that evening Frances still hadn't heard from Harriet. It was *so* unlike her. Slightly irritated, Frances picked up the phone in her private sitting room and called down to her husband's study extension.

'Yes?' he barked, picking it up after the second ring.

'Did Harriet tell you she was going out anywhere today?' she asked Ambrose.

'Don't think so, she's probably still in a bit of a sulk with me,' he said gruffly. 'Why?'

'Oh, I can't get hold of her,' said Frances, suddenly feeling a bit shaky. 'I'm sure she's fine. I'll see you at eight for dinner.'

But by then, she could barely touch the light lemon sole prepared by Cook, who hadn't seen Harriet either. Despite Ambrose's assurances that Harriet was probably with friends somewhere, Frances took his golf buggy and drove down the lane to Gate Cottage. The place was in darkness. She tried Harriet's home phone again: nothing. Frances returned to the house and called Camilla. 'I am trying to get hold of Harriet. Have you spoken to her today?'

Camilla's answer only worried her all the more. 'No, we were meant to meet for lunch at the pub and she didn't turn up. I've been trying to call her all afternoon. I thought maybe she'd forgotten, but it's—'

'So unlike her,' they both chorused together.

Camilla sounded very small and frightened at the end of the line. 'Oh, Lady Fraser, do you think she's all right? It's just, after what happened to the Reverend . . .'

Frances took a moment to answer, and when she did, her voice wavered slightly. 'I'm sure she's fine,' she said unconvincingly. 'If you hear from her, will you let me know?'

She rang off and stared into the darkness outside her window. Her mother's instinct had kicked in properly now. Something was definitely wrong.

After an unbearable sleepless night, at six in the morning she tried both phones again: no answer. She pulled on a wax jacket and wellies over her silk pyjamas and walked down to Gate Cottage. It was exactly as she had left it. Frances tried the back door. It was open. Inside, the air was still and oppressive. As if on autopilot, Frances made her way upstairs to her only child's bedroom. Mouth dry, she pushed open the door, flicked on the light switch and . . .

Nothing. Harriet's bed hadn't been slept in. Harriet was normally very tidy but there were papers and clothes strewn around the room. A vase that stood in the fireplace had been knocked over, dried flowers spilling out over the carpet. Had someone else been in here? Something metallic, half-sticking out from under the bed, caught her eye. Frances knelt down to pick it up. Harriet's mobile phone, with dozens of missed calls on it from her and Camilla. Frances could feel the nausea rising in her stomach. Harriet never went anywhere without her phone. Frances couldn't pretend any longer!

She ran out of Gate Cottage and up the drive, tears streaming down her face. Rushing into the

Hall and up the stairs, she flew into her startled husband's bedroom. He listened to her frantic story and immediately called 999. Exactly twenty-one minutes later, as the village was waking up, two police cars with blue lights on wailed up the drive to Clanfield Hall.

Chapter 45

The following day dawned as if in mourning, dull, grey and wet. Down at the station, Ambrose and Frances were sitting in Chief Inspector Haddock's office waiting to be interviewed by DI Rance. No sludgy brown liquid from the coffee machine for them: they were drinking Earl Grey out of bone china cups, the tea made by Chief Inspector Haddock's secretary. He was on a day off, but had phoned through strict orders to Rance to bend over backwards to accommodate them. Now the daughter of Sir Ambrose Fraser had gone missing, things had taken on a whole new importance. Haddock was just waiting for the Super to call him, apoplectic. The new Police Commissioner Sir Rodney West was a personal friend of Sir Ambrose's.

Rance sat across the desk in front of them. He had a headache, probably brought on by the front page of the *Bedlington Bugle* that morning. 'Serial Killer In Our Midst?' screamed the headline. That was all he bloody needed! The nationals were even worse, after all it wasn't often the daughter of a baronet went missing. Rance hoped the parents hadn't seen the papers. He looked across at them.

'When did you last see your daughter?' he asked carefully.

'The day before yesterday,' said Frances. Sitting perfectly upright in a rather grotty plastic chair, Frances was wearing a navy-blue Valentino suit. As ever, her blonde chignon and make-up were immaculate. Only her pale face and slightly reddened eyes hinted at the turmoil she was going through.

Ambrose, on the other hand, couldn't keep still, and was jiggling his leg impatiently, his cheeks flushed red and raw-looking. He leaned forward. 'I don't care what it takes, man,' he yelled. 'Just find our daughter!'

Rance did not like being shouted at, but he could see the pressure the older man was under. 'Sir, we are going to do everything in our power to get her back to you,' he replied through gritted teeth. He surveyed the couple before asking his next question.

'Any reason for your daughter to run off? Any fights or arguments we should know about?'

'Of course not!' exclaimed Frances. 'I mean she did have a bit of a tiff with her father recently, but it was nothing, really.' Rance raised his eyebrows at Sir Ambrose.

'It was just about the blasted car park for this ball we're having,' he boomed. 'We had words about the best location, and I put her straight. But my wife is right, it blew over. Storm in a teacup.'

All three of them studiously avoided the subject of anything more sinister having happened. After a few more questions, Rance decided to leave it for the time being. He offered to escort them out through the station.

'It was just about the bloody car park,' Sir Ambrose muttered again as the couple walked towards their shining Bentley. His voice had suddenly become quiet and subdued. 'If she'll just come back to us, she can put the blasted thing where she bloody well wants to.'

Everyone was in the incident room looking up at the large white board. A picture of Harriet, looking sunburnt at Ascot the previous year, had been stuck up next to a photo of the Revd Goody. Photos from both bedrooms had also been blown up and pinned there. DI Rance had given a press conference that morning, in which he had gravely informed the assorted press crammed into Bedlington town hall that they were investigating the disappearance of thirty-year-old Harriet Fraser. He emphasized the police were *not* currently linking it to the murder of the Revd Arthur Goody, even though everyone in there thought differently.

'The official line is that we're keeping an open mind and still treating these as two separate inquiries,' Rance told his team. 'But behind closed doors, we could well have a double murder on our hands. We've just got to find the body.' He turned to the wall. 'Both cases have a lot of similarities. Only the master bedrooms of both properties seem to have been disturbed, indicating they may have been attacked in the night when they were asleep. We know Harriet Fraser was a neat person and we assume the Reverend kept his bedroom fairly tidy. Yet, as you will see, both rooms were left in a state of disarray, which does indicate a possible struggle with a person or people unknown. Forensics are dusting for fingerprints at Gate Cottage. As you know, two sets of prints have come back from the bedroom – the Reverend's and another we haven't been able to identify. Let's see what we get back from Gate Cottage. If we get a match, we'll know we're definitely looking at the same guy. If we come up with zilch, it may mean our killer is getting clever and has started wearing gloves. If that is the case, then we have to get him—'

'Or her,' interrupted a female detective.

'Or her,' said Rance. He continued, 'Then we'll have to get the killer another way.'

He let the others digest his words. 'All Harriet Fraser's clothes are still in her wardrobe. Including a signet ring with the family crest that her parents had made for her eighteenth. According to them, she never left the house without it. This also applies to her mobile phone, which was found under the bed. Harriet's wallet has gone missing, which means the perpetrator could have stolen it. I want one of you to get on to her bank – I think it's the same one the Queen uses – and see if her cards have been used anywhere.'

Rance dished out further orders and the meeting broke up, but not before he had instructed DS Powers and PC Penny to do the house-to-house calls again. 'Ooh, can I ask some more questions this time?' squeaked Penny.

Powers looked less than impressed at the prospect. 'Guv, do we have to?' he grumbled. 'We didn't find diddly squat last time. Maybe send someone else, eh? A fresh pair of eyes?'

'I want *your* eyes, so button it,' said Rance crossly. 'You've both got a head start, you know the patch.

So get yourselves out there again.' Powers stood up muttering, only slightly mollified at the thought of seeing Angie and Caro's chests again. He left the room with PC Penny trotting at his heels like a faithful Yorkshire terrier.

Chapter 46

Camilla was utterly distraught at her best friend's disappearance. Like Frances and Ambrose, she couldn't bring herself to think the worst had happened. The whole Standington-Fulthrope family, dreadfully upset themselves, all rallied round her. Her parents called twice a day from Barbados to check up on her and see if there was any progress on the case. Camilla started having dreadful nightmares and waking up screaming and drenched in sweat, so Calypso shared her bed on the nights she wasn't with Angus.

Camilla also handed her notice in at work. 'I was going to anyway, for the wedding.' She spent hours walking Errol Flynn, working on the ball, and feverishly cleaning No. 5 The Green. Anything that would keep her busy and stop her thinking what could have happened to her dear, dear Harriet. Her absence was like an awful, yawning chasm. The pair had been in contact every day for most of their lives; if not seeing each other, then by phone and 'Forever Friends' cards and, later on, emails and text messages. Camilla didn't know what to do without Harriet.

She couldn't face up to the fact she might be dead.

Ambrose was taking it badly as well. At night, Frances would hear him restlessly pacing the corridors of Clanfield Hall, then by day he would shut himself away in his study. A six-figure reward put up by the couple had gone unclaimed. There had been several false leads, including one from a deranged-sounding caller from Hull who said he'd seen Harriet working as a topless go-go dancer at the local working men's club. DI Rance and PC Penny had endured a hellish four-hour drive up there to find out that 'Harriet' was actually a transvestite called Helena who looked no more like Harriet Fraser than Rance did Sylvester Stallone. He had cursed about wasting police time all the way back down the M62.

A week after Harriet had disappeared, Frances had been overcome with helplessness. Desperate to feel like she was doing something, she had worked long into the night making up posters of Harriet, and the next day she had asked Jed to drive her round so she could pin them up. It had ended up taking them three days, and Frances had had so many kind words from the well-wishers she came across, it had threatened to crack her famous poise on several occasions.

The posters were pinned up on every village notice board, shop window and telegraph pole in the county. The word MISSING stood out in searing red letters, above a picture of Harriet that Ambrose had taken of her in the garden last summer. The sunlight had caught the auburn tones in her hair perfectly, and laughter danced in her eyes. Devastatingly, the posters yielded nothing. Every time Frances drove through the village and saw one of them fluttering in the breeze, every time she saw the same picture flash up on the news, she thought her heart might break into a million pieces.

With Ambrose shutting her out through his own grief, Frances tried to seek solace with Devon at Byron Heights. She had become quite fond of the Victorian monstrosity, spending hours walking in the gardens, and taking comfort in the simple, home-cooked meals Nigel made at night. Occasionally, Devon would find Frances crying on the terrace or elsewhere. Then he would sweep her up in his arms, carrying her to bed to make tender love to her, making her feel wanted and cared for, letting her forget just for a short precious time the tragedy she was going through.

Although he didn't like to talk about it to Frances at that moment, Devon's music was going from strength to strength. He'd even managed to track down the members of his old backing band, who'd all been doing their own thing for years, and persuade them to come to Byron Heights for the weekend. When the 'Three Ts' – Taz, Terry and Todge – turned up, the years fell away instantly. It was as if they'd never been apart. Like others before them, they were gob-smacked at the quality of the songs Devon was playing, and after a few bars of his second track, they had told him they were definitely in. The four of them spent all weekend in the studio reminiscing and then jamming. When they left that Sunday evening, the Three Ts had privately agreed Devon Cornwall was on the best form of his life. The public were not going to know what hit them.

The month dragged on, and so did the investigation. The police learned that Harriet had taken fifteen hundred pounds out of her bank account the day before she disappeared. But according to her mother, she had been planning on buying some new furniture for the cottage, so it could have been for that. No other transactions or withdrawals had been made. The police, armed with dozens of sniffer dogs, had made a painstaking search of the grounds of Clanfield Hall. Rance had told Sir Ambrose and Lady Fraser that he was looking for evidence, but they had all known what he was really looking for. Watching from her sitting room window as the distinctive black and white uniforms combed every inch of the estate, Frances had thought her heart might break.

One morning towards the end of October she was in her dressing gown in the powder room, applying her make-up, when there was a knock on the door. 'My dear, may I come in?' Ambrose's voice called out.

Frances was surprised: he hadn't been in that room for years. 'Of course, the door's open.'

Ambrose entered. He was wearing his staple outfit of tweed trousers, shirt and bow tie, with a dark-green wool jumper over the top. Frances thought that in the past few weeks he had aged twenty years: his face was tired and lined, the once-sparky eyes defeated and flat.

Ambrose sat down on the overstuffed chaise longue, which ran the length of one wall, and let out a long, deep sigh.

'Am I a bad man, Frances?' he asked his

wife. 'You must tell me, I know you'll be honest.'

Frances stared at him in shock. She had never heard him speak that way. 'Ambrose, of course not! My goodness, whatever makes you say that?'

Her husband appeared not to have heard her. 'I must be a bad man, to have this happen to us. Why else would it?'

'Ambrose—' Frances started, but he carried on.

'Or am I just a bad father?' He sighed again. 'Is this someone's way of punishing me? Lord knows I've been hard on Harriet over the years, but it was only because I thought it was the best thing for her.' He swallowed. 'I've been a fool, Frances, a stupid, bloody-minded old fool.' And with this, Ambrose started to cry: racking, great, unfamiliar sobs that took over his body. 'Now I might have lost the best thing that ever happened to me, and I won't ever be able to tell her that!'

Frances's eyes were welling up now, and she crossed the room to embrace her husband. They felt each other's pain but drew strange comfort from it. They were the only ones who really understood, and now they had each other again. 'We'll get through this, my darling, we've got to!' whispered Frances.

Afterwards, she knew what she had to do. When Frances went over to Byron Heights and told Devon she would always treasure their friendship, but that she could no longer carry on with its physical side, he felt he had been kicked in the stomach. But he told her he understood. He did, to a certain extent. Devon didn't have any kids, but he knew how he would feel if he lost Nigel, who was the closest to family he had. Frances was telling him she had to be there for her husband, and in a funny way, it made his feelings for her even more powerful. Her compelling decency – which had so attracted him in the first place – was back, stronger than ever.

As Frances drove away from his house that evening, she felt a mixture of sorrow and regret. It hadn't just been about sex with Devon, he'd brought out a side of her she had never known existed. The thought of never again lying in the four-poster bed at Byron Heights, lazily chatting and laughing in a post-coital glow of happiness, brought a lump to her throat. She fought back the tears and took a deep breath, steeling herself.

She was Lady Frances Fraser. She had a duty to her husband – and daughter – to invest her all in keeping the family together.

Frances wasn't the only one in the village to suddenly see life more starkly. Camilla was about to drop the most enormous bombshell on Angus. Ever since Harriet had disappeared, he'd done his best to comfort her, but unfortunately, Angus didn't possess one sensitive, empathetic bone in his entire body. He was, in his own way, extremely shaken by the disappearance of Harriet, but his idea of cheering Camilla up was driving an even bigger gulf between them. It involved trying to roger her senseless, taking her for bone-jarring rides in his old Land Rover or inviting her to play drinking games with his farming mates down the pub. Although Camilla knew he was trying to help, when Angus suggested she take all her clothes off and run round the bar setting light to her farts, she just felt infinitely worse.

It wasn't that there wasn't a decent chap under all the bluff and bluster, just that Angus struggled when it came to feelings or matters of the heart. He had only ever cried once in his life, and not at either of his parents' funerals, but long before, when he was six years old and his older cousin Edward had accidentally run over and killed Angus's rabbit Ace with a BMX bike in the farmyard. When Angus had burst into tears over the untimely demise of his beloved pet, Edward and his friends had teased him so mercilessly that the young boy had sworn to himself he would never cry again.

Camilla had already postponed her wedding-dress fitting twice, telling everybody she was too upset about Harriet. They understood, and Camilla was telling the truth, but a little bit of her did wonder guiltily if she was using Harriet as an excuse as well. If she had been feeling confused about the wedding before, she now felt a million times worse. Ironically, the only person in the world she felt she could really have talked to wasn't there. Camilla felt utterly lost.

Things finally came to a head at the end of October. The nights were drawing in, and several lashing thunderstorms had reduced the country-side to a sodden mass. The brilliant sun which had so dominated the summer crept down in the sky earlier and earlier, only occasionally throwing out milky, luke-warm rays.

Camilla and Angus were having a night in at the farm. His spring-clean hadn't lasted very long. Camilla looked round in despair at the piles of dirty washing everywhere and the muddy footprints that trailed through the house.

Angus was sitting across the kitchen table from her, boots up on the table, drinking a beer and reading a copy of *Trout Weekly*, his large goofy mouth moving slightly as he read aloud to himself. Letting out a large belch, he looked at Camilla for praise, then scratched his crotch and went back to his paper. Angus looked as happy as a pig in muck, and it suddenly dawned on Camilla that he was never going to change. Angus was happy with things as they were, but she knew she never would be.

'Angus, we need to talk,' she said nervously.

'What's that, sweet cheeks?' he said, putting down his paper. 'Does the naughty filly want little Angus to give her a good seeing-to again?'

That was enough. 'No!' she shouted, pent-up frustration and emotion pouring out.

Angus was startled. 'All right sexpot, keep your hair on. What is it, then? Bored, are you? I've got a British Lions DVD next door if you fancy it, bloody good game of rugger, that.'

It was like they were communicating in different languages, she thought despairingly. 'Angus, do you ever think we're too different?'

Angus paused to consider for a moment. 'Not apart from the fact I'm hung like a rogue elephant, with a swinging set of balls to match. But you don't want those, do you?' he chortled.

'Angus, will you stop joking for just ONCE!' she shouted. 'Please, I'm trying to talk to you.' She paused, suddenly quite weary. 'Oh, I just can't go on like this. What with Hats and now this . . .'

By now, it was sinking into Angus's thick skull that something was wrong. 'Now what?' he asked nervously.

Camilla wondered how on earth to work the conversation round. 'What do you want from life, Angus?' He looked perplexed, not being used to such searching questions.

'Well, to live on a farm and grow and shoot things, but I've got that already.' He looked around. 'Er ... to go on the beers with the chaps, maybe have a jolly in Will Thorpe-Jones's box at Twickers every year, er ...'

'Anything else?' asked Camilla pointedly.

He thought for a few seconds. 'Beat the Snifferman's record of drinking a yard of ale in 4.8 seconds. If I can do that, I'll die a happy man!' he guffawed.

Camilla looked at him. 'What about *me*?'

'What about you?' He smiled at her indulgently. 'You're my foxy little filly, who's going to live here and pop out lots of manly sons I can go shooting and hunting with. Oh, and who'll carry on the family name at Harrow. There's been an Aldershot there in every generation for the last hundred and fifty years!'

'What if I *don't* want that, though?' Camilla cried. 'Maybe I want to go and do a degree or go travelling or something instead.'

Angus looked at her blankly. 'But why would you want to do that when you've got Highlands? If you fancy getting away, we can always go up to Aunt Gwendoline's estate in Perthshire ...'

Camilla knew then there was no hope. She walked round the table and knelt by her soon-to-be-ex-fiancé, holding his bear-like, muddy paws. 'Angus, you're a wonderful man and you're going to make someone very happy,' she whispered. 'It's just not me.'

He stared at her for a second, uncomprehending. Then the blood started draining from his face. 'You're calling the wedding off?' he said shakily. Camilla nodded unhappily. 'There's no way I can convince you not to?' he asked, and she shook her head.

'Oh, I'm so sorry,' she sobbed, covering her face with her hands.

Angus pulled her into a hug; his huge body a comforting mass around her. 'Come on, old girl, don't get yourself into a state,' he said, in a tender voice she didn't think him capable of. 'Can't have you spoiling that pretty face with tears!' His own eyes brimmed for a second, but his cousin's long-ago taunts of 'Cry baby!' came to mind and he blinked them away.

Camilla pulled away and looked at him. 'You're not cross? I thought you'd hate me.'

Angus shook his huge head. 'I'd never hate you, Camilla Standington-Fulthrope.' He sighed. 'Truth is, I kind of expected it one day. I could never believe you agreed to go out with me in the first place. You're so bright and stylish and pretty . . . How a great big clod-hopper like me got his hands on you, I'll never know.' He smiled at her proudly, a flash of the old Angus back.

'Angus, please don't say things like that, they're not true,' pleaded Camilla.

'They are,' Angus said firmly. 'And if I'm honest with you, Camilla, I can't give you the things you want. You should go and travel, study ... the world's your oyster, you fine filly. As for me,' he gestured around the room. 'My world is here and I'm happy with it. It's just a pity I can't share it with you.'

The next day, Camilla rang the bridal shop and cancelled her gown. Three days after the engagement was called off, Camilla, Caro and Calypso went out to a wine bar in Bedlington. There were lots of tears, for Harriet and for Angus – and consoling hugs. By the end, after many reminiscences, among them Calypso's funny story about the time an infant Camilla had gone for a number two in one of Clementine's prized flower pots, Camilla had finally started laughing.

She ended up getting so sloshed she'd wobbled out at closing time and fallen face-first into the memorial flowerbed on the market square, right opposite the police station. DS Powers, working late inside, heard the whoops and shrieks, thought it was a local gang of troublemakers and rushed out with multiple arrests – or at least a caution – in mind. When he saw it was Caro Belmont, magnificent chest heaving with giggles as she tried to pull a pie-eyed Camilla to her feet, he offered the sisters a lift home instead. At Calypso's request, Powers even put the flashing blue siren on, the three of them helpless with laughter in the back as she made inappropriate remarks about his truncheon and helmet.

Powers dined out on the story in the staff canteen for months after, although his version had him turning them down for a threesome: 'Bit unprofessional on duty, lads, and besides, there's the wife to think of.' No one had believed him.

The next day, all three girls woke up to hideous hangovers. Feeling worst, Camilla spent all morning throwing up into a bucket by her bed, and didn't surface until lunchtime. Despite vowing never to drink again, it had been exactly the release she had needed.

Chapter 47

'More bubbles, darling?'

Lucinda Reinard offered her plastic flute up.
'Please.' As her friend Charlotte Stamford refilled
Lucinda's plastic glass with Möet, she glanced at
the sky. It was looking ominously grey: angry black
clouds scudding overhead. 'I hope it doesn't start
raining,' she said. 'Hero hasn't got her waterproof
and she hates getting wet.'

'Mmm, yah,' said Charlotte, and poured the last
of the liquid in her glass. She turned to her
husband, a beak-faced man with huge bushy eyebrows who was rummaging through the back of the
battered Volvo estate the two women were leaning
against. 'We need another bottle, Barnaby,' she
called.

'What ho, coming right up.'

'How long before they turn up, do you think?'
Charlotte asked.

Lucinda looked at her watch. 'I'd say twenty
minutes or so. We're at the halfway point.'

As well as Lucinda and Charlotte, there were a
dozen more mothers and several fathers standing
around or sitting in the front of their enormous

4×4s quaffing champagne and eating quails' eggs out of straw picnic-baskets. They were waiting for their offspring, all members of the Bedlington Valley Pony Club, to come past on their ten-mile sponsored ride to raise money for the Save Churchminster Ball and Auction Fund. Fifteen riders in total, led by the formidable District Commissioner Patricia Mountbottom. Lucinda hoped Hero was in a better mood; she'd thrown a complete fit that morning when she hadn't been able to find her best jodhpurs, and had had to settle for the navy-blue pair instead.

'Here they come!' shouted one father, and, sure enough, the distinctive green and blue jumpers of Bedlington Valley were trotting up the road towards them. Hero was at the front, a freckly, gap-toothed girl riding beside her, ginger ponytail sticking out from under her riding hat.

'Mummy, are you looking at me, ARE YOU LOOKING?' Hero bellowed as she drew nearer on Dancer. 'Mrs Mountbottom has let me and Tabitha—'

'Tabitha *and I*, darling,' corrected Lucinda. Hero drew level with the car, both she and the ginger-haired girl wearing bright red armbands.

'We've been made pack leaders because we are the best riders by miles!' boasted Hero, pulling Dancer up. She looked at Lucinda and Charlotte. 'How much are you going to sponsor me, then? Jake Winsted-Cleverly's dad is giving him a hundred pounds a mile!' At that point Jake, a small, skinny boy on a huge, brown horse that was far too big for him, thundered past, screaming, towards the main road.

'Hero! It's rude to talk about money,' reprimanded Lucinda, as Patricia Mountbottom, her huge thighs wobbling, galloped up from the back of the pack to rescue Jake.

'Heels down, Tabs,' said Charlotte, rushing over and rubbing the mud from one of her daughter's boots with the outside pages of her husband's *Daily Telegraph*.

'Where's your brother?' Lucinda asked Hero. Before she could find out, a bawling Jake was brought back, led by a grim-looking Patricia.

'*You* need to be the master, not him, Jake,' she bellowed.

'I want to go home!' wailed Jake.

'Oh, don't be such a wet lettuce,' ordered the District Commissioner, sounding like an army drill sergeant. She looked around. 'Right, are we all here, troops? Lead on!'

Hero turned around as she trotted off. 'Mummy, you'd better be at the finishing line to see me or I'll be *really* cross.'

'Little horrors, aren't they?' said Charlotte fondly, as they watched the ride go past. Lucinda tried to wave to Horatio, who she spotted riding next to a pretty, blonde, well-developed girl on a dappled grey, but he put his nose in the air and ignored her.

'Darling, I must say you are looking very trim at the moment!' remarked Charlotte, as they started to pack the car up. 'Are you still going to Fit 4 U? I hear that trainer Henry is quite a task-master in the studio!'

Lucinda could think of several ways Henry took her strictly in hand, none of which she could tell

Charlotte. Her friend leaned in conspiratorially. 'I hear he's having a hot and heavy affair with one of his clients!'

Lucinda went cold. 'Really?' she croaked. 'What makes you say that?'

Charlotte was busily packing up the picnic-hamper, oblivious to Lucinda's paling face. 'Well, Beverley – she keeps the house tidy for me – has a son Darren, who goes out with Amy, who is the sister of Becky who works in reception. Apparently Becky found a *very* saucy pair of knickers in Henry's office a few weeks ago, and empty condom packets behind the cross-trainer *two weeks running!*'

Lucinda blushed, they were normally so careful. At least she knew where the La Perla French knickers she had bought from the boutique in Bedlington had gone, the bloody things had cost her a fortune.

'Apparently, one can tell from the bulge in his shorts he has the most *enormous* member!' said Charlotte excitedly. 'Have *you* noticed it, darling? Ooh, it must be true what they say about black men.'

'Charlotte!' said Lucinda.

'What?' asked her friend. 'I'm just saying it. I'm rather jealous actually.' She turned to her husband. 'Darling, what did you say about the woman who's having it off with Henry from Fit 4 U?' Lucinda cringed. Christ – did the whole county know?

'I said, when we see a middle-aged yummy mummy in cycling shorts doing the "John Wayne" walk down Bedlington High Street, we'll know who she is. Haw haw, haw haw!' Barnaby collapsed into guffaws of laughter, his wife following suit.

Lucinda smiled weakly and pressed her legs together.

Chapter 48

Three days later Caro was unloading the Waitrose shopping bags from the 4×4 outside Mill House, when someone pinched her bottom. It made her jump, and for a fleeting second, the ridiculous thought flashed through her mind that it might be Benedict Towey. She whirled round to find her husband standing there. 'Boo,' he said softly.

'Seb!' Instinctively Caro looked at her watch to check the date. 'But it's Thursday. What are you doing back?'

Sebastian flashed his wolfish grin at her. 'What, aren't I allowed to miss my wife any more?' He looked like he'd come straight from the office: dressed in his black and white pinstripe suit, teeth dazzling against a recent spray tan. His Louis Vuitton overnight bag was casually slung at his feet.

'Of course not, it's just that I wasn't expecting you until Friday,' replied Caro, heaving the remaining bags out with no offer of help from her husband. 'I haven't got much for dinner, I was just going to have lentil soup,' she said. 'Oh! The cleaner's not coming until tomorrow, either, the house is in a complete state. Why *are* you home, darling, is there something wrong at work?'

Sebastian's grin disappeared. 'What are you, the bloody Gestapo?' he asked. 'I just fancied coming back today, OK? Anyone would think you're not pleased to see me.' He picked up his bag and stalked down the front path into the house. Caro sighed. She'd said the wrong thing again. Seb had caught her off-guard. But it was more than that, she admitted to herself. Maybe she *wasn't* that pleased to see him. Sebastian had been spending so much time in London over the past few months that Caro had got rather used to being by herself. She'd even grown to like it. Tonight, she had been looking forward to having a long, hot bath, putting on her pyjamas, and then sitting on the sofa and watching *The Devil Wears Prada* DVD she'd borrowed from Camilla. Well, that certainly wasn't going to happen now. Her arms full, Caro kicked the car door shut with her foot, looked longingly at the GU chocolate orange soufflé for one resting on top of the bags, and followed her husband inside.

Sebastian's early arrival – like most things in his life – did have an ulterior motive. Fed up with London and his mistress, he'd come home to get some TLC and undemanding company from his wife. Dear, sweet, predictable old Caro, at least she didn't give him constant shit like bloody Sabrina. Or so he'd thought, until she'd started asking him twenty bloody questions as soon as she'd clapped eyes on him. Christ!

That Monday, Sebastian and Sabrina had rowed furiously when he had let it slip that Luciana, the stunning waitress from Italy, was coming to do work-experience at his office. Actually, Sebastian had let the admission out on purpose: Sabrina had become far too bloody demanding recently. She needed a harsh reminder that there were plenty of younger, less high-maintenance options out there.

Usually Sebastian liked having arguments with her, and knew exactly what buttons to press, because of the great make-up sex afterwards. But this time, the silly bitch had actually had the nerve to throw him out of her house like he was some kind of nobody! After hissing imploring words through the letterbox, to no avail, Sebastian's pride had kicked in and he'd ended up going back to his cold, empty flat and having to make do with a cursory wank under his White Company bed sheets instead.

Sebastian had sent Sabrina conciliatory flowers the next day, even though he was boiling underneath at the way she'd treated him. But he'd learned by now that life was so much less bloody complicated when Sabrina wasn't in one of her infamous sulks. Plus, at this point his balls were swinging like bloody Space Hoppers, and the only thing to cure that would be to take full advantage of the 'all off' Californian bikini wax Sabrina was currently sporting. But the flowers had been ignored and it was only when Sebastian got his secretary to phone with an invite for dinner on the chef's table at Gordon Ramsay's restaurant the following evening that she returned his call. Stupid, selfish, spoilt Sabrina, he had thought derisively. She was so easy to read, and even easier to buy.

The evening hadn't started well. Getting ready

together at hers, Sabrina had walked in on Sebastian dying his chest hair with a home high-lighting kit from Boots. 'What the fuck are you doing?' she asked him, aghast. Mortified, he whirled around from the mirror, plastic gloves on both hands and chest hair covered in great streaks of gloopy white gunk.

'Haven't you heard of knocking, you stupid cow?' he howled. In spite of herself, she couldn't help giggling. Sebastian looked so angry and absurd with those ridiculous gloves on and a spatula in his hand! She leaned forward to look closer. My God, was that a bit of ginger? How come she had never noticed it before?

'I am not a fucking ginger!' he roared defensively, as if reading her thoughts. 'My chest hair is just a bit auburn in places, OK? I need to dye it to match the rest of my body hair.' He furiously applied another streak, watching himself in the mirror as he did so. 'Especially if you keep buying me those ridicu-lously low cashmere V-necks.'

'Don't be so fucking ungrateful,' Sabrina yelled. 'It's not my fault you're a, you're a . . .' Before she knew it, another giggle burst out.

'I am NOT a ginger. *Comprende?*' he bellowed again. By now hysterical with laughter, Sabrina fled the bathroom before he did serious damage to her with the spatula.

Two hours later, after she had spent the entire cab ride telling him redheads were sexy – 'Think of the actor Damian Lewis, darling, half of London's dying to sleep with him' – Sebastian was just about talking to Sabrina by the time they'd reached the restaurant. Anticipation of the evening that lay ahead had raised his spirits even more. His work colleague Charlie Simpson had just closed a lucrative business deal and, to celebrate, had booked Ramsay's coveted chef's table. As well as Sebastian and Sabrina, Charlie and his German wife Irina had invited Ferdinand Chatsfield, one of Charlie's polo-playing friends, and his new girlfriend, a stunning six-foot underwear model called Bunny. Sabrina was not good with competition; Sebastian knew she'd hate the model on sight.

They were met by the maître d' and led through the restaurant. Sabrina, tanned, tousled and immaculately made-up, was wearing a black cutaway dress by Julien McDonald that barely covered her gorgeous body. Revelling in the open-mouthed glances she was attracting as she pouted past a mirror, Sebastian caught sight of his own reflection in his new dark blue Oswald Boateng suit and smiled. He really was a handsome fellow! Ego fully restored, he strode through the restaurant, looking down his nose at those not so well-connected, handsome or rich enough to be able to sit at Gordon Ramsay's best table.

Then, suddenly, like an apparition in some awful nightmare, Benedict Towey was standing in front of him, wiping the corners of his mouth with a snow-white napkin. Sebastian, momentarily fazed, stood there, mouth agape. 'What are *you* doing here?' he said eventually. A nasty taste found its way into his mouth as he remembered the bitter defeat meted out to him by Towey at the Save Churchminster Fun Run. The bastard!

'Business dinner,' Benedict said coolly. 'You?' He looked pointedly at Sabrina, who was now smouldering provocatively at this mysterious, handsome stranger. God, he was gorgeous! She didn't think she'd seen such devastating good looks since an ex-boyfriend had made her watch *Butch Cassidy and the Sundance Kid* and she'd ended up lusting after a young Robert Redford. Next to this man, Sabrina thought with a stab of satisfaction, Sebastian looked positively ordinary. And the stranger really *was* a natural blond!

'Hello, I'm Sabrina,' she purred.

'Hello,' Benedict said, giving her a cursory once-over. He turned back to Sebastian, who by now was making a big show of looking round the room un-interestedly. 'Friend of yours?' Benedict asked him, unsmilingly.

'Yah, something like that,' Sebastian said nastily. 'Now, if you don't mind? We're eating at the chef's table tonight and I'd like to talk to Gordon about the menu.'

'Of course, I'm sure you'll have a wonderful dinner,' Benedict replied. 'Even if Gordon can't be there. He's not working tonight. I just spoke to him.'

'What, best friends, are you?' Sebastian snarled.

Benedict gave him an amused, quizzical look. 'I wouldn't go that far. Anyway,' he stepped back to let them pass.

Irritation, humiliation and disappointment seeping out of every pore, Sebastian gave him one final murderous look and dragged a pontificating Sabrina off in his wake.

His evening went from bad to worse when Sabrina, already shooting daggers at Bunny across the table, found out that Bunny had won a modelling contract that Sabrina herself had been coveting for weeks. 'Accidentally' spilling her red wine all over Bunny's white Balenciaga dress, Sabrina had unconvincingly pleaded a headache and stomped off home to sulk.

Back at the marital home a few days later, Sebastian was watching his wife unpack the shopping. As she leaned up to put something away, her top rose up, showing off her slender shape. Sebastian ran his eyes over her lasciviously. 'Have you been on a diet?' he asked. Caro turned round to face him, a packet of couscous in one hand. She blushed, it made her look endearingly pretty.

'Not really, I've just been watching what I eat,' she half-lied, not having the courage to tell him it was because she was so bloody miserable.

Sebastian slipped off the bar-stool he'd been sitting on and made his way towards her. Caro looked at him uncertainly, almost fearfully. 'It's all right darling, I'm not going to bite,' he whispered. 'Not yet, anyway.' He was pressed against her now, his hands running greedily over her body. 'You look fucking sexy,' he told her, as his hand slid up her jumper and into her bra.

Caro winced as he tweaked her nipple roughly, his tongue hot and insistent in her ear. This was what she'd wanted for months, wasn't it? To have physical contact with her husband, to feel wanted and loved again. But there wasn't an ounce of affection in his touch. Caro wished he would just leave her alone. She could feel his rock-hard manhood pressing against her, and knew she should unzip his trousers and take it in her mouth, enthusiastically pleasuring him the way she used to. But instead she just kissed him back half-heartedly, arms hanging by her sides as if paralysed.

Sebastian groaned and slid his hands into the front of her knickers. Caro winced again as he stuck two fingers up her. 'You're as dry as a bone!' he exclaimed. 'Make a bloody effort, darling.' He plunged them up her again, merciless and probing.

Caro couldn't stand it any longer. 'Get off, GET OFF!' she shouted and pushed him away from her. Shock, then confusion, and finally contempt crossed his face.

'What the fuck is wrong with you?' he asked coldly.

'You haven't laid a finger on me in months, and then you just turn up and expect it *like that*?' Caro was crying now, but she was angry too. 'It's not on, Sebastian!'

He stared at her, arms folded across his chest. 'Well, what do you want, *darling*? First you're moaning I don't come near you, then when I do, you act like a frigid fucking bitch! I mean, cut me some slack here! What am I supposed to think?'

'What *about* bloody you?' Caro shouted at him. 'It's always about you! What about *me*? What about your son? You spend so little time here, you're like a bloody stranger to him.'

As if on cue, Milo started crying in his nursery upstairs. Sebastian took a step towards her and then stopped. His face was an icy mask. 'That's a bit rich coming from you,' he sneered. 'Every time I come home or ring, that bloody baby is crying in

330

the background. Handling him a bit roughly, are you?'

That was enough. Caro took the nearest thing she could find – the packet of couscous – and threw it at Sebastian. It hit him squarely on the head, and he flinched as it burst open, grain spraying all over the kitchen.

'How DARE you!' she screamed at him, shaking with rage. 'Get out with your disgusting insinuations. Go on, get OUT!'

Sebastian thought about going over to calm her down, but there was a strange, wild look in his wife's eyes that made him stop. 'Suit yourself,' he said contemptuously, and went over to pick up his bag and the keys to his Aston Martin. He had an old school friend who lived near Oxford in a stately home; he'd crash there. Not that he'd tell Caro that. He wanted her to lie awake racked with guilt all night, wondering if he was shivering in a lay-by somewhere.

As he drove off, Sebastian thought about his week. Kicked out by the mistress *and* the wife! He laughed out loud. The boys were going to have a field day with this one. Who'd have thought Caro had it in her? At least it spiced things up a bit at home, and he'd win her over soon enough.

Back at the house, Caro held a now-sleeping Milo to her chest. Silent tears streamed down her face. She couldn't go on like this.

Chapter 49

'Night, princess, speak soon, yeah?'

'Goodnight, Devon, I'll call you when I can. Look, I'm going to have to go, Ambrose is calling me. Bye for now.'

There was a click and a dialling tone. Frances had gone. Devon slowly put the receiver down. Even though the physical side of their relationship had stopped, they still found strength in phone calls to each other. God, she was a gutsy woman. Frances had thrown herself into running the Hall, preparing for the ball, looking after her husband and ringing the police every day to find out if they had learned anything new about her daughter. Devon didn't know how she was coping, but he knew he couldn't have handled it. He was also worried Frances was living in denial.

'Until they find a body, I won't think any different,' she had told Devon shakily a few nights ago.

But by now Devon, like the majority of the village, was convinced Harriet had been bumped off by the Revd Goody's murderer. It had become an open secret. No one dared bring it up in earshot of the Frasers or even the Standington-Fulthropes, but they were all thinking it. Harriet was such a sweet, home-loving girl. How could she just disappear into thin air?

Just after eleven o'clock that night, Freddie was climbing into his Land Rover outside the Maltings. Angie had retired to bed with a copy of *Homes and Gardens*, and Archie had been in his bedroom with Tyrone for hours, the familiar thud of music accompanied by incense smoke wafting gradually downstairs.

For most of the evening, Freddie had been working on his accounts in the study at the bottom of the stairs. He had thought it strange that, even after Angie had cooked him the most delectable duck for dinner and he'd finished it off with his usual biscuits and cheese, he was having the most incredible cravings for sweets. Freddie was salivating at the thought of Yorkie bars and Fruit Gums, all washed down with a chocolate milkshake. After a disappointing rummage through the cupboards and fridge, his cravings became so strong that there was only one thing for it: a late night trip to the Texaco garage on the outskirts of Bedlington. He put on his waxed jacket and opened the front door.

Outside, the crisp night air hit him like a sledgehammer. Christ, he felt weird! Spaced out, was that what they called it? Maybe he was coming down with something. Struggling to fit the key in the car door, Freddie eventually climbed in.

Fifteen minutes later, he was wandering around the harshly lit aisles of the Texaco garage. He homed in on the confectionery. With their brightly coloured wrappers lined up and glinting at him, they looked like rows of glittering jewels. He no longer knew what he fancied, but wondered if that was because he suddenly fancied everything. Freddie started throwing bars of chocolate into his basket. Dime bars, a box of Roses, family-sized bags of Revels. Eventually, he made his way to the checkout. Now, where was his wallet?

There was a giggle behind him in the queue. 'Check it out, that old geezer has got some *serious* munchies!' Freddie turned around to find two teenage girls in tracksuits and matching ponytails staring at him.

'Hmm, what's that? Munchies?' he said absently. 'I've got a packet of them in here somewhere.' He turned around again, patting his pockets. Where was his blasted wallet? He just couldn't bloody remember.

The two girls burst out laughing. 'He is *off* it!' one of them cackled. Freddie eventually found his money and slowly counted out £28.73p for the bemused cashier. 'Sure you don't want some *Rizlas* with that?' the girl said, and they both cracked up laughing again. Freddie peered at them hazily through bleary eyes; their voices sounded miles away. Like they were underwater. Extraordinary. Shaking his head he delved deep into a packet of chocolate-covered raisins and made his way back to his car. It was parked haphazardly on the forecourt with the windows open.

Freddie climbed in and drove off slowly, forgetting to put his headlights on. By Jove, the Snickers bar was good. He couldn't get it in his mouth fast enough! After a few minutes, the country lanes once again yawned open ahead of him. He didn't know if it was his eyesight, but he was finding it damned hard to concentrate. Now, where was that green triangle one in the Roses?

Suddenly, blue lights appeared in his rear-view mirror, accompanied by the wailing of police sirens. A car chase, thought Freddie dreamily. For some reason he burst out laughing and, with some difficulty, pulled the Land Rover over into a grassy lay-by and waited for the police car to pass. But to his surprise, it stayed behind him, lights flashing insistently in his mirror. Freddie cut the motor. Must have a flat tyre, he thought, pulling out a caramel toffee with which to ponder the situation.

Moments later, there was a rap on the window. Freddie wound it down and peered out into the gloom. He was confronted by a stern DS Powers and red-nosed PC Penny.

Powers took in his red, unfocused eyes and the discarded sweet wrappers all over the passenger seat. 'Do you know why we stopped you, sir?' he asked grimly.

Freddie shrugged, his mouth half full. 'No idea, officer, got a flat have I? Can I offer you a sweet?' He thrust a box of chocolates in Powers's face.

'No, thank you.' DS Powers slapped away PC Penny's gloved hand, hovering hopefully around the sweets, and fixed Freddie with his scariest police officer look. 'You were driving erratically. Not only that, you have no lights on. Were you aware of that?'

'Golly, no!' replied Freddie, more intent on looking for the giant-sized fruit and nut bar he knew he'd bought. Locating it in the plastic carrier bag, he pulled it out. 'I like a good nut, don't you?' For some reason, Freddie found this hysterically funny and started chortling uncontrollably.

'This one's away with the fairies, isn't he?' Penny whispered excitably.

Powers had seen enough. 'All right Penny, let's get him out. By the look of it, he's stoned out of his mind.' He sighed, what with the missing body and now poshos on the funny fags, he wondered what this sodding place was going to throw up next.

Freddie caught the tail end of his sentence. 'Hang on, you're going to stone me?' he said indignantly. 'That's a bit much, I only had the bloody headlights off!'

Powers opened the driver's door and pulled Freddie out. 'Ow, what are you doing?' Freddie stood unsteadily as Penny leaned across him, pulling the keys out of the ignition and pocketing two Ripples in the process.

Powers shone a flashlight into Freddie's eyes, then leaned in and sniffed him, like a bloodhound. The sweet, heavy smell of marijuana was unmistakable on his clothing. Satisfied, Powers snapped the torch off, facing Freddie with an iron grip on his arm.

'You're accompanying me down to the station, sunshine, on suspicion of driving whilst under the influence of Class B drugs.'

Freddie stared at him, uncomprehending. *'What?'*

Powers tightened his grip. 'Don't make this worse for yourself. Penny, put this gentleman in the back of the car and mind his head while you do it. And no, you can't handcuff him.'

*

It was 1 a.m. before Angie turned up in her pyjamas and full-length wax jacket at Bedlington police station. She was in a state of shock, having been woken by a phone call informing her that her husband was being held in one of the cells.

'But I don't understand, what's he done?' Angie wailed to the grumpy desk sergeant who was fantasizing about his warm bed. 'Fred's never been in trouble in his life. Oh, this must be some kind of horrible mistake!'

DS Powers appeared at the sergeant's shoulder. 'Are you Angelica Fox-Titt, spouse of one Frederick Fox-Titt of the Maltings, Churchminster?'

'Yes!' Angie cried. 'Where's Freddie? What's going on?'

'Madam, if you'll come this way,' said Powers ominously and led Angie through to one of the interview rooms.

'He's done *what*?' asked an appalled Angie five minutes later. She was sitting next to her husband, who was slumped beside her, moaning slightly.

'Smoking drugs? *Freddie?*' She stared into her husband's face, finally recognizing the dopey expression and bloodshot eyes for what they really were. 'Oh Fred! In our house! With Archie there! What on earth were you thinking?'

Freddie was finally coming out of the stupor that had gripped him all evening. 'Drugs? What are you going on about?' he cried. 'I just got a bit peckish, that's all!'

DS Powers ignored him, leaning in towards Angie. 'Mrs Fox-Titt, can you remember when the first signs of your husband's drug abuse started?'

'Now hang on a minute—' started Freddie.

'Mood swings, irritability, secretive or out-of-character behaviour?' Powers continued.

Angie thought for a moment. 'None of these things!' she said desperately. 'He'd got a bit absent-minded recently, but I thought it was early onset dementia.'

'Thanks very much!' Freddie said indignantly.

Powers wasn't giving up yet. 'Any drugs para-phernalia stashed away in his sock drawer?' he persisted. 'You've never come across the smell of unfamiliar smoke in your home?'

Angie looked at Freddie. He shrugged, utterly confused. 'I suppose the only smoke I've smelt is from my son Archie's incense candles,' she said apologetically.

'Bloody things, they stink my study out,' grumbled Freddie.

'I have asked him to open his window and get a bit of fresh air in,' Angie told Freddie.

He rolled his eyes. 'You're all right darling, you can escape to your shop! I'm stuck at home with those hippy candles burning like funeral pyres all day long. I don't know why people like them, they give me a right bloody headache.'

Powers was watching this exchange with mount-ing interest. He fixed Freddie with a questioning eye. 'Mr Fox-Titt. You are categorically saying that you do not use marijuana, even though you are showing clear signs of being exposed to it?'

'I certainly don't!' said Freddie.

Powers and Penny looked at each other and then back at the Fox-Titts. 'This son of yours,

Archie, is it? How old is he?' asked the detective.

'Seventeen,' replied Angie impatiently. 'But I don't see what this has got—'

Powers cut her off. 'And these funny smelling incense candles? How long has he been burning them in your house?'

Angie and Freddie looked at each other again, their minds frantically working overtime. Archie, their only child, who, in recent months, had become withdrawn, moody and unsociable. The light switch finally flicked on. Angie's face drained of colour and her eyes brimmed with tears. 'My baby!' she sobbed into her hands.

'The little sod!' Freddie yelled. 'I'm going to bloody kill him!'

The Fox-Titts left the police station at 3.04 a.m. Once he had established that Freddie was an unknowing victim of passive smoking, DS Powers had exercised his discretionary powers and released him without charge. The couple sat in silence as Angie drove home, and before she had pulled up outside the house Freddie was already opening his door. 'Oh Fred, can't this wait until tomorrow?' Angie pleaded. They were both so tired and over-wrought, she didn't think she could handle a showdown with her son right now.

Freddie looked back at her, his mouth set in a straight line. 'Sorry, darling, it can't.'

Angie sighed: 'OK, let me park the car. Let's do this together.'

Even hours later, they could detect the rank, sweet smell inside that had been perfuming their house for so many months. Incense candles, their son had told them. I know better now, thought Freddie grimly.

As he walked up the stairs, Angie close behind him, the smell became stronger. Freddie was at Archie's door and turning the handle before he knew it. He fumbled for the switch along the wall and flicked it on. Harsh light flooded the room.

The room stank. Lying on his bed on top of the covers, face down and fully clothed, with the end of a gone-out joint in one dangling hand, was Archie. He was dribbling, a large pool of spit collecting next to his mouth on the duvet. Sitting on a bean bag in the corner was Tyrone, fast asleep, his head back and mouth open. Angie gasped, the place was a pit! Magazines, Rizla papers and empty beer cans were strewn everywhere, the remains of a takeaway pizza on the floor in front of them. In the middle of the chaos was a small clear plastic bag, half-full of what looked like dried herbs. Freddie scooped it up.

Neither boy stirred, then after a few moments Tyrone slowly opened one bleary eye. Trying to focus on Freddie and Angie, he yawned loudly. 'What's with the light, man? Easy now!'

That was it. 'All right you two, up. UP!' roared Freddie. He went over and shook his son roughly by the shoulders. Archie moaned but didn't wake up. Freddie got a pint glass of half-drunk water that was sitting on the chest of drawers, and emptied it over his son's head.

It did the trick. Archie jumped up, awake now and in shock, his top soaking and hair plastered to his head. He stared indignantly at his father. 'What are you doing? I'm all wet!' Suddenly aware of

Tyrone's presence, he sucked his teeth derisively at his parents and looked at his friend. 'Check out the olds. Aggro!'

'Stop that bloody awful rap star act when we've given you a perfectly good education!' Freddie shouted.

Archie flinched. His dad was seriously het up. 'What are you doing in here?' he asked, sounding sulky and slightly more contrite.

'What are *you* doing, more like,' thundered Freddie. 'Smoking drugs in my house!' Archie's eyes widened momentarily and he scanned the room in panic. 'Looking for this?' Freddie asked him, thrusting the bag in his face.

Flattened by his father's rare show of anger, Archie looked to his mother for support. But Angie bit her lip and turned away, disappointment and unhappiness in her eyes. Archie turned back to Freddie and spread his hands in a placating gesture. 'Dad, I can explain . . .'

'Explain what, exactly? The fact that you've been smoking drugs under my roof while your mother and I feed you, clothe you and send you to bloody college? I've just been pulled over by the police and very nearly arrested because I've been inhaling all the smoke that's stinking out the house.'

Tyrone whooped. 'You got pulled over by the Feds? Bruv, respect!' He went to high-five Freddie but was met by a look that could have curdled milk. He shrank back into the bean bag instead.

Freddie continued. 'You've put yourself at risk, me at risk, your mother at risk . . . I ought to bloody lynch you!'

'Dad, I'm sorry!' pleaded Archie, on the verge of

tears now. 'Honestly, I didn't mean to upset you and Mum.'

'It's too late for that,' Freddie said ominously. 'You are grounded indefinitely.'

'You can't do that!' howled Archie, 'I'm seventeen!'

'I can, if I confiscate your car and stop your allowance. You'll get a lift to and from college and that's it. If you aren't back in your room by seven o'clock every night doing your homework, the car and allowance are gone for good. Understood?'

The fight had gone from Archie, and he nodded moodily just as a loud snore shattered the tense standoff in the room. They all turned to face the sleeping Tyrone. 'I want him gone by morning, Archie,' Freddie told his son. 'He's been nothing but bloody trouble.' With that, suddenly exhausted by the last few hours, he ushered his wife from the room and they finally went to bed.

The next morning Freddie, worried the drugs might have seriously affected Archie's brain, phoned the college from his study to enquire how Archie's studies were going. He was horrified to hear his son hadn't been to a lesson in two months. 'We thought he'd left. A shame because he was a bright boy,' Archie's genial form tutor told him.

'I can assure you he hasn't,' Freddie informed him grimly. 'He'll be in first thing on Monday. I want every free hour of his timetable filled so he can catch up. Can you see to it?' The tutor gave his word he would and Freddie hung up. Sighing, he ran his hand over his face and thought about the morning's events. Tyrone had slunk out early,

342

Freddie had flushed the rest of the drugs down the downstairs loo, and Archie was still sulking in his bedroom, probably vowing never to speak to his parents again. Freddie leaned back in his big, leather desk chair and sighed again. Children, who'd have them? At least he wouldn't be putting on any more weight, now he'd stopped mindlessly shovelling down grilled Mars bar toasties. What had those two girls called it, 'the munchies'? Shuddering at the thought, Freddie vowed to go on a diet until Christmas.

Chapter 50

On Saturday, 31 October, the Jolly Boot put on a Hallowe'en party, 'fancy dress optional'. Jack and Beryl had spent hours decking the pub out like a ghoulish grotto, and it looked fantastic. The ceiling was covered with midnight-blue sheets, dotted with hundreds of silver stars. Green and purple lights cast an eerie glow over the bar. Through one of Jack's old mates, who worked in a travelling theatre, they'd managed to secure a huge painted backdrop of Dracula's castle, sat high atop a craggy cliff, ferocious-looking wolves circling the wild land below. It was stretched across an entire wall, and Beryl had added her own touches, adorning it with rubber snakes and spiders. In one corner sat two large plastic buckets, waiting to be filled up with water for an apple-bobbing competition, a chalkboard hanging on the wall above to mark the contestants' results.

Much to Pierre's horror the normal menu had had to make way for Bat Burgers, Pumpkin Eye Pie and Scary Soup. He had thrown a hissy fit and refused to cook, complaining that if any of his fellow Michelin-starred friends heard about this, he would be an industry laughing-stock. Jack, mindful of keeping his star attraction happy, had given Pierre the night off and pulled in his deputy head chef Sammy instead.

While her parents had been running around downstairs preparing for the party, Stacey Turner had been upstairs trying on her costume. A few of the local lads she fancied were coming tonight – but she also wanted to show that Jed Bantry *exactly* what he was missing out on. Stacey had decided to go as Elvira, Mistress of the Dark. Her blonde hair was covered by a waist-length, straight black wig and she'd spent an hour on each eye perfecting the Gothic, catlike make-up. Then there was the dress. Put simply, if Stacey had gone out in any town centre that night wearing it she would have been arrested for causing a public disturbance. Made of purple velvet, it was a long, floor-skimming creation that indecently hugged every overripe curve of her body. Two thigh-length slits either side gave a flash of her lacy black knickers every time she reached for a glass, but the *pièce de résistance* was the neckline. It was so low and plunging, a drop-jawed male could see a flash of a nipple if he waited long enough. Finally, just in the almost impossible event her chest wasn't getting enough attention, Stacey had added a long, blood-red pendant that nestled glittering in her cleavage like the Holy Grail. As she looked in the mirror in her bedroom for the umpteenth time, she felt very pleased with the outfit indeed.

Her father had other ideas. 'Bugger me, you are NOT wearing that!' he croaked in shock as she sashayed down at seven o'clock that night to start

345

behind the bar. Jack, in a pirate's hat and Beryl's eyeliner, was giving the bar a last wipe down. He was dressed as his namesake Jack Sparrow from *Pirates of the Caribbean*, while his wife, in a large pointy hat and swishing black gown, looked maturely delectable and witch-like.

'I *so* am!' said Stacey testily to her father. 'What's wrong with it?'

'You might as well be topless with a flashing sign above your head saying "Look at my tits!" ' he told her hotly. 'Beryl, she can't serve punters looking like this. We're not a bleeding knocking shop!'

His wife came bustling around the corner, bags of coins for the till in her hands. She cast a quick, practised eye over her daughter. 'I think she looks pretty, Jack,' she said. Stacey flashed a triumphant glance at her father, but he was standing firm.

'We are not opening until you go and put something more decent on,' he told her.

'Daaad!' Stacey stamped her foot, bottom lip starting to wobble. She turned to Beryl. 'Mum, tell him!'

Beryl knew to expect an all-out screaming match if she didn't defuse the situation. She stepped forward and tugged Stacey's dress up a few inches. 'There, that's better! Stace, if I see you pulling that neckline down there'll be trouble for you, my girl.' Beryl turned to Jack. 'She hasn't got time to go and change now, so please just leave it,' she said soothingly. 'Besides, we don't want her in a sulk all night, frightening off the customers.'

Jack sighed; he knew when he was losing a battle. 'If I see those knockers hanging out over the bar, there'll be no tips for you tonight,' he warned Stacey.

'Yes, Dad,' she said obediently, the spark in her eye suggesting otherwise.

Beryl checked her watch. 'Blimey, it's ten past. We'd better get the doors open.'

By nine o'clock the place was packed. It seemed the whole village and beyond had turned out. Even Devon had been cajoled by Nigel into coming along.

'I don't like things like that,' Devon had told his PA when he had suggested it earlier that day.

'Oh come on, party-pooper,' Nigel had said, a firm look on his face. 'It will be good for you to mix with the locals, especially with the ball coming up.'

'Don't remind me,' Devon had replied gloomily. Everything had gone like a dream for him up until now, but he was starting to have a nasty attack of nerves. Several times over the last fortnight, Devon had woken from an awful nightmare in which he was playing in front of the Queen at the ball, but every time he opened his mouth to sing, the nursery rhyme 'The Grand Old Duke of York' came out instead. At breakfast, exhausted and hollow-eyed, he had recounted his fears to Nigel. 'What if it's an omen? What if it's someone's way of saying I'm going to be the biggest fuck-up in music history?' Of course Nigel had told him he'd be no such thing and he was bound to be feeling a bit nervous, but privately even Nigel had been having doubts. Was Devon ready for something like this again? He'd always suffered from performance anxiety, but Nigel had never seen his boss so jittery.

*

As it turned out, Devon was having a good evening. Nigel, rather at home in a blonde wig and satin cocktail dress, was listening agog to Angie Fox-Titt recount a bizarre tale about a local legend called Sir Jonas 'Mad Dog' Winterbottom. Devon hadn't wanted to be Fred Astaire to Nigel's Grace Kelly, so he stood by the bar in normal dress taking in the atmosphere. He'd avoided coming down here so far, not wanting to be stared at all night or given any hassle. But people constantly came up to him, just to wish him luck for the ball and to say how excited they were about seeing him perform. Devon was rather touched. He'd had so many drinks bought for him, he'd had to ask Jack to hide them behind the bar.

Most people were in fancy dress. Camilla and Calypso looked horrifically funny with blackened teeth, false warty noses and gaudy, voluminous pantomime dresses. 'We've come as the Ugly Sisters, although Camilla didn't have to try too hard,' giggled an increasingly sozzled Calypso to anyone who would listen. Lots of people commented on how nice it was to see Camilla out and about again, before whispering something about Harriet in a sad undertone. In actual fact, Camilla had almost backed out at the last minute. Harriet had always loved fancy dress and had once spent two weeks hand-stitching a giant caterpillar costume for their end-of-term sixth-form party. Camilla, overcome by sorrow and guilt about going out and having fun without her, had been given a firm talking-to by Calypso and sent off to get changed into her outfit.

Lucinda and Nico had come as the Two

Musketeers, while Freddie and Angie, minus a grounded Archie, had looked resplendent as Rhett Butler and Scarlett O'Hara in costumes they'd somehow borrowed from the BBC costume department. There was a hairy moment when one of Angie's skirts caught on a candle and started to smoulder, but luckily a nice young gentleman dressed as the camp policeman from 'YMCA' was at hand with his novelty NYPD water pistol.

Sebastian had seen the party as the perfect chance to show off his honed physique, and had hired a very realistic Superman outfit from the fancy dress shop in Cirencester. Most men would feel – and look – ridiculous dressed in a skintight body-suit complete with blue pants and red boots, but Sebastian was positively revelling in it. Caro had made her own cat outfit and was now feeling very self-conscious in a black leotard, her whiskers and ears made out of cardboard. It had looked all right in the comfort of her bedroom, but now, in this crowded bar, if one more person pulled on her tail and said 'Nice pussy', she was going to swipe at them with her claws.

Caro's bad mood was also attributable to her husband. A few days after their blazing row Sebastian had managed to talk her round. Now in an uneasy truce, the tension between them simmered unbearably close to the surface. While Sebastian thrived on it, it was slowly killing Caro. As she looked across the bar and saw him flirtily flicking his cape over his shoulder and chatting up Stacey, she felt like walking straight out of the door and going home.

*

Her sisters, on the other hand, were having a whale of a time. Leaving Calypso showing an astonished group of young men from Bedlington how to light a cigarette using only her toes, Camilla stumbled out into the corridor to go to the loo. Feeling a bit tiddly, she pulled her skirt up with some difficulty and sat down on the toilet. Angus suddenly flashed into her thoughts. She had been a bit worried he might turn up, but to his credit he had temporarily removed himself from the scene. Camilla was grateful for that, and her heart ached at his unfamiliar thoughtfulness.

She pulled up her knickers, pulled the chain and wobbled out of the cubicle. Washing her hands at the sink, Camilla caught sight of her reflection. Cripes, she thought, I really do look hideous! Lucky I'm not about to meet my Prince Charming! She laughed to herself, drying her hands on a paper towel. She opened the door, stepped out into the corridor, and nearly went flying as she collided with a tall, lean figure in an all-in-one skeleton suit, complete with grinning skull's face. 'Oops, sorry!' she giggled as the skeleton went to catch her. 'Bit too much to drink.'

The skeleton remained silent as it slowly peeled off its facemask. Underneath was Jed Bantry, face chiselled and black hair tousled, his extraordinary eyes taking her in.

'Oh!' said Camilla, not knowing what to say. 'It's you.'

'Are you OK?' Jed asked her, still holding her by the elbow. 'You banged your head on the door just then; is it hurting?'

Camilla had never heard him say such a long

sentence before. 'Er, yes, I'm fine,' she said, rubbing her head for bumps.

Jed stepped closer. 'Here, let me,' he said softly, and before she knew it she could feel his strong fingers gently caress her head. Standing this close, she could also smell the spicy, masculine scent of his aftershave and feel the warmth from his body. Her skin turned to goose-bumps. The moment seemed to go on for ever, and then he pulled away and looked at her. His eyes almost drove through her with their intensity, and Camilla felt completely powerless to look away. At that moment the door to the bar swung open, filling the corridor with noise. The spell was broken. Self-consciously, she stepped away from him.

'Oh, excuse *me*!' cried a sarcastic voice. Suddenly Stacey was in front of them, voluptuous and seething.

'I just bumped my head, Jed was helping me,' stuttered Camilla, remembering when she'd caught them unawares at the French evening.

Stacey raised a theatrical eyebrow. 'So? Why are you telling me?' With an imperious look at Jed, she swept into the Ladies.

Camilla started edging away, not entirely sure what had just happened. 'Er, I'd better be getting back.'

Jed stared at her again, holding her gaze. 'Just be careful, all right?' he said, something unfathomable dancing across his eyes.

Back in the bar, Caro was downing her fourth glass of Dom Perignon when the door to the pub swung open, bringing with it a cold wind. Automatically, everyone shivered and turned to see who it was.

Standing on the doorstep, legs astride and hands on his hips, was Benedict Towey. Dressed in a Superman outfit exactly the same as Sebastian's, his body was taut, powerful and rippling. He looked like a natural-born super-hero, and there were 'Oohs' of admiration from several females around the room.

Benedict stepped back and held the door open. A stunning girl glided in dressed as Cleopatra, her eyes bewitching against a jet black wig, and her toned, sensuous body shown off perfectly in a white toga dress that looked like it had come straight off the rack at Gucci.

As she watched them make their way to the bar, so perfectly in tune and familiar with one another, Caro wondered why she felt so wretched. Maybe it was because they clearly had what she and Sebastian didn't, she thought, watching Benedict tenderly brush a stray hair from the woman's face.

Before she knew it, her husband was at her shoulder positively fuming. 'I can't believe that twat has got the same costume as me!' he spat furiously. 'Stupid bloody cow in the shop told me there was only one. I'm getting a refund, that's for sure.' He stared at Benedict and then turned to his wife. 'I look better than him, don't I?'

'Yes, darling.' They both knew it was a blatant lie. Benedict had the kind of God-given body that no amount of hours in the gym could match.

As he paid for the drinks, Benedict scanned the room, eyes soon resting on them. He said something to the beautiful girl, and to Caro's mortification they headed over, Benedict's hand resting in the small of her back.

'Hi,' he said moments later, holding out his hand. For one excruciating moment, it didn't look like Sebastian would take it, then he grabbed it, squeezing as hard as he could.

'Towey,' he said ungraciously. 'Nice outfit, although my wife here was just telling me how much better I look in it than you.'

Benedict looked at Caro, one eyebrow raised in a slight look of amusement. 'Were you, indeed?' he asked.

'Er, it wasn't like that, exactly,' said Caro, feeling more stupid than ever in her amateur costume. She turned to the girl. Close up she was even more ravishing. 'You must be Benedict's girlfriend, I love your outfit,' she told her.

The girl let out a delightful peal of laughter. 'He'd be lucky! But thank you for the compliment.' She noticed Caro's perplexed expression and quickly added, 'He's my brother.'

'Oh, I see,' said Caro, annoyed at how relieved she felt.

The girl stuck out her hand. 'I'm Amelia, I've heard lots about you.' She had an air about her that put Caro at ease.

'Have you?' she laughed, shaking Amelia's hand and shooting a quizzical glance at Benedict. 'Not all bad, I hope!'

Amelia smiled. 'Of course not.' Her gaze travelled on to Sebastian and cooled slightly. 'I've heard lots about *you*, too.' Sebastian's lips curled up into a smile; he didn't quite know what to make of her.

'I think you've said enough for now, little sis,' said Benedict, giving her a gentle warning look. 'Let's go and get some food, I'm starving.' He added curtly to Caro and Sebastian, 'Have a good evening.'

'Nice to meet you, Caro,' Amelia shouted over her shoulder as Benedict propelled her away.

'You, too!' Caro called after her. 'She seemed lovely,' she said to Sebastian.

'If you ask me, she's just as full of it as her brother.' He sniffed dismissively and looked at his empty glass. 'Go and get me another drink, will you?'

At midnight the party was in full swing, and no one seemed to have any intention of going home. Jack Turner had already had to prise apart a pair of fornicating pumpkins he'd found in the disabled toilet. Freddie was so drunk he'd fallen asleep face first in his Scary Soup, and had to be pulled out and shaken by Angie until he showed signs of consciousness again.

Someone else was feeling the effects of all the booze, as well. Devon, more than a little tipsy and already regretting the hangover that would surely follow, had somehow been coaxed by Calypso into singing her one of his new songs. After protesting for five minutes he'd finally given in. 'This is a song about someone who means a helluva lot to me,' he had told her. Taking a deep breath, both physically and metaphorically, he had tentatively eased into the first verse of 'Heart Catcher'. He'd never felt so vulnerable, without instruments or his backing band; just him on his own, to be judged accordingly.

As it happened, his fears were misplaced. The effect was spellbinding. One by one the rowdy crowd fell silent as his voice – raw, powerful and haunting – filled the very eaves of the building. Devon could feel that high he remembered from years ago as he opened his soul and held the audience in the palm of his hand. They were reacting just as he wanted them to. Jack and Beryl stopped working for the first time that night, and swayed against each other behind the bar. Lucinda Reinard, sitting on her husband's knee, whispered intimately to him during certain lyrics in the song. When Devon finished and trailed off uncertainly, the room remained quiet. Then, suddenly, somebody cheered – and the whole place erupted.

'Devon, that was like, totally amazing!' gasped Calypso, wiping a tear away, as Devon was besieged by people congratulating him and slapping him on the back. Through the hubbub, he searched for Nigel, and found him staring back across the bar, his eyes brimming with pride. They smiled at each other in understanding. Something big had happened here tonight.

Over in the apple-bobbing corner, things were taking a decidedly dangerous twist. The game had proved hugely popular and people had been queuing up all night to take part. So far, Babs Sax's date, a young man dressed as Lester Piggot complete with a full-sized fake horse, was in the lead, with six apples pulled out in one minute.

After avoiding him all evening, Sebastian was immensely annoyed to find himself standing next to Benedict Towey. 'Come on, chaps, let's have a

Superman stand-off!' said Brenda Briggs's husband Ted, who was manning the corner and writing up scores on the board. Just as Sebastian was about to tell the silly old sod where to shove his apples, Benedict turned round and faced him.

'Up for it?' he asked casually, but there was no mistaking the challenge in his eyes. The gauntlet had been well and truly thrown.

'You bet,' Sebastian replied viciously.

Both men knelt down in front of their respective buckets. By now, quite a crowd was gathering. It wasn't every day one saw two Lycra-clad Supermen engaging in an apple-bobbing contest.

'Right gents, you know the rules,' said Ted. 'As many apples as you can get out, using only your mouth, in one minute. No hands, feet or any other foul play. On your marks, get set, GO!'

Sebastian plunged his head into the water. It was freezing cold, making him gasp. He realized the carefully styled kiss-curl on his forehead would be ruined, and his desire to whip Towey's arse burned even more. Looking across at his adversary, he saw he already had his perfect teeth clamped around an apple and was manoeuvring it to the side of the bucket to get it out.

Sebastian whipped his head back into his own bucket; he was damned if he was going to let that bastard Towey beat him twice in a row! At first it seemed an impossible task as the apples merrily floated away, but finally he managed to secure his first one by taking a huge bite. He flung it triumphantly down beside him.

Benedict was just depositing his third apple and, for a second, the two men stared at each other, water running down their faces in rivulets.

'Had your mistress long, then?' Benedict asked him, just low enough so no one else could hear.

'Long enough,' spat Sebastian. 'You should try getting one, Towey. Might make you a bit less uptight.'

Benedict stared at him with distaste, then plunged his head back into his bucket, Sebastian following suit. His blood was boiling as he chased another apple around. The fucking impudence! After about twenty seconds of frantic splashing, both men pulled out at the same time again, dropping their catches down and gasping for breath.

This time, Benedict leaned in towards him so close, their noses were almost touching.

'You don't deserve her, Belmont.'

At this point Sebastian, chest heaving from lack of oxygen and the unimaginable prospect of losing again, flipped. 'Fuck you, Towey!' he roared, propelling himself towards his rival. Grabbing Benedict's head, he plunged it straight into his bucket of water and held it under. Someone screamed.

'All right lads, calm down!' shouted Ted Briggs, waggling his piece of chalk at them furiously. Under his hands, Sebastian felt strength surge through Benedict as he suddenly reared out of the bucket, sending Sebastian flying. Before Sebastian could collect himself Benedict had grabbed him by the shoulders and plunged his head under the water in his own bucket.

Sebastian struggled, but he was caught in an iron grip. Gasping for air, and with water filling his

357

lungs, he started to choke. My God, I'm going to die, he thought to himself. A strange, shrieking noise filled his head, getting louder and louder.

Just as he was sure he'd taken his last breath, the hand around his neck hauled him out. Heaving and spluttering, he collapsed on the floor as Benedict Towey stood up, breathing heavily.

The strange, shrill noise turned out to be Caro. 'What are you doing? You could have drowned him!' she screamed at Benedict. Shock and anger coursed through her as she faced him, her whole body shaking with emotion. 'Why don't you go and molest someone else's wife instead, you bloody adulterer?'

Confusion flickered across Benedict's face, then he eyed her coldly. 'I think that's something you should ask your husband about,' he said, and turned on his heel.

Caro stared after him for a second, before turning back to Sebastian as he lay wheezing on the ground. He stared up at her spitefully: 'Something I'm missing here, darling? You shagging him or what?' There were a few scandalized gasps from the onlookers. Caro went white as she went to help him up.

'Don't be so ridiculous,' she said in quiet mortification.

There was a brief, deafening silence, then a cry from Jack. 'All right, show's over, folks, let's get back to the party.' An excited babble of voices started up again as everyone watched Caro drag a dripping Sebastian out through the bar.

Chapter 51

Some bright spark had used their camera phone to record Devon singing, and by ten o'clock the next morning, the clip was up on *YouTube*. At the end of the day, the grainy but clearly audible footage had received a staggering hundred thousand hits. Nigel was inundated with calls from record labels wanting to sign Devon up. The singer refused to discuss it, however, saying he was going to get the Churchminster ball out of the way first. His reticence only succeeded in creating even more hysteria, and Devon had great pleasure in telling his old record company, who had dropped him like a hot potato when he started to go off the rails, where to stick their offer. 'What goes around comes around, Nige,' he said sagely, and padded off barefoot down the corridor to his studio. Rehearsals were in full swing now, and the Three Ts were turning up later, ready to eat Nigel out of house and home again.

A few nights later, there was a dramatic turn of events in Churchminster. It was around midnight, after the pub had closed, and Jack Turner was putting the bins out. Suddenly feeling he was being watched, Jack glanced across the deserted green and saw a shadowy figure lurking near the Merryweathers' cottage. With no thought for the fact that he might be confronting Churchminster's serial killer, Jack shouted at the figure and ran towards the cottage. But by the time he'd reached the front gate, there was no one to be seen.

Jack looked around, scanned the green and pulled his mobile phone out of his back pocket. After a few rings, he got through to Bedlington police station. 'Jack Turner here, landlord of the Jolly Boot,' he told the operator. He turned to look at the cottage. A light had come on downstairs: Eunice and Dora had been woken by the disturbance. For the first time, Jack considered what might have happened if he hadn't spotted the sinister figure, and his blood ran cold.

'I'd like to report a suspicious character in the village. I've just seen him outside No. 3 The Green. Yeah, just standing there, dressed all in black. Up to no good if ever I saw it, thought it might be the guy you're looking for.' He listened to the person on the other end: 'OK, I'll stay put. See you in a bit.'

Behind him, the porch light flicked on as the front door creaked open a few inches. 'Hello?' a shaky voice called out.

'Eunice, Dora, it's me, Jack,' he said, striding up the path. 'Sorry to wake you.'

The door swung fully open to reveal the sisters, hairnets on and quilted dressing gowns pulled tightly around them. 'Jack?' said Eunice, a look of concern on her face. 'What's going on?'

He reached the door. 'I'm sure it's nothing to be worried about, Eunice, but I just spotted a dodgy looking figure lurking outside the front here.' He gestured to the spot.

'Here? Outside ours?' cried Dora. 'Oh Eunice, it's the murderer! I knew we'd be next. My horoscope said I was about to encounter danger.' Bursting into tears, she covered her face with her hands.

Her older sister whipped out a lace handkerchief from her dressing gown and gave it to her. 'There, there dear,' she said consolingly, but Eunice had gone as white as a ghost.

She looked at Jack. 'Oh, how dreadful!'

'Don't upset yourselves,' he said reassuringly. 'I've called the police, they're on their way over.'

Dora looked up from her handkerchief, eyes red. 'The police? Coming here? Oh, but we don't want to cause any trouble!' She retreated back behind the lace, weeping in the most heartrending fashion. Jack felt awful. The figure had been a big enough shock for him, let alone these two old dears. He was surprised it hadn't finished them off.

'Would you like to come in?' Eunice asked him.

Jack looked back at the pub. 'I'll just call Beryl and tell her where I am, and to lock the doors – we don't know if he's still about somewhere.' At this there were fresh cries from Dora, and Jack shot Eunice an apologetic look. She nodded understandingly and ushered her sister back inside the house.

By the time Jack had finished talking to an alarmed Beryl, a police car was pulling up outside. DI Rance sprang out, followed by a sleepy looking PC Penny. He gave Jack a brisk nod. 'Thanks for calling us, Mr Turner. This was the property you saw the suspect outside?'

Jack jerked his head. 'There, just by the front gate.'

Rance stared at the grassy area. 'Penny, go and check for footprints,' he ordered. 'Look for anything else he might have left behind: cigarette butts, chewing gum, his bloody calling card if we're lucky.' He glanced at the front door. Eunice had appeared again, her hands held fearfully to her mouth. 'Can we come in, madam?'

'Of course,' she said. 'If you don't mind going in to the sitting room. There it is, first on the right. I'm afraid the rest of the house is a bit of a mess. Knitting seems to take on a life of its own, Inspector. We've got wool and needles everywhere!'

Rance smiled politely at her. Oh God, these were the two Powers and Penny had moaned about. The most ineffectual witnesses you could ever have the misfortune to come across. He'd probably be stuck here for hours talking about fluffy bunnies. Rance sighed and stepped into the sweltering cottage. Like lots of old people, the Merryweather sisters were permanently cold. By the looks of them, both had several layers of night clothes and God knows what else under their dressing gowns. Thermal all-in-ones most likely, thought Rance, shuddering.

The sitting room was the most claustrophobic space Rance had ever been in. Ornaments of woodland animals covered every shelf, table and surface, pictures of old-fashioned countryside scenes hung from every available piece of wall, and draped across the two uncomfortable-looking armchairs that faced out on to the green were a hideous set of chintzy lace covers. A tiny, floral-covered sofa heaped with owl-embroidered cushions made up the rest of the furniture. Rance wedged himself uncomfortably on it while Eunice and Dora sat in the armchairs and Jack hovered by the gas fireplace.

'Can you tell me what time you saw this figure, and what you were doing, please, Mr Turner?' asked Rance.

'It must have been about forty minutes ago. I was just putting the bins out like I always do,' Jack recounted. 'Something caught my eye over the green and when I looked, I could see a figure standing by Eunice and Dora's here.'

A squeak came from one of the sisters, Rance couldn't tell which one. 'Can you tell us what this person looked like?' he asked Jack. Jack furrowed up his brow in concentration.

'I couldn't see his face. I mean, I thought it was a bloke because he was quite tall. About six-foot I would say. And sort of lean-looking.'

Rance felt a flash of excitement. It sounded like their suspect, all right. 'What happened next?' he asked.

'Well, I shouted at him and ran over,' said Jack, 'but by the time I'd got here, the bugger had disappeared. That's when I called you.'

'Ooh, you are brave, Jack,' cried Dora. 'Isn't he, Eunice?' Her sister nodded enthusiastically.

Rance turned to the sisters. 'Now then, ladies,' he said. 'Did you see or hear anything before Jack got here?'

'Not a thing,' said Dora, clutching the handkerchief to her chest. 'We'd been asleep for hours by then.'

'Anyone hanging around recently you thought was a bit out of the ordinary?'

'No one, Inspector!' declared Eunice. 'Oh, we are such silly old things, not being able to help you. This isn't how it happens on *Midsomer Murders*, is it?'

Just then, a breathless Penny came into the room. 'Nothing, Guv,' he said. 'Ground's so hard a JCB would have a job to leave a mark.'

Rance breathed out heavily. For a while, it had seemed as if they were about to catch their suspect, only for him to disappear again, like a wreath of smoke before their eyes.

He got to his feet. 'All right, I think we'll leave it there. Mr Turner. Eunice and Dora Merryweather. Do let me know if you see or hear anything else. In the meantime, make sure you lock up and have a good night's sleep. Thank you.'

'What do you think, Guv?' asked Penny as they drove back to the station. 'Sounds like our man, doesn't it?'

'I just don't know,' said Rance wearily. 'I've got a feeling in my guts. Something about this case doesn't quite add up.'

Chapter 52

November seemed to fly by for the Save Churchminster Ball and Auction Committee members. They now met every few days, to keep everyone up-to-date on progress and make last-minute preparations. They'd had to hastily build a helicopter landing-pad at Clanfield Hall for Mick to land safely, and there had been a hairy moment when the uber-cool fashion designer's studio had nearly burnt down, which would have meant waving goodbye to the coveted work-experience slot. Luckily the fire brigade had got there just in time.

There was no doubt about it, though, this was a cause that struck a chord with the public. Another anonymous benefactor had kindly donated five hundred thousand pounds to the fund, and through yet another generous contact, Angie had managed to secure lunch with a top supermodel. This would surely go down well with the testosterone-fuelled bidders at the auction.

All in all, the organization was running wonderfully smoothly, far better than anyone could have hoped. Poignantly, this was largely down to

Harriet and her role as site manager before disappearing. Frances had taken over, as much as she was able, but Harriet had planned everything in such fine detail that the site arrangements practically ran themselves. As they sat round the large dining room at Fairoaks one evening, Harriet's absence had never been so conspicuous or felt so tragic. Several committee members were in tears as Clementine told them what a marvellous job she had done.

Halfway through the month, Ambrose and Frances had an extremely upsetting meeting with DI Rance. After weeks of being plagued by Frances's daily calls for updates on her daughter's investigation, he had decided enough was enough. He had phoned Clanfield Hall and asked if he could visit them. They insisted on driving to the police station, and so it was in a rather squalid and dingy back room that Rance quietly told them that, although they were still doing everything they could, it was more than likely their daughter was dead. A single tear ran down Ambrose's face, and he collapsed into the nearest chair. Frances, chalk-white face and rigid shoulders, declined the offer of a lift home and calmly drove them both back to the Hall.

Once she'd sat by her husband's bed and watched him sob himself to sleep, Frances got back in her car, drove to the furthermost field of the estate and, for the first time since it had happened, truly let her emotions pour out. Jed Bantry, in the area checking for rabbits with myxomatosis, thought the noise was a wild animal wailing in pain. As he got to the boundary of the field, he found Frances on her knees, crying into the ground. Face paler than ever, Jed took a step forward to console her, then changed his mind and silently retreated. Lady Fraser would not have wanted him to see her like this.

The next day, Frances invited Camilla round for afternoon tea. Her hand clasping the younger woman's, Frances relayed the meeting with Rance. She'd expected to be the one to comfort Camilla, but found herself breaking down again. Camilla, sheet white, held her tightly, struggling to keep her own emotions in check. Frances had finally confirmed what she had been too scared to let herself believe all these months.

Harriet was gone.

The next day, Frances received a phone call from Clementine. Clementine was desperately concerned for her and Ambrose, was she *sure* they wanted the ball to go ahead?

'Clementine, I've never been so sure of anything,' Frances told her, voice wavering. 'Churchminster was Harriet's life. It's what she would have wanted.'

Chapter 53

The auction for the Meadows on 10 December was going to be held in Bedlington town hall. Clementine was beginning to feel rather sick about it all. After the murder of the Revd Goody, and the mystery of poor Harriet, and the effect of these two tragedies on the whole village, she really couldn't bear to consider the prospect that they wouldn't raise enough money.

Even more worryingly, someone had leaked Sid Sykes's application plans to the press. It was worse than they had thought. Not only did he want to build the housing estate, Sykes now planned to put in a betting shop and a themed pub, too. He had also had a lucrative offer from a waste-disposal firm to locate one of their tips on the outskirts. Outraged, Clementine had been straight on the phone to Humphrey Greenwood at the council. Surely this wasn't allowed? But after learning that, due to a ridiculous new legal loophole, Sykes could include these additional proposals, Clementine was in despair.

The cold, wet November weather had crept over the village like a bad mood. One day late in the month, Camilla drove up to Gate Cottage. She didn't know why, perhaps part of her hoped futilely that she might find her best friend there, as though nothing had happened; but another part just wanted to be close to the house they had had so many good times in.

It was a grey day, chilly, with heavy clouds gathering in the sky. Camilla wondered if there might be snow. They had said on the weather forecast that it was possible. It would be wonderful if they had a white Christmas, she thought wistfully as she drove the familiar route to the Clanfield estate. But then the reality of spending it without Harriet hit her, sending her heart plummeting again.

Camilla parked the car in her usual spot by the side of the cottage and made her way round the hedge and into the front garden. The weather was making it worse, but the house and garden looked dreadfully sad and unlived in. A wooden bench sat under the living room window. It was a fantastic sun-trap in summer, and she and Harriet had wiled away many a lazy afternoon on it, gossiping, chatting and laughing.

Now Camilla made her way over there, carefully picking up a luridly bright ceramic dragon that had been kicked over, probably by the police when they searched the cottage. She smiled as she looked at it; Harriet had bought it when they'd gone to the Chelsea Flower Show some years ago. Camilla had thought it was perfectly hideous and told her best friend so, but Harriet had loved its kitsch appeal and bought it anyway, saying if ever an intruder tried to get in they'd be frightened off by its sheer bad taste. The smile suddenly left Camilla's face. Despite her hopes, the dragon didn't appear to have saved Harriet from God knows who or what terrible fate.

'Hats, I miss you!' she cried, sitting down heavily on the seat. Her eyes welled up and she put her head in her hands. God, there was so much she wanted to talk to her friend about. The ball, Angus, life; even mundane things like what she was going to cook for dinner and whether she should cancel her subscription with *Country Life* and switch to *Tatler*.

Suddenly, a shadow fell across her and she jerked her head up. To her surprise Jed Bantry was standing there in his work clothes, a toolkit in one hand. 'You scared the life out of me,' she cried.

Jed stared down at her for a second, his strangely impassive look again seeming to reach deep inside her. 'Sorry. I didn't mean to scare you.' He sat down on the other end of the bench.

Camilla glanced away quickly; she found his gaze unnerving. 'I just thought I'd come and sit here for a bit,' she said. 'It probably sounds silly, but I feel close to her this way.'

Jed looked out into the trees beyond the garden. 'It's not silly at all,' he told her. 'I often come round here and do little repairs,' he gestured to his toolkit. 'I used to think it would look nice for her when she came back. But now . . .' He trailed off.

Camilla turned and studied him properly for the first time. 'You think a lot of her, don't you?' she asked softly.

Jed looked down at his feet. 'She's always been there, you know? When we were growing up and

370

stuff. It feels like a part of me isn't here any more. If I ever find out who did this to her . . .' His voice broke, and he stayed silent for a moment.

Camilla felt tears surge up again, and blinked them away. 'I know how you feel, I really do. We just have to hope the police catch them.'

Jed turned to her again, and this time Camilla didn't look away, taking in the sharp contours of his face, the long dark eyelashes and those mesmerizing, khaki green eyes. Slowly but surely, he brought his hand up and caressed the outline of her cheek. She could feel his rough, calloused fingers on her skin, it was the most comforting, yet erotic sensation she had ever experienced. What on earth is going on here? she wondered. Am I really feeling like this about Jed Bantry?

He kept his hand there, cupping her face.

'You're not alone, Camilla.' For some reason she felt thrilled as he used her name for the first time.

She thought he was going to kiss her, but his hand dropped away. She felt a stab of guilt at her disappointment: she was here to remember poor Harriet, not cop off with Jed Bantry! But he looked at her again, a little nervously, and asked, 'Do you fancy going for a drink some time?'

Camilla went bright red but didn't hesitate. 'Yes! Sorry, gosh, I mean, that would be great!'

He eyed her carefully. 'Thursday? It's not very exciting but we could go to the Boot.' He gave her a cheeky smile that illuminated his solemn features. 'Of course, if you're too embarrassed to be seen with the hired help we could go into Bedlington or something.'

Camilla gave him a mock-indignant slap on the

arm. 'Of course not! The Boot is just fine.' She smiled at him. 'Unless you're worried about Stacey emptying a pint over you.'

Jed laughed; it was a deep, throaty sound. 'I think I can handle it. From what I've heard she's got a new fella anyway, and knowing Stacey, she'll have forgotten my name by now.'

Camilla smiled. 'Great. So that's a date? I mean, er, a drink . . .'

Jed grinned back. 'It's a date, Camilla.'

He offered to walk her to her car, but Camilla wanted to sit for a while longer. As she watched his handsome form stride out of the garden, Camilla wondered if she should really be doing this. Was it appropriate, in the circumstances? The wind rustled across the garden and Camilla glanced round. Did she just hear someone laughing? A weird sensation spread over her and for a while she couldn't place it. Then she realized: for the first time in months – and arriving in the surprising form of Jed Bantry – she was looking forward to something.

Thursday arrived, and with it Jed and Camilla's date. As he was the first man she'd been out with since Angus, Camilla hadn't told anyone. But when Calypso came bounding into Camilla's room that night as she was getting changed in a mist of perfume, she guessed instantly.

'Oh my God, you have totally got a date!' she exclaimed, throwing herself on Camilla's bed and watching her.

Camilla blushed. 'Mind your own business,' she said.

Calypso whooped. 'Ooh, touchy! C'mon, who's it

with?' Her face dropped suddenly. 'Yuk, it's not Angus, is it? Don't tell me you guys have got back together.'

'No, of course not, and don't talk about him like that,' said Camilla crossly, hunting for her pale-pink Lancôme lip gloss.

'Who then?' asked Calypso impatiently. 'It's not like you have a life and go and meet people and stuff.' She clapped her hand over her mouth. 'Fuck, is it someone from the village?'

'Might be,' said Camilla, looking through the drawers of her dressing table. Where was the bloody thing?

'The tall, blond and mysterious Benedict Towey? He is like, HOT,' said Calypso.

'No.'

'Not fit-but-fat Peter, the one who works for the brewery and is always in the Boot pissed out of his head?'

'No way!'

Calypso screwed up her face in frustration. 'But there isn't anyone else, unless you count the farming lot, and Angus seems to have put you off them for life. Urgh, you're not having an affair with a married man like Freddie Fox-Titt are you? Ma and Pa will go off their rockers!'

'Sometimes you are too much,' Camilla scolded. She looked at her sister warily. 'If you must know, it's Jed Bantry.'

There was a pause. 'As in Jed Bantry, the Frasers' gardener?' exclaimed Calypso.

'Yes, why so shocked?' asked Camilla defensively.

Calypso studied her. 'Well he's hardly landed

gentry is he? He's not going to give you the big house in the country you've always banged on about.'

'Well, maybe I don't want that any more,' Camilla told her huffily. 'Don't be such an awful snob.'

Calypso lay back on the bed and laughed. 'I'm not! I'm just surprised, that's all. He's not your usual type. His teeth are normal-sized, for a start.'

Camilla threw a cushion at her head. 'Watch it!'

'I'm only joking,' protested Calypso. 'He is really fit y'know.' She sat up. 'Omigod, are you going to let him shag your brains out tonight? First date's always a bit tricky, do you put out or not?' Giggling, she put her arms up defensively as another cushion narrowly missed her.

As it happened, the most Jed and Camilla did that night was have a brief, lingering kiss outside her house after he had walked her home. Heart thudding and knees weak, Camilla promised she would see him again soon.

The evening had taken her totally by surprise. She had been worried she wouldn't know what to say to the enigmatic Jed, and she'd had awful visions of them sitting in the bar in stone-cold silence. But he showed a side Camilla never dreamt existed; a dry sense of humour, an interest in what she had to say, and most importantly, he didn't try to be anything he wasn't. Camilla had never met anyone like him before, and she liked that a lot.

As Jed started the walk home afterwards, the delicate scent of her lip gloss still on his lips, his heart was beating as hard as hers, but for entirely

374

different reasons. Tonight had been one of the best nights of his life. But it still hadn't been the right time to tell Camilla he'd been in love with her since he had first clapped eyes on her, aged eleven, riding her bicycle across the green. That would surely have scared her off, and now Jed had her in his sights he never wanted to let her out of them again. He wasn't religious, but as he looked up at the moon shining benevolently down over Churchminster, Jed Bantry prayed that, after all these years, his feelings would finally be reciprocated.

Chapter 54

Amidst a flurry of hugs and kisses Johnnie and Tink arrived home for their traditional month-long stay over the Christmas period. They'd come back a few days earlier than normal, for the ball, and were filling a table with much-missed friends and family. Party animal that she was, Tink was beside herself with excitement at the thought of a good night out, especially as her hero Mick Jagger would be playing.

On their first night back, the whole family sat down to a welcome dinner at Fairoaks.

'You both look so well!' Caro said enviously to her parents. 'I feel half-dead in comparison.'

'Nonsense, darling!' her mother cried, but it was true. With their tans and the glow that came from outdoor living in an agreeable climate, the couple had brought back with them a much-needed waft of Barbados colour and glamour.

Johnnie, tall, grey, and distinguished – but with a frequent boyish grin that made him look all of twelve again – looked round the table and sighed contentedly.

'All my girls together in one room. I feel on top of the world,' he said.

'Hear hear!' echoed Clementine.

Johnnie raised his glass of 1995 vintage Taittinger in a toast: 'To us and a bloody good Christmas!'

'And to the ball!' added Calypso, and they all raised their glasses in unison.

Just then, Brenda bustled in with steaming hot bowls of asparagus soup. She'd forgotten to buy fresh asparagus and had had to rush out and get cartons of Covent Garden soup instead, but to her relief no one seemed to notice. In fact, it went down a storm, and when she received several surprised-sounding compliments afterwards, Brenda didn't think it prudent to tell the truth. It makes my life a lot easier, she thought, wondering if she could get away with giving Clementine M&S microwave meals for one now and again.

The main course was served as everyone filled Johnnie and Tink in on the village gossip. Tink's eyes widened like saucers as Clementine relayed Freddie's inadvertent brush with the law and Archie's subsequent grounding. 'I know I shouldn't laugh, but oh!' said Tink, putting her hand to her mouth. 'Poor old Fred!'

Clementine nodded. 'Goodness, I have never seen him so angry.' She let a smile cross her face. 'I can't imagine Archie will have a very merry Christmas, he's only being allowed out to go to college and the library.'

The conversation took on a more serious note. 'Still no word about Hatty, then?' Tink asked Camilla tentatively. Camilla gave an almost imperceptible shake of her head.

'Nothing, Mummy, it's awful.' Her eyes filled up, but as her family offered consoling remarks, she fended them off. 'I'm not to get upset tonight, not when you've just got back,' she told her parents stoically.

'It must be *so* awful for Frances and Ambrose,' Tink said. She shivered. 'The thought of the murderer still being at large is quite unsettling!'

Tink had an extremely fertile imagination, and the rest of the family had decided not to tell her about the recent sighting outside the Merryweathers'.

'I agree with Camilla, let's move on to cheerier things. Are you all set for the ball, Ma?' asked Johnnie. He forked a potato into his mouth and winced as the rock-hard root vegetable almost broke one of his teeth. 'Christ! I'd forgotten about the delights of Brenda's cooking.' Everyone giggled as Clementine looked at him indulgently. Johnnie was her only son, and she adored him.

'It's all going very well,' she replied. 'We've got people in tomorrow to set up the stage. All the tables and chairs are in already; it's going to look wonderful.' She gave a fatalistic sigh. 'It's all running so smoothly, one keeps thinking that any minute now it's all going to go horribly wrong!'

'Oh, it won't be like that,' said Tink. She had a habit of making people feel better. A vibrant, youthful blonde, her appearance was made even more delightful by dancing hazel eyes, the exact colour of Camilla and Calypso's. 'You've done the most incredible job – everyone has – and it will run like clockwork. I'm sure of it!' She looked at Clementine. 'Is it true Devon Cornwall is really playing? I used to have such a crush on him when I was younger!'

Her husband shot her a mock-hurt look. Tink laughed. 'Other than you, my Prince Charming!' Johnnie clasped his hand over his heart theatrically as Tink blew a kiss over the table at him.

Watching her parents flirt like a pair of love-struck teenagers, Caro could only think about her own desperate situation. Sebastian was conspicuously absent tonight: he'd cried-off the night before. It had been a very tense phone call.

'Sorry, darling,' he had drawled, sounding anything but. 'A frightfully important business meeting has just come up. I really need to stay in town for it. I'm still at work now, you know. *Hell* of a day.'

The background noise had sounded more like a busy bar than the office, but Caro hadn't had the energy to give him a rollicking. 'Fine,' she'd said wearily. Then, to her dismay, she had distinctly heard a woman's voice asking Sebastian something in the background.

Mouth dry, Caro demanded to know who was with him. Sebastian had told her she was being paranoid, it was just his secretary staying late to work on some figures. Caro had angrily reminded him he'd told her Bethany was in hospital having liposuction on her love-handles.

'Oh, darling, calm down!' Sebastian had responded patronizingly. 'Look, it's just voices from the street, I was joking with you.'

Sick of his excuses, Caro had hung up. Unfortunately her suspicions were justified. Far from being in the office, her husband had been dining at an intimate Italian restaurant off Sloane Square. His dinner companion, looking innocently ravishing in a simple black dress, had been Luciana, the waitress he had met in Italy.

When Luciana had asked hesitantly who had called, he had smoothly told her it was no one important, and refilled her wine glass. Then, putting on his most sympathetic voice, he had asked to hear all about her family's escape from Croatia. Luciana's eyes had filled with tears. He was such a gentleman, so kind and interested in her family.

'A bit more of this sensitive shit and I'll be in her knickers in no time,' Sebastian had thought triumphantly.

Now, at dinner with her family, Caro was still dwelling on their argument. She'd known what a flirt her husband was from day one, but had always tried to laugh it off or give him the benefit of the doubt. 'Oh, you know Seb,' she'd say, in an over-cheery manner to anyone who hinted that he was behaving inappropriately. Now, as she passed Calypso the salt, she thought, with despair, that it was becoming increasingly impossible to write off anything he did as harmless.

Her mother seemed to read her thoughts. 'Where did you say Sebastian was again, darling?' she asked.

'He's got a meeting,' Caro said shortly.

Across the table, her father raised one eyebrow. 'He can't make it down here for one night to see his wife and gorgeous son?'

'Oh, leave it, Daddy!' Caro snapped. The table went quiet; it was so unlike her.

Johnnie threw his wife a questioning look. 'Sorry, sausage, I didn't mean to upset you,' he told Caro. Aware of everyone's eyes on her, Caro attempted a smile.

'No, it's me who should be sorry. I don't mean to be a grump. I'm just tired, that's all. Milo hasn't been sleeping well again.'

Tactfully, her mother changed the subject. 'Well, I'm home now, and I am dying to spend more time with my handsome grandson,' she informed Caro. 'I can take him whenever you want a break.'

Caro flashed her a grateful smile, and not just for the babysitting offer. 'Thanks, Mummy.'

Johnnie looked more closely at Caro, properly scrutinizing her appearance for the first time since they'd arrived. He was worried. Caro had always been the curviest of his three daughters, but now she was as slim as a rake. Her cheekbones looked elegantly prominent, but her face was pale and wan. He opened his mouth to ask if she was eating properly, but his wife, who had an uncanny knack of knowing what her husband was going to say next, gently kicked his leg under the table.

Tink moved on to slightly safer ground and turned to Camilla. 'How are you feeling at the moment, Bills? Have you seen Angus at all?'

Camilla put her knife and fork down. 'Not once, Mummy. I get the feeling he's staying out of the way at the moment. Which is good, I suppose. It puts some distance between us.'

Johnnie looked at his second-eldest daughter, this time admiringly. 'I must say, heartbreak suits you, Billy Goat Gruff. You're looking positively radiant!'

'Darling!' Tink admonished her husband.

'It's true,' he protested. 'Isn't she looking a million dollars?' Camilla *was* looking radiant and alive at the moment, and this was even more obvious because she was sitting next to poor tired, flat Caro. Camilla blushed slightly.

'Oh, stop it, Daddy! I'm just happy. It was an awful shock breaking up with Angus, but, oh, I don't know, I feel like me again. Does that sound odd?'

Her mother nodded wisely. 'Not at all. Angus was an awful sweetie, and I would never have said this if you had ended up marrying him but...'

'Pleased to hear it,' Johnnie told his wife in trepidation of what was coming next.

'Oh, shush!' she said. 'I'm not going to say anything dreadful! No, Angus was a good old stick really, but he wasn't quite – how does one say this ... the most sensitive or inspirational of souls, was he? Oh, poor Angus!' She smiled ruefully at Camilla.

'*She's a woman in love* ...' Calypso chose this moment to introduce her own version of the Barbra Streisand classic.

Camilla looked at her sister in horror. 'Shut up, you!'

'Ooh, is there someone new on the scene?' Tink asked excitedly. 'How romantic!'

Camilla blushed again. 'Not really. Well I mean sort of, but it's early days. We've only been on a few dates.'

Camilla and Jed had met up twice already since the Jolly Boot night, both times for long walks in the surrounding countryside, well muffled-up against the winter weather. It was a new experience for both of them, and Camilla couldn't believe how easily she could talk to him about everything and anything. As for Jed, this was the first girl he didn't just want to have sex with and leave. Admittedly, the thought of taking Camilla to bed made him dizzy with desire, but it went a lot deeper than that. For the first time, he didn't just want to ask her what position she'd like to get into next, but silly stuff like what she'd had for lunch and whether she said, 'Hello, Mr Magpie, how's your wife?' whenever she saw one of the black and white birds, too. These feelings were alien. They both excited and scared him.

'Will we meet him at the ball?' asked Tink. Camilla nodded, and her mother clapped her hands. 'How thrilling!'

Johnnie looked at his wife in despair: she was worse than all three of his daughters put together, sometimes. 'For goodness' sake, darling, you are so childish,' he told her fondly.

Still blushing, but this time at the sudden thought of Jed doing something positively indecent to her, Camilla decided to get her own back on Calypso.

'Why don't you tell Mummy and Daddy about Sam?' she suggested sweetly. Calypso shot her sister a deathly look, but it was too late, her father had swivelled round in his chair to face her, and become the Spanish Inquisition.

'Yes, what *did* happen there, Muffin? I know one shouldn't really pry, but I must confess I was looking forward to meeting this Sam. Sounded like a thoroughly decent chap.'

For once lost for words, Calypso opened her mouth like a goldfish, and then shut it again.

Camilla, quickly feeling guilty, was about to intervene when Clementine stepped in from where she was sitting at the head of the table.

'It just didn't work out, did it?' she said, looking directly at Calypso. Stunned, her granddaughter managed to shake her head weakly in agreement. Clementine continued, 'What with Calypso living here and doing such a marvellous job on the committee, and Sam down in Brighton, I think it just got a bit too much. Heaven knows, these long-distance relationships can be a blasted nuisance.' She looked around briskly at her family, signifying an end to the subject.

Her intervention worked. Johnnie shrugged in a 'that's life' way, and sat back in his chair.

'Anyone for pudding?' Clementine asked. 'Brenda's made a brandy and mincemeat tart. I can't vouch for its safety but we can give it a go.' She rang the silver bell on the wall beside her, and several moments later Brenda fussed in to clear away the main course. Camilla and Tink started chattering about what they were going to wear to the ball, and Caro went upstairs to check on Milo.

Amongst the hubbub, Calypso caught her grandmother's eye. 'Thank you,' she mouthed gratefully. Clementine winked and gave her a conspiratorial smile.

She might be ancient, but my gran is *seriously* cool, thought Calypso as she went to bed that night.

Chapter 55

Saturday, 1 December dawned. It was show time. Clementine, who had spent half the night awake worrying, was fully dressed at six o'clock and drinking litres of Earl Grey tea in the kitchen. By 7.15 a.m., as the first milky white streaks of dawn started to filter across the dark sky, she had decided to don her wellies and Barbour and take Errol Flynn for a walk up and around the Meadows.

Outside, the air was crystal clear and cold. Clementine crunched her way across the frost-covered grass and out through a side gate on to Bramble Lane. Around her the birds were starting their morning wake-up calls, their chirps cutting across the silence enveloping the village.

Errol Flynn, seemingly unperturbed by the prospect of skidding along the ice on his well-covered bottom, bounded ahead of Clementine, tail wagging furiously. 'Don't run off too far!' she instructed, and the Labrador obediently sat and waited until his mistress had caught up. By the time they had cut through the stile and walked up the grassy path to the edge of the wood, dawn had broken. Clementine's prayers had been answered:

they were going to have one of those gloriously clear, crisp winter days. The sun was rising steadily in the pale blue sky as she and Errol made their way through a field. Long grasses were bowing down under the weight of the frost and bare tree branches glittered in the weak morning rays. It looked like someone had flown overhead and let off a bomb made of fairy dust. Pausing to look around, Clementine thought the place had never looked so beautiful. Or vulnerable.

How fitting, she thought, that her day should start here, where it all began. It was like the calm before the storm, a chance to reflect and galvanize herself for the battle ahead. Clementine closed her eyes for a moment. Oh please, let us raise enough money to keep the Meadows, she prayed. Then she heard a familiar voice next to her ear, as clear as day.

'You can do it, Clemmie old girl, chin up!'

Bertie! Clementine opened her eyes and looked round. There was no one there. Had she just imagined her husband's voice? But it had sounded so real . . . A firm, resolute look came into her eye. 'We *are* going to do this!' she said aloud. Errol Flynn trotted over and shoved his huge wet nose in her hand. She looked down at her pet: dear loyal old Errol, who had been her constant companion in recent years. 'Come on boy, let's go get 'em!' she said fervently.

A few hours later, at Byron Heights, Devon was going through a similar crisis of confidence. It was only eleven o'clock, and already a group of fans and photographers had gathered at the end of his drive, hoping to glimpse the pop star on the day of his grand comeback. Devon had looked out of the window, gulped and drawn the heavy curtains across it. He flung himself down on the sofa and turned on the television, trying to take his mind off what lay ahead. The pretty face of the newsreader on the local news station flashed up. She announced solemnly:

Today is the day of the Save Churchminster Ball and Auction. The biggest event the area has seen in many years: a whole host of celebrities are attending, including Mick Jagger. But the REAL focus of the night is on comeback king, Devon Cornwall, playing his first live performance in almost two decades. Critics are divided as to whether he will be able to reclaim his throne. Music supremo Simon Cowell is adamant that . . .

Devon could stand it no longer. 'Arggh!' he yelled and clicked the set off, throwing the remote across the room. Nigel, hearing the commotion down the corridor, rushed in looking alarmed. He found Devon lying face-down on the sofa, a cushion pulled over his head.

'What on earth is wrong?' he cried, running over to him.

Devon slowly lifted his head up and gazed at him. 'Nige, I don't think I can do it. I thought I was ready for it, but now it's here, I can't. I'm bricking it!'

A voice sounded from behind them. 'Devon, you can do it. I know you can. Come on, darling.' Devon sat up and they both turned to face the door. Looking effortlessly chic in a navy-blue polka-dotted scarf and blue quilted riding-jacket,

Frances was leaning against the doorway. She looked apologetic. 'I did knock but no one answered. I hope you don't mind me letting myself in.'

Nigel smiled in relief. If anyone could talk Devon round, it was Frances. 'Not at all, come in,' he said. 'I'll leave you to it.' He gave her arm a grateful squeeze as he passed, and she smiled at him reassuringly.

'Now then, what's all this?' She sat down next to Devon on the sofa.

He gave a loud groan. 'Frances, I can't do it, man! What if I go down like a lead balloon? What if they hate all my new stuff? I'll never recover from that.'

Frances took Devon's chin in her hand tenderly and looked straight into his eyes. 'Devon Cornwall, you are the most talented man I have ever met. You are going to bring the house down tonight, no question.' He began to protest but she stopped him. 'It's just last-minute jitters, darling, which are entirely understandable,' she said soothingly.

Devon started to look slightly less stricken. 'But what if me nerves fail me?'

'They won't,' she told him firmly. A pained look flashed across her eyes. 'Devon, you need to do this. Not just for you, but for the village. For Harriet . . .' Her lower lip wobbled.

Devon sat up straight, guilt flooding over him. What a selfish git he was being. 'My beautiful Frances,' he murmured, hugging her. 'You're right, of course I'll do it. There's a lot at stake tonight, and it's not just my bleedin' career.'

Frances closed her eyes and clasped him tightly.

Around lunchtime Clementine went down to Clanfield Hall to see how everything was going. It looked slightly chaotic. At least a dozen cars were parked outside the magnificent building, ranging from a white florist's van with bright pink roses painted down the side to a dusty looking lorry from which several muscular men were unloading pieces of the stage. Several more people were shouting across to each other, staggering as they carried large flower displays and boxes of food and drink across the gravel drive. Someone had dropped a tray of eggs by the front door, the yolk spreading out in a big, gloopy yellow puddle. A workman in overalls, with a pencil stuck behind his ear, cursed as he stepped in it, lifting his dripping boot up and looking around unsuccessfully for somewhere to wipe it.

In the middle of all this, a short, excitable young black man was standing beside a black Saab shouting furiously down the mobile phone he had clamped to his ear.

'What do you mean, you forgot to pack my CDJ 1,000s!' He had a high-pitched, slightly manic voice. 'What am I supposed to do, rig up to the old guy's gramophone?' The man paused as a babble of protest could be heard down the line. 'G-Man, I don't care if they've fucked up your weave at the hairdressers, get your sorry boy ass down the M4 now!' He lowered his voice slightly. 'And don't forget my wheatgrass juice, it's in the fridge, yeah?'

Clementine stared at the stranger in bemusement. He had braided hair, worn incongruously in bunches on either side of his head. Big diamond studs glittered in both ears, while immaculate white trainers with some kind of tick down the side dazzled on his feet. The man was wearing a full-length brown fur coat, which fell aside as he jiggled round impatiently, revealing a huge oversized T-shirt with the words 'Dirty Dawg' emblazoned across it. Irritably he snapped the tiny diamanté phone shut and, looking round, noticed Clementine for the first time. His whole face lit up in a beaming smile, revealing even more diamonds in his dental work.

'Hey, girl!' he called out in a friendly manner. 'Can you tell me where I can find the lord of this manor?' He proceeded to moonwalk across the drive towards a very disconcerted Clementine. 'I'm Dawg!' he said, turning round and pointing with both hands to his T-shirt. 'Just like it says on the tin!' He gave a booming laugh and extended his hand in greeting. The name rang a bell.

'Dawg? Mr Dawg, are you performing tonight? I think my granddaughter Calypso has been in charge of the arrangements,' she said formally.

'You're Calypso's gran? Damn, good looks run in the family!' Dawg slapped his thigh and chuckled again. 'Yeah, I'm the Dawg, *DJ* Dawg, if you'd be so kind.' He eyed Clementine's tweed trouser suit critically. 'Man, that country look is so yesterday! Why don't I get my assistant G to bring up one of our 'Dawg's Bitch' tracksuits for ya? It would look *well* fly. My old ma loves hers, wears it out for bingo with a pair of heels.'

'No, thank you,' a slightly thrown Clementine told him.

He shrugged good-naturedly. 'If you change your mind, let me know. "Dawg On Dawg" is one of Selfridges' bestselling lines at the moment.' Suddenly loud barking rang out from nowhere, making Clementine almost jump out of her skin.

'Chillax, it's just my ring tone,' he told her, amused, as he pulled his phone from his pocket. He slapped his thigh again. 'P Diddy! My main man! What's going down?'

'Laters, home girl,' he said to Clementine, and wandered off to take the call.

What's later? How does he know I like staying at home, she wondered, feeling rather perplexed. Reeling slightly from this encounter, Clementine walked in through the enormous oak front doors, which had been propped open. As she stepped over the threshold she was assailed by the smell of fresh pine, and her confidence was restored. A huge, beautifully dressed Christmas tree stood in the centre of the sweeping entrance hall, a man in overalls perched precariously on a step ladder as he reached to put a decadent silver star on the top. The whole place looked positively festive.

'Isn't it wonderful? It was Ambrose's idea,' said Frances, appearing behind her, her arms full of bottle-green sprigs of mistletoe. 'We thought this would get everyone in the mood at the drinks reception.' She had just returned from Byron Heights, having left Devon in an encouragingly buoyant mood.

'It's really very kind of you,' said Clementine gratefully. 'Good old Ambrose!' She looked concerned. 'How is he holding up?' She studied Frances. 'How are *you* holding up?'

Frances smiled bravely. 'To be honest, tonight has been the only thing that's kept me going. One tends to sit and dwell less when one is so busy.' She leaned in confidingly. 'I have had serious doubts about Ambrose, but he's seemed a bit brighter in the last week.' She laughed ruefully. 'You know my husband, he can't bear not to be involved!'

'I can't put into words how grateful we are for all this. You've been so brave,' Clementine said emotionally. The two women smiled and clasped each other's hands.

At this moment there was a loud crash from the back of the house, followed by an angry babble of distant voices.

'Ah, I was going to pop in and see how Pierre was doing,' said Clementine.

'I wouldn't, if I were you,' Frances warned her. 'The last I heard, the suppliers had delivered partridge instead of prawns, and one of the sous chefs dropped a saucepan on his foot and had to be carted off to A and E. I believe Pierre is in one of his more *fraught* moods.'

Another noise made them jump as a loud barking sounded out at the front.

'What *is* that awful racket?' asked Frances, craning her neck round the door. Her face was a picture as she caught sight of Dawg, answering his phone, holding it with one hand, the other stuck down the front of his baggy jeans rearranging his particulars.

'Ah, I don't believe you've met the DJ yet, have you?' said Clementine delicately.

Chapter 56

After a thorough inspection of the car park and newly erected cloakrooms and toilets, Clementine was satisfied everything was ready. Driving back through the village, she saw Babs Sax wandering across the green, carrying a long, canary-yellow dress on a hanger. Babs waved the car down and Clementine stopped begrudgingly. A straight-forward, no-nonsense woman, she really couldn't see the point of silly, affected people like Babs.

'Just picked my dress up from the dry cleaners,' Babs announced shrilly. She stuck her bony face through the window and Clementine got a disconcerting waft of gin-fuelled breath. 'Got the bloody thing covered in green gloss at Lucien's – that's Lucien *Freud*'s – painting party last year. I was beside myself they wouldn't be able to get it out, but they did! Otherwise I don't know *what* I would have done.' She held the dress up to the window. 'Marvellous, isn't it? I got it from a fright-fully expensive boutique off Portobello Road.'

It was hideous, thought Clementine. On closer inspection, the clingy fabric would have looked more at home in an ice-skater's closet. It was also covered with yellow feathers, and someone appeared to have attacked the jagged hemline with a pair of gardening shears. Billowy chiffon sleeves hung off each side like a pair of limp windsocks. The whole effect was absurd and strangely terrifying.

Clementine decided to exercise her tact. 'It's very original,' she told Babs, and looked at the clock on the dashboard pointedly. 'I must be off, Brenda's due round at Fairoaks to babysit Milo soon.' The artist stepped back from the car with a flourish.

'Of course,' she cried. 'See you later!' She swayed dangerously, like a tall poppy blowing in a gale-force wind. For a worrying second, Clementine thought she was going to fall over. But Babs managed to right herself and wove off back towards Hard-on House. As Clementine drove off she made a mental note to make sure Babs was served the non-alcoholic champagne at the drinks reception.

The invitation stated guests were to arrive from seven o'clock. Dinner was at 7.45 p.m., the all-important auction starting at nine thirty. At eleven o'clock, Devon Cornwall was opening the live entertainment on stage – hopefully still with an appearance from Mick Jagger. For those who were still standing at midnight, DJ Dawg would be spinning and mixing his choice of dance-floor fillers. Carriages were at two o'clock and Ambrose hoped to be tucked up in bed with a tot of single malt scotch by 2.10 a.m. 'Maybe a *trifle* ambitious, darling,' Frances tactfully informed him.

By six o'clock, all the committee members were

down at the Hall doing last-minute preparations. Her granddaughters did scrub up well, thought Clementine admiringly, as she watched them rush about clutching clipboards, to-do lists and table plans. She had been slightly worried Calypso would shame the family by arriving dressed as a Soho streetwalker, but her youngest granddaughter was the epitome of elegance in a long, gold, strapless dress, her normally messy bed-hair swept up in a sophisticated topknot. Camilla was making the most of her fabulous legs in a short black dress. Long-sleeved, it had a low scooped back that showed off her honey-coloured skin, courtesy of the fake tan she'd had done at the Sunshine beauty salon in Bedlington the day before. It made her hair look blonder than ever, and her eyes smouldered under artfully applied smoky make-up. No wonder Jed Bantry, helping to bring the last few crates of wine in, couldn't take his eyes off her.

In his rented dinner jacket and with his black hair swept back, exposing his imperious cheekbones, Jed looked every inch the young aristocrat. Clementine smiled wryly as she thought of the look that would surely appear on some people's faces tonight when Jed opened his mouth and exposed his country roots. She was rather relieved he had finally made his move on Camilla. Clementine's beady eyes had missed nothing over the years, and she probably realized the extent of Jed's feelings towards her middle granddaughter before he did. For all her breeding and connections, Clementine was not a snob and was more concerned with manners, decency and honesty than which school someone had been to or what their father did for a living. She had encountered far too many boorish, unscrupulous Hooray Henrys in her lifetime.

This was why she was so worried about Caro. She had never seen her granddaughter look so stunning. But at what cost emotionally? Her slim shape was clad in a beautiful olive-green dress that hugged her in a bodice and flared out at the bottom into a fishtail shape. Exquisite diamonds, given to her on her twenty-first by Johnnie and Tink, glittered at her ears, neck and wrists. Her hair, freshly streaked from the hairdressers, had been artfully put up in a sexy, almost casual chignon, a few select strands falling about her neck. Any man would be proud to have her on his arm, Clementine thought.

Aware of being watched, Caro looked up from a table plan and glanced at her grandmother. She smiled, but it failed to mask the sadness and hurt in her eyes. As if a fist was being squeezed around it, Clementine's heart contracted in sorrow and anger. She had seen Sebastian Belmont for what he was from the moment she'd met him. But Caro had been so head-over-heels in love Clementine hadn't been able to bring herself to interfere. Now, she wondered if maybe she should have. She had hoped Milo would tame Seb and give him a sense of responsibility for the first time in his life. To her dismay, he seemed to have had the opposite effect.

'All ready, Granny Clem?' Calypso appeared beside her, patting the back of her hair to check it was still in place. 'It's five to; I'm going to stand by the front door to welcome the VIPs.' Clementine nodded, feeling slightly nauseous as nerves and anticipation stirred in the pit of her stomach.

Calypso squeezed her grandmother's arm. 'It's going to be fine!' she assured her.

'I hope so, darling!'

Calypso hurried off and Clementine looked around the ballroom for the umpteenth time. It looked fabulous. Fifty tables decorated in the finest white tablecloths and laid with gleaming solid silver cutlery, a glorious winter flower display the centrepiece on each. An intoxicating scent from the flowers wafted across the room, mixed in with the heady smell of recently polished mahogany. Three huge arched windows ran along each side of the room, and floor-to-ceiling silk magenta curtains framed each one perfectly, pulled back to show the twinkling velvety night sky outside. The heavy, ornate chandeliers had been turned down low, casting a decadent, romantic glow over the room.

We've done our absolute best, thought Clementine. The rest of it was in the lap of the gods.

A few minutes later, the first headlights appeared at the bottom of the drive. They were swiftly followed by more and more. Angie, who was standing at the entrance, thought it looked almost biblical, the bobbing, swaying lights moving nearer like a procession through the distant darkness. Everyone suddenly galvanized into action, burly looking security men in dark suits with ear sets shouting instructions into their walkie-talkies, and the valets and car park attendants milling about expectantly. Inside, waiters in dicky bows hovered, champagne flutes at the ready.

A few minutes later the first car, a midnight-blue

Bentley, pulled up outside. The smartly dressed valet, who didn't look a day over sixteen, stepped forward and opened the door reverently and an old man, dressed in black tie, with splendid white whiskers, emerged. He turned to help his companion out, a grey-haired regal-looking woman in a lavender ball gown. Looking around as if they owned the place, they walked slowly up the front steps. They were followed by a younger, similar-looking couple.

'The Earl and Countess of Radmore,' Calypso whispered to Angie. 'That's their son Rollo behind, with his wife Millicent. Between them, they own half of Warwickshire. Oh look – there's the Marquess and Marchioness of Havensbury.' She smiled winningly as the guests swept imperiously in.

After that the floodgates opened. Car after expensive car pulled up and deposited their rich, famous and privileged guests. By 7.30 p.m., one could barely move in the car park for Bentleys, Rolls Royces and Mercedes, the chauffeurs standing around and chatting to each other. For most it would be a long night's wait, but they were used to it.

A sleek, black BMW pulled up, tyres crunching on the frost-covered gravel, and out stepped Elizabeth Hurley, looking every inch the superstar in a long, red, figure-hugging dress and fur stole. A dashing Indian man climbed out of the other side of the car and walked round. 'That's her husband Arun Nayar, quite cute, isn't he?' Calypso whispered to Angie. Linking arms with Arun, Elizabeth glided up the steps, her dress moving like flowing water. Across the entrance hall, Camilla looked on with admiration as Calypso greeted the couple, complimenting the celebrity on her outfit and beckoning over attendants to take coats. She is not the slightest bit star-struck, thought Camilla. Moments later, Calypso was air-kissing a debonair-looking Bryan Ferry and sharing a joke with the upper-crust environmental campaigner Zac Goldsmith. The whole Goldsmith clan was there, Zac's sister Jemima Khan looking impossibly glamorous in a cream Chanel number. When an over-excited male admirer rushed up to fawn over her, Calypso stepped in from nowhere and smoothly directed him away in the direction of the champagne.

Camilla jumped as she felt a soft pair of lips brush her neck. She whirled around to find Jed standing there. Her heart missed a beat. Under the soft light of the chandeliers Jed's chiselled face looked like a Grecian statue.

'You look beautiful,' he said softly.

Camilla blushed. Why did he make her feel like a giddy schoolgirl? 'Thank you, so do you,' she managed. 'Well, not beautiful. Handsome.' They smiled at each other. 'Oh, are you sure about sitting with me on Mummy and Daddy's table? Won't it be a dreadful bore for you?'

Jed caressed the top of her hand. 'I'm looking forward to it, don't worry.' One of Johnnie and Tink's friends had pulled out that morning with a nasty bout of tonsillitis. They had generously given the place to Jed. Camilla had readily accepted and phoned Jed straight away, but now she was regretting it slightly. What if her parents didn't get on with him? She couldn't imagine the easy-going Johnnie and Tink having a problem, but she would still have preferred a less full-on introduction for Jed.

Calypso was on cloud nine. Getting stars to confirm they were attending was one thing, actually seeing them turn up was a completely different story. To her delight, they had all arrived, including a famous American pop star and her new toy-boy husband, who swanned in looking fabulous in sunglasses and matching black tuxedoes. They were followed by a gamine-looking Kate Moss in a striking Alexander McQueen dress. Her trademark rock-chick locks had been cut into a startling peroxide blonde crop. The other guests started chattering wildly when they saw her, and Calypso fervently hoped the photographers loitering at the end of the drive had got a picture. The supermodel's new hairstyle would be all over the papers tomorrow and give them even more publicity.

'Urgh, what's *she* doing here?' Calypso made no effort to stop her nose wrinkling as a heavily made-up Sabrina slunk in, wearing a rather tarty short pink satin dress. She was accompanied by a tall, thin brunette with legs up to her armpits, and a hard, knowing face.

'Who?' asked Camilla. She'd just had a furious snog with Jed behind a suit of armour and had reluctantly disengaged herself to bring her sister a glass of champagne and to see if she needed any help. Caro was still rushing around the ballroom like a madwoman, making sure all the name cards were in the right place.

'Sabrina Cox. And boy does she love them! She's

a low-rent model from Chelsea who makes a living out of latching on to rich playboys. Until they get bored of her, or vice versa. I hear she's shagging some Mafioso billionaire now.' Calypso looked her up and down as contemptuously as only she could. 'God, what does she look like?' She took the glass from Camilla. 'Thanks, Bills. I think all the VIPs are in now, trust old slaggy pants to come in last and try and upstage everyone.' She paused and studied Sabrina, who was looking around at the crowd like a meerkat. 'I heard she was after Sebastian as well.'

'*Caro's* Sebastian?' exclaimed Camilla. She watched as Sabrina grabbed a flute from a waiter, unsubtly yanking the neckline of her dress down to expose even more cleavage. 'He wouldn't, would he? I mean, I know he's not perfect but . . .'

'Bloody hope not,' said Calypso dismissively. 'One thing I *do* know is that that old trout is about fifteen years older than she tells everyone. A girl who works at the Botox clinic she goes to told me she's *ancient*. About forty-three at least.'

As the glamorous guests filled the room, the place reeked of power, fame and money, both old and new. Caro was just using her compact to put on a hasty application of lipstick when she saw Benedict Towey walk in, Amelia on his arm. He'd obviously been away somewhere hot and exotic. His hair was bleached by the sun to a dirty surfer-boy blond, and a deep tan made his blue eyes sparkle. Momentarily he and Caro had eye-contact. He looked at her as if he'd just scraped her off the bottom of his Tod's loafer and turned sharply away.

In spite of receiving umpteen compliments on her appearance, Caro was feeling dead inside.

She'd had yet another row with Sebastian just before they'd come out. He'd wanted to wake Milo up to show him off to his awful City friends. They'd come down for the ball and had been gathered in the sitting room downstairs with their equally awful wives, downing glasses of Cristal and bragging about how much money they made. Caro, quite rightly, had refused. After all, she'd just put Milo down, and had to finish getting ready herself.

'Don't be such a precious little bitch,' Sebastian had snapped at her, before stalking downstairs to announce to the entire room that his wife was clearly suffering from a bad bout of PMT and refused to get Milo up. 'No shag for me tonight, then,' he had said, throwing back the last of his Cristal.

'Oh, I'm sure that won't stop you getting your end away somewhere, Sebbo,' one of the men had drawled. The whole room had erupted: the men guffawing into their glasses, and the wives gleefully tittering and shooting nervous looks at one another, maliciously grateful it wasn't one of them in the firing line tonight instead. Caro, standing on the landing getting her tights out of the airing cupboard, had heard every word.

By now the reception was in full swing. Richard Branson was chatting with Naomi Campbell and the Duchess of York, making them laugh at a riotous joke. In the middle of the room, ex-*Daily Mirror* editor Piers Morgan was receiving glowering looks from several disgraced aristocrats he'd done risqué exposés on. Luckily Piers seemed blissfully oblivious to the animosity as he engaged in an intense conversation with Salman Rushdie. A large

group of guests were being entertained by the cele-
brated street magician Dynamo, who was wowing
his audience by levitating one of their solid gold
pens whilst simultaneously body popping on the
spot.

Camilla was standing chatting to Poppy Cadwell,
an old school chum of hers. 'Have you heard Angus
is here tonight?' Poppy asked her. As if on cue,
Camilla caught sight of her ex-fiancé across the
room. He was looking more red-cheeked than ever
in a dusty dinner jacket. Beside him was a horsy
looking girl. She was about Camilla's age, but
matched Angus for height and broadness of
shoulders. She was wearing an unflattering
mustard-yellow taffeta dress, her long brown hair
pulled back with a black Alice band. Angus said
something to her and she threw back her head and
brayed with laughter, exposing huge, buck-like
front teeth. He gazed at her as if she was the
prettiest girl in the world.

'That's Tamara Knatchbull-Drake, I hear she's
Angus's new girlfriend,' said Poppy, looking
anxiously at Camilla. She needn't have worried.
Camilla watched as Tamara downed a glass of
champagne in one gulp and promptly put the glass
on her head. Angus roared with laughter, and
Camilla couldn't help but smile.

'Poppy, I think they're absolutely perfect for each
other. I mean it.'

'Phew,' said Poppy. 'I thought things were going
to get a bit hairy, then.' She took a sip of her
champagne. 'I say, what on earth is wrong with
Lady Fraser? She looks like she's seen a ghost!'

Camilla swivelled her head round. Frances was

standing in the middle of a group of men and women. She was looking as elegant as ever in a simple black cocktail dress, and had obviously been holding court when something had made her stop in her tracks. Her guests were looking at her with a mixture of bemusement and concern. Every drop of colour had drained from Frances's face, even her lips. She was standing stock still, staring through the crowds towards the front door.

Instinctively Camilla followed her gaze. What on earth was Frances looking at? At the door, she could see that some guests were gathered, drinking and laughing, while a pretty brunette had just walked in. Several men were eyeballing her with interest, but the girl seemed oblivious, surveying the room as if she was working up the courage to go further in. She looked vaguely familiar. It must be one of the celebrity guests, Camilla thought.

Then she looked again. And nearly keeled over as the features she knew so well suddenly fell into place. Later, she described the moment to her parents as like watching television with bad reception and suddenly getting the aerial fixed.

'Harriet?' she tried to say, but it came out as a croak. It couldn't be!

She was snapped out of her shock by a long-drawn-out scream. Camilla turned around just in time to see Lady Frances Fraser slide gracefully to the floor in a dead faint.

'But where have you *been*?' asked Sir Ambrose Fraser shakily. He, Frances, Camilla and Harriet were in a small, cosy sitting room at the back of the house.

'Does it matter? She's back with us now, and that's all that counts.' Frances had recovered sufficiently, and was lying on a chaise longue, a glass of water in her hand. She looked at her daughter and her voice broke. 'Oh darling, we thought you were dead!'

Harriet rushed over and threw her arms around her. 'Oh Mummy, I am so sorry! I had no idea the police had got involved. I feel so terrible.' As mother and daughter embraced, Ambrose gazed at Harriet in wonder. She looked like a different person entirely.

Gone was his podgy, dumpy daughter with her frizzy mop of hair, unflattering wardrobe and ungainly walk. In her place was a stunning young woman. Harriet must have lost at least two stone, and her hair, which Frances had so despaired of, was now a poker straight, glossy chestnut, and styled in a flattering layered cut. Harriet's once-pasty complexion was tanned, and she looked beautifully elegant in a long, white chiffon dress and strappy silver heels. She stood up again and looked at her father. A tear-stained Camilla moved next to Harriet, arm linked in hers. She hadn't stopped crying or hugging her best friend in the last fifteen minutes.

'Where have you been, Harriet?' Ambrose asked again.

She looked round at them and smiled hopefully.

'I've been in South East Asia. Back-packing. *Don't* look like that, Daddy, it was the best thing I have ever done! The place, the people . . .' Harriet looked at Ambrose imploringly. 'I had to get away. Please understand.'

'But why?' he croaked. 'I've always made sure

405

you've never wanted for anything. You're Sir Ambrose Fraser's only child, for goodness' sake.'

Harriet threw out her hands despairingly. 'But that's exactly why! Can't you see? I know you have my best interests at heart – both of you – but I felt like I was suffocating here. I was never allowed to be my own person, and too scared to stand up to you or for anything else I believed in. Because I wasn't a boy, I always felt like a disappointment.'

Ambrose opened and closed his mouth again, for once struggling for words.

Frances understood and nodded weakly. She knew what her faults had been as a mother. 'How long had you been planning it?' she asked gently.

Harriet gave a small smile. 'I hadn't, really, it was just a knee-jerk reaction. One minute I was gazing out of the window wondering what to do with my life. The next I'd booked a ticket with Trailfinders for a flight out of Heathrow that evening and was suddenly running around like a mad thing trying to get packed!'

'Why didn't you tell us where you were going, so your mother didn't have to go through all this?' asked Ambrose, a familiar hint of irritation creeping into his voice.

Harriet stared at him, aghast. 'But Daddy, I did! I left two envelopes, one to you and Mummy and one to Camilla, on the desk in your study. I couldn't face telling you face-to-face because I knew you'd probably talk me out of it. Oh, please don't tell me you didn't get them . . .'

Now it was Ambrose's turn to look horror-struck. 'Two white envelopes with purple handwriting?' Harriet nodded.

'I thought they were another set of those God-awful invites!' Ambrose looked at each of them in turn, with a pleading glance. 'I'm too old for all this gallivanting around, I'd had enough of the blasted things.'

When Frances spoke, her voice was dangerously quiet.

'What did you do with the letters, Ambrose?'

He turned to her, shame-faced.

'I threw them away.'

Frances's face darkened in anger. 'For God's sake, man! Can't you for once in your life stop charging around like a bear with a sore head, with no thought for anyone but yourself? Look where your bloody-mindedness has got us!'

In all their years of marriage, Frances had never questioned or criticized her husband. Harriet, expecting the Third World War to kick off, threw herself in-between them. 'Mummy, please don't take it out on Daddy. He didn't know what he was doing.'

Ambrose exhaled loudly. It sounded like a thousand regrets in one breath. 'Your mother is right,' he said quietly. 'I've been a bloody fool. You're better than a dozen sons!' His voice cracked. 'I know I've always been hard on you, but I thought I was doing the right thing. Will you forgive me?'

Harriet threw her arms around him. 'There's nothing to forgive, Daddy.'

Eventually, she pulled away and looked around the room at them. 'Oh, I've missed you all so much! I'm sorry I made you all sick with worry.' She shot Camilla a pleading look. 'Bills, do you hate me?'

'Of course not, you dolt!' Camilla said tearfully. 'I'm just so pleased you're home again!' She hugged her friend. 'We have got *so* much to discuss!' she whispered in her ear.

Harriet laughed. 'So I see,' she told her wryly. 'When I was plucking up the courage to come in I saw you with Jed. Are you happy?' Camilla nodded. Harriet clapped her hands in delight. 'I always knew he had a soft spot for you, how romantic!'

Ambrose put his arm around his daughter's shoulders. 'Are you sure you want to go ahead with this tonight?' he asked her.

Harriet nodded. 'I wouldn't miss it for the world. Besides, we've got a village to save, haven't we?'

As they got up to leave, Frances stopped her daughter. 'Darling, there is one thing I must ask you. I hope you don't think it's inappropriate but how did . . .' She trailed off uncertainly.

Harriet, intuitive as ever, grinned at her mother. 'I've discovered the joys of hair-straighteners, Mummy!'

Pierre had excelled himself. As the courses were brought out, guests 'oohed' and 'aahed' over the exquisite plates of lobster, foie gras and roast veal. The dark chocolate mousse was so delicious that dozens of guests asked for the recipe afterwards.

Just after coffee was served, Stephen and Klaus approached Clementine at her table. 'Would you like to come and meet Belvedere? He's just arrived,' asked Stephen.

The famous auctioneer was pulling off his coat in

a small study off to the side of the ballroom when Clementine walked in.

'Delighted, dear lady!' he cried. 'I've heard so much about you and the Meadows, thrilled I can be of service!'

Clementine smiled. 'It's very much appreciated.' Belvedere Radley was a short, rotund man with a small, neat moustache. With his immaculate well-cut dinner jacket covering his portly frame, he reminded her of David Suchet's Poirot.

'What kind of result are you hoping for?' Belvedere asked her briskly.

'A lot,' admitted Clementine. 'We've raised a significant amount already, but we really need to raise at least ten million.'

Belvedere raised an eyebrow, reflecting on the amount. 'I've seen a few familiar faces as I walked in,' he said. 'If they're in a generous mood tonight, we'll be laughing all the way.'

'And if they're not?' she asked.

'Don't even think about it,' Belvedere muttered darkly.

'Oh dear,' said Clementine faintly.

By nine thirty on the dot, the coffee cups had been cleared away and the waiting staff had retired discreetly. Voices and laughter filled the very eaves of the impressive, stately room. Harriet, sitting with her parents at one of the head tables, was by far the most sought-after person of the evening, and had a constant flow of people coming up to clasp her hands and marvel at her miraculous reappearance. At one point Ambrose, his nerves fortified by several large single malt whiskies, became so fed up with the interruptions that he started chasing the unfortunate well-wishers away with a solid silver candelabrum.

At the far end, the stage had been set up with various speakers, microphone leads, and a red and black drum kit. The dance floor was immediately in front, and a portion of it had been set up for the auction. When Belvedere Radley regally climbed up to his wooden rostrum and surveyed the room, the audience's attention was instantly claimed. As the chatter faded away naturally, it was for sheer effect that he brought his hammer down loudly, three times.

'He's a showman, I'll say that,' whispered Tink to Clementine from their table. 'Look at him working the crowd!'

Belvedere studied the crowd more closely, nodding solemnly at the people he knew. Then, clearing his throat, he addressed the audience.

'Ladies and gentlemen, may I take great pleasure in welcoming you to the Save Churchminster Ball and Auction,' he announced. 'I would like to thank Lord and Lady Fraser for opening their charming home to us, and I would like to thank the SCBA Committee, as I believe it is called round these parts, and all who have worked so tirelessly to put on this splendid night for us.' He cleared his throat again. 'Now, I am sure you are all aware of the real reason we are here tonight—'

'Drink, eat and hopefully get a shag!' a young voice brayed from the back of the room. The Countess of Radmore and several of the older guests frowned in the direction of the heckler. Belvedere allowed a ghost of a smile to flicker across his face, and smoothly moved on.

'The reason we *are* here tonight is, of course, the Meadows,' he told them. 'An area of outstanding natural beauty, it is even mentioned in the Domesday book.' Clementine raised an impressed eyebrow; the man had clearly done his homework. 'Now it is under threat of disappearing, as are *many* other places like it. Concrete jungles, busy roads and other such horrors are descending in their droves upon the countryside.' The little man was getting quite worked up now, his forehead and bald spot shining under the lights. He gripped the sides of the rostrum and leaned forward. 'It's up to you folks tonight to put your hands in your pockets and do the decent thing. Save the Meadows and save Churchminster!'

Cheers resounded around the room as Belvedere pulled a spotless white handkerchief from his pocket and swiped at his brow dramatically. Then he raised his hammer aloft and cried, 'Let the auction begin!'

Brochures listing each item had been left on each guest's chair and now they studied them intently, remarking to their neighbours and pulling faces at some of the guide prices. A door opened to the side of the dance floor and four men in dark suits and shiny black shoes emerged, carrying between them a large, ornately patterned rug.

'Lot 1, a Tabriz carpet from north-west Persia, early twentieth century,' Belvedere informed the crowd. 'Approximately twenty-two feet by nineteen feet, original flat woven end finishes. Bidding starts at £71,000. £71,000 do I have anyone?'

Things did not start well. Belvedere's worst prediction seemed to have come true: the crowd were not in a buying mood and showed little interest in the items displayed before them. The eye-catching Persian rug went for barely above the reserve price, while the early Louis XV table and chairs donated by the Frasers was sold for £125,000, half the price the set was really worth. An oil painting by a seventeenth-century landscape artist went for a scandalously low £23,000. One of Babs Sax's more successful paintings, a murky grey and brown affair called *A Vagina's View of Berlin Pavements*, didn't get one bid. 'At least people here have got good taste,' Calypso tried to console Clementine. Afterwards, the highly offended Ms Sax stormed out, leaving a trail of yellow feathers in her wake.

'That's the problem with these things, one has just seen it *all* before,' the sour-faced wife of one of Sebastian's friends announced loudly. Caro winced as several people on the nearby tables turned around. This wasn't going to help the situation! As she glanced around nervously, she noticed an over-made-up blonde woman in a very short pink dress hovering by their table, and staring directly at her. Caro wondered if they had met, and smiled at her. But the woman shot her a dirty look and walked away, making a great show of squeezing past Sebastian's chair as she did so. Sebastian didn't even look up from his brochure, but something about the way his shoulders tensed made Caro feel as though an icy droplet had fallen into the middle of her heart. She quickly took a large glug of her wine.

On the Fox-Titts' table, worry was etched across Freddie and Angie's faces. They were swiftly realizing that if it carried on like this, they'd barely be able to buy one square foot of the Meadows.

A few tables away, Clementine looked so stricken her companions were left feeling utterly helpless, unsure of what to say.

Meanwhile, a huge, ten foot by fifteen foot canvas was wheeled out. A mixture of schizo-phrenic green, purple and yellow streaks, Clementine thought it looked like the work of a two-year-old child in the midst of a tantrum. Her heart sank further; there was no way anyone was going to buy this rubbish. They were finished!

Then, something wonderful happened. As the canvas was put in place, a buzz broke out in several parts of the room. Belvedere quickly put his reading glasses back on. 'Lot 5. *Urbane Jungle* by Ezru.'

The chatter was growing louder now, some people standing up from their chairs to get a better look.

'Oh, I've heard about this!' Johnnie said excitedly. 'Ezru is a 43-year-old African elephant from Zimbabwe. He's been doing the most extraordinary self-portraits from his zoo pen. Apparently the old boy suffered from dreadful depression for years. Nothing was making him better until his trainer read something about animals expressing them-selves through art. He gave him a paintbrush and easel and old big ears hasn't looked back since. Experts reckon he's the best since Dali!'

'Looks like a load of rubbish to me,' remarked Jed wryly. Johnnie burst out laughing. In spite of Camilla's earlier fears, Jed and her parents were getting on like a house on fire, and Jed's good looks were certainly wowing the other ladies at the table.

413

'I agree, old boy!' cried Johnnie. 'Not my cup of tea at all. But ever since Ezru trampled Robert Mugabe on a state visit to the zoo two years ago, the damn creature has become some kind of national hero. There were furious calls to have Ezru put down, but someone influential in the Mugabe camp turned out to be an animal lover and the elephant was saved. Now the paintings are going for ten times as much!'

The noise from the audience had almost reached fever pitch by this point. Clearly there were a few serious art collectors amongst them.

'Can I start at seventy thousand pounds, a snip at seventy thousand!' cried Belvedere. A well-fleshed man on Elizabeth Hurley's table put up his hand, signet ring glittering in the candlelight.

'Eighty thousand, do I have eighty thousand pounds?' asked the auctioneer. This time a flurry of hands shot up in the air. One forty-something Swedish woman in an opulent ruby necklace already had her chequebook out, the tall, thin man sitting on her right bidding on her behalf.

And so it went on. Clementine had never seen anything like it. When bids reached five hundred thousand pounds she could barely continue to look. *Urbane Jungle* eventually sold for a whopping £1.7 million pounds, to a small, shabby-looking man with an unkempt grey beard and moth-bitten dinner jacket. She later learned that he was one of the richest men in Europe.

The appearance of the painting seemed to awaken a thirst in the crowd. Soon after, the two week work-placement with the uber-cool designer went for £56,000, while a meet-and-greet with

George Clooney, one week's hire of the Bahamas island and ten sessions with Madonna's personal trainer reached a staggering £1.25 million between them.

The more lots there were, the more frantic the bidding became. One could almost smell the testosterone dripping from some men in the crowd as they tried to outdo each other. When a tortoiseshell hairbrush owned by Marilyn Monroe, and with a few of her blonde hairs still stuck in it, went for £169,000, Johnnie nearly had to get the smelling salts out to revive his mother.

Finally, it was over. Everyone slumped back in their chairs, suddenly exhausted by the tension and drama that had been coursing through the room for the last ninety minutes. Clementine was still trying to take it all in when an exuberant Angie Fox-Titt flew across the room.

'Oh Clementine, I think we've done it!' Overwhelmed with emotion and alcohol she burst into tears.

'There, there,' said Clementine soothingly and handed Angie her napkin, but she too could feel the hope and excitement bubbling up. 'We've got to get it all added up, but, what with all the other donations and fundraising we've done . . .' She broke off, not daring to say it out loud.

Angie promptly burst into floods of happy tears again.

There was a short break while the auction paraphernalia was cleared away and the stage prepared for Devon. A number of harassed-looking men with long hair and Def Leppard T-shirts began running around doing last-minute sound and lighting checks. The star attraction was nowhere to be seen, having spent the last thirty minutes throwing up in the toilet.

Nigel eventually found him, looking pale and weak, by a stairwell at the back of the house.

'Devon, what on earth are you doing here?' he gasped. 'You're on in five minutes. The Three Ts are screaming blue murder, thinking you've run off or something.'

'I was seriously thinking about it, Nige,' Devon said, not managing to meet his eyes. 'Was all set to slip out the back and take off across the fields. But I dunno, at the last minute I bottled it.'

Nigel had to sit down on the bottom step. 'Well, I am extremely relieved you didn't,' he said weakly. His voice became firm. 'Devon, no matter how many times Frances and I say you can do it, it's no use if you don't believe it yourself.'

'I know, I know,' Devon told him. He looked at his friend earnestly. 'Nige, I do know I've got it in me. It's just been a long time coming.'

Nigel smiled at him and put on a very bad American accent. 'Just a walk in the park, buddy!'

'You doughnut,' Devon told him, punching his arm affectionately. 'What would I do without you?'

'I dread to think,' Nigel replied, quickly turning all businesslike. 'Right! Mick's PA just called me, the helicopter has been fixed. Mick took off a few minutes ago and is heading our way.'

A look of determination came into Devon's eyes. 'Well then, let's get this show on the road!'

*

416

Back in the ballroom, fuelled by alcohol and sheer anticipation, the crowd were becoming restless.

'Where's Devon?' a woman called out.

'Fuck that, where's Jagger?' shouted one of her male companions. Cheers and heckles rose up from some of the younger guests.

'What *is* keeping the man?' Clementine asked worriedly. 'People are going to start walking out in a minute!'

'Chill, Granny Clem,' Calypso told her from across the table. 'Devon's probably just—'

She never had the chance to finish her sentence as an ear-splitting drum-roll reverberated around the room. The stage lit up with what seemed like a thousand lights to reveal the Three Ts in their trademark black T-shirts and drainpipe jeans, brandishing their respective instruments. The audience began cheering loudly. Another loud drum-roll faded away into silence, and as the audience quietened down all that could be heard was the faint crackle of the amplifiers.

Just as Tink wondered if she might wet herself from the suspense, the black curtains across the stage were slowly drawn back and there, looking like a total rock god in a white, billowing shirt and tight black leather trousers, was Devon Cornwall. All trace of fears and nerves had been eradicated as he stood before them with the stance and supreme confidence of a born superstar. Across the room, Frances felt all of eighteen years old again.

'Well, folks, I hear there's a bit of a party going on tonight,' Devon said into the microphone in front of him. He smiled knowingly, sharing a secret joke with the hundreds of guests, making each one feel he was speaking to them directly. 'I'm not too late, am I?'

That was it. The whole place went off. A few women started shrieking, while some of the men were up on their feet, clapping. Gradually the whole room joined in, with one thunderous round of applause. Devon Cornwall was back!

Nigel, watching from the stage wings, was quite overcome and had to fight to swallow the proud, emotional lump in his throat. After all these years Devon could still turn an audience to putty in his hands.

People gradually settled back into their seats and Devon waited until there was total silence before speaking again.

'As some of you might know, I've been away recuperating for a few years.' He smiled wryly and the audience did, too. 'But like they say, you can't keep an old dog down.'

'I love you, Devon!' shrieked a rather matronly middle-aged woman in a mustard ball-gown.

Devon looked out at her lazily, sexily. 'Fancy a drink later then, darlin'?' Everyone laughed as the woman shrieked and pretended to faint, a man next to her joining in the charade and frantically fanning her with his auction brochure. Watching the scene unfold, Nigel had to smile. Devon was in full-on performer mode now and it was a joy to watch.

'So you want to hear some songs, then?' Devon asked the room.

'Play "Pistol Nation",' one man shouted.

Devon nodded his head. 'All in good time me old mucker. I've got a bit of a mixture tonight.' He bent one knee forward, leaning into the microphone as if they were friends. 'This is a new one, a racy little number called "Upstreet Girl". Get up and dance if you feel like it. Lads?' He looked to his backing band, poised ready for Devon's cue.

'*One, two, three!*'

The next thirty minutes passed like a dream for Devon. He'd never felt so at home on the stage, and the audience had never been so responsive. During the faster, up-tempo songs everyone was dancing. A white-haired old man with a handlebar moustache even put his back out trying to copy one of Devon's snake-hipped moves and had to be carted out by two St John ambulancemen.

Devon had just finished his most heart-rending version of 'Heart Catcher' yet, leaving many women sobbing in abandon, when a distant, whirring noise could be heard. It grew louder and louder until it was a deafening roar, and bright lights streamed in from the garden. Devon looked towards the window and smiled. 'Ladies and gentlemen, Mick Jagger is about to enter the building!'

The crowd went wild. Ambrose jumped to his feet, shouting frantically. 'The heliport is on the other side of the house!' Too late, the helicopter squatted above the grass like a giant insect, and lowered carefully. Frances, pulling her husband back into his seat, thought of the thousands of pounds they'd spent on reseeding and planting that spring, and winced.

Moments later, the double doors at the back of the hall were flung open and Mick Jagger strode in. Dressed in black, his hair fashionably messy, and wearing sunglasses, charisma simply radiated off him. Everyone was on their feet cheering as the rock legend moved through the crowds like a champion boxer, kissing the women and shaking hands with the men. He leapt up on to the stage and embraced Devon.

'It's good to see you, matey,' Devon told him over the din of the crowd, overcome with gratitude and emotion.

Mick stayed to do three songs with Devon before leaving for another charity function. Between them, the stars had put on the performance of their lives. As Devon came to the end of 'This Heart's for the Takin' Not the Breakin'' there was a standing ovation that continued for ten minutes. Afterwards, several music-industry bigwigs who had been dotted around the room almost came to blows trying to sign him up.

For now, Devon wasn't interested in thinking about his future. He was trying to take in what had just happened, revelling in the moment. Nigel found him backstage, soaked in sweat, happiness oozing from every pore.

'That was fucking amazing!' he shouted, throwing his arms around Nigel ecstatically. *I'm back, baby!'*

By midnight the dance floor was heaving. A few of the older committee members had been seriously concerned that DJ Dawg would play awful robotic music and drive people away in hordes, but Calypso had managed to persuade them the DJ would be a sure-fire hit. Looking around now, Clementine could see her granddaughter had been right. Dawg was playing a surprisingly eclectic mix of music, with lots of disco and Motown classics thrown in. Clementine watched the young man bopping around behind his decks, bunches jiggling, and a beatific expression plastered on his face. Despite her earlier reservations, she smiled. DJ Dawg had such energy and enthusiasm, it was hard not to be affected by it.

In front of her Lucinda Reinard was being twirled around by Nico. She looked fantastic in a floaty midnight-blue dress, and Clementine watched as Nico pulled his wife in close and whispered something in her ear. Lucinda threw back her head and laughed. How different she is to the stressed, neurotic woman of a few months ago, thought Clementine. She had heard from Brenda that Fit 4 U was up for sale, as Henry had got a new job in Australia; but from the look of things Lucinda wasn't missing her lover too much. Clementine smiled wryly. She would never condone infidelity, but in these circumstances it seemed to have worked wonders for Lucinda's self-esteem, and her marriage, too. Clementine had never seen Nico so attentive.

Sebastian and Caro were still seated at their table. He had been telling yet another story of his skiing prowess, while the City wives sipped their wine and cast him coquettish sidelong glances.

Caro was sick of these people, with their ostentatious greed and self-centred, superficial lives. As the evening wore on, she had become steadily quieter, finding solace in the bottom of her wine glass instead. After one and a half bottles, her bladder was fit to burst, so she quietly excused herself. Sebastian, deep in the middle of an anecdote about how he'd been told he had the same speed and agility as an Olympic skier, didn't even notice her go. Still smarting from the way she had disobeyed his orders earlier, he'd barely said two words to her all evening.

Slightly unsteadily, Caro made her way out of the ballroom into the main hall. Most guests were dancing now, apart from the odd canoodling couple, heads pressed together as they flirted drunkenly. The ladies' powder room was half-way down a corridor to the left. Caro pushed the door open wearily, smiled at the female attendant who was sitting in a chair by the sinks, and went into the cubicle at the end.

She pulled her dress up and sat down on the loo, her head in her hands. God, her life was a mess! She was so desperately unhappy in her marriage, yet somehow couldn't see a way out of it. Milo needed a father, and she needed to be part of a family unit that actually felt important to her. She laughed derisively at her inability to do anything, even to walk out of a relationship that was utter misery. Some family I've made, she thought bitterly.

The door swung open, bringing a blast of cold air and a snatch of distant music with it. Two women chatted as they stood in front of the mirror applying make-up. Their voices sounded vaguely familiar to Caro.

'I can't believe she's bloody turned up, the sheer cheek of it,' one said.

'I know! If any of the little floozies Tarquin takes up with showed their faces at a party we were at,

I'd give him bloody what for!' replied her companion. 'I don't care what he does when he's away from home but I've told him, if he dares bring any of those little whores within five miles of me, I'll take him for every penny he's got.' She paused. 'Not that I'm not doing that already!' The two broke into thin, malicious laughter.

'What horrible creatures,' Caro thought. 'I wonder which poor woman's life they're going to pick apart?'

She heard the squirt of a perfume bottle and moments later the musky, heavy scent of Thierry Mugler's Angel floated over the cubicle door. Then the first voice spoke again, and Caro froze.

'Of course, Sebastian can get away with pulling this sort of crap because his wife is such a wet fish.'

'Yah, what's her name again? I keep forgetting. She's a right little mouse, no wonder he's shagging the brains out of Sabrina Cox.'

Caro felt numb, as if the blood was slowly freezing throughout her body. She was stone cold sober now.

'Bit of a slut, isn't she?' said the first voice. 'If you ask me, she looks like a prostitute in that awful pink dress.'

'You're probably not far wrong there, darling,' remarked her friend, and they burst into laughter once more. The door swung open and shut, and they left a deafening silence in their wake.

Sitting in her darkened cubicle, Caro felt her world collapse around her. A scream was going round and round in her head, growing louder and louder, but when she opened her mouth, nothing came out. She felt dazed and disorientated, but at the same time everything suddenly became clear as day – the blonde woman from earlier, Sebastian's over-studied nonchalance. Bringing his infidelity here, to Churchminster? How could he do that to her?

The taste of betrayal rose like bile in her throat. Those two witches had been talking about her life and marriage as casually as if they'd been discussing where they were going on holiday next year. And who else knew? Pain, shock, humiliation and hurt flowed over Caro, as she stood up slowly and leaned against the wall, trying to take it all in. But she felt an entirely new emotion, too, one that had been bubbling under the surface for so many months and was now forcing its way out.

Anger.

Caro stumbled out of the cubicle. The attendant looked at her white face and shaking hands curiously, but seemed too bored to care. On autopilot, Caro made her way back into the ballroom. A vaguely familiar face came up to her, drunk and happy, but she barely registered it.

As she walked to her table, she could see Sebastian was still sitting there. To Caro's horror, the blonde woman had slunk into the seat – *Caro*'s seat – beside him. The woman's jaw was working furiously, and she seemed to be having a go at him, while Sebastian looked around with a bored expression on his face.

He locked eyes with Caro, and a look of panic flittered across his face momentarily. Throwing down his napkin, he got up to waylay her. 'Darling, where *have* you been?' he asked in an over-solicitous voice. A voice that now made her skin crawl. 'I was just talking to an, er, old work colleague.'

Caro couldn't even look at Sabrina.

'Don't you mean your mistress, Sebastian?' she asked him, fighting to keep her voice steady.

Their friends were watching them now. 'Oh shit, Sebbo's for it,' muttered one of the men. He turned and gave Sabrina a dismissive look. 'I'd fuck off if I were you.' Sabrina opened her mouth to object, saw Sebastian and Caro standing nose to nose, and thought better of it. She stood up with as much dignity as she could muster (which wasn't much), tossed her hair over her shoulders and sashayed away.

In the meantime, Sebastian was trying his best 'surprised yet hurt' expression. It had worked wonders in the past with previous girlfriends who'd caught him red-handed. 'Darling, what on earth are you talking about?' he exclaimed, putting a placatory hand on her arm. 'What a ridiculous thing to say.'

Caro shook it off. 'I *know*, Sebastian,' she said quietly.

He spread his hands out, trying again to placate her. 'Know what?' he asked brightly. 'Come on, darling.' He cast an eye at his friends, rolling his eyes theatrically at them. They sniggered like a pack of hyenas, waiting to watch the kill. 'You've probably had a bit too much to drink, let's get you a cab home, eh?' He stepped forward and tried to put an arm around Caro's shoulders.

Caro had had enough. 'Just stop it! STOP IT!' she screamed at him. 'I know about you and that blonde woman. Sabrina, isn't it? She's your lover!'

By now, other people were starting to turn around. A few tables away her father stood up, concern etched across his face. Camilla and Calypso were also half-out of their seats, unsure of what was going on.

'For God's sake, keep your voice down, people are looking!' Sebastian hissed, glancing around. 'You're making a total fool of yourself.'

'*Me*, making a fool of myself?' A strangled laugh came out of her. 'And what about *you*, Sebastian?' she asked him. 'You've been making a fool out of me since the day we met. God knows how many women there were before this one.'

Sebastian couldn't help himself, and smirked, looking at his friends again.

Caro stared at the stranger in front of her. It was like she was seeing him properly for the first time. The eyes that had once captivated her looked hard and selfish; the face she had thought so handsome for all those years was now a cruel mask. How could I ever have loved him and found him attractive? she wondered. How could I have let him hurt me so much?

Sebastian was rapidly losing his temper. 'Sit down, woman, for Christ's sake.' She didn't move an inch. 'What the fuck is wrong with you?' he spat.

When Caro spoke again, her voice was calm and steady. 'I want a divorce.'

Sebastian stared at her for a moment, uncomprehending. 'What are you talking about? Don't be so bloody ridiculous.'

'I mean it. Go home and get your bags packed. I want you out of the house tonight.'

As her words sunk in, Sebastian's mouth twisted

into a sneer. *'You're* divorcing *me*, darling? Well, that's a fucking joke. I think I deserve a medal, not a divorce, for putting up with you. Not exactly Lay of the Year, are you?'

'That's enough, you bastard.' Johnnie had stepped in-between them, white with rage. 'You've been walking a fine line for too long. If you ever come near my daughter again, I'll knock your head off.'

Sebastian stared at his father-in-law contemptuously. 'You're fucking welcome to her, old boy,' he said, and he turned on his heel and stalked off. Johnnie looked after him and shook his head in disgust. Then he turned back to comfort his daughter.

But Caro was nowhere to be seen.

Chapter 57

Caro ran blindly down the huge sweeping drive of Clanfield Hall. She had fallen out of the front door, tears streaming down her face, the valets and security men watching open-mouthed as she took off into the darkness. She'd been holding it together so well until then, but Sebastian's last comment had hurt and humiliated her beyond belief. And the fact that it had all taken place in front of her father was almost more than she could bear.

She was stumbling more than running now, great sobs racking her body. The moon suddenly went behind a cloud. Barely able to see in the pitch black, Caro tripped over a bit of uneven ground and went flying. The adrenalin from confronting Sebastian for the first time in her life was being swiftly replaced by a realization of where it had left her. She was getting divorced. A sick feeling of fear took hold, and she sobbed even more loudly.

She thought she could hear footsteps behind her somewhere, getting closer and closer. Oh no, her dad hadn't come all the way out here, had he? The footsteps were nearly upon her now, and she turned round. 'Oh, Daddy . . .' she started to say tearfully, and stopped. It wasn't her father. It was Benedict Towey.

She stared at him for a second. He was slightly out of breath, bow tie undone and hanging round his neck. 'What are you doing here?' she said shakily. I must look such a fright, she thought. The bottom of her dress was ripped, her Emma Hope heels were covered in mud, and her mascara had to be halfway down her face by now.

Awkwardly Benedict reached out to touch her cheek but something stopped him and his hand fell away. 'Caro, are you all right?'

Benedict had never used her name before, and it felt ridiculously intimate. Her eyes welled up at the surprising tenderness in his voice, and she looked down at her feet, not wanting to blub like a fool. But Benedict walked over and put his strong, powerful arms around her. It was such a gentle, comforting gesture that Caro found herself melting into his chest, the tears coming freely.

Benedict stroked her hair. He smelt of woody aftershave, and a delicious warmth radiated from his perfect body. 'Ssh, ssh, my darling,' he told her softly. For the first time in so long, Caro felt secure and wanted in a man's arms. This thought made her cry even harder.

'I'm d-d-divorcing Sebastian,' she stuttered. Benedict looked down into her eyes. 'I know, I overheard,' he said with a wry smile. 'I think the rest of the village did, too.'

'I can never show my face around here again,' Caro sobbed.

'Bullshit,' he told her fiercely. 'Sebastian's the one who needs to disappear.' He smiled again.

'Everyone had a go at him after you ran out. Your sister Calypso even emptied a bottle of Delaforce vintage port over his head.'

In spite of herself, Caro smiled back. 'It's like a bloody episode out of *Jerry Springer*,' she sniffed, drawing away from Benedict. He handed her a handkerchief from his pocket, and she blew into it loudly. 'I'm getting a divorce,' she said again, sadly. 'I'm going to be someone's ex-wife, can you believe it?'

'If you were my wife, I'd never let you go,' Benedict said softly. 'Sebastian's not good enough for you, I knew it from the start.' As if embarrassed by what he had just said, his face went blank, and he quickly stared off into the distance.

Caro studied his profile. 'Why are you out here, Benedict?' she asked again. 'I thought you couldn't stand the sight of me.'

His strong, handsome face suddenly looked sad and vulnerable. 'Is that what you really think?'

'Well, yes I do,' she sighed. 'We've got off to such a bad start as neighbours, every time I see you I seem to say or do something wrong . . .'

Benedict gave her the ghost of a smile. 'I can be an awkward sod, Amelia is always telling me that.' He looked into her eyes. 'I'm sorry I gave you that impression. The truth is nothing like that.'

Despite all that had happened that night, Caro felt an unexpected lurch of happiness in her stomach.

Benedict looked up into the starry night, searching for the right words. 'I don't know how to explain myself, really. I'd promised myself I'd never fall for . . .' He stopped, took a breath and tried again. 'After Caitlin . . .' Caro looked at him in confusion. Who was he talking about? 'She was my wife,' Benedict explained. 'Well, ex-wife now, actually.'

The memory of the conversation Caro had overheard in the church came back and stung her, and the hurt she'd felt made her anger flare up again. 'The one you left for another woman?' she asked coldly.

Now it was Benedict's turn to look angry. 'I don't know who you've been gossiping with, but you've got your facts all wrong,' he snapped.

There was an awkward silence for a few moments, before Caro spoke. 'I'm sorry. It's just that I heard . . .' She stopped and waved her hand feebly. 'Village gossip.'

Under his tan, Benedict had gone pale. 'Someone did run off in our marriage,' he said quietly. 'But it was Caitlin, not me. With my twin brother, Harry.'

Caro's jaw dropped in horror. 'Oh, my God!'

Benedict shook his head. 'It's all right. It's in the past now. She probably did us both a favour, the marriage was never going to last.' A bitter note entered his voice. 'I just wish it hadn't been with my own brother.'

Caro tried to imagine how she would feel if Camilla or Calypso ever betrayed her in such a way. It was too awful to contemplate, even though she knew they never would.

'It tore our family apart. Mum and Dad were killed in a car crash when Harry and I were both in our twenties, so it was up to us to keep things going and look after Amelia. Then I met Caitlin, and a few years later she went off with Harry.' He laughed humourlessly. 'And for all that, it didn't even last six months. Caitlin met someone else at their local tennis club. The last I heard she was still shacked up with him in some palace in Dubai.'

'And Harry, do you speak to him now?' Caro asked. Benedict gave an almost imperceptible shake of his head.

'Oh Benedict, you should forgive him,' she said. 'Family is so important—' Benedict's next words cut across her like a knife.

'Harry's dead. He died a year after Caitlin left me. Bacterial meningitis.'

Caro clapped a hand to her mouth. 'The charity you were running for at the fun run! Oh, I should have realized.'

Benedict didn't appear to have heard. 'One minute he was fine, the next thing I was in hospital watching the life drain out of him,' he said tonelessly. 'He'd been phoning me every week since Caitlin had left, trying to make amends. I wouldn't take his calls, wouldn't see him. Amelia was more forgiving; she'd been trying to talk me round for months. The day before he died, I'd decided to call him and make it up. But I never got the chance.' A funny noise sounded in his throat. 'Life's a bitch, and then you marry one.'

His grief was palpable. Caro thought her heart would break. 'Oh Benedict, I am so sorry.' This time it was she who enveloped him in a comforting embrace. His tall, muscular frame leaned into her and they stood as if they were one, entwined by sorrow and understanding.

Finally Benedict drew away. 'It's destroyed me for long enough,' he said shakily. 'I should think about the future now.'

He hesitated and looked at her intently. 'Caro, I know this is probably totally the wrong thing to say at the moment, but do you think we might have some kind of future together?' Caro was silent for a few moments and Benedict looked embarrassed. 'Of course not. You've got all this shit going on with Sebastian. How bloody stupid of me.'

Shaking slightly, Caro took his hands in hers. They were firm and dry, with long, capable fingers that were surprisingly elegant. Momentarily she imagined what they could do to her, and shivered. She looked deep into his eyes and smiled. 'It's not stupid at all, believe me.' In the background, as if by magic, fireworks started to go off, illuminating the black sky.

Long after the party had finished and the drama died down, Jed and Camilla consummated their relationship back at No. 5 The Green. The passion was certainly there, but it was also so tender and loving that it felt like Jed's first time with a woman. The detached, self-fulfilling need he'd had with Stacey, and all the girls before her, had gone. As he lay there afterwards and kissed every inch of Camilla's body, he told her he loved her.

Looking at his naked, muscular body, Camilla couldn't quite believe how sexy he was. Her body was still trembling from the blissful orgasm Jed had brought her to five minutes ago. They were so different, yet so in tune with each other. 'I think I love you, too,' she whispered back, her hand edging down to find his perfect cock again.

Chapter 58

The next day there were some extremely sore heads round the village. Freddie woke up in bed next to Angie, naked apart from a diamond tiara on his head, and spent all day ringing round frantically trying to track down the owner. Angie, who felt nearly as hungover, managed to stagger out of bed at a reasonable hour to get over to Fairoaks. The previous night, in her euphoric drunkenness, she had promised Clementine she would help her add up the money they had raised overall.

As she walked up the path, Angie realized she was feeling rather sick, and it wasn't just to do with her hangover. What if last night had just been a wonderful dream? What if they didn't reach the target?

But as soon as Clementine flung the front door open, Angie knew it was good news. When the older woman took her into her study, showed her all the sums and finally told her the amount, Angie went weak at the knees and had to sit down. Her hands only stopped shaking when she took the first glug of an extra strong G and T, hastily mixed for her by Brenda.

The final amount was a staggering £16.6 million.

'Enough to buy the Meadows *and* have change in our pockets!' cried Angie. She leapt up and did a little jig of joy around the room. 'Sid Sykes is never going to match it. Hurrah!'

For the first time, Clementine felt confident she was right. She had just finished a phone call with Humphrey from the county council office. 'You know I would never say something I didn't mean, old bean,' he had told her. 'But I really do think you've got it in the bag. Fifteen mill really is top whack for that place. No one else has that kind of money to throw at it, not even Sykes.'

Clementine smiled at Angie. 'My dear. As one would say, I do believe we have got it in the bag.'

Over at Bedlington police station, Detective Inspector Kevin Rance was about to have one of the most extraordinary days of his career.

He was alone in the office, having just finished an extremely boring traffic-accident report. Sighing, Rance pushed his chair back and gazed up at the ceiling. For someone who lived, worked and breathed the job, he couldn't remember a time when he had felt more disillusioned. The Revd Goody murder inquiry had ground to a complete halt. Most of the team had been pulled off the case to work on other, more pressing matters, and only Rance and PC Penny were left to go over old ground and wait in vain for new lines of inquiry to materialize.

Not that they were going to at this rate. Earlier that morning, Rance had got an astonishing phone call from Sir Ambrose Fraser to inform him his daughter Harriet had turned up safe and well. As much as Rance could understand Ambrose's delight, the other half of him wanted to go down to Gate Cottage and give Harriet Fraser a piece of his mind. Surely one bloody phone call home to tell everyone she was alive and well wouldn't have been too hard? Rance didn't pause to consider why the considerate and home-loving Harriet might have acted in the way she did, or the complexities and traumas that Fraser family life entailed. Facts, figures and results were all that mattered to Rance. Some stupid Hooray Henrietta buggering off to find herself – probably on daddy's credit card, he thought savagely – did not.

Penny came rushing into the room, eyes more bulbous than ever, face red with excitement.

'There's someone outside I think you should see, Guv!' he gasped.

'Cheryl from Girls Aloud?' asked Rance grumpily. Then he realized he'd never seen the young constable quite so het up, and sat up straight.

'Who is it, Penny?'

PC Penny could hardly get the words out. 'It's . . . it's a man who says he was with the Reverend Goody the night he died!'

Rance was out of his chair now, bounding round to the other side of the desk.

'This bloke says the Reverend wasn't murdered, that they were playing some kind of sex game!' squeaked Penny. Rance stopped in his tracks. 'The Reverend was gay?' he asked, astonished.

'Too right! This bloke met him in some internet chat room and the Reverend invited him over to the rectory for some hanky panky or something. Apparently they were into some pretty kinky stuff . . .'

Rance hitched up his trousers grimly. 'Let's get to the bottom of this – no pun intended – right away.'

They were in interview room two. The man sitting across the small square table from DI Rance looked like he wouldn't say 'boo' to a goose. Average height, he had short thinning dark hair, a round, slightly petulant face, and rimless half-moon spectacles which he kept taking off and polishing nervously with his shirt sleeve. He had just told them his name was Gareth Hebdon and he was a 34-year-old librarian from Birmingham.

'I can't live with it any longer!' Gareth wailed, small mole-like eyes filling up with tears. 'I wanted to protect Arthur, and all I've done is let him down! My poor Arthur!' Gareth burst into snorts of noisy tears.

Penny was instantly there with a Kleenex, waving it solicitously in front of him. Gareth accepted it gratefully. 'Th-th-thank you,' he said from behind the tissue.

Rance wasn't so sympathetic. He leaned over Gareth ominously.

'Do you want to tell me what the hell is going on?'

It took twenty tortuous minutes, punctuated by sobs, before the whole sorry story was out. By the end of it, DI Rance wanted to grab hold of PC Penny's baton and shove it somewhere where the sun didn't shine. He couldn't believe this bloody bloke!

It transpired that the two men had been conducting a secret affair for six months. They had indeed first met on an internet dating site, and after a clandestine meeting in an Oxford library they had begun a full-blown love affair. Gareth claimed he was sick of hiding in the closet, and wanted to leave his wife and come out to the world as the Reverend's other half.

'Is that where you've been all these months, then?' barked Rance. 'In the bleeding closet?'

'You're *married*?' squealed Penny.

'Arthur begged me not to tell the truth! He said he'd dedicated his life to the church and it would ruin everything. I told him not to be so stupid, that there are more gay vicars around than you can shake a cassock at these days . . .'

At this particular revelation Penny's eyebrows shot into his hairline.

Gareth carried on, 'Arthur wouldn't listen to me. He said if we were to go on seeing each other, it would have to be in secret. No one else knew about us. That was the only way Arthur wanted it.' He sniffed loudly. 'I loved him so much, I went along with it.'

'Would you like to tell me what happened on the night the Reverend died?' asked Rance grimly. Gareth went pale and seemed to baulk at the memory.

'It was awful. I decided to go and have a bath and left him listening to Radio 4. When I came back, he was dead.' Gareth shuddered. 'He was just *hanging* there from a hook on the door with the scarf round his neck.' He burst into loud, noisy sobs again. 'I've had auto-erotic asphyxiation experiences plenty of times and it's never gone wrong before!'

'Auto what?' asked Penny, clearly baffled. What was this bloke talking about cars for?

'Auto-eroticism Penny,' Rance informed him. 'It's a sexual practice when people strangle themselves to reach orgasm. Something about cutting off the blood supply to heighten the senses.'

This time, Penny's eyes looked like they were about to pop out of his head.

'I – I came back and when I saw poor Arthur there, I panicked,' said Gareth. 'I went over to revive him, but he was obviously dead.' Gareth's pudgy bottom lip wobbled. 'I was in a state of shock, but eventually I untied him from the door and dragged him over to the bed. I couldn't bear to leave him just lying there for the world to see. People would have put two and two together and our – his – secret would have been out. I know what it's like, people would have made his life sound sordid, and he wouldn't have been there to defend himself.' Gareth blew noisily into his sodden tissue.

'Even if what you say is correct, you *did* leave him there, didn't you, Mr Hebdon?' barked Rance. 'I don't need to tell you you're in *very serious trouble*. A possible murder suspect, perverting the course of justice, wasting police time . . . Don't you watch the news, man? We've had a full-scale murder hunt going on!' Rance exhaled angrily. What a cock-up.

'Don't you think I've wrestled with my conscience every day!' wailed Gareth. 'I haven't been able to eat or sleep, I've left my wife because I couldn't go on living a lie. Every time I went to phone the police, I'd hear Arthur's voice saying: "We can never tell anyone."' Gareth wiped his nose on the back of his sleeve. 'It was horrible to let people believe Arthur had been murdered, but I thought anything was better than the truth. I wanted him respected in death, as he was in life.' He looked at the police officers through red-rimmed eyes. 'You do understand, don't you?'

The months of hard slog and frustration had come to a head. Rance slammed his hands down on the desk, making Gareth and Penny both jump.

'No, I bloody don't understand!' he roared. 'We've been running around here like blue-arsed flies for the past five months while you've been living in cloud bloody cuckoo land!'

'I'm here now, aren't I?' Gareth said plaintively. 'I'm a law-abiding citizen y'know.'

'Ha!' shouted Rance. 'I don't think so. For all this sob-story malarkey, may I remind you that you are under suspicion for the killing of the Reverend Arthur Hillary Goody!'

At this, Gareth went into meltdown, wringing his hands. 'I'm not a murderer, you've got to believe me!' he shrieked. 'I know I should have come forward earlier, but I was in turmoil!' He put his face into his arms and started sobbing violently.

Rance studied the man caustically. He'd seen enough crocodile tears in interview rooms to spot them a mile off, but he didn't believe Gareth Hebdon was a cold-blooded killer. Self-obsessed and highly-strung as he was, the guy just didn't have it in him. Not that Rance was going to tell him that just yet.

'You, Mr Hebdon, are not going anywhere until you answer a few more questions,' Rance told him. 'Let's get on with this, shall we?'

Penny had heard that tone of voice before. He looked at the snivelling witness in front of him, and knew his day was about to get much, much worse.

Caro and Milo ended up staying at Clementine's on the night of the ball. When she cautiously returned to Mill House the next day, having waited to give Sebastian enough time to pack his belongings, Caro's heart was in her mouth at the thought of what she might find. Perhaps he would have gone ballistic and taken everything with him; or maybe he'd have trashed the place out of spite. Even worse, he might still be there, simply refusing to leave. As she put the key in the front door, Caro's heart sank at the thought of another confrontation.

Instead she was greeted by silence. It should have been a horribly isolating moment of realization, but Caro took a deep breath and felt only relief. She made her way up the stairs and into their bedroom. Sebastian had gone. It wasn't the empty wardrobe or the absence of face serums and pore strips in the bathroom that told her this. All the tension and misery in the place seemed to have evaporated. Even when Sebastian hadn't been at home, he had somehow managed to distil negativity into the very bones of the house. But today it felt welcoming and happy for the first time. It was almost like an exorcism had been performed, driving away Sebastian's nasty spirit.

Caro looked in the mirror above the fireplace and smiled at her reflection tentatively. The smile felt natural and good.

'I think I'm going to be OK,' she said aloud.

Chapter 59

Detective Inspector Rance was furious again. In fact, he was completely boiling. It was two days after the ball and he'd just been summoned to Chief Inspector Haddock's office. After Gareth Hebdon had come forward, a second pathologist had been ordered to go through the Reverend's post-mortem results one more time. She had come back with conclusive evidence that the death was not suspicious. If the original pathologist, Bernard Trump, hadn't been several sheets to the wind that day in the mortuary, he would have arrived at the same conclusion. Trump was promptly hauled up in front of a disciplinary hearing, with rumours of an immediate retirement and a trip to a drying-out clinic in the West Country.

Despite this farrago, Rance had been ready to slap several lesser charges on Hebdon, including failure to report a death. Then Haddock had called him in and ordered him to let Hebdon off. Muttering on about too much bad press around the case, and the police looking like a laughing-stock, Haddock had said he wanted the whole furore to die down naturally. When Rance had tried to object, his superior officer had angrily informed him that he could like it or lump it, before adding in a scathing tone that, under the circumstances, Rance should be thankful he still had a career in the police force. 'Can't believe you didn't realize her passport was missing, man.'

Furious at Haddock and even more furious at himself, Rance stormed down the corridor, flinging open the door to the main office. DS Powers, head buried in the sports section of the *Bedlington Bugle*, looked up in bemusement. 'Don't ask, Powers, just don't ask,' Rance growled, and threw himself down in his chair.

The mystery of the hooded figure and suspicious car was solved that evening. Once again putting out the rubbish at closing time, Jack Turner saw a dark mysterious shadow, wearing a full-length hooded cloak, loitering near the Merryweathers' cottage. This time Jack was quicker off the mark. In a heroic, silent dash across the green he launched himself at the figure and rugby tackled it to the ground.

It quickly transpired the sinister figure was actually not very sinister at all. As the two rolled around on the grass, distinctly female shrieks came from the figure. When Jack rolled off, aghast, he was confronted by a tall, skinny, middle-aged woman wearing a pink 'Devon Is Heaven' T-shirt under her cloak. She got up and breathlessly intro-duced herself as 45-year-old Valerie Higgins from Oxford. Wild-eyed and even wilder-haired, Valerie claimed to be Devon Cornwall's number one fan, despite the fact that she had spent months driving round the village unsuccessfully looking for Byron

Heights. 'I thought he lived in a castle somewhere!' she cried. 'I only wanted to knock on his door and ask him to sign my memorabilia.' At that point, a whole load of Devon photos and fanzines had fallen out from under her cloak.

At first Jack thought she was having him on. But when Valerie told Jack indignantly that the cloak was one of only fifty limited editions made for Devon's 1982 Pop Phantoms tour, and assured him she had no intention of murdering or robbing anyone, he decided she was fairly harmless. Still reeling from the fact that he'd rugby tackled a woman, Jack gave Valerie Higgins a sharp reprimand for stalking one of his punters and sent her on her way with a flea in her ear.

Chapter 60

Devon and Frances were walking round the garden at Byron Heights arm in arm. The mist had finally lifted and it was turning into a rather nice, if chilly winter's day. They passed the two stone lions at the end, still poised stoically on their platforms, their majestic faces covered with the remnants of early morning frost. 'Do you realize this was where we first—' Devon said, but Frances interrupted him with a squeeze of her hand.

'As if I'd ever forget,' she said, smiling.

They continued walking in the easy, companionable silence that had become so familiar to them. 'How's Harriet?' Devon asked eventually, pausing to pluck a winter flower off a bush and hand it to Frances.

Her face lit up as she took it. 'She's good, really good. She and Ambrose are getting on so much better, as well; it makes such a difference to everything.'

Devon looked at her, one eyebrow arched humorously. 'The old man's giving the poor girl a break at last, eh?'

Frances playfully hit his arm. 'Stop that! Ambrose

isn't a complete ogre.' She sighed. 'If anything, I'm the bloody wicked witch of the west. I keep thinking about how I've treated Harriet over the years. Always going on at her about the silliest of things, making dreadful comments about her weight.' She sighed again. 'I think it all said more about my own insecurities than hers. Harriet wasn't the one who needed to change, *I* was. I am trying now. I just hope she can forgive me.'

Devon stopped and wrapped his arms around her in an embrace. 'Don't give yourself a hard time, princess. You're a cracking mum. I am sure Harriet feels the same way.' He kissed her forehead and made her smile again.

'You are wonderful for one's self-esteem, darling,' she told him.

'Just returning the favour,' he said. 'I wouldn't have got anywhere near where I am now without you, Frannie.'

They stopped walking for a second, staring at each other and luxuriating in the moment. Then Devon spoke quietly. 'Frances, I . . .'

He stopped mid-sentence and Frances looked concerned. 'What is it? Are you all right?'

He tried to laugh. 'Oh, I'm more than all right! This morning I signed up to a five-album deal with Sony records. You'd think by the way they were acting that the bloody Messiah had been found alive and well living in a phone box in Chipping Norton.'

Frances clasped his hands; 'Darling, that's wonderful!' She studied him. 'Why the long face?'

Devon shuffled his feet a bit. 'They want me to go on a tour first, "Re-engage with my fan base", I think is how they put it.'

Frances looked even more uncertain. 'That's still good news, isn't it?'

Devon kicked a stone along the path in front of them, and it went flying off into a sparse-looking rose bush.

'It's for four months, worldwide. Then they want me to go straight into the recording studios in Miami. They're the best in the world for equipment and facilities,' he explained.

Frances paused and studied him carefully. 'In my heart of hearts, I knew this day would come,' she said. 'You're too big for Churchminster, Devon. You always were.'

'But *you're* here, Frannie,' he said, gripping her hands fiercely.

She smiled. 'I'll always be here, Devon. It's where I belong, at Clanfield.'

Devon understood what she was trying to say. 'I can't persuade you to run off with me, then?' he joked sadly.

'One person in the family running off is *quite* enough, thank you,' Frances said, and put her arms around him so he wouldn't see her tears. It didn't work.

'Hey, you'll always be my princess,' Devon said huskily into her hair. It smelt of apples.

Late that night Devon and Nigel were asleep in their respective wings of Byron Heights, Devon in the middle of a very pleasant dream in which he was being awarded an OBE for services to the music industry by the Queen at Buckingham Palace. Suddenly there was a loud bang downstairs, and Devon shot up in bed gripping the duvet.

Bang! There it was again. Devon, his mind racing with every imaginable horror from ghosts to mad axe-men, was paralysed with fear. When someone knocked softly on his bedroom door, he nearly had a heart attack.

'Devon! Are you awake?' Nigel's voice whispered urgently. Devon leapt out of bed and ran across the room. Unlocking the heavy wooden door, he pulled it open to find a white-faced Nigel standing there in his striped pyjamas. Devon pulled him inside and hastily locked the door behind them.

For once, Nigel looked positively unsettled. 'Did you hear that noise?' he asked Devon anxiously.

' 'Course I bloody heard it! Now do you believe me? This place is bloody haunted. I knew I should've bought that new build in Cheltenham instead!' Devon was interrupted by another loud bang downstairs, followed by a bloodcurdling guttural howl. It went on for several terrible seconds before fading into the depths of the house.

Devon clutched Nigel. 'That's what Frances and I heard before! Is there a fucking werewolf down there or something?' His teeth were chattering violently, and not through cold. 'I-I wish Frances was h-h-here. She'd know what to do.'

Nigel tried to disengage himself from Devon. 'We've got to go down there,' he told him. 'It could be a burglar.'

'Are you off your flaming rocker?' Devon hissed. 'I'm not going down there!'

Some of Nigel's common sense was returning now. 'Come on, and pull yourself together, there's probably two of us against one of him,' he said firmly.

'Or "it"!' Devon retorted, his eyes two round saucers of horror.

'I'm going down there, with or without you,' said Nigel, collecting a poker from the fireplace and moving back towards the door.

Devon was in a quandary. 'Shit!' he wailed. 'You know I can't let you go by yourself.' Nigel didn't say anything, and Devon looked half-heartedly round the room for a weapon of his own, eventually settling for a rolled-up yoga mat that was propped by the side of his bed.

'Going to stretch the intruder to death, are you?' enquired Nigel.

'Oh shut up! I don't know how you talk me into these things.' Devon positioned himself behind Nigel, the yoga mat raised above his head like a baseball bat. 'Let's go and get killed, then.'

Nigel silently unlocked the door and pushed it open. Outside, the wide sweeping corridor was a yawning chasm of darkness. There was another bang downstairs, this time followed by the unmistakable tread of slow, heavy footsteps. Devon gave a squeak of fear. 'It's coming from the kitchen!' he whispered.

They crept down the stairs, Devon still hiding behind Nigel, his hands clawing at Nigel's pyjama sleeves. 'Ouch, let go,' Nigel whispered angrily. 'I can't move with you clamped on me like a baby koala!' As they reached the bottom, Devon reluctantly prised himself off and reached out to flick on a light switch. 'Don't do that!' hissed Nigel. 'We don't want to warn them we're coming!'

'Yeah, or maybe we'll be able to see when they come for us,' said Devon unhappily, his hand dropping away from the wall.

They were half-way down the corridor, heading towards the back of the house and the kitchen. The only sound to be heard was the 'tick tock' of the grandfather clock in the hall, cutting through the air with a sinister precision. Devon could taste the rank, bitter flavour of fear invading his mouth. What were they going to encounter? Was it going to hurt them? Just when his life had turned around as well. He stifled a sob.

They had nearly reached the kitchen when another low howl came out of the darkness. 'No way!' Devon murmured. 'I am outta here!' But Nigel's hand had closed on his arm like a vice. The two men tentatively rounded the corner and stared through the kitchen doorway.

The sight that greeted them was more horrifying than Devon could ever have imagined. A tall, large apparition swathed in white was standing in the middle of the room. Instantly aware of their presence, it slowly swivelled round, but in the inky darkness Devon couldn't make out any features, human or otherwise. Then it started to glide silently towards them, one claw-like hand stretched out, searching, grasping . . . Beside him, Devon could feel Nigel rooted to the ground in shock. As if independent of his body, Devon's fingers started frantically scrabbling for the light switch by the doorway.

The figure was mere feet from them now, and Devon could smell an acrid, damp decaying smell. The stench of death, perhaps, as though it had been lying in a grave for a long, long time . . .

Devon couldn't stand it any longer. He let out a terrified, high-pitched scream just as his fingers finally found the switch and flooded the room with light.

The apparition blinked, and then said crossly, 'What the dickens do you think you're doing creeping up like that? Almost gave me a bladdy seizure!'

Standing in front of them was no headless ghost or machete-wielding burglar. Instead they were confronted with the bizarre sight of a wild-haired old man dressed in an old-fashioned nightshirt. His white hair and beard were yellowed around the edges and clearly hadn't been washed for some time. The man glared at them as he ran a gnarled hand across a red, beaky nose criss-crossed with broken veins.

Devon gaped as the man nonchalantly wiped his hand on his gown. 'Who the bleedin' 'ell are you?' Devon spluttered. 'And what the 'ell are you doing in my house?'

Despite his ragged appearance, the old man had a commanding air. 'So you're the new owner, are you?' he asked in a crisp, well-spoken voice. 'Don't think much of the way you've decorated the place.'

Devon was lost for words. 'Who *are* you?'

The man drew himself up straight. 'Sir Jonas Winterbottom,' he said proudly.

Nigel, still silently rooted to the spot, thought the name rang a bell. What was that story Angie Fox-Titt had told him at the Hallowe'en party? ' "Mad Dog" Winterbottom?' he asked uncertainly. 'Killed a grizzly with your bare hands on a hunting trip to Alaska, and once fought off a ship of pirates while sailing a yacht single-handedly round the Pacific Ocean?'

The man smiled, revealing a ghoulish set of broken teeth, and winked at them. 'At your service.'

Devon gazed at this strange, fearsome-looking creature and then back at Nigel. 'Am I missing something here?' he asked in astonishment.

It was all coming back to Nigel now. 'Sir Jonas "Mad Dog" Winterbottom is a bit of a local legend around here,' he explained. 'Correct me if I'm wrong but as legend goes, your father, Sir Percy Winterbottom, built Byron Heights at the end of the nineteenth century. Jonas was quite the adventurer and the apple of his father's eye,' he told Devon. Jonas beamed happily at them. 'But after an unfortunate, er, diving accident in Peru was it?' Nigel looked at the old man questioningly.

'Bog snorkelling,' Jonas replied darkly.

'Sorry, bog snorkelling,' apologized Nigel, 'Jonas came back a different man. He shunned all contact with society and went to live in a cave somewhere round the Malvern Hills.' He turned to the wild-looking old man. 'But you were meant to have died, no one's seen you for years!'

Jonas tapped the side of his nose knowingly. 'People don't know where to look, do they? And I don't like people looking. I've been living quite happily in the cellar here for a while now, with no one bothering me. Until you two moved in.' He glared at them.

'So *that's* where all the food keeps going!' exclaimed Nigel. 'I thought Devon was having secret midnight pig-outs.'

Jonas looked slightly bashful. 'My knee's playing

up these days, I can't get out poaching as much as I used to.'

Devon was staring at him. 'The howling, is that you?' he said faintly.

'Keep banging my shinbones on your damned furniture!' said Jonas. 'Bladdy stuff everywhere.'

'What about the scratches on the skirting boards?' asked Nigel. 'The ones the Rodent-Kill man found months ago?'

'Ah yes, that was where I stashed my tobacco behind one of them and made rather a mess getting it out. I'm quite handy with a plane,' Jonas offered. 'I can always sand it down for you.'

Nigel wondered if a Candid Camera crew were going to pop up at any second. Was this really happening? They'd had this strange, aristocratic tramp living in the house for God knows how long? How could they not have noticed?

'Keeping your friend up, are we?' remarked Sir Jonas cheerfully. It had all proved too much for Devon. Nigel turned to find the pop star slumped on the floor in a dead faint.

Chapter 61

Like a loud, imperious knock on the front door, 10 December arrived. The auction for the Meadows would take place at eleven o'clock. That morning, the entire Standington-Fulthrope clan made their way over to Bedlington together, Caro and her parents in Clementine's mud-splattered Volvo estate, while Camilla and Calypso followed behind in Camilla's Golf GTI.

Camilla had only just taken the 'Young Farmers Do It In Combine Harvesters' sticker off the back window. It had been there so long, she'd almost stopped seeing it, until Calypso let out a big 'Urgh!' as they climbed in. 'Like that is *so* sad, I'm not going anywhere until you get rid of it.' As Camilla acquiesced and peeled off the offending item, it seemed a symbolic gesture. That part of her life was a long distant memory now. Big, boorish Angus, the many nights out with his ruddy-faced friends as they joked about sheep-shagging and drank their bodyweight in cider, and all those cold, windy weekends sitting in the car watching tweed-attired men grouse shooting.

Now she was with Jed. As Camilla thought of

what he'd been doing to her the night before a delicious thrill flickered up her spine. She'd had a few boyfriends before Angus, but never a lover like Jed. He was so in control and yet gentle at the same time. Teasing her to the brink of orgasm until she could bear it no longer, and then thrusting masterfully until she cried out his name over and over. Camilla was getting hot and bothered at the memory of it. She sighed happily.

'Oh, try not to be nervous, Bills,' said Calypso, sitting in the passenger seat. She'd misinterpreted her sister's lusty exhalation for one of anxiety. 'It's all going to be fine. Granny Clem spoke to Humphrey from the council again this morning. It looks like only Sid Psycho and us are putting in anything in the way of substantial bids. And this Humphrey thinks Sykes won't go higher than ten mill. The bloke's known for being a wheeler dealer and never pays top whack for anything. We are, like, so going to walk it.' She patted her sister's knee reassuringly.

Camilla blushed guiltily. Here they were, on the most important day in Churchminster's history and she was fantasizing wildly about Jed's manhood. She chided herself. 'I'm sure you're right, Muffin,' she told Calypso, flicking on the indicator and turning left into the town hall's car park.

The car park was packed with vehicles. Every resident from Churchminster, and indeed half the county, seemed to have turned out. As they walked over to the hall they saw Humphrey and his po-faced cronies from the county council, along with someone from the Land Registry. It was unheard of at a land auction around these parts for so much to be at stake – and for so much money – and there had been ominous mutterings that this was the shape of things to come. There were even a few photographers and reporters milling around outside the entrance. The fate of Churchminster was still very big news, especially after the press surrounding the vicar's supposed murder, and the far more cheerful publicity surrounding the ball and Harriet's reappearance.

Clementine led her family inside, ignoring pleas from the assembled press for a quote or picture. There was hardly a seat left, but Angie and Freddie waved them up to the front where they had saved some places. It was a rather dreary, grey room. The central heating had broken down and it was bitterly cold inside. Most people were still muffled up in their coats and scarves. It seemed an incongruous backdrop to the enormous amounts of money that would shortly be thrown round the room, thought Clementine, as she walked down the aisle.

'Feeling confident, old girl?' Freddie asked as she sat down next to him.

'As much as I let myself,' she confided. 'I keep thinking we've miscounted the final amount and it's been a horrible mistake!'

Angie leaned over him. '£16.6 million, there's no mistake about that,' she whispered happily. Clementine looked around, there did seem to be a positive atmosphere in the air, the expectant faces and excited chatter of a battle already won.

Despite her naturally cautious nature, Clementine began to relax. She hadn't seen any sign of Sid Sykes yet. 'Maybe he's had second thoughts and decided not to turn up,' she said to Tink, who was on her other side.

No such luck. At 10.59 a.m. Sid Sykes sauntered in, accompanied by two bull-necked henchmen who made the Kray twins look inoffensive. He was dressed in a cheap-looking shiny grey suit, and gold rings and chains flashed at his hands and neck. As he took a seat across the aisle he flashed Clementine an oily grin, revealing yellow rodent-like teeth. She managed to nod at him frostily. Why did he feel the insufferable need to always look so pleased with himself? Just then the land auctioneer, a tall, stern-looking man in a brown suit, stood up behind his wooden desk at the front of the room and shouted for quiet.

'Good morning, everyone,' he announced. 'We are here today for the sale of land commonly known as the Meadows. The highest bid is final – no cheques or IOUs.' He allowed himself a slight smile as his joke received a few titters. The auctioneer continued. 'Let's have a good, clean auction. No heckling or time-wasters please. Right! The guide price is eight million pounds.' There were a few sharp intakes of breath. 'Show your hands, please, ladies and gentlemen.'

As Angie was used to attending auctions in her line of business, she was the one putting her hand up to bid for Churchminster. The committee members sat around her like an impenetrable wall. It felt reassuring and gave them all strength. A surprising number of hands shot up with hers at first, including that of a well-known Cotswold business-man who owned a string of luxury health clubs, and a noisy, well-dressed American Angie had overheard talking about building a rehab centre for the rich and famous. 'Kinda the country equivalent to the Priory,' he had announced, puffing on a giant cigar. Clementine's heart sank; maybe there were more contenders in the running than they thought.

Her fears were short-lived. As soon as the bids reached twelve million, most of the interested parties shook their heads and dropped out. It was just Churchminster and Sid Sykes left.

Suddenly, events took a worrying turn. According to the information they'd been given, Sid Sykes should have dropped out long ago. But as soon as Angie put her hand up, he was right on her tail, outbidding her and flashing obnoxious, secret smiles back at his henchmen. The price carried on climbing. And climbing. When it reached £14.2 million, Clementine shot an anxious glance at Humphrey. This wasn't supposed to happen! To her great concern, he was looking distinctly unsettled as well. Catching her glance he shrugged uncomfortably and dropped his eyes to the ground.

The bidding had now reached a staggering fifteen million pounds. The room was utterly silent, everyone watching with bated breath as the two sides slugged it out.

'Do I have fifteen million?' asked the auctioneer.

Angie tentatively put her hand up, but no sooner did she, than Sykes shot his in the air. It was starting to feel like he was playing a game with them.

'What the fuck is going on?' Calypso whispered to Caro. 'That's the maximum it's meant to go for. We're going to run out of money soon!' Caro shook her head in confusion.

Now the bidding crept up by a hundred

thousand at a time. By the time they had reached sixteen million pounds, even the auctioneer was starting to sweat.

'Sixteen million, do we have any takers for sixteen *million* pounds?' he said, as he if couldn't quite believe the amount.

Sitting ramrod straight in her chair, Clementine was starting to feel positively sick. She had a very bad feeling about this! 'Clementine, what shall we do?' whispered Angie frantically.

'Carry on, we've got to,' she told her. 'Maybe Sykes will drop out now.'

He didn't. As the bidding steadily climbed, an atmosphere of stunned disbelief settled round the room. When bidding reached £16.5 million, Angie turned and looked at them all with an air of finality.

'This is it, we're down to our last hundred thou,' she told the committee shakily. They looked at her with white faces, most now clutching the person sitting next to them.

Just as Angie was about to raise her hand for the last time, Sid Sykes spoke out. His coarse, nasal tones rang mercilessly through the room.

'Let's get this wrapped up, shall we?' he said to the auctioneer. 'I'm a busy man, and I've got places to go, people to see. A bid for twenty mill should do it, eh?'

Clementine felt as though she had literally been punched in the stomach.

The auctioneer looked at Sykes, flabbergasted at the amount, but also clearly annoyed at being told what to do. He looked over to Angie and raised his eyebrows. 'Madam? Would you like to bid against this gentleman's offer?'

Angie shook her head and slumped back in her seat, eyes filling with tears. Freddie, looking equally devastated, put his arm around her shoulders in an attempt to console her.

An angry babble of voices grew louder around her as the residents started to protest, but Clementine could neither hear nor see them. She was in her own private hell. 'I'm sorry Bertie,' she murmured.

After that, all hell broke loose. 'You bloody promised us we'd get it!' howled Calypso, running over to confront a stunned Humphrey.

'We had no idea it would go for that much,' he protested, looking distinctly uncomfortable as the suits around him looked anywhere but at Calypso. 'Nothing here has ever come close to a sum like that before!'

'Ssh, sit down,' soothed Tink, pulling Calypso back in her seat. Her daughter burst into noisy tears, and Tink looked ready to follow suit as she tried to comfort her.

Meanwhile Jed Bantry, standing at the back of the hall with his mum, shot Camilla a bewildered look. In the second row, Lucinda and Nico sat white-faced and immobile, unable to speak to each other. Even Babs Sax looked genuinely upset, noisily blowing her nose into the paper tissue Brenda Briggs had found in the bottom of her handbag. Reporters were clustered around the entrance on their mobiles, excitedly relaying their copy to their editors back in London.

In the midst of it all, Sid Sykes looked over to Clementine and gave her a leery wink. 'Bad luck,' he mouthed. He and his henchmen turned to snigger at one another. Clementine was shocked at the force of hatred that burned through her.

The auctioneer raised his voice. 'All right folks, calm down. Calm DOWN!' The hubbub subsided until only a few stunned whispers and sobs could be heard around the room.

The auctioneer didn't look happy that the Meadows was going to Sid Sykes, either. Sighing, he cast a regretful eye over the audience. 'Right! Twenty million pounds is our final bid, to the gentleman in the front row. Going, going . . .'

Clementine closed her eyes, but before he could finish his sentence, there was a flurry of commotion at the back of the hall as the door burst open. To everyone's astonishment, a dishevelled and red-faced Archie Fox-Titt came flying in. He had his slippers on and no coat, and was brandishing a thick book in one hand.

'Stop, STOP!' he shouted, skidding to a halt in front of the shocked auctioneer.

Freddie stood up, appalled. 'Archie, what the hell do you think you're playing at?'

Archie swivelled round, and Clementine could see he was breathing heavily, sweat running down the sides of his face. He flapped the book at them. 'I knew I'd seen it somewhere!' he gasped, scrabbling through the pages. Clementine could read the title now: *Rare and Endangered Birds of Great Britain*. 'I've seen it in the Meadows a few times,' Archie continued, 'but it was only when I went to the library this morning that I realized *what* it was.'

Sid Sykes was on his feet now, making his way over. ''Ere, what's going on? Seen what?' he asked suspiciously. 'Are you going to get on with it and sell me my land?'

'Hold on a minute,' the auctioneer ordered. He turned to Archie, who was jiggling up and down on the spot with excitement.

Archie stopped on a page. 'Here it is!' he yelled triumphantly. 'The Lesser Spotted Gull Beak! This is the one I've seen in the Meadows!'

'The Lesser Spotted *what*?' Calypso whispered to Caro. The auctioneer rushed out from behind his desk to look at the book. A keen ornithologist, he spent most weekends out in the countryside with a pair of binoculars. He couldn't quite believe what he had just heard.

'It can't be!' he gasped. 'The Lesser Spotted Gull Beak has been extinct in this country for half a century.'

'That's what *I* thought,' Archie told him. 'But then I got close enough to take a picture on my camera phone and it *is* the Gull Beak – look!' He showed the auctioneer his mobile, and the middle-aged man studied it intently. A look of astonishment crossed his face.

'By Jove!' he cried. 'I think you're right!'

Archie turned back to face his audience. 'I've done a bit of research,' he said almost shyly. 'And, well, if the Lesser Spotted Gull Beak *has* settled in the Meadows, the place has got to be left as it is. There's a law to protect the habitat of endangered species.'

Scarcely believing her ears, Clementine felt a surge of emotion bubbling up inside her.

'This is the biggest discovery the bird world has seen for years!' exclaimed the auctioneer. 'Bill

Oddie is going to think all his Christmases have come at once!'

'What a load of crap,' rasped Sid Sykes. 'It's my fuckin' land now and there ain't no friggin' bird going to stop me building on it.'

Several people winced at his language and some covered their children's ears. The auctioneer took great pleasure in what he said next.

'In case you didn't notice, your bid hasn't yet been formalized. And even if it had been, *Mr* Sykes, you wouldn't have been able to build anything on it. As this young man just pointed out, it looks like the Meadows will be staying as it is.'

Sykes's eyes blazed furiously. 'This is a fuckin' fit-up!'

'Mind your language,' thundered the auctioneer. 'Now get out or else I'll make sure you're black-listed from every land auction in the county!'

Sykes was white with anger. 'You'll be hearing from my lawyers!' he hissed, and stalked from the room, his henchmen glowering as they followed.

Within seconds, everyone was crowding round Archie, congratulating him. 'Arch, have I missed something here?' a perplexed Freddie asked. 'Since when did you become interested in *ornithology*?'

Archie flushed and grinned. 'Since I've been grounded and spent half my life in the library. I just picked up a book on it one day and thought it was really interesting. I've been going down to the Meadows after college to see what birds I can spot.' His face grew anxious. 'You're not going to bollock me, are you, Dad?'

Freddie hugged his son fiercely. 'I've never been so proud,' he told him.

'Does that mean I'm not grounded any more?' Archie asked hopefully.

'Don't push it,' Freddie said. He roared with laughter. 'Just joshing! I think you've learnt your lesson. At least you've started speaking like a human being again.'

As it dawned on everyone that, at the last second, the Meadows had been saved, the room went wild. Overcome by emotion, and much to the disgust of Stacey, Jack and Beryl Turner started kissing passionately, while Calypso burst into tears again. Amidst all the whooping and hugs, Johnnie picked up his mother and swung her round in delight.

'This Christmas is going to be the best we've ever had!' he shouted.

'Hear hear!' everyone chorused back happily.

The next day, the whole saga made front-page news across the country. An explosive exposé on Sid Sykes's disreputable business practices ran in one tabloid, and his associates and backers quickly deserted him in droves. A team from the RSPB had been promptly despatched to the Meadows and, to everyone's surprise and delight, they found a whole family of Lesser Spotted Gull Beaks in residence there. The next day the land was declared a natural habitat for endangered species under the 1981 Wildlife and Countryside Act. As Gull Beaks normally stayed nesting in one place for years, the area was also designated a 'site of special scientific interest', and all plans to sell it were called off indefinitely.

After a lengthy discussion, the committee

members decided to divide up all the fund money and donate it to various charities. But not before Clementine insisted they bought two more much-needed new pews for St Bartholomew's.

Chapter 62

Six months later . . .

Village life had finally returned to normality. A few weeks after the sensational outcome of the auction, an ancient Roman settlement had been discovered by a mushroom collector in the Forest of Dean. As artefact after priceless artefact was dug up, it was hailed as the greatest find in modern-day history. Suddenly Churchminster was old news, and to the relief of the residents, the coachloads of tourists and the press abandoned the village for the West Country.

It was a gorgeous sunny June day as Caro drew up outside Mill House. Turning the engine off, she climbed out of her 4 × 4 and went round to open the boot. She carefully heaved out the large potted plant she'd bought from the garden centre that morning, and with the fob of her car keys gripped between her teeth, staggered up the path. Since Sebastian had left, Caro had been busy redecorating the house in softer, feminine colours. It felt like a different place.

Her front door opened. 'Let me help.' Benedict strode towards her and took it easily, flashing her a perfect smile. Caro's heart quickened, and it wasn't just from the exertion of carrying the plant.

'Has everything been OK with Milo?' she asked, following him back into the house.

Benedict carefully put the plant down in the hall. 'He's been great,' he said. 'We read *Elmer and the Lost Teddy* and then I put him down for his afternoon nap like you said.'

'Thanks for looking after him again, Benedict,' she said gratefully.

'My pleasure.'

They looked at each other for a second, before Caro lost her nerve and broke eye-contact. 'Come through to the kitchen,' she said brightly. 'I made some lemonade earlier.'

Benedict took a seat at the breakfast bar, as Caro bustled around getting out a pitcher and two glasses. Once again, she marvelled at how well Benedict had fitted into her and Milo's lives. If Sebastian hadn't had a paternal bone in his body, Benedict Towey was put on this earth to be a father. He doted on Milo, and whenever Caro wanted some time out, or her grandmother or sisters couldn't babysit, it was Benedict who happily stepped in. Once, when Caro was suffering from dreadful toothache, he had even cancelled an important meeting in London to come home and take care of Milo, so Caro could get an emergency dentist's appointment. Milo adored Benedict in return. Whenever he laid eyes on him, his little cherub face lit up in delight, and he held out his arms. It was a world apart from Milo's relationship with his father, who was a virtual stranger to him now.

Caro had put the divorce petition in shortly after New Year. There was no going back. As hard as it was at times, she knew if she didn't push on, Sebastian would try and wheedle his way back into her life. The divorce papers had been sent to Sebastian. All they needed was his signature and the process would be under way.

Up until recently, the couple had only communicated through solicitors, and Sebastian hadn't bothered to make a single arrangement to see his son. But recently he had been on the phone every few days asking how they both were. Caro wondered if he'd undergone some sort of miraculous transformation and finally discovered where his conscience was.

In fact, Sebastian was just beginning to realize what a good deal he'd had with Caro. After their showdown at the ball, he'd invited himself on a skiing trip with some bachelor friends in Aspen. Christmas and New Year were spent drinking, skiing and vowing to get as much sex as possible over the next twelve months. When he returned to London, convinced that Caro would be hysterically pining after him, Sebastian had maliciously decided to cut all communication for the time being. That would teach her a lesson, let the silly cow see what she was missing! He had left instructions for Caro to put all his belongings into storage, and promptly moved in with Sabrina.

It was far from the shag-fest he'd been expecting. After a few weeks, it quickly dawned on him that while Sabrina was the perfect mistress, she was God-awful to live with. He became irritated with the piles of mess and clothes everywhere, and the fridge that never had anything in it apart from champagne and Sabrina's nail varnish. The pressure of daily domesticity was new to both of them, and their sex life started to dwindle. Unfortunately, sex was the only thing they'd ever really had in common, and Sebastian quickly learned to despise Sabrina's slovenly ways and selfish, moody temperament. It never occurred to him she might be feeling the same way, and after a blazing row one morning, he'd packed his bags for good and left. He'd been back in his huge, stark penthouse flat in Clerkenwell for six weeks now, and its appeal was starting to wear off.

While Benedict was making headway with her son, Caro still found she couldn't let him get close to her. For all the time they had spent getting to know each other, their relationship was still strictly platonic.

A few months earlier Benedict had tried to kiss her one night in the kitchen, but Caro had frozen. 'I'm sorry,' was all she could say and she had busied herself opening a bottle of wine so she didn't have to see his expression. Benedict hadn't pushed her or made any kind of move since.

It wasn't that she didn't want to reciprocate his advances. Christ, if only he knew! Night after night she had lain awake tossing and turning, imagining what it would be like to have him lying next to her. His mouth on hers, his strong hands running over her body . . . Caro had wondered if, just a few feet away next door, he had been feeling the same. Or perhaps he'd got fed up with waiting and started dating someone else? The thought had made her feel sick. It wasn't just Benedict's heart-stopping good looks that she had fallen for, or the tiny crow's feet around his eyes that she longed to trace with her fingers. It was him as a person. Every day he surprised her with another aspect of his character. Tender, kind, funny . . . All the things Sebastian was not. In the darkness of those long, interminable nights, Caro had stared at the ceiling and wondered if her marriage had crippled her emotionally for life.

Later that day, after Benedict had carried the new plant out to the garden, Caro asked him to stay for a glass of wine. As it was a warm, early summer evening they sat outside on the patio, watching the sun's rays dip over the ripe, blooming flowerbeds.

Caro was luxuriating in the moment when, across the wooden table, Benedict cleared his throat. She looked at him expectantly. 'I was wondering,' he said tentatively, 'if you'd do me the honour of letting me take you out to dinner tomorrow night.'

Caro felt her heart start to pound, and tried to keep her cool. 'Oh! That would be lovely.' She thought for a second. 'I could always ask Granny Clem if she'll have Milo for the night.'

Now it was Benedict's turn to redden. 'I hope you don't mind, but I've already taken the liberty of asking your grandmother.' At the age of nearly eighty Clementine was well past swooning at the opposite sex, but when Benedict Towey had turned up on her doorstep the evening before, bearing a bottle of vintage French burgundy, she'd found herself smoothing her hair back and rapidly agreeing. No woman was immune to Benedict's blond, god-like beauty, no matter how old, wise or battle-scarred. Besides, over the last few months

470

Clementine had begun to think very highly of the man. And when the final financial paperwork for the Churchminster fund had arrived from the bank that morning, accidentally revealing the identity of the mysterious million-pound benefactor, Clementine's opinion of Benedict Towey had taken on reverential status.

'What do you think?' Benedict asked Caro.

She smiled at him cheekily. 'I suppose I can always Sky Plus *EastEnders*. I'm joking. It sounds wonderful.'

All Benedict had told Caro was that he'd be picking her up at 7 p.m. that night and the dress code was smart.

'I wonder if he's taking you to Raymond Blanc's new place near Cheltenham. I've heard it's *amazing*,' said Calypso that afternoon. They were out in the garden and she was lying on Milo's blanket tickling his tummy. He gurgled happily. 'You are just too cute!' she said, ruffling her nephew's hair. 'It's amazing how much happier he's been since bloody cockface has gone,' she remarked briskly.

Caro had to smile. Calypso's outspokenness and fierce loyalty was one of the reasons she loved her.

'So what are you wearing, sis?' Calypso asked.

Caro got up from her deckchair. 'I'll show you. It's this dress I saw in a boutique in Cheltenham a few weeks ago.' She paused. 'I'm not sure if it's really me, though.'

'Crap, I bet you look great. Go and put it on,' urged Calypso. 'Let me have a sneaky preview of what Beautiful Ben Boy has in store for him later.'

When Caro reappeared a few minutes later and

stood in the open French window, Calypso let out a long, low whistle. She sat up to get a better look. 'Come out here so I can see you properly. Oh, wow!'

Caro had never looked so stunning. She was wearing a soft gold, halter-neck dress made of a fabric that flirted with every contour of her body. It stopped just above the knee and showed off Caro's slim, lightly tanned calves. Sewn in around the neckline, tiny gold bejewelled stones lit up Caro's face and set off her chocolate-coloured eyes. She had pulled her freshly washed hair out of its ponytail and it cascaded round her shoulders.

'Fuck, he is not going to know what's hit him!' Calypso cried. She held Milo up. 'Look at your gorgeous yummy mummy.'

'It's not a bit OTT?' asked Caro. 'He could be taking me to Pizza Express for all I know.'

Calypso laughed. 'Somehow I don't think that's Benedict Towey's style. You look fucking hot, sis.'

Caro was reapplying her lip-gloss in the hallway mirror when the doorbell sounded. She looked at her watch. He was bang on time. She took one last glance at her reflection and opened the front door.

Benedict was wearing a beautifully cut midnight-blue suit and white shirt, unbuttoned at the neck. His hair had been cut that day, and his strong, firm jaw gleamed from a recent shave.

'You look beautiful,' he said appreciatively. Caro blushed. Benedict held out his arm. 'Shall we?'

As Caro took it, she noticed a black Bentley at the end of the path, gleaming spotlessly. 'I thought you were driving?' she asked, stunned to see a chauffeur get out and hold open the passenger door.

'Ma'am,' he said courteously as she climbed in.

Inside, the cream leather seats smelt gorgeous, and she sank down into them. 'How fantastic, I wasn't expecting this at all!' she told Benedict as he climbed in beside her, and the car silently pulled away.

He smiled. 'Let's hope you enjoy the rest of the evening as much.' Leaning forward, he pressed a button on one of the mahogany panels. 'Now for my James Bond moment.' A tray slid out, holding an ice bucket with a bottle of champagne and two flutes in it.

'Hope you've got a license to chill with that,' said Caro.

'And I hope the champagne's not as bad as your jokes,' Benedict replied, smiling as he poured her a drink.

The car had been purring through the darkening countryside for twenty minutes or so, before it slowed and turned into a large entrance. Huge stone pillars stood on each side and the iron gates had been pulled open to let the car through.

'Chowdry Castle, I played here a few times when I was younger!' exclaimed Caro. 'A friend of mine lived about five minutes away.' She looked puzzled. 'Isn't it derelict?'

Built in the mid-1800s, Chowdry Castle had once been a beautiful sprawling country house. Unfortunately it had fallen into the hands of a disreputable earl, who gambled away his fortune on horses and prostitutes. He had ended up bankrupt, destitute and syphilis-ridden in a mental asylum down on the south coast, and creditors had seized

Chowdry Castle. But nothing was done with it, and it was a great travesty that the once-elegant building had fallen into such a state of disrepair.

Benedict grinned as the car bumped down the overgrown drive, the chauffeur wincing. 'It was until Felix, a friend of mine, took it over. He's restoring the whole thing, going to make it into a smart country hotel for the London set to escape to. I think he's marketing it as the next Babingdon House.' Caro could now see the huge dark outline of the house in front of them, its jagged, tumbledown silhouette framed against the night sky.

Benedict saw the look of alarm on her face. 'I'm not taking you in there, don't worry,' he said in amusement. The car suddenly swung down a little track to the left. 'Thanks, Tony, you can stop here.'

Benedict opened the door and helped Caro out. They were standing in a small clearing, surrounded by trees. 'Now's the bit where you have to trust me,' he said and put his hands over her eyes. He guided her gently forwards and Caro felt the smooth grass change to more uneven ground underfoot. A minute later, after she had tripped and nearly sprained her ankle four times, Benedict pulled up.

'Ready?' he whispered. 'One, two, *three*!' He took his hands away.

Caro blinked and it took a few seconds before everything swam into focus. Her jaw dropped. 'Oh Benedict,' she gasped. 'It's beautiful!'

They were standing at the beginning of a long, narrow, tree-lined lawn. Hundreds of tea lights were dotted on the ground along either side, their flames flickering in the gentle night breeze. Above their heads, Chinese lanterns in every colour of the rainbow swayed gently from branches. At the end of the lawn stood an elegant, wrought-iron gazebo. A table for two had been laid inside, and as she drew closer, she could see a pristine white table-cloth and ornate candelabra. A silver bucket was hooked to the side of the table and another bottle of champagne nestled in the ice.

She turned to Benedict, overwhelmed. 'But, how, why . . . ?' she said.

He smiled, putting his hand in the small of her back to guide her forward. His light touch made her shiver. 'Gorgeous, isn't it? Apparently all of this was overgrown with weeds and God knows what else until they started clearing it. To everyone's surprise, they found the gazebo underneath. It's been here since Victorian times and was in pretty bad shape with rust and whatnot, but Felix had it lovingly restored, and here it is. It's going to be quite a selling point.' He paused. 'And now we're the first to use it.'

They'd reached the gazebo now, and, as if by magic, an impeccably dressed waiter appeared. 'Madam, sir,' he said solicitously, and pulled their chairs out. Benedict waited until Caro was seated before he walked round to his chair.

Caro was only just remembering how to speak. This was probably the most romantic setting she had ever known.

The waiter appeared again and handed them two thick white menus embossed with gold lettering. 'Shall we?' asked Benedict. Caro realized she was absolutely starving.

*

475

The next three hours passed like a dream. Caro didn't know how or where it had been prepared, but a mouth-watering three-course meal was served to them. She ate sea-fresh prawns and exquisitely tender lamb and laughed until her sides hurt at a story Benedict told her about one of his eccentric clients. Benedict told her all about his design agency The Glass Ceiling. 'It's been a hard slog setting it up these past few years, but it finally seems to be paying off,' he said, leaning across the table to refill her glass.

'And you've got a place in London?' asked Caro. 'Stephen and Klaus mentioned it . . .'

Benedict smiled at her teasingly. 'Oh, you've been checking up on me? Yes, I've got a place in Chelsea: Montague Mews. Stephen and Klaus live a few doors down. They've been very generous to me.'

Caro hesitated. 'Now the agency is doing so well, will you move back to London permanently?'

Benedict's eyes scanned her face. 'I don't know,' he said softly. 'I've become rather attached to Churchminster.'

Caro wanted to whoop with joy.

As coffee was served, she looked across the table at Benedict, reflecting. For the first time in her life, Caro felt she could be herself with a man; that she wasn't going to be sneered at or put down. He was actually interested in everything she had to say. Benedict made her feel bright and alive, even laughing at her stupid jokes, which Sebastian had always dismissed as childish and puerile. She gazed at him, noticing how his handsome, carved features were accentuated by the shadows of flickering candlelight. 'Can I ask you something?' she said.

Benedict's strong fingers caressed the bottom of his wine stem. 'Fire away.' The corners of his mouth turned up. 'Are you going to press me for my deepest, darkest secrets?'

It was Caro's turn to smile. 'Of course not. Not unless you try to press me about mine. Not that I've got any.' She got a bit flustered. 'I mean, I suppose I *have* but they're not that bad. I mean . . .'

Benedict's right eyebrow rose in amusement, and Caro quickly composed herself, taking a deep breath. 'That night at the ball,' she continued, 'you never did tell me why you seemed to hate me for so long.' Caro lifted her hand and gestured around. 'All this is just wonderful. The time we spend together is wonderful, but it feels like two different lifetimes.' She leaned forward hesitantly. 'Why the change, Benedict? I mean, what really explains that?'

A bleak look came over Benedict's face, and he stared over her shoulder into the distance, as if remembering something he didn't want to.

'Caro, I . . . When I met you, all the joy had gone out of my life. What with the divorce and Harry.' His voice cracked. 'I was an empty shell. I didn't think I deserved any happiness and was quite determined to lead a solitary life where I could never hurt anyone or be hurt myself.' His face softened as he looked at her. 'Then I met you, and you were everything I was trying to avoid, everything I'd told myself to hate and stay away from.' He laughed derisively. 'What a fool I was.'

Spellbound, Caro sat perfectly still.

'The moment I met you outside your house, it

477

was like all the lights in the world had switched on again. I felt something I'd never felt before, and I tried to fight it all the way. I didn't want anyone in my life again, so I tried to push you out.' He smiled wryly. 'Unfortunately that just translated into me being the rudest bastard imaginable.'

'You were, rather,' Caro teased.

Benedict held his hands up. 'Guilty as charged,' he said. His face turned solemn again. 'But after the ball, what Sebastian did to you . . .' Caro's face fell at the memory and Benedict trailed off, not trusting himself to speak for a second. 'Caro, you had every right to kick me into touch after the way I've behaved. You *still* have the right. My only defence is that I was a proud idiot and, thank God, I realized I can't live my life like that. I've changed.' His strong, warm hand reached for hers across the table. '*You've* made me change,' he whispered. He squeezed her hand. 'Caro, will you forgive me?'

Apart from Milo's birth, Caro couldn't remember a single moment when she had felt happier. 'I've never been very good at holding grudges,' she whispered back, and squeezed his hand in return.

By midnight they were back in the Bentley, gliding towards Churchminster. At dinner, the conversation had flowed easily, but suddenly the atmosphere changed and they sat in silence, like strangers forced to share a small space together. Caro wondered if Benedict could feel the sexual tension radiating off her, but when she glanced across at him, his elegant profile stared thoughtfully ahead into the darkness.

They continued in silence until they reached the

outskirts of the village, by which time Caro was beginning to despair at how it had all gone so suddenly wrong, when Benedict finally spoke.

'Are you over him, Caro?'

Caro was momentarily thrown off-balance by the question. She turned to Benedict and their eyes met. She smiled. 'Yes, I really think I am,' she said softly.

The car pulled up outside Mill House, and after tipping the driver generously, Benedict walked Caro to her front door. She fumbled round in her bag for her door keys. 'I don't know where to start thanking you, I've had the most wonderful time,' she told him. Suddenly flustered, she quickly thrust the key into the lock.

As she turned it, Benedict's hand enveloped hers. 'You're worth it,' he said gently. She felt a jolt of electricity that made her stomach flip upside down. At that point, Caro knew there was no going back.

'Would you like to come in?' she asked.

He trailed a finger slowly down her cheek. 'Are you sure?'

'More than I've ever been,' she said, and pulled him inside.

The door shut behind them, and they stood in the darkness like a pair of awkward teenagers. Moonlight streamed in from the window above the door, illuminating Benedict's perfect features. Stepping towards her, he cupped her face in his hands. 'Oh my darling, I have waited for this moment for so long,' he said shakily, and lowered his head to kiss her.

His full lips were tender and practised, and he tasted vaguely of mint as his soft, probing tongue found its way into her mouth. Caro felt her body melt. Running her hands over his lean, muscular back, she felt her nipples harden and the long-forgotten pulse start between her legs.

Benedict nuzzled her neck and moaned slightly. Through the fabric of his trousers, she could feel his rock-hard erection straining to get out. Benedict ran his hands up her bare thighs to her buttocks, pulling up her dress. He lifted her up into his strong arms and she wrapped her legs round his waist. Still kissing passionately, he began to walk down the hall, carrying her as if she was as light as a feather. Up the stairs they went, kissing, licking, and unbuttoning each other until they reached the top. Kicking the bedroom door open with his foot, Benedict carried Caro in and put her down gently.

She pulled his shirt off. His body was better than she had ever imagined. Strong sculpted arms, broad shoulders and a six-pack stomach that tapered into a narrow waist. Caro's fingers traced the V-shape leading to his groin, and he groaned again. 'I want to see you first,' he said, voice thick with desire, and Caro felt her halter neck being undone. He pulled her dress down over her body and she stepped out of it, kicking it away. Underneath, she was wearing just the skimpy black Agent Provocateur G-string she'd bought months ago but never had the guts to wear. His eyes ran over her hungrily, and he caressed her full, firm breasts before slipping his fingers down beneath the lacy triangle.

Caro couldn't wait any longer. She pulled his trousers and Abercrombie & Fitch boxer shorts down over his powerful thighs. Her fingers found his cock, gloriously long, wide and hard. Benedict groaned louder. He picked her up again and pushed her against the wall, splaying her legs apart. Caro gasped in pleasure as he slid inside her. They moved rhythmically together, slowly at first, and then harder and faster, building up to a crescendo.

'Oh my God, oh my God,' gasped Caro as she arched her back against the wall, wrapping her legs around him tightly to drive him in deeper.

'Oh Christ,' he moaned. 'Oh my beautiful Caro . . .'

They both cried out as their orgasms exploded together, hearts hammering and bodies bathed in sweat.

'I love you so much. Will you marry me?' gasped Benedict.

Caro held on to him tightly, feeling every nerve in her body tingle. 'Yes, my darling,' she sobbed happily. 'Yes, yes, yes!'

Chapter 63

Three days later Caro was sitting at the breakfast bar, laughing as she watched Benedict trying to feed Milo. The little boy was in his highchair, clearly not impressed at the organic yoghurt and fruit purée on offer. At this stage most of it was in Benedict's hair.

'He obviously gets his table manners from his mother,' Benedict said, wiping a bit of strawberry off his ear.

'Watch it, you,' said Caro smiling. She was handing him a piece of kitchen roll when the phone on the wall rang. Reaching across, she picked it up. 'Hello? Oh, it's you. What do you want? No, I didn't mean it like that. I just wasn't expecting to hear from you.'

She listened for a moment, a frown crossing her face. 'I don't know if that's a good idea.' She listened again and sighed. 'OK, but I can't meet you for long. No, don't come here. I'll see you in the Jolly Boot at one.'

She hung up and turned to Benedict. 'That was Sebastian. He wants to meet me at the pub at lunchtime.'

Benedict studied her, holding Milo's little wrists to keep the sticky grasping hands away from him. 'Will you be OK? I can always come as well.'

Caro giggled. 'Can you imagine the look on his face? "Sebastian, I'd like you to meet my fiancé." I don't think his ego would be able to stand it.' As Caro wasn't officially divorced yet, they had only broken the news to their immediate families. Naturally everyone had been delighted.

'I think I'll hold my own,' she continued. 'Anyway, it's a good chance to hurry him along with the divorce papers.'

'I'll be on standby if he tries anything,' said Benedict darkly.

'My hero!' Caro said teasingly and leaned over to kiss him.

It was a fine, dry day as Caro made her way over to the pub a few hours later. As she crossed the green, she realized the cramped, anxious feeling she was used to getting before seeing Seb had gone. She wasn't looking forward to the meeting, but there was no dread there, either. Caro felt strangely calm.

The pub door was open and as she ducked her head under the low beam, she could see Sebastian had arrived before her. He was standing at the bar, clearly trying to chat up Stacey Turner. Once upon a time the scene would have made Caro's heart clench in misery. Now she just thought how worn and pathetic he looked.

She walked over and tapped him on the shoulder. 'Seb?'

He turned around from leering down Stacey's

top, and his eyes widened in surprise. 'Christ, you look amazing!'

Caro did. She was in fantastic shape, but the glow of being in love illuminated her more than any make-up or toned figure ever could.

'I'll get you a drink,' he said. 'Sauvignon Blanc, isn't it?'

'I'll have a Perrier,' she told him. She wanted all her wits about her, she didn't put it past him to try something funny like announcing he was going for sole custody of Milo. 'I'll find us a table.' Caro walked over to one in the corner, feeling Sebastian's eyes on her bottom.

'So how are things? How is my wonderful son?' he asked over-heartily a few minutes later.

'Milo is great.' Caro took a sip of her drink. 'You can see him whenever you want; I'm not going to stop you.'

Sebastian cleared his throat and looked around the room evasively. 'Yah, you know how it is,' he said. 'I've been so busy. Work's simply a *bastard* at the moment.' He fixed Caro with his most beseeching look, trying to garner sympathy.

It didn't work. She had heard it all before, and simply didn't care enough to challenge it. Sebastian was so transparent, it was laughable. Caro had a sudden urge to get out of there.

'When are you going to sign the papers?' she asked. 'They've been with your solicitor for months now.'

Sebastian took a glug of his vodka tonic, eyeing her over the glass. 'Ah yes,' he said lazily, a sly smile playing at the corner of his lips. 'I've been meaning to talk to you about that.' He smiled patronizingly. 'Don't you think you've made your point, darling?' He held his hands up in an insolent gesture. 'All right, so I'm *sorry*! Sebastian's been a naughty boy, and now he's had his wrists slapped.' Laughing, he took another slug of his drink. 'Let's just stop all this divorce crap and go home, shall we?'

Caro sat perfectly still. 'You really don't think I'm serious, do you?' she asked evenly.

Sebastian sat back smugly and put his hands behind his head. 'I know you too well. The ball-breaker act just doesn't suit you.'

'You don't know me at all,' she said quietly. 'You never have. Because even if you were the last man on earth, I still wouldn't stay married to you.'

He laughed indulgently. 'Sweetheart!' His tongue ran revoltingly across his lips. 'Mmm, I like it when you play hard to get.' Sebastian reached over and put his hand on her thigh. 'Stop it now, though, darling. You know we're both dying to shag and make-up.'

Caro pushed his hand off and stood up. 'Sebastian?' she said quietly. He looked up like the cat who'd got the cream, arrogant and smirking.

She looked down at him. 'Go fuck yourself.'

Her words took a second to sink in. Sebastian's jaw dropped slack with shock. 'But, but . . .' he stammered.

Without a backward glance, Caro turned her back and walked out of the pub, ready to live the rest of her life.